THE PULP /
EXPERI

As science fiction has moved increasingly beyond its pulp magazine roots, readers have begun to sense that they missed a genuine phenomenon. For those who wish to capture something of that experience, there are literally hundreds of anthologies reprinting the colorful, fast-paced tales that filled the pages of the old pulp sf mags. In and of themselves, the titles of these magazines generated and foreshadowed the level of cosmic thrills (aka their "sense-of-wonder" factor) to be found inside—*Astounding, Astonishing, Fantastic, Super-Science, Wonder Stories*—and, of course, **Amazing**, the first of them all, often billed as "the aristocrat of science fiction."

The problem with most anthologies of old pulp magazine tales is that while they supply the feeling of the stories, they do not really supply the feeling of reading the pulps themselves. Sans the original illustrations, editorials, letter columns, and back-of-the-magazine advertisements, such anthologies are at best a pale imitation of what readers of the original magazines felt. In order to savor the total experience, one needs to savor the pulp magazine in which the stories were originally embedded.

However, publications from the Golden Age of the Pulps sell for $100 and up apiece, and are far beyond the price range of the average reader. That is why Experimenter Publishing Company is proud to present this new series of licensed replicas drawn from the best issues of *Amazing Stories'* groundbreaking 90-year run. At last, modern readers can recapture the full pulp experience, for a modest price—without having to take out a mortgage on their home or bankrupt their savings accounts.

BOOKS PUBLISHED BY
THE BEST OF AMAZING STORIES

Amazing Stories: Giant 35th Anniversary Issue
The Best of Amazing Stories: The 1926 Anthology
The Best of Amazing Stories: The 1927 Anthology (Aug. 2015)
Seeds of Life: A Novel of Evolution's Fires by John Taine
Amazing Stories Replica: May 1944

AMAZING STORIES REPLICAS

"FIRST IN SCIENCE FICTION SINCE 1926"

The Complete Issue

May, 1944 – Vol. 18, No. 3

Editors, 1944
RAYMOND A. PALMER
Editorial Director
B. G. DAVIS

Publishers 2015
STEVE DAVIDSON
JEAN MARIE STINE

An Amazing Stories Classics Publication
Produced by Digital Parchment Services
This authorized replica licensed by The Experimenter Publishing Company.

ISBN: 9781500785109

Amazing Stories Classics are produced by Digital Parchment Editions, Inc.,
under exclusive license to Experimenter Publishing Company, publisher of
Amazing Stories and owner of the Amazing Stories registered trademark(s).

*For the best in new science fiction, plus breaking news of the world of science
fiction books, movies, television, games and more, visit Amazing Stories at*
amazingstoriesmag.com

INTRODUCTION

Science Fiction got its start in the magazines.

There was this guy, see, and his name was Hugo Gernsback. He arrived in the United States from Luxemburg just after the turn of the 20th century. Hugo was the embodiment of the 20th century man. He didn't just bring himself to America, he brought a design for a new type of battery and a head full of other ideas with him.

Not finding success with his battery (it was too costly to manufacture) he turned to the new science of radiotelegraphy. Radio, as it came to be known, was still so new that everyone talked about the message Marconi had propagated through the aether the way some of us still talk about Armstrong walking on the Moon.

Hugo invented an inexpensive radio set that eager enthusiasts could build for themselves at home. Discovering that the parts were not readily available, he opened an import business and started publishing a catalog—one that quickly turned into a magazine. And then another magazine, and another, and another.

Some of this may seem a bit odd to people born towards the close of the 20th century (and even odder to those born after the start of the 21st). That's because, among other things, 100 years ago there were no radio stations, no Wal*Marts, no factories in China, no Amazon. If you wanted to ship something overseas, you had to arrange for it to be packed aboard a steam freighter. Many people did not have telephones. Comic books hadn't even been invented yet.

Hugo had been a science and technology geek his entire life and soon discovered that when he had emigrated to the United States, he'd arrived in the home of science and technology. But there was one thing that bothered him. Not enough people shared his enthusiasm, even though the benefits of doing so were in evidence all around them.

Since he was already in the magazine business, Hugo decided to do something about this problem. His magazines began to feature how-to articles, chronicling the latest discoveries and inventions and even turning its hand to fiction that captured the spirit of inventiveness and discovery.

And then Hugo created something that wouldn't even have a name until a few years into the 21st century: Social Networking. He started with the Wireless Association of America, an organization for radio enthusiasts that was promoted and supported through several of his magazines. The letter columns in those magazines were used to recruit, the magazines were used to recruit, the association gave them a focus and before you knew it, they were lobbying Congress.

And THEN. Then Hugo realized that while the success he'd had with radio was unprecedented, it was too narrow a focus. Science and technology were not limited to radiotronics; there was physics and chemistry and biology and... Hugo needed and wanted to broaden the scope of this newly created enthusiasm.

So he invented Science Fiction.

Sure that's an overly broad statement, but it does capture the gist of what actually happened. Hugo was looking for stories that would inspire people, stories that would make scientists seem like cool cats, stories that would open up visions of what the future might hold and at the same spur their readers into creating that future.

He looked around and discovered that H.G. Wells, Jules Verne, Edgar Alan Poe and a handful of others, like Edgar Rice Burroughs, Murray Leinster and William Wallace Cook, were writing the kind of thing he was looking for. Then he floated the idea of a magazine devoted to those kinds of stories to his readers, and they promptly rejected the idea.

Undeterred, Hugo waited a few years for things to gestate, and they were. *The Thrill Book* hit the stands and faded away. *Weird Tales* hit the stands and was at least a partial success. But both contained fantasy and even memetic fiction. Hugo decided it was time to try science fiction once more.

In March of 1926, a new kind of magazine was revealed for all—*AMAZING STORIES*. It was flashier, larger, thicker and more expensive than all of the other pulps on the stands and its 100,000 copies quickly sold out.

Here's a little of what Hugo Gernsback had to say in his opening editorial:

"By 'scientifiction' I mean the Jules Verne, H. G. Wells and Edgar Allan Poe type of story—a charming romance intermingled with scientific fact and prophetic vision... Not only do these amazing tales make tremendously interesting reading—they are always instructive. They supply knowledge ... in a very palatable form... New adventures pictured for us in the scientifiction of today are not at all impossible of realization tomorrow... Many great science stories destined to be of historical interest are still to be written... Posterity will point to them as having blazed a new trail, not only in literature and fiction, but progress as well."

From the pages of *Amazing Stories* (and Hugo's later magazine, *Science Wonder Stories/Wonder Stories*) would spring forth not only the first science fiction written as science fiction, but also the community known as Science Fiction Fandom.

Hugo Gernsback was nothing if not prophetic: "Posterity will point to them as having blazed a new trail, not only in literature and fiction, but progress as well." Here we are, well past the first decade of the 21st century and you are holding in your hands a reproduction of an issue of Amazing Stories. A reproduction that was created using technologies many of which were forecast within those stories that intermingled scientific fact and prophetic vision.

Steve Davidson
Publisher
Amazing Stories

I, ROCKET by Ray Bradbury

SEE BACK COVER

AMAZING STORIES

MAY 25c

MURDER IN SPACE
By DAVID V. REED

Will postwar, super-duper SHAVING CREAM
make shaving a pleasure?
YOU CAN BET YOUR WHISKERS, IT WON'T!

In every way worthy of the name, because made to the Listerine standard of quality

Byron said it: *"Men for their sins have shaving, too, entailed upon their chins, —a daily plague"*

In the great days after victory, we may get flying flivvers, tireless tires, and plastic bathtubs. But despite all the wonders of wartime chemistry, there is no relief in sight for shavers.

Your daily reaping in black pastures will continue to be, as it is today, a nuisance and a bore. So drown your sorrow, tomorrow morning, in a faceful of pure, foaming lather brushed up in a jiffy from Listerine Shaving Cream.

Now it would be pleasant to promise that Listerine Shaving Cream puts magic and music into wearisome shaving. But we have dedicated ourselves to proclaiming our no-hokum lather. And though our cream is blest with a good name, whiskers don't wilt at the mere sight of it on the tube. Nor do they stand erect for slaughter at the first moist slap of your brush.

It is a fact, however, that in every fractional inch of this quality cream there is lots and lots of good, rich lather... which does as much as any reasonable man can expect in providing aid and comfort for his steel-scraped face.

Our package designer, with an artist's instinct, has made the tube sea-green and white to suggest that the stuff inside is cool.

Is it? That's for you to say after using it. So we suggest that you meet Listerine Shaving Cream face to face. Ask for it at any drug counter. The price is low, the tube lasts long; so it is just as smart to buy as it is smartless to use. LAMBERT PHARMACAL CO., *St. Louis, Mo.*

LISTERINE
SHAVING CREAM

35¢ TUBE LASTS AND L-A-S-T-S
month after month after month

LISTERINE
brushless
SHAVING CREAM

REMEMBER, THERE ARE 2 TYPES OF LISTERINE SHAVING CREAM
Out of this tube come swell shaves for men who prefer no-brush cream

AMAZING STORIES
REG. U. S. PAT. OFF.

MAY 1944

» STORIES «

» FEATURES «

Front cover painting by Malcolm Smith illustrating a scene from "Murder In Space"

Back cover painting by James B. Settles depicting the "Rocket Warship"

Illustrations by Hadden; Arnold Kohn; Lew Meyer; Julian S. Krupa; Brady; Malcolm Smith; Robert Fuqua

Copyright, 1944, ZIFF-DAVIS PUBLISHING COMPANY
Member of the Audit Bureau of Circulations
William B. Ziff, Publisher; B. G. Davis, Editor; Raymond A. Palmer, Managing Editor
Howard Browne, Assistant Editor; Herman R. Bollin, Art Director; H. G. Strong, Circulation Director

AMAZING STORIES MAY 1944 Published bi-monthly by ZIFF-DAVIS PUBLISHING COMPANY at 540 North Michigan Avenue, Chicago, 11, Ill. New York Office, 270 Madison Ave., New York, 16, N. Y. Washington Office, Earle Building, Washington, 4, D.C. Special Washington representative, Col. Harold E. Hartney, Occidental Hotel. London editorial representative, A. Spenser Allberry, Chandos Cottage, Court Road, Inkenham, Uxbridge, Middx., England. Entered as second class matter November 9, 1943, at the Post Office, Chicago, Illinois, under the act of March 3rd, 1879. Subscription $2.50 a year (12 issues); Canada $3.00; Foreign $3.50. Subscribers should allow at least two weeks for change of address. All communications about subscriptions should be addressed to the Director of Circulation, Ziff-Davis Publishing Company, 540 North Michigan Ave., Chicago 11, Ill.
Volume 18
Number 2

Despair

ARE YOU IN THE CLUTCHES OF INSECURITY?

ARE you too young to fail — and old enough to admit that each conscious moment affords a possible *opportunity?* Do present circumstances compel you to make drastic changes in your future? Is someone *dependent* upon you to guess or *think* your way out of your dilemma? Perhaps you are in a sort of suspended animation — awaiting what will happen — wondering what to do next.

Do you know that certain hours are best to seek promotion — and to *start new ventures?* Do you know that there are forces of your mind which can — profoundly and properly — *influence others* in your behalf? Do you know that *you can mentally create* many passing fancies, fleeting impressions, into *concrete realities?* As a human you exist in a sea of invisible, natural *Cosmic forces.* They can be utilized by your greatest possessions—*self and mind.*

Let the Rosicrucians, a Brotherhood of learning, reveal the *sensible* method by which these things are accomplished. Use the coupon below for the fascinating booklet explaining how you may share this knowledge.

The ROSICRUCIANS (AMORC) - SAN JOSE, CALIFORNIA

EVERY time we are bursting with things to tell you, we find this column cramped for space. So for the next 154 lines we are going to throw it at you hot and heavy!

FIRST, in this issue: another great Reed novel, as fine as "Empire of Jegga." This one's an answer to our "scientific detective" fans, and also an answer to critics of "Carbon-Copy Killer." This one is *perfect,* and we say it with all possible bombast! Nobody's going to disagree, so we're letting the ego ooze! Read "Murder in Space" (note the *terrific* cover by Malcolm Smith) and agree with us. If you don't, you're not honest!

SECOND, one of those "fine" stories we automatically put in a "special" class. Ray Bradbury presents "I, Rocket," and it's the first time a piece of machinery ever brought tears to our eyes! Thanks, Ray, for a swell hunk of stuff!

TO MACHINE-GUN you into helpless ecstasy, and complete our rapid encirclement of your enjoyment, Edmond Hamilton — Emil Petaja — Berkeley Livingston—Helmar Lewis. Just names, but oh, boy! Read 'em and weep—because there aren't more!

NOW, BIG news! Next—July—issue will be written *entirely* by fighting men! Yes, that's right; our fighting authors have come through with some of the finest science fiction yarns they've written, for this special issue. Each and every man has given up long hours of his precious free time to appear in this issue! Most of these stories, readers, were *written* in camp! One was written *overseas!* In Africa. Not only that, every article, every filler, every letter, is by service men. Strangely enough, all stories but one were written by members of the air forces. We list their names here with pride!

Pfc. David Wright O'Brien, AAF
Sgt. William P. McGivern, AAF
Pvt. E. K. Jarvis, AAF
Sgt. P. F. Costello, AAF
Pvt. Robert Moore Williams, AAF
Sgt. Gerald Vance, AAF
Pvt. Russell Storm, AAF
Lt. William Lawrence Hamling, USA

Pfc. John York Cabot, AAF
Cpl. Arthur T. Harris, USA
Sgt. Morris J. Steele, USA
Pfc. Julian S. Krupa, USMC
Pvt. Virgil Finlay, USA
Pvt. Henry Gade, USA
Cpl. Kingsley Kellior, US
Frank R. Paul (Assigned to USN)
Lt. Russell Milburn, USMAC

A fine bunch of names, authors and artists, and the list will be longer! Don't miss this issue. The stories are tops and the artwork brilliant. This is no publicity stunt. It is the result of a plea by Pfc. David Wright O'Brien to devote a special issue to those writers who have had to give up their writing in favor of fighting—and earnestly desire to keep their names before the readers! Dave, and all you others, we guarantee we'll keep them there! If we have to print that list every issue, stories or no! Thanks, you guys! This is the first time your editor has ever bawled over your manuscripts—and then bought them!

FOR the first time in its history, AMAZING STORIES is preparing to present a true story. But it is a story that you won't find in the newspapers, or in the history books, or in any scientific crime detective annals. Quite correctly, we have presented stories with truth in them, or true fact stories—but we have never presented such a true story as this! We aren't going to ask you to believe it. We are going to challenge you to disbelieve it. Also, we are going to challenge the best scientific minds among you to refute the facts in this story!

WE, THE editors, *believe* the story. We have tried to challenge just one thing in it. We have failed. We may bring down a hurricane of debate and perhaps even scorn and laughter on our heads. But let it come! This is the greatest experience, the greatest thrill, of our years of editing and writing. And because we do not fully understand, we cannot, in fairness to Truth, condemn it. We have no choice but to publish this story.

NATURALLY, because we are editing a magazine designed to entertain you, we consider
(Concluded on page 193)

6

MURDER IN SPACE

BY DAVID V. REED

IT WAS one of those afternoons with which the colonial planet Mirabello is so often blessed. Its twin golden suns blazed merrily from a sky of flawless blue, and little puffs of breezes chased each other through poplars and willows, and the tall grass at the edge of the stream where Terwilliger Ames sat fishing was cool and fresh. If there was a word for such an afternoon, it

Ames was the best detective in the solar system; but when Death rode in on a space ship, mere detection wasn't enough!

was lazy—and if there was a word for Ames, well that was lazy, too.

"Shucks," said Ames, mildly, discovering he had a bite on his line. He turned the massive book he had been reading face down, and, rolling over on his back, he gradually sat up, drew his legs up after him, and prepared to deal with the situation. He handled the bamboo pole expertly enough, though with little of the fiery enthusiasm native to fishermen, and after a few moments of play, he yanked up the line.

A fish came plunging out of the agitated water and swam in a wide arc in mid-air, then plopped down into the grass beside Ames where, thrashing about, it glared at him. Or so, at least, Ames thought as he regarded his strange catch. It was a small fish with blue scales that might have been made of some precious stone, to judge by their luster. Its eyes—they seemed overhung by angry, beetling brows—glared fiercely at Ames as it struggled, and its hooked lips kept opening and closing in an amazing way, until it seemed as if the fish was silently mumbling a string of curses at its catcher.

"Well, now," said Ames, "don't go blaming me. I was just sitting here reading my book when you started up with my hook."

He reached out a hand to take the fish, when it began to change color. The blue paled to white, then the white became pink and the pink red, and the red very red indeed, and all this time the fish was swelling until it had blown itself up to three times its original size. It looked like something having an apoplectic stroke, and Ames, alarmed said, "But I didn't even have anything on my hook!" And at this, as if his words had been the final insult, the fish exploded.

Ames jumped back and stared at the spot where the fish had lain. A little shower of hard, purple scales came floating down like the petals of a blossom, and there was nothing left of the fish but its lips, which were still cursing away as they hung from the hook.

He was still sitting there, perplexed, when a twelve year old boy came running through the grass toward him, calling his name. "Mr. Ames! Oh, Mr. Ames!" the boy cried, running up to him.

"There's a lady who wants you to be—" He stopped short and his gaze followed Ames'. "Oh," he said, seeing the hook, "you caught a crazy-baiter, huh?"

"A what?"

"A crazy-baiter, Mr. Ames," said the boy. "Gee, Mr. Ames, you don't know nothin' about Mirabello, do you?"

"I'm afraid I don't know much, Willy," said Ames, getting up. "You mean you can tell from what's left that I caught a fish?" He kept looking at the hook, and he scratched his sandy head.

"Sure," said Willy. "They're little fish that get awful mad when you catch 'em, and they start turnin' colors like they were crazy, and then they explode and there's nothin' left but their lips— but that's the best part of it, because their lips are about the best kind of bait there is for other fish. That's why we call 'em crazy-baiters."

"Hmmm," said Ames, with a thoughtful grin. "Had me for a minute, I guess. You'd think that with all the trouble they went to, planting Earth trees and grass and flowers, and getting Earth birds and things, that somebody'd remember to bring Earth fish too."

"Oh, there's plenty of them," said Willy, "only they usually wait for crazy-baiter lips before they bite. Seems to me you should know that, Mr. Ames —you been goin' fishin' every day for four months, ever since you came here. Didn't you never catch no fish before?"

TERWILLIGER AMES grinned again. "Guess not," he said. "I kind of lost interest since I left Indiana. Got too much to read these days." He picked up his book and marked the place. "Now what's that you started to tell me, Willy?" he said, gingerly removing the hook and throwing it, together with the lips, into the stream, where it sank from sight.

"There's a lady down at your office, Mr. Ames. She says she wants you to be her lawyer."

"Huh?" said Ames, startled. "Anybody put you up to this?"

"No, sir, Mr. Ames. It's the truth."

"Well, why didn't she go to Lawyer Farley?"

"I don't know, sir. All I know is she came into the office and asked for you. She asked me, 'Where is Mr. Terwilliger Ames, Attorney at Law?' and I said, 'Fishin'. Why?' and she said, 'I want him to be my lawyer. Can you get him?' and I s'posed I could."

"Hmmm," said Ames, thoughtfully. After a moment he picked up his fishing pole, tucked his book under his arm, yanked a fresh grass stem which he chewed deliberately and said, "Well, Willy, I guess we'd better get back to town."

So down the dusty road they walked, leisurely, of course, because Ames wasn't a man built for hurrying. He was a tall, gangling sort of young man, with long arms and bony wrists and a big Adam's apple that bobbed around when he spoke, and from the way his face and arms were sun-burned, you'd never have guessed he was a lawyer, because law is, after all, generally an indoors occupation.

A mile or so off, a bit in the valley, lay Mirabello City, with its population of 10,021. It was hardly a city, though it called itself that; but for that matter, neither was Mirabello a planet. It was really a planetoid, pushed far out into the system, a few days' jump from any of the larger system groups, but it was a peaceful, prosperous place—peaceful, that is, when the miners weren't shooting each other, and prosperous when conditions were right. Conditions like the Hive, for instance, about which you'll hear more later.

For Mirabello City, like most of the towns on Mirabello, and there weren't a great many, was a mining city. It had its other industries too, like medicine farms and canneries and a bottling works—the Famous Mirabello Miracle Water—and cattle and dairy places, but mainly it was a mining place. It had been originally settled by miners who came to dig orium in the surrounding asteroid belt, and who had chosen beautiful Mirabello as their headquarters. And like most mining towns, it had remained more or less a frontier place, and therefore somewhat wild and woolly. And as long as the big ships came in for orium, and were Mirabello's blood stream, bringing in supplies, mail, news, even occasional settlers like Ames, just so long would Mirabello remain a frontier, and all that that meant.

And now, as Ames and Willy walked toward the town, Mirabello City seemed half asleep in the heat of the warm afternoon. Not that there wasn't plenty of life in the center of town—Mirabello City was a busy place indeed—but the center isn't the town. It reminded Ames of the town he had grown up in, in Indiana. Maybe that was why he liked it so much, and was so determined to make good in it and stay.

"Gee, Mr. Ames," said Willy, kicking a stone, "I'm just like you. I don't like work neither."

Ames grinned and said nothing, though he wondered how many adults shared Willy's opinion of him. Ames liked work as much as the next man, and better than some, but he was the kind of man such things didn't show on. And coming to this town hadn't been the easiest way to start a practice; Lawyer Farley and his friends had seen to that. If Ames had had his way, he'd have gone on fishing trips a good deal less. . . .

WHEN they reached town, Ames gave his fishing pole to Willy to hold, though it fooled no one. Here and there he nodded self-consciously to people he knew, and he buttoned his shirt and straightened his tie, and wished he were wearing a coat. He might have sneaked in the back way if his client hadn't been waiting out front. She was sitting in Ames' big rocker on the porch, right under his Attorney at Law sign.

"Here he is, ma'am," said Willy. "He was fishin', just like I said."

Ames bowed politely, caught the words: "I'm Miss Sue Wylie," and held his book so that she could see its title, *MacDougal's Interplanetary Torts and Laws*, and said he was pleased to make her acquaintance.

To tell the truth, Willy hadn't prepared him for her, though one could hardly have expected more from a young boy. Because Miss Sue Wylie was beautiful. She was a slender, ashen-haired girl, with a face and figure like those you get on good calendars. Ames took it in in one glance, and he took in more than that. When he met the direct gaze of her hazel eyes, he saw the trouble that lay in them, and for all the girl's good control, he knew that she was close to the breaking point.

"Mr. Ames," she said, quietly, "I want to retain you as attorney for my brother, Bruce Wylie. He has just been arrested on suspicion of murder. Will you take the case?"

"Yes," said Ames. "Of course I will. And now, if you'll sit down again, I'd like to hear some of the details."

Which was a strange way for Ames to have spoken, for he didn't usually accept a case before he knew the details—that is, he hadn't done it when he practiced in Indiana and later in New York; this was his first case in Mirabello. But his answer had come out as directly as the girl's question. He nodded to Willy to leave, and waited.

Sue Wylie said, "I don't think there's anything I can tell you that hasn't already appeared in the *Twin-Sun*."

"The . . . the . . . ah . . . what?"

"The *Mirabello City Twin-Sun*," said the girl, a trifle puzzled. "The town newspaper."

"Ah, yes," Ames acknowledged. "You say the paper published the story this morning?"

"This afternoon."

"I haven't seen the afternoon edition," said Ames, mildly. "Is that a copy that you have with you?"

"Yes," she said. "They publish only one edition a day."

Ames took the paper without a word. The arrest had been given a sizable splash on the front page. The headline read: *Ex-Convict Arrested On Suspicion Of Murder.* Under that: *Buck Wylie, Notorious Gunfighter, Held In Connection With Mysterious Disappearance of Scotty Purdom.* A short, meager story followed. Scotty Purdom had disappeared several days before. An investigation by the Colonial Attorney for the Regency office had uncovered certain facts which warranted the arrest of Wylie. These facts were being kept secret until the indictment proceedings that afternoon, when the grand jury was meeting.

At the end of the article appeared a small note advising the reader to turn to the editorial page for further comment. Ames read the editorial. It was a plea for speedy justice and the refusal of bail in the event that Wylie was indicted. *"The past criminal record of Buck Wylie,"* it read, *"should convince the Court of the danger of allowing such a man liberty, especially since he can well afford forfeiting any bail and making his escape."*

"Nonsense," said Ames. "They can't refuse him bail." He had spoken half to himself, and now, addressing the girl, he said, "Tell me, Miss Wylie, is your brother a wealthy man?"

"He owns the Wylie Lode."

"The . . . ah . . . Wylie Lode," Ames repeated slowly. His face brightened and he said, "Of course. I knew the name was familiar. You see, I'm rather a stranger here; I've only been here four months. Perhaps you knew who this Scotty Purdom man was, Miss Wylie?"

"I thought everyone knew that. Purdom owned the Silver Spoon Mine, the famous bonanza."

"I must have heard of it," Ames observed. "Now then, this business of your brother's criminal record—exactly what is that about?"

SHE hesitated. "I don't know much about it. I don't live with my brother. Six year ago he was convicted of killing a man in a gunfight over a mine in Tyuio. Gunfights were nothing unusual there. He was given six months in prison and a suspended sentence of five years. When he got out, he sold his interests and wandered around. Two years ago he came here and struck the Wylie Lode."

"I see," said Ames. "May I ask whether your brother knows you are retaining me as his attorney, Miss Wylie?"

"Not exactly, Mr. Ames. When my brother was arrested I went to him and told him I meant to fight this thing out at his side. He asked me to get a lawyer. I went to Mr. Farley. He said he didn't have the time to take this case. I think he didn't want it. So I came to you."

Ames said, gravely, "Thank you for your frankness. And now, if there are any other pertinent facts?"

"I don't think we have time," said the girl. "The indictment proceedings begin in half an hour."

Ames rose. "If you'll excuse me for a few moments," he said, and started to go inside. He paused at the threshold. "May I ask you, Miss Wylie—though you needn't answer—whether you believe your brother to be guilty?"

Sue Wylie said, "I don't know. I know neither the facts of the case nor the specific charges. And I think if I did know, I probably wouldn't tell you."

Ames nodded and went in. He changed to a blue worsted suit and put on his new shoes. He knotted his tie several times before he gave up. If there had been more time, he would have fought the tie to the bitter end. As it was, he came out on the porch, blushing furiously, his lawbook and portfolio in his hand, and he said, "May I trouble you?"

She looked up at him, and for a moment her troubled eyes cleared, and Ames thought he liked the way she smiled. Talking to her, he had felt how badly he had messed up their initial contact. He had felt more than that; he had been unable to shake off the feeling that he had started something the end of which he could not foresee— something that left him uneasy. Now, momentarily, he felt better.

II

THERE was a large crowd around the courthouse, and the constabulary had its hands full keeping it in order. People sat on the steps and milled in the corridors, and many of them nodded politely to Sue Wylie. More of them stared at the gaunt, blue-clad man who strode beside her, his head towering above them, as if they couldn't quite place him. Once, someone said, "Why, that's Lawyer Ames! Didn't know him without his fishing pole!"

Possibly Ames didn't hear that. He had other things to think about. The suit he was wearing, for instance. He was the only man in Mirabello City that afternoon who wore woolens, he had discovered, for when Mirabello wasn't working it wore tropical whites, it being a sort of tropical place to begin with. It wasn't quite Indiana, Ames was discovering. There were differences, small ones, but subtle, and they confused him. He wished he had spent more time studying the town instead of his law books. As for his books, right then he was probably wishing he had finished the one he held in his hand.

But he took his large steps calmly, and he was calm indeed when he sat in the courtroom, waiting for the prisoner to be brought in. He had introduced himself to the judge, a portly, good-humored man named Averill, and he had said something about wishing he had time enough to meet his client before the arraignment.

"Makes no difference to me, Mr. Ames," said Judge Averill. "I'll postpone it if you say so, but I can tell you all you need to know. Your client says he doesn't know a thing, and the C.A. hasn't opened his mouth about the evidence he means to bring out. So where are you?"

When they brought out Buck Wylie, Ames studied himself casually. He was hardly any older than Ames, a big, well-built man with Sue's light eyes and her determined mouth, dressed simply enough in rough whites. He shook hands with Ames, and said, "I don't know what it's all about." Evidently, Ames thought, directness was a family trait.

Soon the Colonial Attorney, a harrowed-looking man of forty, got up and made a short speech to the grand jury. He asked them to pay attention and do their duty. Then he presented the facts of the case.

On the morning of the 10th, Scotty Purdom had put out in his craft for his mine. As was well known to everyone, the famous Silver Spoon mine was a mystery, as far as its location went, which Purdom had guarded well since he had discovered it ten years before. On this occasion, Purdom had borrowed an additional craft, because of unsettled asteroid conditions, and towed it with him, meaning to bring back a double load of orium, thus guarding his shipping contracts in case the weather subsequently turned bad.

He had been due back, the C. A. continued, eight days later, at the outside. He had not returned. His craft was equipped, naturally, with an AV and alarm signals, but no word had been received from him. Then, two days ago, on the 24th, Purdom's craft had been seen being towed by the craft which he had originally borrowed. Some hours later, Purdom's craft had been found in free space, empty and drifting, with a demolition mine bomb and time fuse in it. Purdom was still missing.

"The prosecution," said the C. A., "intends to show that Wylie was the man who lent Purdom a vessel; that Wylie later returned with his and Purdom's vessel; that the bomb found in Purdom's craft came from the Wylie mine. From inferences drawn from these facts, the prosecution intends asking this jury to indict Buck Wylie for murder."

Ames had been sitting and listening only too painfully aware of what he didn't know. But this was too much.

"OBJECTION!" he said, and he was startled at how loud his voice sounded. He rose, and with a puzzled frown, said, "Is the defense to understand that the prosecution is asking for a murder indictment on the basis of *inferences?* The prosecution has made no mention of the *corpus delicti.* How can a murder indictment possibly be granted without the preliminary introduction of a body? Unless the Honorable Colonial Attorney has made an oversight in his presentation, I ask the Court to dismiss the jury."

Ames looked around, in the hush that followed his words, and he saw that Judge Averill wasn't the only one who was staring at him. Even Sue Wylie had that peculiar look on her face. The jury seemed astonished; the C. A. let his mouth hang open.

Judge Averill cleared his throat noisily and rapped his gavel. "The Court declares a fifteen-minute recess," he said, solemnly, then, pointing a finger at Ames, he said, "May I see you in my chambers, Mr. Ames?"

So Terwilliger Ames followed the judge to his chambers. The judge kept looking at him for a few minutes, offered Ames a cigar, and waited until Ames had lit both of them before he spoke.

"Mr. Ames," he said, "this is your first case in Mirabello, is it not? Yes, I thought so. Heard so, in fact. You haven't practiced much colonial law, have you, Mr. Ames? I thought so. What kind of law have you practiced, Mr. Ames?"

"Contract and corporation, sir."

"Where?"

"New York City, sir. Four years of it."

The judge nodded. "May I ask what made you come out here?"

"I wanted to be a lawyer again, sir, not a bookworm—that is, not a highly specialized bookworm. And I wanted to see a little of the system. I moved around for a year or so before I came to Mirabello, and I fell in love with the place." He let the silence continue for a moment before he said, "Is anything wrong, sir?"

"I think so," Judge Averill nodded. "I think so, Mr. Ames. A man's life may lie in your hands—yours to defend as ably as you can. I'm not sure that your ability warrants such a trust."

"But why, sir?"

"Because you don't know your law, Mr. Ames. Don't you know that Regencies outside the regular police areas of the I. P. have their own criminal codes? Don't you know that our code does not necessarily need the production of a dead body to indict and convict for murder? Think of it a moment, Mr. Ames. We aren't living in an orderly, highly integrated community with a large police force. Murder is a simple crime when millions of miles of free space surround one. A murderer could dispose of a hundred bodies in space, or in any one of a dozen convenient hiding places hidden in space. If we insisted on the *corpus delicti* in every instance, we might never convict anyone of murder. We might—"

"Excuse me, sir," said Ames, quietly. "You're perfectly right, of course. I knew better than that. I guess I was confused for a moment by the . . . ah . . . the . . ."

"The what?"

"The talk about the various craft and the necessity for borrowing other vessels because of unsettled conditions —the weather and that kind of thing. I just— It's all very new to me, you see."

"You mean you didn't understand what the C. A. was talking about when he summed up the case and explained about the loan of the craft?"

"Yes, sir. That's about it, I guess."

The judge shook his head. "That's terrible," he said. "You haven't the vaguest notion of what's going on. Do you want my advice, Mr. Ames—advice I intend giving your client? Give up the case."

Ames puffed furiously on his cigar a moment, then, laying it down, he said, "Thank you, sir. I have no intention of giving up the case. I've never given up a case before." He stood up and added, "I might also say that I've never lost a case before." He spoke very quietly, and he looked at his watch and said, "I've still some eight minutes left, sir. With your permission, I'll go back to my client."

Judge Averill nodded solemnly and watched him go out.

AMES went into one of the antechambers, where he found Wylie and Sue. He sat down with them and said to Wylie, "Before I say anything else, tell me one thing, Mr. Wylie—are you guilty?"

Buck Wylie looked at Ames curiously. "That's a hell of a question!" he said.

"I know it is. What about the answer?"

"I'm innocent," said Wylie. "Absolutely."

"All right," said Ames. "Judge Averill just advised me to give up this case. He's going to tell you the same thing. But I don't want to give it up. If you're innocent I'll clear you. Listen to me," he said, in dead earnest, "I've never lost a case in my life. I'm probably going to make more mistakes, but if you keep your confidence in me, I'll promise you that I'll win this one for you. I've got my own reasons for wanting this case. Will you let me stay on it?"

"Got a cigarette, Sue?" said Buck Wylie. He lit it deliberately, studying Ames' lean, earnest face. "Haven't run into many like you, Mr. Ames," he said, at length. "Guess I'll string along. For a while, anyhow. Don't know what else I can do."

"All right," said Ames. "Now explain that boat business to me. Tell me exactly what you know and what you did."

"Easy enough. About two weeks ago, a day or two before Scotty went out, I got a call from him. He wanted to see me. I was surprised, but I went to see him."

"Why were you surprised?"

"Why? Because I'd never been especially friendly with Scotty. Nobody ever had been, I guess—or don't you know that? Sure, he was a kind of a hermit, a miserly one at that. I hear he used to be all right until he struck the Silver Spoon. After that he stuck to himself. He was always afraid someone was going to steal his mine from him—or that they'd follow him to it and stake a claim inside legal limits and share the orium with him.

"So it was odd, his wanting to see me, and it was even more odd when he said he wanted to borrow my boat for a big haul."

"Why was it so odd?" Ames asked.

"Because as far as I knew, Scotty had never asked anyone for a loan of a boat. He never seemed to give a damn about weather, and he never had worried much about keeping his shipping contracts on time. He pulled so much orium he didn't have to worry."

Ames hesitated, then said, "I'm afraid I don't understand this business of the weather and this boat borrowing. Would you mind explaining it to me?"

Wylie looked at his sister, then back at Ames. "Where the hell have you been keeping yourself?" he asked. "Don't you know anything?"

Ames colored a little at this, but he didn't let it bother him. He just met Wylie's eyes and waited, and after a minute Wylie said, "I guess you don't know many miners, Mr. Ames. You see, some of the miners who work the asteroid belt have to pass through bad areas. Every now and then there'll be a blow—what you might call a sort of storm—"

"Vacuum impact?" asked Ames. "You mean that or spacial glides?"

"Impact, I think," said Wylie. "Anyway, it means trouble. When those asteroids start acting up because the Hive's going crazy—"

"The Hive?" Ames asked doggedly.

"That's a big nest of them, close together, all sizes and shapes and full of crazy motions. When they start acting up, you daren't get your ship anywhere near the whole belt. Sometimes that means a miner's got to stick close to his mine for days because the weather—we call it the weather—is so bad. Meanwhile the big cargo boats keep coming in here for their shipments, and if a miner's late with his shipment, he stands to lose considerable.

"So they pay close attention to the weather, and if it looks bad, they try to borrow an extra ship in advance so's they can get to their mines, load up fast, and bring both boats back before the blow sets in. The extra load gives them time, you see."

Ames said, "Does this happen often?"

WYLIE shook his head. "Couple of times a year, maybe, and generally most miners are stocked up well enough not to have to borrow a boat. So that was another funny thing, as I said, because Scotty used to pull out plenty on every trip."

"Did you ever lend anyone your boat before?" Ames asked.

"Sure," said Wylie. "I've got four boats alternating all year, and my mine's way the hell out at the end of the belt, so the weather never bothers me. I've lent my boat out a dozen times. I've got all the money I can use in one lifetime, I guess."

Ames said, "So you lent your boat to Scotty?"

"And no questions asked," Wylie nodded. "He told me where to meet him and I was there. Then I got back in his boat and he—"

An attendant poked his head in the door and called, "Recess is over, Mr. Ames. His Honor is coming in."

"I guess you'll hear the rest of it soon enough," said Wylie, as he went back to the courtroom with Ames.

They stood until Judge Averill was seated, then the judge motioned for Buck Wylie to come to the bench. A whispered conversation followed, at the end of which Wylie returned to his chair. He didn't have to tell Ames what the judge had spoken to him about.

"After due consideration," said Judge Averill, "the Court has refused the plea of the defense to dismiss the jury. The prosecution will continue its presentation."

"Call the first witness," said the C. A. "Harvey Franshaw!"

Franshaw, a mild-mannered man of about fifty, took the stand. His evidence lasted less than a minute. He said he had been sitting in the Rocketeers Cafe, at the bar, when Scotty Purdom used the telephone. "The phone was right near the end of the bar, where I was," he testified. "I heard him speak to someone he called Buck. He said he wanted to see him the next morning, and Buck evidently agreed."

"Thank you, Mr. Franshaw," said

the C. A. "Has the worthy counsel for defense any questions to ask the witness?"

"None," Ames said, quietly.

"The prosecution calls Timothy Saunders to the stand. Mr. Saunders, will you tell your story to the jury, please?"

Saunders carefully smoothed down his thinning hair. "Ain't much to tell," he said, grinning a bit foolishly. "I seen Buck Wylie with Scotty Purdom the morning of the tenth. They were talkin' together, standin' at the number three gate of the Standish blastport. A few minutes later, I seen both of them goin' off to where they had their boats on the field. Then they both blasted off, stayin' close together."

"When did you see them again, Mr. Saunders?" asked the C. A.

"Later that day. They came back, then Scotty had his boat fueled up, and after he'd brought his stuff aboard, he blasted off again, and Buck Wylie was in the other boat, goin' with him again. That's all."

"Thank you, Mr. Saunders. Has the estimable counsel for the defense any questions to ask the witness?"

"None."

"The prosecution calls Harry Reichard to the stand. Mr. Reichard, where were you on the afternoon of the twenty-fourth, two days ago?"

"I was out in my boat, hovering around the Grey Mountain area, checking a valve leak that had been giving me trouble."

"What made you go to so lonely a place, Mr. Reichard?"

"The valve leak, as I was saying. I didn't want any other craft around me because I was testing my boat, and I got some speed out of her every now and then."

"Did you see anything unusual, Mr. Reichard?"

"Yes and no, Mr. Whitley. I mean I didn't think it was unusual when I saw it, but later on it turned out to be unusual." He held a hand up to the C. A. "Hold on, I'm getting to it," he said. "What I saw was Buck Wylie's boat, the one that's known as the *Hellcat*, towing Scotty Purdom's boat."

"In what direction were these two vessels traveling?"

"South by east, land compass. That would be about 3 point 7. I didn't think anything of it then because Buck Wylie has his own blastport down that way."

"Mr. Reichard, did anything unusual happen at that time?"

"Yes and no, Mr. Whitley—that is, I didn't think so then. I stuck out my signal flag and gave them a friendly hello. I didn't get any answer, though they couldn't have missed my signal. I thought maybe they were in some kind of trouble, but when I started coming closer, the first boat just opened the throttle and roared away. I figured maybe Buck Wylie was having one of his black days and let it go at that."

"Thank you, Mr. Reichard. Has the learned counsel for the defense any questions to ask this witness?"

"Just one," said Ames. He half rose from his chair, crouching over, as if his question didn't warrant getting up. "Mr. Reichard, did you see either of the occupants in either of the boats?"

"No, sir. I was too far off, but when I started getting up—"

"Thank you," Ames interrupted, sitting down.

COLONIAL ATTORNEY WHITLEY was facing the small audience that had been permitted into the courtroom. He looked toward a heavy, florid-faced man whose grave, important manner distinguished him from the small group in which he sat, and he shrugged and smiled. The gesture was meant as much for the jury as for the man. It implied that the C. A. neither understood nor was concerned with anything Ames said or did.

Ames leaned over to Buck Wylie. "Who's that man there?" he said.

"John Murchison," said Wylie. "He's the publisher of the town newspaper, the *Twin-Sun*."

"Could have guessed as much," said Ames, turning back to the C. A.

Whitley said, dryly, "If my honored colleague is through conferring, I will call Robert Halloway as witness for the prosecution."

An old, white-haired man, dressed in miner's clothes, walked slowly to the stand. The judge and he exchanged nods, and the C. A. said, "Bob, suppose you tell us what happened to you the afternoon—"

" 'Twas evening," the old man said, crisply. "Almost night."

". . . the evening of the twenty-fourth," Whitley finished.

The old man stretched his legs and settled back in the chair. "I was just comin' in from my diggin's. Been away 'bout three weeks, so I didn't know Scotty'd gone out and was overdue. I was sailin' along at four thousand, gettin' ready to pick up the Standish beam for a landin', when I saw Scotty Purdom's boat. I didn't know whose boat it was then, and I didn't care, because I'd almost run smack into it.

"The damn boat was idlin' along at my level, goin' in a small circle, without no runnin' lights, no signals or nothin'. If my alarm hadn't popped off, I'd have been sheared in half by her. Well, sir, I let out a howl they heard in Standish—I'd just opened my AV to tell 'em I was comin'—and I cut over and came up alongside. I tried to contact her on the AV, but she didn't answer. She just kept goin' round and round in a quarter-mile circle over the ridge near Grey Mountain, and not a sign of life in her anywhere.

"So I hove to and drew up closer, till I contacted her. With the grapplers, I mean. I tied up fast to her and burned her lock open with a torch and went in, lettin' her carry my boat with her. And the first thing I saw—right smack in the middle of the main deck, near the control board—was a big five hundred pound son-of-a-gun demolition bomb, and a time fuse attached to her blazin' away.

"Well, sir, I was about half a minute from goin' to my eternal reward. I just flattened out and dived on that fuse and put it out with my bare hands, gettin' a fine burn for it."

He held up his palms. They were covered with ugly, seared blisters that reached along the inside of his hands to his wrists.

"Don't want no bandages," he explained, half defiantly. "Sun's the best healer there is. You let the sun get at you and you'll live—"

"What about the boat, Bob?" Judge Averill said, tolerantly.

"Yep, the boat. Well, I put the fuse out and disconnected the bomb. I tried to call Standish port on the AV, but it had been put out of commission. I went through the boat, and there wasn't a soul on her. Then I looked at the bomb. The fuse'd been goin' about ten minutes, and the bomb had Buck Wylie's seal and registry number on her. Then I went back to my boat and called Standish, and came on in. They wanted me to detach Scotty's boat, but I wouldn't hear of it. Made the best landing—"

"Thank you, Bob," said Whitley. "Has the—"

"None," said Ames, dryly.

The C. A. turned to the jury with the air of a man whose job had been too simple. "Mr. Wylie," he said, politely, "may I prevail upon you to answer a few questions?"

Ames pulled Wylie back to his chair. "The defense requests that all questions to Mr. Wylie be submitted in writing," he said.

"Really, Mr. Ames," Whitley objected, "this is not a trial—"

"As I am well aware," Ames drawled, "though it has been conducted as such. Evidently the prosecution has gathered more than enough evidence to prove its indictment. That it has presented such evidence seems to me to indicate an attempt to force my client to defend himself prematurely—in other words, to indicate his line of defense—"

"Objection!" Whitley cried. "I object to this innuendo!"

"Mr. Ames," said Judge Averill, surprise in his voice, "do I understand you to say that you agree with the indictment of your client?"

AMES hesitated briefly before he spoke. From the corner of his eye he glanced at Sue Wylie, and he saw that her brother had not missed that sidewise glance. "Yes, sir," Ames said, quietly. "I believe the prosecution can present enough evidence to warrant an indictment."

It was like dropping a bomb into the room. Ames flushed and seemed to shrivel under the eyes that looked at him. He sat down and met the astonished gaze of Buck Wylie, and he started to say something and changed his mind and was silent. He turned to regard the C. A., who had been completely taken by surprise by Ames' statement.

Slowly, the C. A. regained his composure. He faced the jury, threw his hands up helplessly and said, "That's it, gentlemen. The prosecution stands by the words of the counsel for defense."

Judge Averill rose to declare a recess, but the jury foreman, who had taken a quick look around the panel, said, "Your Honor, we don't need any more time. We're ready to bring in—"

The Judge brought his gavel down sharply. "You'll take the time!" he said, snorting. "May I remind this jury that it is their duty to return a verdict based *solely* upon the evidence presented, and not upon its evaluation by either the prosecution or defense. In fewer words, the prosecution's claim that its evidence is good enough does not make it so. Neither does such a statement from the defense have any validity in this matter." He paused, looking at Ames, and added, "I might point out that counsel for defense merely stated he believed enough evidence *could* be presented—not that it *had* been presented. The decision rests with you, gentlemen. Recess."

As the jury started filing out, Buck Wylie grabbed Ames' arm. "What the hell are you doing?" he demanded, fiercely. "He hadn't shown a thing yet. He didn't have anything on me!"

Ames said, "What would you have answered if he'd asked you where you were during—" He broke off. "Excuse me. The judge wants me."

Ames walked up to the judge, who had motioned to Ames from the door to his chambers. "Mr. Ames," he said, closing the door, "may I ask what motive you had for your strange statement regarding the evidence?"

"I'm sorry. I'd rather not answer that."

"I see," said Averill, thoughtfully. "You are aware that it is the duty of the Court to protect a defendant even though he may be represented by counsel?"

"If counsel is incompetent, yes, sir."

"I must ask you to bring your credentials to me, Mr. Ames."

"Yes, sir. May I ask when?"

"I'll give you twenty-four hours, Mr. Ames."

An attendant knocked. "The jury's back, Your Honor," he said.

As Ames sat down beside Wylie again, he noticed how drawn Wylie was. "Relax," he said, quietly. "You'll be indicted, all right. I'm saving my guns for the fight for bail."

Sue Wylie asked, anxiously, "You think they'll refuse bail?"

"Not if I can help it," said Ames.

The foreman of the jury had risen. He handed a sealed envelope to a clerk, who opened and read it. "The grand jury hereby indicts Buck Wylie for the murder of Scotty Purdom."

Judge Averill rapped for silence and instructed the clerk to enter the verdict. He called Wylie before the bench. Ames stood up with Wylie and said, "May I petition the Court to release my client in bail sufficient to maintain security?"

Whitley was up like a flash. "I ask that the defendant be denied bail, Your Honor!" he cried. He opened a folder and flourished a newspaper clipping. "In connection with this request for bail, may I read this editorial from the Twin-Sun which—"

"Objection," said Ames. "The opinions of a newspaper have no bearing on my client's legal claim to liberty before he has been found guilty. May I cite the case of Worth vs. Worth, Northwest proceedings, Volume 122? I object, moreover, to the introduction of hearsay evidence intended to harm the reputation of my client. In this connection, may I cite the case of Mars Trading Corp. vs. Jackson, Mars Superior Court, Volumes 34 and 35?"

Colonial Attorney Whitley stood amazed by Ames' speech. He took a deep breath, snapped, "Not at all!" and crossed quickly to the rail. After a hurried consultation with Murchison, Whitley took a briefcase from Murchison and opened it. He took out a sheaf of papers which he brought to Judge Averill's bench.

"Your Honor, I submit here certified evidence of the defendant's criminal record, and point out that his wealth makes any bail a mere pawn in his struggle for freedom. I further point out—"

"Objection," said Ames, raising his voice slightly. "May I point out to the Court the abnormal interest taken in these proceedings by the editor of the *Mirabello Twin-Sun?* I charge him with attempting to influence this Court, and maintain that his editorial is grounds for an action holding him in contempt of Court."

Judge Averill waited a moment before he spoke. "Objection over-ruled," he said, very quietly. "Mr. Ames, this Court is quite capable of arriving at decisions without the aid of newspapers." He studied the papers carefully. Presently he looked up. "In view of the defendant's previous conviction, and after consideration of his present ability to forfeit any bail this Court may set, and after consideration of the nature of the indictment herein returned, this Court grants the petition of the prosecution. Bail denied."

"But that's impossible!" Ames exclaimed. "That's penalizing a man for being wealthy, as well as persecuting him for a previous crime! In the case of Trotter vs. the Appelate Division of—"

"Mr. Ames, another word and I will hold you in contempt of Court!"

Ames stood there, his fists clenched. Watching the armed guards escort Buck Wylie from the courtroom, he thought, for no especial reason, of the fish he had caught that afternoon. This had been another fish. He had caught it, only to have it explode in his face. . . .

III

AMES watched the girl crying quietly. He wished he was more useful in a situation like this. He was helpless before a crying woman, and this time, maybe because the woman was so beautiful, and because at least part of the reason for her crying lay with him, he felt especialy helpless. But it was more than that. He didn't really understand what had happened.

He had forseen most of it, he thought, right up to the end. He had been certain he would have Wylie out on bail. Perhaps then he would have had a chance at getting to the bottom of things. Right now they were pretty hopelessly confused.

He touched the girl's shoulder again. They were the only ones left in the courtroom. "Please," he said, "there's no reason to cry. Nothing's happened yet. I was sure he'd be indicted—"

She looked up then, and her eyes were strangely dry. "Why?" she asked. "You didn't fight for him. You let them indict him."

"I had to," said Ames. "It was either that or they'd have convicted him here without a trial. If I'd let them make the points they wanted to make, he'd never have been able to look forward to a fair trial. That publisher Murchison would have had all the ammunition he wanted. I don't know what he's up to, or why he's so hellishly bent on seeing your brother in jail, but I'll get to the bottom of it."

"No," said the girl, slowly. "It's impossible. We can't let you be Buck's attorney. You'll kill him. It isn't your fault, but you'll kill him if we let you."

"What?" said Ames, bewildered. "I don't understand."

"That's it," the girl said. "There's too much you don't understand. I didn't know why you angered Judge Averill so much by implying that Murchison was doing something wrong. Now I see it was because you didn't know."

"Didn't know what?"

"That Murchison was Scotty Purdom's only friend. That he was a partner in Scotty's mine. That his interest in this case was the most natural thing in the world." She stood up and picked up her bag. "I see you're astonished again," she said, quietly. "Well, that's the way it is. Murchison only wanted justice, but now you've made him an enemy who won't stop at justice alone."

She started walking out and Ames, grabbing his book and briefcase, followed her. "What are you going to do?" he asked her.

"I'm going to try to see my brother now and make other plans."

"I can't let you do that," said Ames.

"I'm afraid you've no choice. I'll pay your fee, whatever it is."

They were on the courthouse steps now, and the curious crowds were looking at them. Ames walked along beside the girl, conscious of the stares. "Hey, Mr. Ames!" someone called, "tell us what happened in the case of Ames vs. Whitley, Volume I!" There was a roar of laughter at this. Ames flushed, realizing that the account of the indictment was spreading through the town. He had a long way to go, and the road was far from clear.

Sue Wylie turned off at the next corner, and seeing Ames still beside her, she stopped. "I'm going with you," Ames said, doggedly. "I've got to show you that I'm the lawyer for you. Please," he said, heading her answer off, "do me just one favor. Don't express any opinion to your brother until I've talked to him. Pretend you still have faith in me until then."

She looked up into Ames' clear eyes.

Ames said, quietly, "Please. Trust me."

"I'll go with you," said Sue.

THEY hardly spoke during the ten minutes it took them to reach the jail and be ushered into Buck Wylie's cell. When Ames went in, he saw that Wylie's face was as dark as a thundercloud. Wylie looked from his sister to Ames and said nothing, waiting.

"We've only ten minutes," Ames said, sitting down with Sue, "so we'll have to be quick. Believe me, I know everything that's going on in your mind, but there are reasons for what I did."

"For instance?" said Wylie, staring at the floor.

"You wanted to take the stand," said Ames. "I stopped you because you would have been asked questions you couldn't answer. Suppose Whitley had asked you where you were for a few days previous to the time that old man said he saw your ship towing Purdom's — what would you have said?"

After a momentary silence, Wylie looked up quickly. "I'd have told the truth," he said. "I was out on a prospecting trip."

"Alone?"

"Yes."

"How long were you gone?"

"Five—no, six days."

Ames nodded. "Well, there's one answer. You have no alibi."

"I don't get what you're driving at."

"I think you do," said Ames. "Whoever was in your boat two days ago, towing Scotty's boat behind it so that Bob Halloway could see it—whoever was in it knew two things: first, that you were going away on a lone trip; second, that you were due back that day. Suppose you told the jury that during the time someone followed Scotty to his secret mine, killed him, then brought his boat back—that during that time you were on a lone prospecting trip? How much water would that story carry?"

"I don't give a damn how much water it would carry!" Wylie said. "I was out prospecting. Everybody knows I go out regularly the third week in the month."

"Hmmmm," said Ames. "If *everybody* knows it, that complicates matters. But you could theoretically have gone to Scotty's mine in that time, killed him, and then brought his boat back."

"Why should I bring his boat back?"

"Because you were afraid to leave it at the mine. Or maybe you wanted to blow it up, have the explosion heard, have the wreck found, and establish Scotty's death as an accident right here on Mirabello."

Wylie sat quietly a few moments. "It's a good theory," he admitted, at length. "But if I wanted to make it an accident, I'd have had Scotty's body aboard, so it would look as if he'd been killed in it."

"Hardly necessary," said Ames. "An explosion of a five hundred pound bomb could be assumed to have destroyed the last vestige of Scotty Purdom, especially if it had taken place over a wild, mountainous terrain as Grey Mountain seems to be." He nodded, adding, "Still, the fact that the murderer didn't include Scotty's body aboard a ship he was certain would be exploded inclines me to think he *couldn't* take Scotty's body back with him. Otherwise he might even have undertaken that slight detail."

Again Wylie was silent.

Ames said, "You didn't run across anyone while you were on your trip? Anybody who might be a witness for you?"

WYLIE shook his head. "I make sure nobody knows where I'm going. That's the only way to protect a strike till it's yours on paper. Every miner knows that."

"Yes," Ames sighed. "The murderer knew it too. He knew you'd be left without an alibi if he timed things right. . . . Tell me," he said, "exactly what did you do with Scotty that day you loaned him a boat?"

"Nothing much. He went with me to my blastport where I fueled the ship with my own fuel. I showed him what to watch out for, because the *Hellcat's* a tough boat to tow sometimes. Then we went back to the Standish port and Scotty fueled up, and we both went off together. We went out about fifty miles and stopped. Scotty took me aboard his ship and brought me back to my own port. Then he went back to where he'd space-anchored the *Hellcat* and took her in tow, I guess."

"Why such a complicated routine?"

"I don't know. I guess Scotty wanted to make sure I couldn't follow him. He was pretty careful, you know."

"Was anybody at the blastport when Scotty took you back?"

"Any witnesses, you mean? No. It was a Saturday night."

Ames sighed again. "When was the next time anyone saw you?"

"That night, about two hours later."

"Who?"

"Never mind who," said Wylie. "Somebody saw me."

"All right," said Ames. "Can you count on that somebody to be a wit-

ness for you—to prove you returned?"

Wylie nodded, and Ames noticed he avoided Sue's eyes.

"Not that this witness is too important," said Ames. "The prosecution could claim you'd followed Scotty before and knew where to find him. Then, when you were supposedly off on a prospecting trip, you went to his mine and killed him."

"Hell," said Wylie, somberly, "you're my lawyer and you make out a case against me that's ten times as strong as the one that louse Whitley tried to cook up."

Ames stretched his long legs. He said, "It's the case I saw him getting ready to cook before your eyes . . . if you took the stand. . . ."

Wylie said, quietly, "How did you know all this?"

Ames replied, thoughtfully, "I knew you didn't have an alibi, or Whitley would never have tried to indict you. What's the sense of indicting a man who's going to bring an air-tight albi to his trial? So I knew you'd only hang yourself if you spoke. . . .

"But I had another reason. I had to stop Whitley from trying the case then and there, which he would practically have done if he could have cornered you on the stand. Once your story was out—and spread through the town, as it would be—we'd have little chance to get an unprejudiced jury. Murchison's paper tried the indictment before it reached the Court; if you'd spoken, you'd have given *Twin-Sun* its chance to conduct the trial in its editorial columns." He looked at Sue as he added. "When I admitted the indictment, I stopped Whitley from turning it into a trial. You understand that now, I think?"

Presently, Wylie said, "What about the trial? I still have no alibi. What am I going to say then?"

Ames seemed lost in thought. After awhile, he said, "I don't know. We're up against thorough opposition. You saw how the case began to unfold, with every detail in place, with every move of yours witnessed when it was necessary. I think we'll find witnesses at every point in this story. What I've got to do is follow the prosecution's trail and stop at each of these points, and analyze them carefully. . . ."

"I've got to have some kind of action," Wylie said.

Ames looked at Wylie and saw the darkness in his face, and though he'd instinctively that Buck Wylie was a strong man, he understood how helpless he must feel. Ames looked at his watch and got up as the turnkey's footsteps echoed along the planking. "I'll be back tomorrow," he said. "Maybe something'll break."

He thought of shaking hands with Wylie, but Wylie was staring out of the tiny window. When he and Sue left, Ames had the feeling that Wylie had turned to look after them. Ames was surprised to find himself thinking what he felt was a curious thought, but he took his hand away from Sue's arm just the same.

THEY were almost at the outside door when Sue turned to Ames and said, "I'm sorry about the things I said. I'll never doubt you again." She took his hand and whispered, "I think you're a wonderful lawyer."

"Thanks," said Ames, feeling hot and cold.

It happened instantly. As Ames openend the door for Sue, the flexiglass shivered and fell out. It seemed to melt away from a spot, where, for an instant, a neat little hole had appeared. Ames would have stood there, fascinated by the thing, but Sue Wylie grabbed him and pushed him against a wall. The next moment the air danced in shimmering, conical form and a hole appeared in the wall where Ames had been standing a moment before. It was about a quarter inch in diameter, with edges that smouldered . . . about the size a Foster II heat pistol would make.

Later, when Ames had finished with the guards who had come running to the scene, and when he had a chance to draw his breath, he said to Sue, "I guess someone else decided I was a good lawyer."

They were very quiet as they walked along, going, as if by some silent agreement, toward where Ames lived, until Ames gathered courage and put it in words. "Will you have dinner with me tonight?"

She looked up at him as if she hadn't heard. "Tomorrow morning you'll take out a pistol permit," she said, her eyes clouded.

"We'll talk about at dinner," Ames said.

"Dinner?" Sue repeated, musing.

"You're coming, aren't you?"

"Of course," she said. "Of course I am. I'm afraid to leave you alone now. You don't know this town. You don't know how capable of violence this sleepy little place can be." A little shiver ran through her. "You'll need someone to take care of you."

They were almost at Ames' house when the boy Willy came bounding down from the porch. "Mr. Ames!" he cried. "You just missed your friends! They left about five minutes ago."

"What friends?"

"You know—the men you sent to get your papers. They went in and took them. They said for me to tell you."

Ames didn't wait to hear the rest of it. He ran up the steps and into the house. A moment later, when Sue followed, she found Ames in the midst of an office that looked as if a hurricane had hit it. The bookshelves had been torn apart, a filing case had been opened and ransacked, the desk drawers lay on the floor. Papers and books lay everywhere.

Ames sat down on the floor and began going through a brown envelope. He searched through other papers before he got up. He didn't seem to be too worried about matters. He smiled wryly at Sue and said, "It wasn't much. It seems they found out that Judge Averill wanted me to present my credentials—"

"When was this?" Sue asked, puzzled. "Why did he ask for them?"

"This afternoon. I guess the judge didn't think I was much of a lawyer." Ames grinned as he surveyed the littered room. "Looks like there are two schools of thought on that, all right. Not only did they take a pot shot at me, but now they've stolen my credentials."

"But why?"

"Because if I don't have them over at the judge's tomorrow, I have a feeling Averill may bounce me off the case."

"But that's impossible! Buck needs a lawyer—he needs you!"

"Well," Ames said, "he could always order Lawyer Farley to take the case. Maybe your brother would like that."

"You mean you haven't a duplicate set of credentials?" Sue said, slowly. "It'll be weeks before you can have another set shipped here!"

"I don't think so," Ames grinned. "A thing like this might have been serious in other circumstances, but I'd say our friends missed the target again. . . ." Even as he spoke he became thoughtful, and he had to remember to keep the grin alive because Sue was watching him. He thought to himself: *unless I've made the greatest mistake of all. . . .*

IV

SHORTLY before noon the next day, Ames was seated in the living room of Judge Averill's home. He had begun by telling the judge that he could not present his credentials, and he had told him why. All the time he was speaking, the judge sat gravely, listening without once interrupting, until finally, when Ames had finished his short recital, his voice had dropped away until it was barely audible.

"Well, Mr. Ames," Averill said, after a moment or two, "I'd hardly know whether to believe you or not if I hadn't heard that you were shot at when you left the jail house yesterday. Why didn't you mention it?"

"I didn't think it mattered," Ames said. He opened the briefcase he had brought with him and took out a thick yellow scroll. "I didn't know what you'd think, sir," he said, "so I ethergraphed to New York to some friends of mine and asked them to vouch for me. I received this about an hour ago."

Averill sat up. "Ethergraphed to New York, did you?" he said. He took the yellow scroll that was the graph and opened it. For several minutes thereafter he read in complete silence. Once or twice he paused to look at Ames. Finally, when he had finished, he let out a sigh and slowly lit a cigar. "I think, Mr. Ames," he said, "that I owe you an apology."

Ames felt his face growing red. He gulped and said nothing.

Averill blew smoke out. "Why didn't you tell me you were *that* Ames—the Terwilliger Ames of Consolidated?"

"Well, sir, I hardly thought . . . that is . . ."

"I see," said the judge. "You seem to be suffering from chronic modesty, you man. Did you think your reputation hadn't reached Mirabello," and

Air danced in shimmering form . . . a hole appeared in the door here Averill smiled, "or didn't you think an old country judge like me would bother to read the Law Review?"

He stood up and offered his hand to Ames. "Here," he said, leading Ames to one of the bookcases that lined the room, "every issue of the past eight years, and about thirty years more stored away in the attic." He pulled out several copies and thumbed through them, stopping at one. *"Corporate Liability And Recent Criminal Laws,"* he read aloud, *"by Terwilliger Ames,"* put the periodical down and snorted, "Why, I must have read a dozen of your articles. I never imagined that you—"

And here he looked at Ames curiously and asked, "But what *did* bring you out here, Ames? What makes a brilliant young lawyer with a system-wide reputation come to a place like Mirabello?"

"I don't know," Ames sighed. "I guess —" He smiled and threw up his hands. "One of these days I'll be glad to get together with you, sir, and discuss philosophies of living, but I confess right now I've so much on my mind I can't think straight." He added, "May I assume that I have your permission to continue with this case?"

Averill said, slowly, "I wish I knew whether you enjoy joking."

"Thank you, sir," Ames said, with evident relief, "but it was no joke for me a couple of hours ago, before I knew what you'd—" He stopped speaking, in sudden embarrassment.

"Before you knew I'd what?" asked the Judge.

"It doesn't matter, sir. I'm very tired; I'm talking too much."

"I see," said Judge Averill, reflectively. "You didn't know whether I'd accept this graph from your friends as evidence of competence? But why shouldn't I? Why not . . . unless you imagined I was persecuting you . . . or wanted you to give up this case?" Sud-

denly the judge looked directly at Ames and said, "You must have been wondering whether I was involved in what seems to be a plot to get you out of this case. All right, you needn't answer. You've every right to be careful after what's happened. But if you get into any trouble, and you decide you can trust me, come to me. Maybe I can help."

"Thank you, sir," Ames said, sincerely.

Later, when he had started the first leg of his long itinerary, Ames wondered whether he might not have to ask Judge Averill to postpone the trial. He had only ten days, hardly time enough to turn around in. He had a lot of things to do in that time.

HE returned home and changed into old clothes, and then he walked out to the edge of the town where the Standish blastport was.

The Standish port seemed out of place in Mirabello City. It had something definitely—as Ames thought— big-time about it. It was a large, efficiently run port. Half the field was given over to the freighters that came to Mirabello for orium; the other half, or most of it, was used by the various miner craft. The miner craft were of all sizes and makes, from the ancient *Blakes* to fairly recent, slick berylium jobs. They sat on the port aprons together, their holds open to the sun, their bows looking at the sky, as if impatient to be off again.

There were miners everywhere, talking, laughing, drinking. Their calling was a hard one, but it made men. The representatives of the orium companies knew that, and so did the crews from the freighters.

Ames walked around the port for awhile, taking in the hustle and hurry of the place, trying to feel its tempo before he undertook talking to any of the men who belonged there. He wound up, finally, at a bar, drinking Jovian rum. He spoke casually with the men on either side of him before he introduced Scotty's name.

Instantly the conversation ceased. When Ames tried to open it again, the miner on his left said, "What are you after, Mr. Ames?"

Ames swallowed his drink. "How do you know my name?" he said.

The miner unfolded a copy of the *Twin-Sun*. The front page carried the story of Buck Wylie's indictment, but what got Ames' attention was a two-column picture of himself. It had evidently been taken on the street some time after the proceedings, for Sue Wylie's hand rested on his arm, where her picture had been cut away. The caption read: *T. Ames, The Man Who Defends Wylie.*

"Well," said Ames, "I'll tell you what I'm after. I wanted to talk to someone *who knew* Scotty Purdom. I wanted to find out what kind of a man he was."

One miner nodded to another, and the first one said, "Did I hear you say somethin' about buyin' the next round?"

It was seven or eight rounds later when Ames walked unsteadily back to his house. From the vast amount of anecdotage and lore he had listened to, he had come away with little. Scotty had been secretive to extremes; no one knew much about him. All kinds of rumors were rife—that Murchison had been only a quarter partner, or less, or more. That Wylie had been on the verge of partnership with Scotty; that both had actually been partners in a new, secret venture; that Scotty had probably been killed accidentally but that Wylie wouldn't talk until he had first protected the new claim legally. All agreed, however, in one particular: that

John Murchison had loved Scotty and would do anything to get his revenge on the man who had murdered him.

Ames wrote it all down when he got home. He barely kept his eyes open until he finished, then he fell asleep on his desk.

When he woke, Sue Wylie was standing beside him, shaking him. He looked at the steaming pot of coffee she had prepared, and though he flushed, he drank it gratefully. "I'm immersing myself in the intimate details of the case," he explained, adding ruefully, "Maybe I got too immersed."

A little while later he went out again, heading for the editorial offices of the *Twin-Sun*. He had wanted to meet John Murchison, and now that he did, he spoke plainly. He found Murchison purposeful and straightforward. The big man offered him a chair as calmly as if he had been expecting Ames.

AMES said, "I see you've got my picture on the front page."

"You don't object to publicity, do you?" Murchison smiled. "A big New York lawyer like you should be used to it."

Ames couldn't help reacting. He flushed and said, "You might have mentioned the fact that I was shot at and had my office ransacked."

Murchison frowned, puzzled. He reached for a copy of the paper and opened it before Ames. "I see you didn't get past the front page, Mr. Ames," he said. "The *Twin-Sun* prints all the news—even when it's liable to be phony news."

Ames looked up from the paper. "You don't believe I was shot at?"

Murchison smiled. "I'm sure you were. I'm not sure who did the shooting."

"What do you mean?"

"I mean," said Murchison, calmly,

"that your worthy client Buck Wylie could have had one of his men shoot at you."

"But why?"

"Need I explain?" Murchison smiled. "It isn't a bad idea to have a defense attorney shot at. It not only creates sympathy, but it seems to imply that there are—shall we say—extra-legal parties interested in the case? It's fine build-up to claim dark plots are afoot." He let his smile fade away. "On the other hand, Mr. Ames, there is always the possibility Wylie arranged the thing just to convince *you*. And there is still a third possibility. Care to hear it? It isn't pretty."

"By all means."

"You'll know the answer to this one better than I." Murchison leaned back in his swivel chair. "It may be that Buck Wylie doesn't like you, Mr. Ames. Maybe you've been asking him too many questions. Maybe you've made him feel uncomfortable enough for him to do something about it. Wylie's a man of action."

"I see," said Ames, rising to leave. "However, all these theories are based on the assumption that Wylie is guilty, aren't they?"

Murchison rose with him, leaning against the door. He nodded soberly. "He *is* guilty, Mr. Ames; make no mistake about that. You see, you don't know Wylie—but the more you investigate him, as I hope you will, the more you'll come to agree with me. But I'll tell you this: I am prepared to use every honest means at my disposal to see that Wylie pays the penalty for what he did to Scotty." He had pounded his fist on the desk as he spoke. Now, grimly, he added, "And I may even allow myself a little leeway in deciding which means are honest. Do we understand each other, Mr. Ames?"

"Somewhat, Mr. Murchison," Ames

said. "Good afternoon, sir."

It was now close to five o'clock, and Ames went to the local ethergraph office. The dozens of minute details and impressions he had already gathered were buzzing around in his mind, and he couldn't make head nor tail of any of them. He needed someone to talk to, someone like Judge Averill. Sue Wylie would have been fine, but he preferred neutrals in cases like this. The only question now was whether Judge Averill was really a neutral. Ames muttered to himself, realizing that he was going in circles. He hadn't been able to make a single one of his decisions stick for any length of time.

He walked into the office of System Ethergraph, Ltd. and asked for the manager. A small, dapper man came out to see Ames.

Ames said, "I think you remember me. I was here for several hours early this morning." The manager nodded, and Ames said, "I have another message I want you to transmit to New York and—"

"Won't one of our clerks do, Mr. Ames?"

"I thought you'd be interested in this message," said Ames.

The manager raised his eyebrows. "Certainly, Mr. Ames."

Ames waited until the manager poised his stylus. "To the System Ethergraph, Ltd.; Central Office, New York," Ames dictated. "Attention, Legal Dep't. Notice is hereby served that the undersigned is filing criminal and civil actions against your company, as per Communications Statutory Laws, Section 885. Will charge that the manager of the Mirabello branch office did wilfully reveal the contents of an ethergraph addressed to the undersigned— Terwilliger Ames."

"Is that all, Mr. Ames?"

"I think so."

"The charges will be twenty-four dollars. May I thank you for your patronage?"

AMES paid and left, feeling tremendously relieved. He had satisfied himself that it had been the manager and not Judge Averill, who had told Murchison of Ames' standing in New York. The graph itself was worthless; he had no proof and no case, but the manager's calm demeanor in the face of a serious charge had told Ames what he wanted to know.

A moment later Ames laughed savagely at himself. It was still possible that *both* the manager and Averill had told Murchison! He was letting the details entangle him. He consulted his memorandum and headed for the Bureau of Meteorology. He would stay with the details. It was the only way he knew how to work.

At the Bureau he asked for the chief clerk and explained what he wanted. Were the files of the Bureau open for public inspection?

"I'll be glad to be of service, Mr. Ames," said the clerk. "Can you be more specific about which files you want?"

"How do you know my name?" said Ames.

"Why, your picture was in the paper today, Mr. Ames."

Ames nodded. "I want to consult the files on weather conditions for the past two months," he said.

"Can you tell me which areas you are interested in?"

"I don't know," said Ames. "Suppose I were a miner. What areas would I have to watch out for, say, the tenth and eleventh of this month?"

"I can't say anything offhand, Mr. Ames. The miners here are scattered around for hundreds of thousands of miles, at the very least. The main as-teroid belt is over six million miles long, and there are miners all through it. I'd say, roughly, that there were at least two or three areas that had storms during the days you mention."

"All right," said Ames, wearily. "Let's get the files and see exactly how many areas there were and what they were."

An hour later Ames left. There had turned out to be four storm areas, all widely scattered, and none of them violent, though the one at the so-called Double Horn had lasted several weeks. Ames had carefully written down every bit of information.

On his way home he stopped at the library and spent some time with *Ghort's Atlas of the Forty-first System Group*, of which Mirabello was a member. He checked the distances of each storm area from Mirabello and added them to his notes.

When he got home, Sue Wylie was there. She was wearing an apron and she had prepared dinner. "Tonight you'll be my guest," she smiled. Ames could see that she was waiting for him to tell her what he had done that day, but he waited until he had finished eating. He was too tired to eat much.

He sat down on the couch in his little living room when he was done. There was a package lying on a table, and atop it lay an envelope. Curious, Ames looked at Sue and opened the enevelope. Inside was a folded certificate for a pistol permit. It had been signed by Judge Averill.

"When did you see Averill?" he asked.

"This afternoon."

"Did you have any trouble getting this?"

"No. He said it was a little irregular for someone to apply for another's pistol permit, but he said he'd make an exception for you." She said, taking a cigarette, "He seems to have changed in the way he feels about you. You haven't told me a thing."

Ames said nothing. He opened the package and his eyes popped. "What do you think I'm going to do with this?" he exclaimed. He gingerly removed the heat pistol and holstered belt that were in the package. He examined it, looked at the permit, then said, "This is a Foster IV! It's practically a portable cannon!"

"They're the only kind my brother owns. I told what happened yesterday and he had one of his men bring it in." She hesitated before she added, "Buck expected you today, you know."

"I had a lot to do today," said Ames.

"Aren't you going to tell me about it?"

Ames said, "I don't know." He put the gun away and said, with his back to the girl, "Tell me, Miss Wylie, what would you say. . . ." But he broke off, sat down again, and took out his notebook. "I'll give you what I've got," he said. He read his notes, summarizing his activities. When he finished, he said, "What do you think?"

"May I ask some questions?"

"I wish you would. It may help me."

"Why did you write down all those absurd things you heard at the Standish port? Why should you be interested in rumors?"

AMES said, slowly, "Because I'm not sure yet what is rumor and what is fact. I've got to see everything for myself. I've got to wade through an enormous mass of facts in the hope that one will mean something. I don't know how to judge the things I know now."

"Why did you hunt up the weather and those distances?"

"Well," said Ames, "there's one re-markable thing about what I do know —Scotty's asking your brother for his boat. Scotty mined the same place for ten years. Weren't there storms there before? What did he do those times? Is it possible that he was engaged in mining a new place—a place where he really needed an extra boat—as he hadn't needed any with his old mine?

"You see," Ames continued, looking at the girl, "suppose we assume that there is some truth to the rumor that Buck and Scotty recently entered into a partnership to work a new mine to-gether. I don't know why they would —but if they did, it explains a lot. For instance, that might be the reason Scotty needed another boat—the new mine being in a dangerous area, while the Silver Spoon obviously wasn't. That would explain why he asked Buck for a boat, of all people. Third, it might tell us where Buck was those six days he says he went prospecting.

"But best of all," Ames said, slowly, "it would provide a better motive for Murchison's determination to be re-venged on your brother. I somehow can't swallow that business of his be-ing so devoted to Scotty—or of anyone being very devoted to him. He wasn't the kind of man that other men felt strongly about, one way or another. It may very well be that Murchi-son hates Buck more than he loved Scotty — because he knew, maybe from Scotty, that he was being sup-planted. . . ."

"Then you don't believe Buck told you the truth?"

"I didn't say that," Ames began. "He may—"

"You think Buck killed Scotty, don't you?"

"Not necessarily," Ames said. "I'm just theorizing, but even if the sup-positions are true, Scotty might have been killed accidentally. If such a thing had happened, Buck might be afraid to tell the truth because of his record. He might have tried to protect himself by bringing back Scotty's boat and attempting to destroy it—which again points to the theory of the new mine.

"You see, Scotty's Silver Spoon was a secret for ten years—so obviously a boat could be left there without fear of its being spotted from space. But if the new mine didn't afford such protection, it would have to be brought back and destroyed. . . ."

He stopped speaking, regarding Sue carefully. He sat down closer to her and said, quietly, "Shall I continue?"

She was smoking very nervously as he spoke. She nodded.

"That's why I'm checking the weather and the distances," Ames resumed. "Scotty left on the tenth. If I could find an area for which the Meteorological Bureau had issued warnings somewhere around that time, I might be able to get an idea of where Scotty had gone. It couldn't have been far if he was due back in eight days, fully loaded. Furthermore, if Buck was gone six days, he would have had plenty of time to make the round trip there and back."

"You've listed four areas," Sue said. "Do any of them fit?"

"Possibly. I can't be sure until I can compare the speeds of both the boats that figure in it. . . . I wonder if you'd do me a favor?"

"If I can."

"Will you take me to Buck's blastport tomorrow? I want to go over the ground, maybe talk to some of his men."

"All right, I will."

Ames sat there, undecided. Presently he asked, "What are you thinking about?"

She was looking at a picture across the room. "I'm thinking I'm glad you're being so methodical about this, because I know you'll get to the bottom of it."

Ames took a deep breath. He went back to the couch, saying, "And you're not afraid of what I'll find when I hit bottom?"

She didn't answer. She continued sitting there, bemused, and Ames made no effort to continue the conversation. He took the volume he had been reading and stretched out. Once she said to him, "You're very tired. Why don't you go to sleep?" Ames said something about having to continue his studies and kept reading. . . .

When he woke up, several hours later, the room was in semi-darkness. The wall clock told him he had been asleep for three hours. Only a table lamp was lit, and across the room, curled up in the large chair, Sue Wylie lay asleep. The Foster gun lay on a chair which she had pulled up near her.

Ames sat up, and his coat fell off him. She had covered him with it and undertaken to keep guard over him. He didn't know what to do. He didn't want to wake her at that hour, and he was too embarrassed to think of asking her to use his bedroom. In the end he covered her up with his coat and laid the gun down beside him on the couch. If there was any protecting to be done, he thought, he would do it. . . .

V

OVER breakfast the next morning, Ames said, "You shouldn't have stayed here last night."

"My reputation, you mean?" Sue smiled. "It'll stand it."

"I mean there was no necessity for it, not only because I'm perfectly capable of taking care of myself, but because there was no danger of anything happening."

She swallowed, then said, "You seem very sure of that."

"It stands to reason. Whoever shot at me two days ago has had innumerable opportunities to do so again. It hasn't been tried, and I don't think it will be."

"Why?" she said, sharing the bacon with him. "Change of plan?"

"I think so. Whoever took that shot at me was a pretty reckless sort. He did it in broad daylight, in the heart of the town. Well, that kind of direct action doesn't jibe too well with the indirect action of stealing my credentials, does it? The man who shot at me would have tried again, being the sort he is—but whoever it was that thought of stopping me by stealing my credentials must have ordered him to lay off." He added, his mouth full, "I think they're laying off because they're curious. They want to know what I'll do. Or maybe they think they can outwit me. Flatters them more."

Sue observed, "That doesn't sound like Buck, then. If he were behind it, he'd have you shot. He likes action."

Ames dropped his fork. "How—how did you know?" he stammered. "You—"

"I looked through your notes after you fell asleep," said Sue, pouring the coffee. She pushed a cup towards Ames and looked into his eyes. "I thought maybe you were sparing me something, and I wanted to know. I read the account of your conversation with Murchison, where he said he thought Buck might have had you shot at."

Ames stirred his coffee. "You don't think so?"

"Not at all. Not a chance of it being true."

Ames said, "You remember the hole that shot left? About a quarter of an inch—from a Foster II." Sue nodded, and Ames said, "Yesterday Buck gave you a Foster IV to give me. I noticed he told you he didn't have any other kind of gun. It might have been an indirect way of letting me know that none of his men had shot at me, because they would have used Foster's IV'S. What about it?"

She put her coffee down and shook her head. "I don't know where you keep it all. Your head is like some huge store-room, with room for all kinds of odds and ends . . . and a little worthless junk too, I'm afraid . . . just a little."

"You know," said Ames curiously, "that's almost exactly what a professor of mine told me once, except that he said my head was like a library with a terribly disordered filing system. . . ." He smiled at the reminiscence. "Comes to the same thing," he mused, "but I'll be damned if I can think of any other way to think a thing out."

"Were you a good lawyer in New York?"

"How do you know I'm from New York?"

"Silly. It's in the ex libris of all your books."

"Oh," said Ames. "I was pretty good, I guess. . . ."

They left shortly afterward, though not without an argument about the necessity of taking along the gun. Ames didn't take it, standing by his analysis. "Here lies Terwilliger Ames," Sue said. "Still standing by his analysis." But Ames noticed she didn't press matters too much; she was learning to trust his judgment.

Sue had called Buck's arrando—it was a Martian word which meant, roughly, a ranch—early that morning, and a gyro was waiting for them when they reached Standish port.

"This is Sour Tom," said Sue, introducing Ames to a lanky, burnt man whose face looked as if a smile would disfigure it. "Tom's going to take us out to the place."

"Don't know if I can get clearance off this danged port," Tom scowled. "Holdin' everything up waitin' for the danged mail freight to blow in. I hope you won't mind waitin' a bit, Miss Sue?"

Sue smiled. "Not at all, Tom. I guess you must be expecting your monthly batch of magazines on that danged mail freighter."

The least bit of a grin crept into the corners of Tom's mouth. "Yep," he said, sheepishly. "Never could fool you, Miss Sue."

A FEW minutes later the Standish port sirens went off with fantastic vigor—a signal used only for crashes and the arrival of mail. When the individual vessels that dotted the apron and the field joined in it meant mail, and a few minutes of utter chaos. People ran about excitedly, shouting to each other in vain efforts to pierce the din, and the control tower broke out a halyard of signal flags. And then the mail freighter flashed in the sky overhead, her silver hull gleaming in the sunlight, her fore rockets easing her off, spluttering with self-importance. Down she came in a graceful arc, landing as softly as a bird. . . .

Fifteen minutes later, Sour Tom came hurrying towards them, a bulky package under his arm. There was a happy light in his eyes, but his face had no share in it. "This way, folks," he sang out, leading them to the south apron. They were off in a few minutes.

The gyro was a fairly large plane, evidently used a great deal to carry supplies from the town to the *arrando*.

Tom got it up to three thousand feet, set the controls and opened the package. "Ahhh," he breathed, contentedly, riffling the pages of one of the magazines. "I'm halfway into the dangest serial I ever laid my eyes on." Ames glanced at the cover of the magazine. It was *Rip-Snorting Wild West Stories*.

The flight lasted almost an hour and a half, taking them deep into country Ames had never seen before. The earth that lay under their wings was green and lovely, and everything flourished in its soil with unbelievable disregard for horticultural laws. Its streams were like bits of gold ribbon, its fields like gardens. Deeper in were jungles, warmed by hot springs that coursed a few feet under the soil, and then, off to the west, the Grey Mountains rose, the peaks like burnished copper above the shadowed slate of the range.

Ames drank it all in, his eyes fastened on the scenes that unfolded before him, but his mind was occupied with other thoughts. Once Sue said to him, "I haven't been out this way in a long time," and he nodded, wondering what lay behind her words.

The Wylie *arrando* stood atop a plateau that climbed out of wild, desolate country. It was a large place, comprising more than a dozen buildings. Farther along the plateau was another group of structures, but these were open-topped sheds that stored orium. Sour Tom brought the gyro down in a small, fenced-off field near the main house, where we led them.

The main house was a two-storied affair with wide piazzas and long expanses of glassine walls. Oaks and aspens surrounded it, and a carefully attended garden ran all around the place. There were paths that led to the other houses, some of which Ames guessed were for the men Wylie employed. And there were barns and stables, for the fields on the far edge of the plateau were cultivated, and the luxuriant range was grazing land for horses and cattle.

Ames hadn't expected anything like it. It wasn't so much the evidence of great wealth and luxury—and of good taste—that surprised him, but the definite effort that had been made to combine the best features that Mirabello offered with nostalgic contributions from home. He breathed the air in deeply and looked about the place with shining eyes. This was no *arrando;* it was a magnificent estate. Ames doubted whether its equal existed on Mirabello.

Some of the men, who were busy around the barns and shed, waved to Sue from their tasks. When they reached the flagstone path, Tom said, "See you later, I hope, Miss Sue. Pleasure, Mr. Ames." He motioned toward the house and his face darkened. "Waitin' for you," he said.

As they went through the gardens and approached the house, Ames saw whom Tom had meant. There was a woman standing on the piazza near the front door. Two Irish setters lay quietly at her feet, and then, seeing Sue, they rose and started running toward her when a sharp word from the woman halted them and brought them back.

SHE was quite a beautiful woman, Ames thought, when he was introduced to her. "Miss Morales, Mr. Ames," she said, quietly. "Mr. Ames is Buck's attorney, Lola." She was in her early thirties, Ames judged, but age meant nothing in a woman like her. She was exotic, with dark, burning, hard eyes, and jet black hair that lay in braids over her bare shoulders. She wore a simple peasant dress that must have cost a great deal, Ames imagined,

because it was made entirely of fibreglass, and the brilliant colors suited her olive skin.

"How is Buck?" Lola Morales asked.

"He's fine," said Sue. "He asked for you yesterday."

"I'm going to see him this afternoon," said Lola. "I tried to get away yesterday, but I had to supervise the paymaster." She issued a call to the dogs. "I must talk to the foreman now," she said before she left. "If you want anything, call Pedro." Then, just before she went down the stairs, she asked, casually, "Does Buck know you're here?"

Sue hesitated briefly, then said, "No; we came out quite suddenly."

A few minutes later, sitting under a huge umbrella and sipping tall glasses of iced *juno,* Ames said, quietly, "Is Lola the witness your brother meant? I mean the time I asked him who had seen him that Saturday night and he wouldn't answer." Sue nodded. Ames said, "I guess she's also the reason you don't live here anymore."

Sue said, "Let's walk around a bit, shall we?"

"Sure," Ames agreed. "And you can tell me about Lola. I'd like to know more about her." He flushed horribly as Sue darted a glance at him. "I mean," he mumbled, "we may need her as a witness and . . . and . . ." Suddenly he blurted, "Excuse me, Miss Wylie, but you're a fool if you think any man would look twice at another woman with you around!" And having said it, he stood stock-still, seemingly paralyzed on the stairs, shocked by what he had uttered.

"Why, Mr. Ames!" said Sue. "What a gallant thing to say!" She looked up at his lean, embarrassed face and smiled. "But don't you think it would have sounded better if you had called me Sue—with such a speech?"

"All right," Ames gulped, "but that goes both ways."

"You mean you want me to call you Terwilliger?" she laughed.

The color in his face deepened. "Call me Ames," he said.

She took his hand and led him. They walked then, going through the stocked sheds and well-equipped barns, talking to the men. Once they saw Lola. She was returning to the house. As if by common agreement they dropped their handclasp. A little while later, a large, stylish gyro rose from the field and Sue said, "That's Lola going now."

It was almost noon when Ames looked at his watch. The time had sped by quickly. "We've spent too long a time here already," Ames said. "I've got most of what I came here for. Now I'll see if I can get the rest of it." He thought a moment, then asked, "This Sour Tom likes you a lot, I know. Does he trust you? I mean, I thought from the way he looked at Lola that he sort of was on your side. Am I right?"

"I think so," Sue said, searchingly. "Ames, you're not thinking of doing anything against Buck, are you?"

"No," said Ames. He let a little sigh escape him. "I told you I've got most of what I came for. Do you know what that was? I wanted to see the kind of place Buck Wylie lived in, to see if I could perhaps understand the kind of life he lead. Well, I've seen it. Buck told me had made enough money for one lifetime and I believe him. He has everything a man could want here. He lives like a prince, but he hasn't flaunted his wealth here. A man like that wouldn't kill for money. . . ." He met Sue's eyes and said, "So you see, I've decided that he didn't kill Scotty. I've quite decided. . . ."

"But what about your theory that

it might have been an accident?"

"I don't know," Ames said, thoughtfully. "That's a bridge I'll come to yet, but it'll be a lot easier to cross than this might have been. Right now I want to see Tom and have a talk with him. Do you know where he is?"

"I think so," Sue smiled. "Follow me."

She led Ames to the farthermost barn and went in. She called out once, "Tom!" A minute later, Tom came sliding down from a hayloft, his magazine carefully folded to keep his place.

"TOM," said Sue, looking at him, "Mr. Ames here is Buck's lawyer. You know that. Mr. Ames is trying to save Buck's life. He's got some things he wants to ask about—maybe some personal things about Buck. Whatever they are, I want you to tell him the truth. Don't keep anything back. Do you understand me, Tom?"

"Dang it all," said Tom, disgusted. "You don't have to go makin' a danged speech like that at me. I'd cut my left arm off for you, Miss Sue, you know that." He added, to Ames, "I'm left-handed, you notice."

Ames said, "Do you know anything about Mr. Wylie's boats—the ones he carries orium in?"

"Guess I do, if anybody does. Any one in p'ticular?"

"The Hellcat, I think it's called. Do you know anything about the speed she can make?"

"Guess I do. Guess that danged boat could do plenty."

"Can you make that a little more specific? For instance, do you think she could do half a million miles in three days?"

Sour Tom scratched his head. "Guess she could. You see, Mr. Ames, the Hellcat's a funny boat. She acts up every now an' then, and we have her over at Hank Miller's more than she's here. Spends more time in his repair sheds—"

"Who is Hank Miller?"

"Why, Hank's the feller that runs the big Miller Rocket Sheds just outside Riverdale. He's got a way with the *Hellcat*, as Buck says. She spends more time in his sheds gettin' her machinery straightened out than she does pullin' orium. Mighty funny boat, she is."

"Do you think you could let me have a look at her?"

"Don't see how I could," said Tom, "seein' as how she's been seized by the law and put in the pound. She and Scotty's boat, both."

"You mean the *Hellcat's* been impounded?" said Ames, puzzled. "It doesn't make sense. Why should they impound her?"

"Guess maybe they figured they'd have a try at her Berry gauge."

"Why? What is a Berry gauge?"

Tom shifted his weight from one foot to the other. "That's the thingamabob that keeps track of the fuel and multiplies that by the time and I don't know what else and adds up the mileage the ship makes. It's a mighty handy gadget."

"You mean," said Ames, eagerly, "that by going through that gauge one can tell how far a ship's been?"

"That's right."

"How far back does it go? I mean, suppose one day I did a hundred miles, and the next day another hundred, and the third day I did fifty miles—how many of those trips would it keep a record of?"

"All of 'em, unless you bust open her seal and started her over again. That danged Berry can go into billions, I guess, with each separate start and finish marked plain from the next. Course, only a licensed mechanic like Hank's

allowed to bust the seal—that's in case of an accident, so's the seal will be intact if they need to investigate."

"Let me see if I understand you, Tom," said Ames. There was an odd look in his eyes. "The seal can only be opened by licensed people because in case of accident it might be necessary to find out where the ship had been? In fewer words, if the seal were intact, one could practically reconstruct a ship's voyage?"

"That's right."

"But suppose I were a criminal and I wanted to hide where I'd been? What would prevent me from breaking the seal myself?"

"You can't break it," said Tom, shaking his head. "The Berry gauge's made of alumalloy all the way through, includin' the seal. We've had wrecks that left nothin' but dust of the ship, but the Berry gauge was there, tickin' away, alive and cheerful. You can't touch 'em without a special nitro key, and you can't git a key without bein' licensed."

"Did Buck have such a license?"

Tom snorted. "Must be less than a dozen men in Mirabello got one of them licenses. Hank's got one, but where would Buck get one?"

"Do you know if Buck had such a key, perhaps?"

"Hell, no—they're harder to git than the license!"

"All right," said Ames. "Why couldn't a criminal burn out the entire gauge—just tear it out of the ship altogether?"

TOM shook his head again and regarded Sue judiciously. "Guess you ain't never been in a minin' craft, Mr. Ames," he said. "That Berry gauge is fixed right smack in the center of the control board. If you tried to take it out, you'd wreck the ship. Ain't nobody can git one of them gadgets out and still have a ship—not even Hank Miller. No, sir!"

Ames leaned against a fence and remained silent, his face screwed up. Sue said, quietly, "What's the matter, Ames?"

Ames let his breath out with a sigh. "I'm not sure," he said. "You remember the testimony established that Scotty's boat was seized while it was circling near Grey Mountain—and it had supposedly just returned from a voyage. From what Tom says, the Berry gauge in that boat and in Buck's boat too, for that matter, must be intact. If that's so, the authorities should be able to reconstruct the last voyage of both the boats and—"

"Excuse me, Mr. Ames," Tom interrupted. "That don't necessarily follow. You could outfox that danged gadget easy enough. Say you aimed to go someplace a hundred thousand miles out, and you didn't want it to show up on the gauge. Well, all you got to do is go out there roundabout—like, addin', say, fifty thousand, and come back the same way—and that's what the gauge would show."

"I see," said Ames, lapsing into silence again.

"Course, that's only if you was up to somethin'," Tom explained. "That's why the authorities havin' Buck's and Scotty's gauges don't mean nothin' to 'em. Scotty was so sly he'd be sure to go roundabout no matter where he was goin'—and I guess Buck'd come back nice and roundabout himself, so the danged gauges ain't worth a—"

"What do you mean by that?"

"By what?"

"By saying Buck would come back roundabout," said Ames, his eyes fixed on Tom. "You sound as if you thought he'd done it."

Tom hitched his trousers up leisurely,

eyeing Sue. "I ain't sayin' what I think, Mr. Ames. I ain't thought about it. All I got to say is, if Buck done it, he must've had a danged good reason. . . ."

Ames took careful note of the way Tom had kept glancing at Sue as he spoke, but he said nothing about it, biding his time. "Tom," he said, "There's just one more thing I want to ask you about. Were you here during the twenty-fourth—the day Buck got back from his prospecting trip?" He added, "That was the same day they found Scotty's boat circling around Grey Mountain, remember?"

"Yes, sir, I was here. I remember Buck come in just before noon that day."

"Did he go out again during the rest of the day?"

"Can't say," said Tom, laconically.

"Why not? You were here all day."

"Can't say," Tom repeated.

Sue said, quietly, "I want you to say, Tom. For my sake."

TOM looked at her as if he hoped she might change her mind. Then he shifted his weight again and said, slowly, "I don't know, and that's the truth. Buck was dead tired when he come in, and he just plumped down into bed and went to sleep—so offhand, I'd figure he couldn't have gone out again that day. On the other hand," he said, hesitantly, "along about evenin', just before I went into town, I decided I'd have a quick look around the place. The other hands had all gone into town, and with Buck asleep, I figured it might be a good idea.

"Well, I went over to the orium sheds, and I was danged amazed to see the *Hellcat* sittin' there in the port. I hadn't seen her come in, and I didn't know how she'd gotten there. The other rocketeers around the place had gone into town the night before, and there wasn't anybody here but Buck who could've brought her in, and he was asleep. I figured Scotty must've brought her back and gone away without me seein' him.

"Well, I went over to the main house and told Lola about it and she said she'd tell Buck. The next mornin' Buck woke me up and asked *me* about the *Hellcat*. I told him what I knew, and he said he'd been asleep all that time. He seemed about as surprised as I was. Well, about an hour later, who comes flyin' in here but the Colonial Attorney. That was the first we knew about Scotty's boat havin' been found the night before.

"Seems the C.A. had found out Buck'd lent Scotty the *Hellcat* and all the rest of it and he asked a lot of questions. Buck told him he didn't know nothin' about it. When the C.A. asked him who'd brought the *Hellcat* back, with Scotty missin', Buck just looked blank. The next mornin' they come here and arrested Buck."

"Thanks, Tom," said Ames, somberly. He took out his little book and added some notes to the ones he had already written. His face was dark as he said to Sue, "I think that's about all we can do here. It's still pretty much of a dead end."

Sue shook hands with Tom, and Tom said, "You wanted me to tell, didn't you, Miss Sue?"

"Yes, Tom. No matter how it looks, we know Buck didn't do it. The only way we can help him is by uncovering the whole truth."

"Well, then, Miss Sue, there's one thing more."

"You mean there's something you haven't told us?"

Tom nodded briefly. "Guess so. You see, Buck lent Scotty the *Hellcat* once before, about five, six weeks ago."

"What?" cried Ames.

"It's the truth. Nobody seems to know about it. I guess Buck don't even know I know. The other hands thought the *Hellcat* was over at Hank Miller's, but I knew Scotty had it."

"Good Lord!" Ames breathed. "Then the *Hellcat* had made that trip before! If there was some way of checking. . . ." He broke off. "Tom, how far are we from Hank Miller's?"

"About an hour up yonder."

"I want you to take me there," said Ames, tensely. "Sue, you'd better go back to Mirabello. I don't know how long I'll be."

"I'll wait here for you . . . at least until Lola gets back. . . ."

He looked down at her sad, frightened face and he wanted to kiss her, but being the kind of man he was, he flushed and said, "See you . . ."

VI

TOM flew Ames in the gyro. In something less than an hour they passed over Riverdale, a small, sprawling town that reminded Ames of an ancient French hamlet in Brittany. He was greatly surprised, therefore, to see the huge repair sheds that flanked Riverdale from the east, for they looked as if they belonged to a great industrial center. Four fat stacks belched green smoke into the warm noon air, and the ground for miles around was torn and blackened with rocket blasts. The repair sheds, of transparent, corrugated *bytly-metal,* distorted the forms of the several ships that lay in them, and the place hummed with activity.

Tom landed the gyro right in the middle of the plant. Without going into the office he led Ames down the length of a shed, past helmeted men who were repairing a set of rocket tubes on a mining craft. At the far end of the shed, in a sort of fenced-off area, sat a middle-aged man in overall trousers and shirt-sleeves. He seemed oblivious to the noise around him as he adjusted the tail fins on a model of an I.P. destroyer.

"Howdy, Tom," he smiled, shaking hands. He adjusted his glasses with an inquiring look at Ames, meanwhile talking to Tom. "Anything new over at the place? That Lola high-handin' it over everyone with Buck out of the way? You hear anythin' 'bout—"

"Dang it all," Tom said, sourly, "you always got time for gossip, Hank. This here's Mr. Ames, Buck's lawyer."

"Thought I recognized the face," said Miller. He wiped his hands on his trousers and offered one to Ames. "Pleased to meet up with you, Mr. Ames. Sure got a lot of trouble on your hands, ain't you?"

"That's what I came to see you about, Mr. Miller. I thought perhaps you could help me." He looked around and held his hands out. "Is there someplace here where we can talk without this noise?"

"Sure," said Miller, smiling. He threw a canvas cover over the model and grabbed Tom's hand, leading them out through a side door.

"Talk, talk!" Tom growled. "All you ever do 'round here."

"Got to keep up with the news, Tom," Miller said, merrily. He led them through the yards and across a road, where, atop a slight hill, a small, neatly painted bungalow stood. He motioned both men to lounge chairs under a gayly colored umbrella and said, "What can I do for you, Mr. Ames? Glad to be of service, if I can."

Ames said, slowly, "Tom here says you and Buck have always been good friends."

"Sure," said Miller. "Fine feller, that Buck. Wasn't what you might call the friendly type, but a fine, hard work-in' lad. Hated to see him get mixed up in somethin' as dirty as that. Trouble with him was he didn't pay enough attention to the things right—"

"Mr. Ames," Tom scowled, "If you let him, Hank'll keep talkin' on any subject till he falls asleep in that chair. Now look here, Hank, Mr. Ames ain't got the rest of the day, I don't think."

Ames said, "Mr. Miller, you were saying that you thought Buck was all right in your opinion. He was also a good customer of yours?"

"My best, maybe. Had four boats, and liked to keep 'em in good workin' order. Why, I remember the time . . ." He caught Tom's disgusted glance and stopped. "Sure," he said. "Fine customer."

"Did you ever do any work on the Berry gauges in his boats?"

"Berry gauges? Now, let me see. I do remember his bringin' in the little one, the one with the Spanish name— Gaucho, that's it. Had some trouble with it not registering, 'bout seven months ago."

"Is that all?"

"Uh-huh. Course, I'd know, because Buck always liked me to have a hand in tinkerin' with his boats. Said I had a way with 'em, and he wouldn't let my boys near them. Scotty—that's funny, my bringin' up Scotty in the same breath, with Buck bein' accused of kill-in' him—now, Scotty was the same way, always wantin' me to work on his boat. Now, there's a man was always foolin' around with his Berry gauge—"

"You also took care of Scotty's boat? Regularly?"

"Sure. I take care of 'bout ninety per cent of the mining boats in Mirabello. Course I don't give 'em all my personal attention."

"You were saying," Ames said, "Scotty was always—"

"Excuse me," Miller interrupted.

"Just remembered some-
thin' 'bout that other
question you asked me.
Funny, my forgettin'
something like that, with
me thinkin' about it only
the other day, when I
read in the paper they'd
arrested Buck. He had
the *Hellcat* in here about five weeks
ago—asked me to set the Berry gauge
on her back to zero."

"He brought the *Hellcat* here himself?"

"Sure. Who else—oh, I reckon you
mean did maybe one of his rocketeers
bring her? No, it was Buck. Funny,
you askin'—"

"And all he did was ask you to set
the gauge back to zero? He didn't ask
you to give him a reading on it? He

didn't want to know what the last figures on the gauge were?"

MILLER laughed. "You're way
ahead of me, Mr. Ames. I'm tryin' to tell you. The day he come down
here, Scotty was here, too. Scotty'd
just come back from a trip and he
wanted me to fix his Berry gauge, same
as always. Well, that Scotty seemed a
heap more interested in Buck's gauge
than Buck himself was. I guess even

Huge repair sheds flanked
Riverdale from the east; looked
like a great industrial center

if Buck had wanted to find out what
was on the gauge, he wouldn't have had
a chance. Scotty kept him tied up in
conversation all the time I was workin'
on that gauge of Buck's."

"And Buck never asked you what
was on it?"

"I'm comin' to it, Mr. Ames. No,
Buck never asked me. Now, the way
I work on a Berry gauge, keepin' it

ethical, I just open it up and spin the
hell out of the dials, mixin' 'em up.
Ain't none of my business what's on
'em. And that's what I would have
done that time, too, if Bax Murchison
hadn't asked me to take special note
of the reading."

Ames sucked his breath in audibly.
"Murchison asked you that?"

"Yep. Asked me once and I said I

wouldn't. Then he pulled out a batch of papers showin' me Buck's criminal record, and he said he was checkin' up on Buck because the paper was goin' to do a big story on him. He wanted to know what Buck was up to."

"So you gave him the reading?" Ames asked, softly.

"Well, I don't do things that way. Course, I didn't know Buck'd had a record, but it still made no difference to me and I said no. The next day Murchison came back. He had a legal paper from Whitley, the Colonial Attorney, givin' me a full authority to do what Murchison asked.

"Well, I didn't have the *Hellcat* in my sheds and I wasn't expecting her, so there wasn't anything I could do, paper or no. Then, about three days later—I'll be danged if Buck didn't bring that boat in! I wanted to tell him what I had to do, but Murchison had said if I breathed a word of it, he'd have the law on me. . . ."

Hank Miller gestured with his hands. "What could I do? I had that danged paper, so I gave Murchison the readings. I thought it was a dirty trick at the time, but three days ago, when I picked up the paper and I seen what Buck'd done—why, I understood that Murchison had only been tryin' to do a public service. Understand me, I ain't sayin' a personal word against Buck; I liked him and I still do. At the same time, I got to admit that Murchison knew what he was doin'. He must have known about that secret partnership Buck and Scotty were goin' into, and he was afraid, knowin' Buck's record—"

Ames broke in. "What do you know about that secret partnership?"

"Well," Miller hemmed, "I guess I don't know much more'n I've heard around. I get to see a lot of people even out here—"

"Gossip," said Tom, scowling. "Pack of old women. Craziest thing I ever heard of, Buck bein' partners with that cooty old Scotty."

"Nothin' wrong with gossip," said Miller, stoutly. "What're we doin' right now but gossipin'? Course, I wouldn't say anything about that whole business—haven't up to now—except that now that you bring it up, why, it's all coming out soon enough anyway, so I guess it's no secret anymore. You're a lawyer, Mr. Ames. Do you think I still got to keep quiet about the reading I gave Murchison?"

"I'LL tell you about that in a minute," said Ames, quietly. "Do you remember what that legal paper said? Did it say specifically that you were to give Murchison Buck's Berry gauge readings?"

"No, it just said I was to do what Murchison asked."

"Tell me, Mr. Miller, do you have any idea where the *Hellcat* had been just before Buck brought her in?" He added, "Or who had used her?"

"No, I don't recall. I guess Buck had her out on a trip. The last big figures on the gauge were around two hundred thousand, but I might be off a good bit, just tryin' to guess at it."

"Has Whitley been here to see you since that time?"

"Not since nor ever before. Never spoke to the man."

"One last question, please," Ames said. "A few minutes ago you said something about Scotty always having you work on his Berry gauge. Exactly what did you do to his gauge?"

"Shift her back to zero," Miller smiled, shaking his head. "I've never known a man like him. Everybody figured his gauge didn't show a thing anyway, with him probably goin' to his mine every which way. But just the same, at the end of every trip, he'd bring his boat in here and have me shift the Berry back to zero."

He shook his head again. "You want to know somethin', Mr. Ames? I ain't sayin' nothin' against him, him bein' dead somewhere and gone to meet his God, but that man didn't even trust me. He'd make me take my glasses off the minute I'd opened the seal, and I'd have to do the rest of the work just feelin' my way. I'm blind as a mole without my glasses, and that's the way Scotty wanted me. Poor old duck."

"Mr. Miller," said Ames, "do you know whether Scotty knew that Murchison had asked you to take down the readings on the *Hellcat?*"

"Can't say," said Miller. "He kept Buck all tied up talkin' to him while I was busy with the gauge, so it might look, judgin' it now, that he was helpin' me. Still and all, knowin' Scotty, I'd say if he knew anything about it, he'd have popped off about it after Buck left. So I guess I'd say he didn't know."

Ames rose to go. He shook hands with Miller and said, gravely, "You asked me something a moment ago, Mr. Miller, about keeping what you know quiet. I'll give you a straight answer. Your life probably depends on whether or not you talk."

Ames' lean face, so seldom revelatory of any emotion, was tightly drawn now, and a curious flame burned in his eyes. "What you know can not only clear Buck, Mr. Miller, but it points directly to the man who murdered Scotty. If that gets out, you may need more repairing than you can get in your sheds. . . ." Miller's hand had gone limp by the time Ames let go of it. "You've been a great help," Ames said. "Thanks again."

"Don't mention it," Miller gulped. "I . . . I . . . won't."

Walking back to the gyro, Tom ob-

served, dryly, "Ain't goin' to be much gossip around these parts for awhile. . . ."

WHEN they returned to the *arrando,* one of the hands told Tom that Sue had gone. Lola had returned from Mirabello and taken Sue back with her, to Mirabello City.

"Don't sound like Lola," said Tom. "She'd just as soon take Miss Sue's eyes out before this happened to Buck. I'll take you in, Mr. Ames."

Ames said nothing. It was as if a fever had seized him during that afternoon. He sat quietly in the gyro, his eyes staring fixedly in the distance. But he couldn't keep his hands still. The long, bony fingers wrestled with each other until they were white from pressure. When they were near town, Ames said, "Don't drop me off at Standish. I want to go to the center of town."

Tom skirted Standish port and landed in the small gyro port near the courthouse. "You know where to get me if you need me, Mr. Ames," he said. "I'm right handy in a fight, if I do say so."

Ames walked the two blocks to the offices of the *Twin-Sun.* He went into the circulation room and asked for the files of the last three weeks. A few minutes later, a side door opened and Murchison himself came in, carrying an armful of newspapers.

"How do you do, Mr. Ames?" he said, sitting down beside Ames. He laid the papers down before Ames. "I hope you find these useful."

Ames hesitated a moment before he took the papers. It occurred to him that he might have gone to the library for the back file, but now that he was here, he wasn't sorry. There was no use deluding himself that Murchison didn't know what he was up to—or that he wouldn't have known soon

enough if Ames had gone to the library.
From here in, Ames thought, the game
would be played open-handed.

Picking up the first issue, Ames
scrutinized the newspapers until he
reached the one dated the 16th. He
took out his notebook and copied the
caption from under a picture. The picture showed Frank Murchison about to
enter a small, private rocketship, the
bow which was emblazoned with two
suns. Murchison was waving to the
camera.

The caption read: *"Mr. Frank (Bax)
Murchison, publisher of the Twin-Sun,
as he left this morning for the two day
convention of colonial newspapers, held
this year at Church's Planet. Mr.
Murchison said, 'Now that the convention has come so close to Mirabello, I
am going to see to it that next year's
convention is held right in Mirabello!'"*

The issue of the 19th carried another
picture of Murchison, taken at the convention. It had been ethergraphed
from Church's. Beside it was a speech
Murchison had made on the function
of the colonial press. Ames kept looking through the succeeding issues carefully, until he had reached the one
dated the 26th, where he gave it up.

"You look disappointed, Mr. Ames,"
said Murchison. "Perhaps I can help
you." He had been sitting there close
to Ames, watching him.

"As a matter of fact, Mr. Murchison,
I am not disappointed. I thought perhaps your paper might have also carried the story of your return from
Church's, seeing the interest with which
it followed your excursion there."

"Well," Murchison smiled, "my editor thought it would please me. I returned on a poor day, however—the
24th, the night Scotty's ship was found,
and the news of the murder seemed
more important. Don't you agree?"

Ames shrugged. "I'm afraid I don't

understand newspaper values, Mr.
Murchison." He re-stacked the pa-
pers, and as he pushed them towards
Murchison, for some undefined reason,
a wave of uneasiness swept over him.
He nodded his good-bye and left.

A few minutes later, across the street
from the jail house, he went into a
phone booth and put in a call to the
Wylie *arrando.* He left a message for
Tom to call him at home as soon as he
reached the *arrando.*

VI

SLOWLY, thoroughly b e m u s e d,
Ames walked across the street to
the jailhouse. A car screeched to a
quivering halt two feet from running
him down. Ames turned absent eyes
in the direction of a series of passion-
ate oaths being hurled at him by the
driver. "Sorry," Ames mumbled and
walked head-on into a man on the
other side of the street.

"Beg pardon," Ames said. "Weather
conditions."

The man inquired blankly: "Huh?"

Ames appeared a bit startled. He
realized he had uttered the thought
weather conditions in a distinctly
audible voice. "Beg pardon," he
apologized, mumbling again, "There's
so damned much to remember." It
didn't occur to him that he had spoken
that thought until he was at the jailhouse door. When he turned around
he saw the man to whom he had just
spoken standing transfixed in the middle of the street. The driver, blocked
again, was shouting curses at his new
target. Ames smiled the least bit.
"Have to stop talking to myself," he
resolved, speaking aloud, and went in.

He went down the corridor to the
chief turnkey's desk. That official,
hearing him coming, separated from
a group of guards and met Ames. He

fixed a dour, noncommittal expression on his face.

"Sorry, Mr. Ames," he anticipated. "Can't do a thing about it."

Ames blinked. "Beg pardon?"

"The order came direct from the C.A.," said the turnkey. "I'm here to obey orders. You'll have to talk to him, and if he says no—"

"Would you mind telling me what you're talking about?"

"The order," the turnkey repeated doggedly. He searched Ames' face and seemed to recognize that something was wrong, and before Ames could speak, he said, "The order that you're not allowed to see Buck Wylie." He added, frowning, "Anyway, it's for your own good, the way—"

"What order?" Ames demanded, coming to life suddenly. "What makes Whitley think he can bar a lawyer from seeing his client? Has he taken to writing in new laws?"

"—the way," the turnkey finished, his voice growing perplexed toward the end, "the way Buck said what he'd do to you if he laid his hands on you," and then, in sudden understanding: "Don't you know you ain't Wylie's lawyer no more?"

Ames took a deep breath. "No," he said. "Who said so?"

"Wylie. So did his sister. She and—"

"Sue Wylie told you that?"

"That's what I'm telling you. She was here about two, three hours ago with Miss Morales. Then they left and half an hour later Miss Morales came back with Mr. Farley. Farley told me he was going to be Wylie's lawyer from now on and to keep you out. A little while after that I got the order from Mr. Whitley, to make it official, I guess . . ." He hesitated. "I thought you knew, Mr. Ames."

"No," Ames said slowly. "No, I didn't." His face had flushed a deep crimson. Now it turned dark and angry as his eyes. He turned and retraced his steps down the corridor, moving slowly.

He was almost at the door when Lola Morales and Farley came in hurriedly. For a fraction of an instant Farley seemed startled, then he regained his stride and his formal, noncommittal expression. The girl glanced at Ames as if he were transparent. They would have walked right past Ames if he hadn't stepped into their path.

"Miss Morales——"

The girl didn't look at Ames. She started to walk around him. Ames followed her movement, blocking her. She stopped a few inches from Ames and behind her Farley came to a halt. The girl's eyes lifted from the floor and met Ames, their black depths filled with hatred.

"I'm not interested," she said in a soft, deadly voice. "Keep away from me."

Her glance fell again and she brushed by Ames. Farley followed her closely, his expression that of a man lost in his own thoughts. Ames watched them until they disappeared down the corridor, then started for the door again.

His face felt hot but there was a growing coolness in his mind. By the time he reached the street he was walking quickly, and then he increased his pace as if his legs were trying to keep up with the speed of his thoughts. He walked through town with his long legs flying, unaware of the people staring after his lanky, urgent figure.

DUSK was falling, gathering the little town into a soft gray bag through which a rising wind blew, playing in the tree-tops. When Ames reached his own street there were already lights in several houses, but he made out the figures of Tom and Sue Wylie sitting on his porch. The sight sent a shiver through him. He tried to tell himself that he had known she would be waiting there, but he knew that he had only hoped and that not until the last moment had he been justified in his inner belief that the girl had not betrayed him.

There was no greeting from either as Ames mounted the stairs. He saw the girl's somber, tear-stained face, her swollen eyes. Tom sat beside her, saying nothing.

Ames leaned against the porch railing. "What happened?" he asked.

At his words the girl broke into tears again and Ames saw that she hadn't spoken because she was holding on. He let her cry until her shoulders were still and then he laid his hand on her arm. Presently she grew calmer. She began to speak very quietly, haltingly at first, her eyes closed.

"Someone spoke to Buck . . . lied to him . . . about us. When I visited him today he was furious. He said I . . . I was keeping you on the case because I . . . we . . ." Her voice fell away then resumed: "—we were having an affair. I couldn't talk to him—he wouldn't listen. When I tried to deny it he asked me if it wasn't true that I had spent last night here. I had to admit it but I tried to. . . . He wouldn't listen. He slapped me and threw me out. He wouldn't . . ." She was crying again.

Ames nodded bitterly. "Yes," he said in a dead voice, then hesitated and left the rest unsaid.

"It's Lola!" Tom spat out suddenly. "She's been tryin' to get rid of you—wants to git lawyer Farley in there!"

"She's gotten him," Ames said. "After Sue left she went out and brought Farley back with her. I just met them together again. They wouldn't talk to me."

He sighed deeply and was silent. He struggled to keep his spirit alive while he pondered this new aspect of an already overwhelmingly complex problem. At times it seemed to him his head would burst, but there was light on the horizon and it was growing brighter. If the unknown enemy's moves were complicating matters they were also tracing a pattern for someone who could read it.

"Yes," Ames said quietly. "Lola Morales has a double grip on him. She's not only his alibi but she knows that Buck has been lying all along. It's the only answer that makes sense . . . the only one . . ."

Sue Wylie was looking up at Ames. She breathed: "Lying?"

Ames softly pounded his thigh with a loose fist. "Yes," he said. "I'll stake my life that there was some kind of connection between Buck and Scotty Purdom—that they were really partners."

"You don't mean that!" Sue Wylie cried. "You can't believe—"

"I'm not saying—"

She seemed beyond reason. Grief had only magnified her loyalty and obscured it with emotion. She rose quickly. "I know what you're saying! You're repeating the lies, the innuendoes—you're taking out your disappointment—"

"Listen to me, Sue!" Ames said loudly. He gripped her arms as she made a move to leave the porch. He was surprised at the energy with which she fought him, struggling to get out of his grasp. He was further confused because he recognized that he was not entirely opposed to her leaving, to avoid the necessity of unravelling thoughts still so tangled that he was uncertain where they might lead. But he could not let her go like this. He had to—

There were loud, excited voices down the end of the street. He saw doors opening, people coming out of their houses. They were calling to the scattering handful of young boys who had descended on the quiet street to hawk their newspapers. The commotion grew louder, and he made out the gist of what the voices were calling. Almost in a dream he heard that Hank Miller had been murdered. The *Twin-Sun* had reason for its extra edition.

For a moment the girl had been still. Tom too had risen and was standing at the edge of the porch. Then the girl took advantage of Ames' relaxed grip and broke free. She ran down the stairs. Ames made no move to follow her. He nodded to Tom's poised hesitation to follow the girl. "Stay with her, Tom. Let me know what happens."

He watched the two figures running down the street towards the center of confusion, adrift in lightless gloom of evening and of his thoughts. . . .

VII

AMES leaned back in his chair and forced himself to nibble at a sandwich, washing it down with draughts of cold, bitter coffee. The light of a single lamp cast disordered shadows in his study, illumining one side of his drawn, thoughtful face. His desk was piled high with scraps of paper, with scrawls and figures and notes, bound only by pencilled lines leading from one to another, as of a man trying to trace a road through inaccurate and incomplete charts of a difficult land. Under the many sheets lay the two-page extra edition of the *Twin-Sun*.

The story was hasty and lurid. Mill-er had been found shot to death in his sheds. Whatever evidence had been found of his murderer had not been revealed. The investigation was proceeding.

Ames glanced at his watch. More than an hour had passed since Sue Wylie had run away from him. He picked up his papers again and studied them. Presently he took a new sheet and began writing, copying bits from the papers spread before him, following the arrows and lines from one to another. Half an hour went by in this manner before he rose up. He pocketed the final sheet and destroyed the others, then turned out the lamp and left his house.

He walked toward the center of town. In early evening the quiet, dimly lit streets, the great, aged oaks, reminded him of the little town in Indiana where he had spent his boyhood. The memory was disquieting. The excitement of an hour before had gravitated to the town square where it was, by then, increasing by the moment, fed by the constant arrival of new people.

Ames caught snatches of their talk as he passed through the square but paid no attention to them. Again and again he summed up the myriad details he had written down and there was no room in his mind for any intruding thoughts. To the people in the square he must have looked a dreamwalker for all the purposefulness of his quick, long-legged gait.

On the other side of town he ascended the hill to Judge Averill's house. Before he passed through the iron-grille gates that enclosed the handsome white house he paused at the hedge. The decision had to be enforced; it could no longer be postponed. Yet for several minutes more he stood there, stiff-jawed, pensive. The judge's study was lit and through the curtained windows Ames heard music as somber and filled with misgivings as he himself was. He went through the gates and rang . . .

Not until Brillov's *Symphony of The Spheres* had concluded did Judge Averill turn to Ames. He had met Ames at the door and quickly and silently taken him back to the study, indicated a chair and resumed his listening. It was the night of the weekly concert from Church's, piped in especially by relay to such small communities as Mirabello. When the last movement, strong and triumphant, had died away, Averill methodically lit a cigar and faced Ames.

"You've decided to trust me, young man?"

Ames nodded and said nothing.

The judge thoughtfully blew out smoke. "Forced to, aren't you?" he asked, almost sadly. "They're moving against you very quickly."

Ames said: "Yes, sir. I've got to do it this way or not at all. If I'm wrong, I'll fail. I must hope I'm right." He waited for Averill to say something and when the silence persisted, he said, "You've heard about Miller, of course?"

"Of course."

Ames said suddenly, "Murchison did it. He had Miller killed just as he either killed Scotty himself or ordered his murder."

Judge Averill kept looking at Ames expressionlessly.

"I can prove these things," Ames said. "I want you to give me the power to prove them."

"How?"

Even-voiced, Ames said, "I want you to confiscate all of Miller's private business records. I want all of Murchison's files and records. I want you to grant me access to the impounded ships, Scotty's and Buck Wylie's."

JUDGE AVERILL contemplated his cigar. He shook his head. "You know I have no right to do what you ask."

"I know. I am hoping that the greater right, the essential justice behind it, will allow you to overlook the minor wrong you may be committing."

"And you believe that if I did what you ask that you could conclusively prove Murchison's guilt?"

Ames met the old jurist's keen eyes. He could not penetrate them. Ames lips thinned. "No," he said. "I can't be sure. I can only hope. I still need facts. Facts, facts—" he leaned forward in his chair, smashing his fist in his palm, his voice intense and low— "facts like links in a chain around Murchison."

"And if you're wrong?" asked the judge quietly, peering at Ames from under his heavy brows. He waited, then added, "I have lived here a long time, Ames. I have devoted my life to the law—"

"Law!" Ames cried out, getting up swiftly. There was anger in his voice now. He advanced to the desk behind which the judge sat. "I'm getting tired of the law!" Ames ground out contemptuously. "What is law in a case like this? What kind of law is it that allows the guilty to use it as a cloak? The law should be impartial —if it can't help the innocent to hell with it! I'll get around it. I'll monkey with it—"

"Yes?"

It wasn't the mildness with which the old man had spoken that stopped Ames short. Rather it was an awareness that his words had taken hold somehow. There was a different look in those wise old eyes. It was gone by the time the judge spoke, but whatever subtle difference had been expressed there now lay, transformed as it were, in his manner. He sounded ironically calm and judicial.

"According to the law none of the things you ask can be done. Why? Because you are not concerned. What protection would an accused man have if anyone was free to tamper with the facts, the details, the fabric of his case? Even as the accused man's lawyer you could not do these things. The law is very clear on such matters—" a cloud of cigar smoke obscured what had been very like a twinkle in his eyes— "as it is on most matters. It has been my experience—and I'm sure you have at some time shared that experience—that it remains clear, although one's view of it may become distorted through various factors."

He sighed, then resumed, "Emotion, for instance," and shook his head. "Or loss of perspective from too great attention to the foreground—the details, you might say, or the—ah—facts. But the law is clear. It says that only the accused, or persons sharing in the accusation, such as material witnesses, may come to the law for the kind of help you want . . ." He paused. "You understand?"

Ames, tensely attentive, had stood quietly listening to the old man. Judge Averill was saying something to him that was buried in his legalistic manner. It seemed to be emerging.

"But how?" Ames asked presently.

"How?" Averill r e p e a t e d. He shrugged. "You, the scholar Ames, ask an old backwoods judge how?"

HE DIPPED his cigar gently into an ashtray and began to putter around his desk, glancing at Ames once or twice. Ames' face was flushed, his eyes directed at the floor, his fists clenched. When finally Ames looked up and started for the door, the judge rose and motioned him to wait. The hand that motioned held a thick, gray-covered, paper-bound volume. He came up to Ames and showed it to him, though Ames knew what it was.

"The May issue of the Law Review," said Averill quietly. "It just came today." He smiled ruefully. "Not as late as usual. The law moves slowly its wonders to perform." He thumbed through the pages and opened it and held it out to Ames.

Ames took it and read: RECENT ENACTMENTS; REGULATIONS; JUDGMENTS: FROM THE INTERPLANETARY COLONIAL COUNCIL. Ames glanced down the index to where, next to GHORT GROUP, a pencil had made a check. He read:

". . . and where a crime has been committed and proven to the satisfaction of the state, and where such crime does cause the heirs and assignees of the estate to suffer monetary, property or real losses, or loss of services which heirs and assignees would not, to the satisfaction of the state, have suffered either in the due course of events or had the crime not been committed, then such heirs, assignees, and such parties listed and enumerated under Sec. 4551, Para. 12 of this enactment, shall have recourse to law both for restitution and for penalty judgment, and that all state claims to forfeiture of estate rights as enumerated under Sec. 23 of the Colonial Penal Code, shall be waived and deemed as transferred to such heirs and assignees. Para. 18: All statements, judgments, etc., listed under Para. 17 of the foregoing shall also apply to heirs and assignees of duly contracted part-

nerships, where such partnerships have been established by law. Para. 19: Sec. 4551 shall be in effect from the date hereinafter inscribed: APRIL 15, midnight, Colonial Central Time. Para. 20: all claims arising. . . ."

Ames looked up and found it difficult to hold the paper-bound volume steady. He stared at Judge Averill incredulously. The legalistic rigamarole of the language was astonishingly transparent, involved as it might have been to a layman. For a moment he could not speak, and then a fierce, quiet exultation seized him.

"In other words," he said softly, "if Buck Wylie is convicted of Scotty's murder, then Murchison, as the legal partner of Scotty, not only inherits everything he and Scotty owned—but he can then claim a penalty judgment against e v e r y t h i n g Buck Wylie owned!"

Judge Averill nodded. "Evidently the Council felt the need for an extension of liability laws for the colonies here. There's been some agitation for this kind of thing ever since it was successfully tried in the Spanish Motanga mandate." He was watching Ames as he went on casually. "It reduced the type of premeditated crime common among—"

"But it's the May issue," Ames said, puzzled, "and today is July 28th." He nodded quickly to forestall Averill. "I know it gets here late, but the law itself—that was passed on April 15th." He had become conscious of Averill watching him. "Why didn't you know this before?" Ames asked. "Wasn't it ethergraphed . . . published . . ." He broke off.

The beginning of an expression was forming on the judge's face. "The law is clear on that, too. The Council ethergraphs its news laws and regula-

tions to the colonies affected—in this case the entire Ghort Group received it—and it must then be published in every local newspaper."

"I know that. Why do you repeat it?"

"To show you that we *both* know it." Ames questioned: "And?"

The expression was more evident now. "You won't have to bother checking it," Averill said. "I have already, without fuss, checked it myself. Murchison's *Twin-Sun* never published the new law."

Ames let his breath out with a soft noise.

"Yes," Judge Averill nodded, his face stern and bitter. "When I read this in the Review today, I, too, decided it explained a good deal. It seems to me that Murchison is undoubtedly guilty. But prosecution for not publishing this law would cost him a small fine . . . where," he nodded again, grimly, "it would appear that true justice calls for a much greater penalty."

IN THE silence Ames worked his hands over his face, rubbing his cheeks until they were red. "Then we both know it," he said. "Conclusive inner knowledge—"

"And no proof."

"No proof!" Ames spat out. But he said no more. His temper, rare to him, hampered his thinking; he was unused to coping with it. He let himself settle to comparative calm, standing there before Averill and saying nothing, but all the while his mind feverish with activity. Then he leaned over the desk, picked up a pencil and a sheet of paper.

"There are two things you can do for me, Judge," he said as he wrote, and added: "Both legal."

"Yes?"

"Send messages for me in Court

code to the I.P. and the Bureau of Claims."

"What for?"

"For facts," Ames said. "Facts, facts . . ." He kept writing for a minute or two more. When he finished he scanned the paper and handed it to Judge Averill.

The judge read what Ames had written and looked at Ames with a bemused, puzzled expression.

"I'll get whatever else I need," Ames said, not offering to explain. "Will you do it?"

"Yes."

"Good. And the rest of it—" Ames grinned horribly—"will be strictly legal, too. Goodnight."

A quarter of an hour later Ames was at a bar in the center of town. He spoke to no one and leaned against the bar, gulping down one drink after another. The buzz of conversation was all around him and he fought off the dizzying effects of the drink and the headache occasioned by the unaccustomed diet and the noise and music. They were still talking about Miller, and, he knew, they were watching him. He stayed at the bar perhaps twenty minutes, then paid for his drinks and walked with only partially feigned unsteadiness to the street and went into another bar on the corner.

Here he repeated the process, drinking a little slower and taken to studying the glasses, occasionally mumbling to himself. He seemed quite drunk by then and he knew he was well noticed. When he called for his fourth drink, the bartender hesitated.

"Think you ought to, Mr. Ames?"

Ames looked up at him, bleary-eyed. "Whazzat?" he demanded, thickly. "Want another drink. Got to have another drink. Make me forget whole damn business, maybe."

The bartender, a kind-faced old man,

looked around then leaned over towards Ames. "Maybe you're—" he hesitated, started again. "Don't take offense, Mr. Ames—no offense meant— but maybe you're taking the whole thing too hard."

"Takin' what hard?" Ames asked. "Think I care I was kicked out of my first case? Don't give a damn!" he said belligerently. He grew more confidential in manner but his voice was too loud as he said: "Got to forget somethin' else." He put a finger across his lips. "Shhhh," he said slyly. "I know something could land the whole gang of 'em inna calaboose. Whole gang, especially Murchison. But don't—"

The bartender, aware of the many curious glances now fixed on Ames, tried to stop him. "Now, Mr. Ames—"

"Don't innerupt," Ames said with annoyance, seemingly oblivious of the attention he had attracted from the moment he had entered, and which was now obvious to everyone near him. "I'm not goin' do anything 'bout it. Let 'em all stew. Let Murchison get away—"

"Mr. Ames, please—"

"Am I gonna get my drink or not?" Ames cried, pounding the bar. "No?" He answered his own question and threw a bill on the bar then turned and walked out, declaring loudly: "Go t'nother place where they don't innerupt."

HE HALF staggered out in the street, wandered a few feet down the block, spun around and caught himself before he fell, and seemingly unaware that he had described a circle and was heading back in the direction from which he had come, re-entered the same bar. He walked back to the bartender he had left a few moments before and greeted him with open arms and a fuzzy smile.

"H'lo, Pop!" he declaimed. "Le's have a drink. Just walked out of a bar 'cause wouldn't lemme have a lil drink." He put down a crumpled bill, and ignoring the bartender completely, put his arm around a small man who stood at the bar. "Have a drink with me, stranger," he smiled loosely, "and I'll tell you a story'll raise your hair." He winked. "Got a fine story 'bout Murchison and Buck Wylie and Farley. Got whole thing worked out up here—" He tapped his temple and winced. "Ow! No good. Hurts a lil." He smiled again, then immediatelly glowered at the bartender who hadn't moved. "Well? Gonna have trouble with you too?"

"I'm sorry, Mr. Ames. I can't serve you."

"Why not?" Ames shouted.

The bartender started coming out from behind the bar. Ames saw him coming and backed away uncertainly. A crowd had gathered around him when he came back and now he faced them.

"Fren's and Romans!" Ames cried. "You're all my witnesses! Murchison's arranged to have me kicked out of every bar inna town because he hates me! And why does he hate me?" he demanded, pointing a long arm at the bartender that kept the old man away effectively. " 'Cause he knows I got somethin' on him—and not only him—" he swept his arm out eloquently —"but Farley and Wylie too! Got 'em all—"

The bartender had quickly moved in under Ames arm and gripped his long frame. With efficient, practiced movements he began pushing Ames out. There were cries from the crowd to let Ames stay but the bartender took Ames, unresisting but still declaming, to the door. He led him to the street

and walked him to the curb.

"Son," he said gently, wheezing a little, "you're going to be a sorry lad in the morning. If you ever had a chance of getting another case in this town, you're losing it tonight. Now why don't you go home and sleep it off?" He shook his head sadly. "You're a good lad. I don't like to see—"

Ames disengaged himself grandly, aware that his audience had followed him to the door. "Unhand me!" Ames shouted. "I'm going home but I'll be back! Gonna make out papers and sue you for a million! Two million!" And he turned and staggered down the street, singing. . . .

He was a good deal steadier when he walked up the stairs to his house but his face was green and his eyes half closed. He went into the bathroom and stuck a finger down his throat. He retched again and again, then went to the kitchen. He mixed a concoction of egg and milk and tobasco which he used to wash down two grains of the Mercurian headache patent medicine, *Nixxir*. Finally, alternately belching and sighing, he retired to his study.

He sat for more than hour studying the diagrammatic sheet he had made up earlier that evening and he was asleep on his feet when he wandered wearily to bed. Five minutes later he was back, fumbling with his thick *MacDougal's Interplanetary Torts and Laws*. He thumbed through the pages until he found something that pleased him, then went back to bed.

THERE was a huge bell in the center of Ames brain and someone was beating it with a stone hammer, standing with both feet on Ames eyes. When Ames finally opened his eyes he saw that there wasn't any man and he decided that someone was ringing the bell downstairs. He glanced at his bedside clock, saw it indicated eleven o'clock, and checked on it by opening his eyes wider to see if there was daylight. There was.

He wrapped a robe around his shivering body and went down. He opened the door to admit Sour Tom and let in enough sunlight to warm and blind himself.

"I thought you were dead," Tom said.

"I'd be better off," Ames moaned. "Come in."

He led the way back to the kitchen and immediately busied himself with making coffee. While he waited for it he took another dose of *Nixxir*. Tom watched him. He hadn't said a word from the moment he had come in.

When Ames felt his voice return he asked: "How is she?"

"Fine," Tom nodded. "Wish I could say the same for you."

"What's the matter?"

"You don't know?"

Ames sighed. "All right."

"What made you do it?"

Ames countered: "What do you think?"

"I ain't sure."

Ames almost smiled. "Then you haven't given me up?"

"Not until I hear you out."

"Thanks," Ames said gratefully. He shook himself, then poured coffee for himself and Tom. He sat down across the small table from Tom and said, "Tell me what you heard. Everything."

Tom sipped his coffee before he spoke: "I heard it all over the place. You went on a binge. Shot your mouth off sayin' you had enough on Wylie and Farley and especially Murchison to hang the lot of 'em." There was a question in his voice the way he said it.

"That's right," said Ames. "What do they think? People, I mean."

"They say you're finished. They don't like to see someone goin' around talkin' mighty because he's been throwed out of a case he didn't have no business bein' in in the first place."

Ames nodded in obvious satisfaction. He finished his coffee and replenished both cups. Then he said, "Good. Anything else?"

Tom studied him before he answered. There was a new expression in his voice, a new life, as he said, "There's talk that Murchison won't like what you're sayin' about him." After a pause, while Ames drank, he said quietly, "That's the way you want it?"

"Yeah," Ames grinned. "Want to help me?"

"Hank Miller was a good friend of mine."

The name erased Ames' smile. "I'm going drinking again," he said.

"In the middle of the day?"

'Day or night, it's all the same. I've got to keep at it until I get what I'm after. You think I enjoy eating *Nixxir*?"

Tom's forehead creased. "All right," he nodded. "But every other round is on me."

The two men exchanged grins.

AN hour later Ames was telling a wizened little miner: "I'm not jus' standin' here making up stories, I'm givin' you fax. Fax. I know, my friend, I *know*."

They were in one of the numerous bars that were like weeds in the vicinity of the blastport. At this time of day the bars were deserted, but the few hangers-on there listened to Ames attentively. Tom, in a seeming state of half-stupor, bent an elbow beside Ames and listened too. Like him, Ames appeared to be more than well oiled.

"And what's this you know?" asked

the miner, eyes bright with interest.

"Ah," Ames smiled mysteriously. "If I tell you everything I know, you'll know everything you know and everything I know, so you'll know more than me, right? But I got enough on Wylie and ole Murch—" and he winked his incessant, wise wink.

From that bar Ames and Sour Tom wandered to another, a third, a fourth. In each Ames grew more loquacious and provocative, his stories more vague and his hints wilder. By three o'clock, after the arrival of a double shipment of orium and a hired mining crew, his audience was a sizable one. But shortly after three, in the fifth bar, the stories came to an end.

Two men came in to the Idle Hour. One was a head taller than the other, but both were broad and muscular and both wore gunbelts slung low from their hips to supplement their deputy's shields. The smaller of the two walked directly up to Ames and touched his arm.

"Your name Terwilliger Ames?"

Ames looked up startled. "Yeah," he admitted belligerently.

"You're under arrest."

"What?" Ames exploded. He stood up to his full height and towered over the short deputy. "Me? Whaffor?" Suddenly he looked crafty. "Got a warrant?" he demanded. "Lessee the warrant!"

The deputy fished out a stiff, folded paper and waved it under Ames nose. "Straight from Judge Averill, signed and sealed, and you're goin' to be delivered. You better come without no trouble."

Surprisingly enough, Ames made no trouble. He submitted meekly and went out to where a large vehicle with wired windows awaited him. If anyone had intercepted the satisfied smile which Ames darted at Tom, it would have surprised them even more. As it was, Tom waved a forlorn farewell and drifted out of the bar.

Everything was ready when Ames was brought in to the courthouse, even to the expectant crowd that greeted his arrival outside. Judge Averill was on the bench, locked in consultation with Farley. Murchison, his face stiff with righteous anger, watched Ames walk up to the bench. Whitley, the Colonial Attorney, came out of a side office. Most of the courtroom was empty—attendants were posted at the doors—but there were more than a dozen men in the first two rows. Ames recognized some of them as having formed part of his audiences the night before and that afternoon.

He hardly listened to the C.A.'s short address to the Court, in which he presented the State's plea. He paid less attention to the men Whitley summoned, one after another, to testify to what they had heard Ames say, a procession halted by Judge Averill after the fourth witness. Farley's speech, in which he alternately pleaded for his client, Wylie, and for himself, was by far the most interesting.

Thickly larded with sarcasm, Farley's speech ended, ". . . and if indeed this drunken oracle knows anything pertaining to this case, then on behalf of my client I feel it is my duty to have Mr. Ames incarcerated and held as a material witness until such time as he can testify under oath before this Court."

Judge Averill nodded. "The Court agrees with the Colonial Attorney and Mr. Farley and finds evidence sufficient to warrant proposed action. However," and he scratched his chin meditatively, "may I ask you, Mr. Farley, whether you believe Mr. Ames actually has any testimony worthy of this Court's consideration?"

Farley sneered. "I view his remarks with the utmost contempt."

"The Court agrees with you, Mr. Farley. Motion to hold defendant as material witness granted." The judge made a notation on some of the papers spread before him, then looked up. "However, in view of counsel's opinion of the defendant's worth as a witness, the Court holds him in bail of five dollars and cautions—"

"Five dollars!" Murchison burst out wrathfully. "Why, that's—"

JUDGE AVERILL rapped his gavel once. "—and cautions him to silence on pain of being arraigned for contempt of court."

Farley, scarcely able to contain himself, gulped: "If it please the Court, counsel submits that Mr. Ames' further liberty might prejudice my client's case beyond repair—"

"The Court has already cautioned him, Mr. Farley."

"But, your Honor, he has already said enough!"

"The Court has entered him as a material witness."

"Your Honor, his innuendoes concerning Mr. Murchison and myself certainly merit some protection from this Court!"

"Are you proposing a separate action, Mr. Farley?"

"If it please the Court, yes."

Judge Averill thought a moment, then said: "Decision reserved."

Farley's face had long since turned crimson. Now it threatened to become violet. "But, your Honor," he spluttered, "a bail of five dollars—*five dollars*—is hardly . . . hardly . . ."

The judge leaned over and surveyed Farley with impartial curiosity. "Come, come, Mr. Farley. You said yourself you had contempt for his value as witness. Surely you don't consider five dollars too high an estimate of your contempt?"

Farley tried to gather himself together. He glanced at Whitley, who stood by rigidly, and at Murchison, whose face was queerly blown up. His lips worked a little and he seemed to be undergoing some internal process that pained him. A new light was beginning to show in his eyes; it shone through his bewilderment. For a moment he seemed on the verge of plunging ahead but he stopped, looking from the judge to Ames. In his stead, C. A. Whitley came forward, officious and flustered.

"Your Honor, the State moves to increase bail to fifty thousand dollars." He paled before Averill's sharp scrutiny. "The State bases its claim on Mr. Ames' reputation."

"Mr. Ames' reputation is well known to the Court," said Averill, slowly. "Petition denied. This Court stands adjourned." He rose from the bench and motioned to Ames. "Mr. Ames, I want to see you in my chambers, if you please."

Ames nodded respectfully and waited until the judge had left the courtroom. He took in the silent consternation Averill had left behind him. Whitley and Farley and Murchison were still regarding Ames, as if they expected their combined examination would yield the answer. With no expression, Ames picked his path through them and followed Averill.

The judge was leaning against a desk. He had taken off his robes and was in the act of choosing a cigar from a case on the desk when Ames came in. He glanced at Ames and rolled the cigar in his fingers. "You're a remarkable young man, Ames," he said dryly, pleased.

"Thank you, sir. You understood, of course?"

"Of course I understood."

"But, but—" Ames fumbled uncertainly, "you're worried?"

"Yes, I am," said Averill. He lit the cigar, regarded it. "I'm worried about what they may do. We didn't fool them, you know."

Ames nodded. "I never hoped to be able to fool them. I'm playing my hand open—so open that it would take—"

A v e r i l l interrupted impatiently. "You still hold to your thesis that Murchison won't use force? That he will play your game, matching wits?" He sniffed at the expression on Ames' face. "Surprised that I'm aware of your strategy, young man? Come now, it's obvious enough. You succeeded in getting yourself held as a material witness, but you went about it in an astonishingly direct way. Why shouldn't you have assumed Murchison would shut you up with a bullet? Why assume he would go to the trouble of having you arraigned?"

"But didn't you think of that last night?" Ames countered. "I take little credit for my success in your Court, sir. You practically told me exactly what to do."

"I'm reconsidering, Ames. I didn't like the way they looked at you out there. I think Murchison is growing tired of the game. It's becoming too dangerous for him. He's the kind of gambler who doesn't enjoy the game unless the dice are his."

Ames looked perplexed. "Granted, then. I assume he will use force, sooner or later, but only when he's sure he's lost. What would you advise me to do? Quit?"

"Why not?"

"Why not?" Ames echoed. "What about that little talk on justice I enjoyed so much? What about your telling me—"

"Words, words," said Averill. "Your life's at stake, Ames. It's a big stake to gamble with."

Ames said slowly: "I won't quit."

THE judge nodded, inhaled and blew out a thick cloud of smoke. He allowed a smile to grow on his face until its warmth had changed him completely from the man he had seemed a moment before. He went to Ames and put a hand on his shoulder.

"I'm glad," he said soberly. "I didn't want you to think that perhaps I was pushing you into something you didn't fully understand. It's been a game until now, but that's over with. Sooner or later, as you say, you'll have to stop being a clever lawyer long enough to slug it out—isn't that the expression?—with them. As long as you know it, I'm not afraid for you."

He returned to the desk and picked up several papers. "I've had these for several hours," he said, offering them to Ames. "I think they answer your questions rather fully."

Ames hastily took the official maroon sheets. They were answers from the I.P. and the Bureau of Claims. Above the jumbled letters of their code the judge had carefully lettered a translation of each.

The I.P. message read:

FROM: I.P. REGIONAL HQ. 41ST GRP. CHURCH'S PLANET. 7-29
TO: REGIONAL MAGIS. B.P. AVERILL. MIRABELLO CITY.
RE: INQUIRY VIZ F. MURCHISON, MIRABELLO CITY AND/OR PARTIES CONNECTED WITH MIRABELLO CITY TWIN-SUN DATED 7-28

ADVISE F. MURCHISON, PUBLISHER MIRABELLO CITY TWIN-SUN MADE INQUIRIES AT CENTRAL I.P. HQ. MARCH 8 CONCERNING CRIMINAL RECORD BRUCE (BUCK) WYLIE. FULL INFORMATION AND DATA FURNISHED MURCHISON ON MARCH 11. AUTHORITY ICC, PUBLIC SERVICE REGULATION, SEC. 122.

The message from the Bureau of Claims read:

FROM: CLAIMBUR, ICC HQ. COMMERCE DIV. URANIAN SEC. 7-29

TO: REGIONAL MAGIS. B.P. AVERILL. MIRA-
BELLO CITY
RE: INQUIRY VIZ BRUCE WYLIE, SCOTT PUR-
DOM JOINT OWNERSHIP FILES, NEW CLAIM
DIVISION, COVERING ONE YEAR, FROM 7-28

THIS PAST FEB. 5 JOINT CLAIM ENTERED BY
BRUCE WYLIE AND SCOTT PURDOM IN FULL
AND EQUAL PARTNERSHIP, LEGALLY EN-
TERED, SEALED AND SWORN BY PROXIES
HERE: HAYES AND HAYES, ATTORNEYS. SE-
CRET CLAUSE INVOKED BY BOTH. LOCATION
CANNOT BE PUBLISHED UNTIL AUG. 5 UN-
DER AUTHORITY ICC CLAIMS REG. SEC. 42,
ALLOWING SIX MONTHS' PRIVATE EXPLOITA-
TION.

WARNING: THIS COMMUNICATION SECRET
UNLESS LEGAL EXCEPTION GRANTED OR UN-
DERTAKEN BY COMPETENT AUTHORITY, ICC
PENAL CODE, SEC. 370. FOR PREMATURE
PUBLICATION RIGHTS APPLY ABOVE.

Ames carefully folded both sheets and returned them to Averill. His face was flushed and eager. He kept his voice restrained with some difficulty.

"That does it," he said. "It proves two things I suspected. It tells me that Murchison knew about Buck Wylie's past as far back as March 11th but kept it to himself for four months. More important, it confirms my idea that Buck and Scotty were partners and have been since February 5th." He paused. "What's this about a secret clause and six months of private exploitation?"

"It's a protective measure usually invoked when miners stake out a new claim. If they had to publish the whereabouts of their claim immediately, it would produce a staking rush. This gives them a chance to get set up properly b e f o r e the territory is swamped."

"I see. Is six months the maximum secrecy allowed?"

"Since Section 42 was passed five years ago."

"And before that? I mean, how is it Scotty Purdom was allowed to keep his Silver Spoon a secret claim for so many years?"

"You see what happened to Scotty. That's why the law was passed; secrecy invited assassination too often—ex-

actly what Wylie is being charged with. Naturally, however, all claims filed before the law was passed do not come under its jurisdiction except by voluntary petition, which Scotty avoided like a plague."

Ames nodded thoughtfully.

Judge Averill picked up the other sheets he had taken and handed them to Ames.

"You wanted these?"

Ames took the papers and read them quickly. They were court orders addressed specifically to one Sam Kaine, Colonial Sheriff in Rheykavike, a smaller city several hundred miles from Mirabello City. There were three of them; one for the seizure and examination of Hank Miller's records, one for Murchison's private files and effects, one allowing Ames access and examination of the impounded *Spoon Special* and *Hellcat*. The petitioner for these rights was listed as Terwilliger Ames, material witness in the case of State vs. Wylie.

Ames picked up a pen and added a notation including the impounding and examination of Buck Wylie's *Gaucho*. He showed it to the judge and handed him the pen. Averill signed underneath. He watched Ames pocket the papers.

"Ames," he said quietly, "I don't really know what you're doing. I have a great respect for you, but I think you still have one valuable lesson to learn —that somewhere you must stop working with paper and start working with human beings. It's quite a different thing." He hesitated, then added: "I do know this—the instant you put this authority into action, you serve notice on Murchison that you're in this to the end. Good luck."

Ames took the proffered hand. "I'm glad you didn't add goodbye," he said, and grinned.

VIII

IT WAS several minutes past midnight when the two official cars sped up to the *Twin-Sun* building and ground to a halt. Colonial Sheriff Kaine, Ames and three deputies got out of the first car. From the second four more men alighted, two of whom stayed behind outside while the rest swiftly entered the building. Downstairs the presses were rolling with noisy thunder.

The men moved with sureness, answering no questions a f t e r Kaine served the managing editor with the court order. They entered Murchison's private office and emptied the files. Other deputies confiscated a duplicate file of the *Twin-Sun*. One of Kaine's men, a bony-fingered, thin fellow, worked on Murchison's safe until it opened under his smooth touch. Ames and Kaine stood by, checking everything taken. The raid had been carefully planned.

The phone jangled and Kaine picked it up.

"Sheriff Kaine speaking." His face tightened. "Sorry, Murchison; court order. . . Averill . . . Today . . .Yes . . . Yes . . . You were served, weren't you? . . . That's your funeral."

He replaced the phone and continued with his checking.

Ames asked, "Your men have trouble at Murchison's home?"

"Some. He refused to open his safe. They threatened to blast."

Fifteen minutes later when they were ready to leave, Kaine picked up the phone, spoke into it. He waited, cursing—Ames caught a reference to his distaste for the hopelessly antiquated telephone on hopelessly antiquated Mirabello—then spoke his name. He listened a moment and hung up. To Ames he said, "It went all right at Miller's. They'll bring his papers in

soon. Nobody tried to interfere."

At Standish Port, Sour Tom was waiting. He had come in from the Wylie *arrando* where deputies had cracked the *Gaucho's* Berry gauge with official keys and copied her listings. Tom had brought a copy, which he gave to Kaine. The party took the official gyro and left the blastport. It was just past one.

By three o'clock they were in the government sheds near Mayville. The large, shadowed forms of the *Spoon Special* and the *Hellcat* rested side by side on their vehicular launching blocks, two ships of seven or eight impounded by the government for one reason or another. The great sheds with their lofty, arching roofs were dark and filled with vast echoes and the men who moved on the stone floors seemed like so many preoccupied ants.

They had trained great lights on both vessels. Inside each two-man teams of specialists worked on the Berry gauges with their nitro keys. The work was tedious and painstaking, and every bit of it was carefully and officially photographed on a continuous film. When the gauges were removed, their listings were slowly unwound before the cameras as part of the record. Other men stood by copying the listings and by the time the raw film was sealed in cans, the operations complete, these men had delivered their copies to Sheriff Kaine.

From there Ames retired to a government office. Kaine and several clerks were with him, working through the night. Papers filled with calculations spread over desks and voices spoke quietly, comparing figures as they were passed to Ames. The hours passed and the shaded lights paled before the oncoming dawn, and still Ames worked on tirelessly, his voice rising now and again above the others to demand a repitition. He seldom sat down, pacing the room with long streamers of papers in his hands, his brow furrowed. He fought off fatigue until his eyes were red-streaked slits in a mask of weariness.

Once Kaine stopped him. He had a flask of whiskey and a paper cup. "Better ease up, Ames," he yawned. "You look dead. Have a shot."

Ames shook his head. "Never touch the stuff," he said.

Sheriff Kaine, in the act of yawning, almost choked. His mouth sagged and he stared at Ames. It wasn't until a minute or so later, when Ames realized that the sheriff had undoubtedly heard of his two enormous drinking bouts, that he laughed at the sheriff's expression. Then he sat down on one of the desks and rested long enough to drink some of the coffee Tom had brought in for everyone. . . .

EVEN the drawn blinds were finally ineffective against the sun. The night's vigil showed in the worn faces of the men around Ames. He himself was finally running down. His head was a spinning mass of bits of information, shooting live sparks that were dates, ratios, mileages, through his body. At half-past eight he gave up. He sat down.

"Finished?" Kaine asked when one of his men roused him.

Ames shook his head. "No. I left a lot of my notes at home and I can't go on without them. But I'm through here. I can't thank you enough, Sheriff."

Kaine smiled sleepily. "If I can go home now, that's thanks enough. I'll see that everything's filed according to the book."

And so it was that Ames and Sour Tom were escorted to the gyro that had brought them to Mayville and took off for Mirabello City. When Ames got home and walked down the dusty road to his house, he leaned on Tom, unable to keep his eyes open. Tom kept shaking him, imploring him to walk straight.

"For your own sake," he pleaded. "These neighbors o' yourn keep seein' you stagger around day after day and your reputation ain't goin'—"

He stopped speaking in silent wonder. He had never heard a walking man snore. And Ames was snoring, deep and rhythmically, as he stumbled on. "I seen everything now," Tom whispered to himself. He took Ames in and undressed him and sat down to sleep in a chair.

When Tom woke he found the bed empty. He started to jump from the chair and was stopped by two things; first, his cramped, aching joints, and second, the reassuring sound of Ames pacing downstairs. He became conscious of the ternal smell of strong coffee, this time mixed with burning food. A glance through the shutters told him the day had become late afternoon.

He went downstairs quietly and passed by the door to Ames' study without being noticed. In the kitchen a griddle had long since melted and burned cheese and toast, and whatever coffee had been in the old-fashioned dripolater had disappeared in clouds of vapor. He busied himself with new sandwiches and coffee. Now and again he heard Ames talking out loud to himself.

At length he brought in a tray to the study. Ames heard him come in, nodded absently and appreciatively, and continued pacing. Tom sat down and bit into one of the sandwiches loudly and sipped his coffee with noisy relish. Ames progressed from inattentiveness to frowning to looking at Tom and ended by sighing. He stopped walking in front of the tray and picked up a sandwich. He took a bite and sat down, eating voraciously until he had cleaned the tray. When he replenished his cup of coffee he took notice of Tom again.

"I've got it worked out," he said. "It doesn't make sense now, but it will because it must."

Tom grunted. "What must?"

"The Hive."

"What above the Hive?"

Coffee in hand, Ames unfurled a large chart on his desk. It was an official mariner's chart of the Forty-First System Group. There were numerous red and blue pencilled lines and markings, with figures and notations liberally sprinkled in the empty areas. Ames began to talk in a low, eager voice about navigation, weather reports, gauge markings, mileages, asteroid belts, vacuum impact and other matters. His fingers kept tracing lines along the chart, and no matter where they started, they always ended in a small area in the upper left of the chart. From the moment Ames first indicated that area, Tom never took his eyes off it, his attention firmly riveted. When finally he spoke, his face seemed older and more deeply lined.

"What're you aimin' to do?" he asked slowly, interrupting.

"It's plain enough, isn't it?"

"I ain't heard more'n half of what you said. All I hear is you sayin' things about the Hive. There's no use talkin' about the Hive."

Ames stopped short. "No?"

"No." Tom gestured with a hand. "You can git there easy enough with a finger on a chart. Goin' there yourself—" He broke off and fixed Ames with his eyes. "Or am I makin' a mistake?" he asked.

"You're right," said Ames. "I'm going to the Hive."

Tom didn't bother answering. He just frowned a little and shook his head and remained silent. He was breathing audibly now, troubled.

"Don't you see?" Ames said. "Every calculation, every—"

"I don't see," Tom cut in. "Suppose you figgered out that you had to go to Kingdom Come for an interview with poor Hank Miller. You think wantin' to go bad enough could make it possible—that and comin' back too?" he added.

"I didn't say I wanted to enter it," Ames said. He waited until Tom's heavy, sad smile faded. "I just want to get close to it."

"How close?"

"That depends."

"On what?"

"On lots of things."

Tom nodded. "Things like those mileages you been figgerin'. How come all these diagrams of yourn end right in the Hive, not just close?"

Ames shrugged and made no answer. He contemplated his chart with a distant air. "You can't talk me out of it, Tom," he said presently. "You can make it tougher for me this way, but I'm going."

Tom regarded him. "Got a ship? Know how to navigate?"

Ames remained lost in thought, then silently began to gather his notes and charts. "I'm going," he said quietly. He continued putting his things together and packed them in a small bag. Then he took out the Foster IV pistol, examined its chambers and stuck it in his belt under his loose coat. His lean, earnest face was calm. He was wondering where he—

"Tell you somethin'," Tom interrupted his thoughts. "I really believe you're goin' to go there, one way or another. Any man's damnfool enough to do that needs a body to look out for him. Guess I'm it."

Ames turned sideways to look at him. Their grins met.

THE *Rainbow* was aptly named, if not for her past glories then for the bright streaks of rust and corrosion and decay that covered her hull. She had once been a privately owned yacht, then an auxilliary vessel for Airways, Ltd. and in the twilight of her career she had been a sort of bus for a mining company, transporting men and materials for small distances. She had, within the last year, made perhaps two short hauls, the more recent of these three months before. She was ancient and cumbersome and far from pretty, but she was spaceworthy and the only vessel Ames and Tom could lay their hands on quickly, so they hired her. Or rather, Ames had hired her. He listened to Tom's objections— the rental was more than she would have brought in an outright sale . . . if they waited a day or two, Tom might swing a deal with a friend of his . . . in any case, if they seemed less anxious and waited—but Ames asked only one question: *Could she make the trip?* and when Tom relucantly agreed that she probably could, Ames took her.

The preparations, fueling, blastpapers, navigation permit, clearance, shipping order, took time. It was two o'clock in the morning when the *Rainbow* was ready in her pit, her stubby nose pointed to the sky. The word had gone round and her departure was not unattended. The story of the preceding night's raids had added to the speculation, and when the Standish port lights switched on, they disclosed clusters of skyfaring men gathered around in a loose circle. Inside the *Rainbow* Tom had settled at the controls, waiting for the tower's blast signal. Ames, a quiet, worn expression on his face, sat beside him.

A white light flashed in the tower. Tom's hand moved and the ship shuddered as her aft tubes exploded. The dark pit became a well of purple and orange light. The tubes went on and off in rotation, the aft port and starboard, the thwartships, the bow, the auxilliaries, the emergency, and then back to the stern. The aft tubes began to roar more loudly and the ship shivered in every strake.

The tower flashed three greens. "Givin' way," Tom murmured, and his fingers played on the control board. The *Rainbow* exploded with a short series of aft blasts that swiftly blended. As if gathering herself or the leap, the ship steadied. There was a single flash of light, a violet streak shot through with brilliant copper, and the *Rainbow* was rocketborne. She bit into the sky like a thing alive.

Moments later, Tom turned to Ames. "She likes being up here," he sighed. "She's a good old girl. Maybe she's got memories."

An hour later, with the vessel fixed on course, Tom switched in her gyropilot and went to sleep. Ames had dropped off almost at the start. He lay tilted back in his seat like a drugged man. Whatever misgivings he had had, whatever troubled visions had flitted through his mind, he knew that at last he had committed himself. There was no turning back now, no matter what the outcome.

With the coming of morning, the golden twin-sunned morning of their little corner of the universe, Ames was in the galley. They ate and spoke of minor matters. Ames remembered little things that had happened to him that amused Tom and the older man was full of anecdotes of the region. Once they spoke of Sue Wylie. Tom had seen her briefly. She was staying with a friend. She had kept trying to see her brother, even begging Farley to intercede for her. It had been useless. Ames knew the feeling. When he thought of her something interfered with his breathing. He had to busy himself. . . .

THIRTY-TWO hours out, the *Rainbow* raised the outlying bodies of the asteroid belt. Green and gray the islands lay in the sky, like stepping stones toward a boundless horizon. The ship slid in past their invisible periphery and slackened speed a bit. Another hour passed and the belt grew thicker, the asteroids appearing in slow-moving groups. It was becoming ticklish to maneuver the *Rainbow* and her speed was dropping off little by little.

Ames stared at the ship's Berry gauge, now and again copying her reading and rapidly working out his calculations. Once Tom, after cutting off a pair of tubes, asked: "How much further?" and Ames shrugged.

"Not much, I think," Ames said, but when he glanced up at Tom's face, he knew the answer was inadequate. He pointed to the notes that lay on the outspread chart in his lap. "I'll try to explain it, Tom," he went on. His fingers traced patterns as he spoke.

"I've got the Berry readings from three ships—the *Spoon Special* of Scotty's, and Wylie's *Hellcat* and *Gaucho*. I've worked them all out to powers of four hundred, to simplify them, and to eliminate s m a l l discrepancies that would be natural in comparing high numbers."

"I don't get it," Tom said.

"It's like this: we know that Scotty took both the *Special* and the *Hellcat* with him. So the readings of both should be more or less the same. They won't be exactly the same for various factors—for instance, Scotty took Wylie back to Mirabello in the *Special* and then returned to the *Hellcat*, which he had space-anchored some fifty miles out, so there's a discrepancy of at least a hundred miles already. Again, the *Special* was found wandering in circles on the twenty-fourth, the day it was found. No one knows how long it wandered, so there'd be another discrepancy there. But the distances both ships traveled are great enough not to allow minor differences—a few hundred or thousand miles—to interfere if you work in large powers. All right?"

"Sounds all right."

"It is. It works. Taking the last twenty readings for the three ships shows interesting results. Buck says that he helped Scotty tow the *Hellcat* out fifty miles, then Scotty took him back, and the next day he left on a prospecting trip. He says he has a witness that he came back with Scotty, but supposing he hasn't, what then? The prosecution—"

"What d'you mean, no witness?"

"I won't go into that now. Let's take the prosecution's case. It hasn't given out its version of the crime yet, but it has two alternatives. If Buck has no witness, it can claim he never came back. It can say he went along with Scotty in the *Hellcat*, behind the Special, and he then killed Scotty and brought both ships back." He held up a hand to keep Tom from interrupting. "Or, if Buck produces a witness, it can claim he knew where Scotty was going and followed him there the next day. He then killed Scotty and brought both ships back—"

"Nuts!" Tom ejaculated. His eyes were on their course. The asteroids were thicker; two points off the starboard bow there was a large group moving toward them slowly. "You can't tell me that Scotty would take Buck along to his secret mine, or that the prosecution would claim anything so stupid. Nobody'd swaller that. And the same goes for Buck knowin' where to foller him."

"I didn't say Scotty went to his secret Silver Spoon. The prosecution said that, but it knows as well as you and I know that it could hardly—" He stopped. "Look, Tom, I'm not trying the case now. I don't want to go into it. Take my word for it that they have their case, and that they can switch it beautifully when the time comes."

"Meanin'?"

"Suppose they claim that Buck knew exactly where Scotty was going because Scotty was going to a mine they held in partnership?"

Bitterly, Tom said: "That the best you can do? Nuts again."

"The fact is," Ames said gently, "that there is proof they were partners in a new claim." He waited until Tom slowly turned his head toward him. "It's true," Ames nodded. "They'll be able to prove it shortly. However, I'm not saying they'll claim that. It's just one of the possibilities I'm ready for. But let's go back to this . . ."

HE HELD up a sheet with three columns of figures. "Here is a comparison of the readings on the three ships. I've got them written from the twentieth to the twelfth, but you don't have to study them beyond the fifteenth —the preceding fourteen are completely divergent, just as the Gaucho's readings are entirely different all the way through."

Tom studied the sheet. It read:

| SPOON | | |
SPECIAL	HELLCAT	GAUCHO
(20) .9	.4	1.4
(19) 76.2	76.2	288.1
(18) .3	.3	112.2
(17) .3	.3	99.2
(16) 76.5	76.5	166.7
(15) .7	.2	343.3
(14) 4.6	81.4	8054.6
(13) 19.4	7.1	655.1
(12) 18.3	322.6	181.9

"Okay," Tom said, presently, handing it back. "But you remember what I told you about it bein' easy to fake them readin's?"

"Exactly. Offhand, no one would claim that the Gaucho had been where the Special and Hellcat had been, from these readings. It goes further than that. First, nowhere does the Gaucho's readings—and I have them much further back—resemble any of the figures on these two. Second, even assuming it was still possible to fake, nowhere is there a reading for point three —something that shows up twice in succession on both the Special and the Hellcat. So, from the almost exact similarity in the readings of two of these ships, I assume they went together and in the duplication of that point three reading, I look for the crux of the matter.

"Suppose we start with 15. It reads .2 for the Hellcat, and that is a root symbol for fifty miles, according to my calculations. Fifty miles agrees with Buck's story: he said Scotty anchored the Hellcat fifty miles out and then went back in the Special. That gives the Special two extra trips of approximately that distance. At 15, the Special reads .7 which is close enough. At 16, both ships traveled the same distance to some objective. They went 76.5, stopped, went 3, stopped again, went .3 and then 76.2 again.

"From this I would say that they concluded the trip there after the first .3. The second was recorded on the return trip, which is shown again by the duplication of the 76-odd figure. Both then stopped, and the Hellcat came in. But the *Special* kept going round and round, as she was seen—which explains why the last recording for the *Special* is .9 compared to the *Hellcat's* .4—in other words, the extra .5 involved may be assumed to have been spent circling. Do you see it now?"

"I'm not sure," Tom said slowly. "According to your figures, where are we now?"

Ames took down the Berry reading, worked a few moments, then said softly, "At 74.1. We're getting close."

Tom looked out of the bow. The *Rainbow* was crawling along at half-speed. The sky was studded with asteroid islands. They swung in their unknown orbits on every side.

"Close to what?" Tom asked quietly. "We're gettin' mighty close to the Hive itself."

"I know," Ames nodded.

Tom looked at him. "There's lots you haven't explained. For instance, you could leave Standish port and travel your 76 distance in any direction—along at least hundreds of lines. What made you decide on this bearing?

Ames shook his head. "There's a complicated answer to that one, I'm afraid," he said, almost smiling. "Let it wait. I may be wrong," he added, and when he looked out, the half-smile vanished.

But Tom was unsatisfied. Irritable and curious he asked "And where in blazes can a jump like that little point three take you out here?" and he swung an open palm in a bewildered, questioning arc.

Ames kept scanning the horizon. "I don't know, I don't know. It is a little jump, isn't it?" He shook his head again. There was no use looking for the answer yet. That would come when it came. By the very nature of its strangeness it would compel attention to itself, in due time. In due time . . .

The phrase kept repeating itself in his mind. When would that time come? Would it be a matter of a split second —would the failure to notice it become a perilous mission?

For the *Rainbow*, moving ever more slowly, was in a dangerous world now. It was a world filled with moving shapes, with smaller and stranger worlds. Above and below the little ship, and in every direction, the sky was filled with forms that gyrated in increasing speed as the ship slowed.

IX

AMES looked at many of them through the navigator's glass. How still they were. There was no life on them. Some were bare, dead worlds of dust and gray moss, with the rotting hulks of strange trees standing stiff and gaunt. Some were beds of lava, thick sluggish balls of brown and red-streaked mud that burst into viscous, creamy bubbles as the surface exploded from the asteroid's fiery heart. Some were perfect little worlds, greening, fresh, alive, delightful miniatures like a child's vision of Paradise, waiting only for the innocent foot of exploration to give itself to a claimant.

The silence of these silent worlds had invaded the ship. The two men sat in the bow, saying nothing, one preoccupied with the management of the vessel, the other with his thoughts, and with the wonder of where the ship had come. How swift these forms were in their flight as they moved one with another in an intricate dance through the sky. . . . He knew they had come to it even before Tom spoke. . . .

"The Hive." The two words fell dry from Tom's tight lips.

Yes, this must be the Hive. It was still a few points dead ahead. It was a place where the worlds were almost infinitely more numerous and tightly packed. They were smaller worlds, some of them hardly a few acres, round and swift. Together their gigantic, swirling mass was too great for the eye or the navigator's glass to encompass, and singly they were nothing. They moved around each other in bewildering, erratic patterns, kept in their course by some strange compulsion that alone understood their being. It was as if some giant, compounded of a force beyond man to understand, had tossed a giant's handful of spheres into the sky, and there they had remained, kept tossing and turning and revolving by the undiminished impetus of the Force, locked in orbits forever. Sometimes they brushed by one another so closely that their flowers— when it happened to two living worlds —could have exchanged pollen. Sometimes they came hurtling through space toward each other as if intent at mutual destruction, only to be caught and swerved aside at the last moment, and they would part and swim from view, lost in the vast sky, in the twilight vastness of distance and followed by more.

But they were so close together, their approaches so sudden and incalculable, that the spaces between them could not be entered into. A brown sphere would emerge from the mass, dance along the edge a little and abruptly be sucked into the whirling vortex. A group would separate from the mass, rotate outside wildly, then break apart and disappear at oddly spaced intervals to rejoin the Hive in a new pattern. The pattern changed from instant to instant. There was no sense there, no meaning. . . .

Ames put his pencil down finally. The Berry gauge had read 76.1 and the *Rainbow* had come to a halt. She lay in the sky near the Hive, an idle, rust-streaked speck. In the silence it seemed to Ames he could hear music remarkably like the *Symphony of the Spheres*. It was a weird succession of harmonies, deep and troubled at times, slow moving and majestic, and then rising quickly to lyrical heights until the body of the music was all but gone and all that remained were great masses of strings being plucked in an evasive, exhilarating melody. Then reeds would echo wildly and the sky break into blue, white-flaked streamers of light and the drums would rumble. Then quiet again.

THERE was something wild and ghostly in the sky, something that penetrated the beings of the two men. When Tom spoke again, after an interminable silence, his voice was low and unsteady.

"We can't go any further."

"Then we'll stay here."

"Here?" Silence again. "For how long?"

"I don't know." Ames' eyes met Tom's. He felt it difficult to speak and yet there was comfort in speaking. It was as if uttering words helped to order his thoughts, the way moments of stress would make him talk aloud to himself. "We'll wait here until it makes sense. Everything else has led me here, a hundred little answers combining to form this one question: where from here? But there must be an answer, and we'll wait here until we know it . . . or until," and he looked out again, somber and thoughtful, "we know that we'll never know any more. Now you go to sleep. I'll sit here and keep looking."

He had no way of knowing when it was that Tom had fallen asleep, but after awhile he knew that Tom had dropped off. From then on there was hardly any time or awareness of it.

There was only this incredible small universe and the music of its existence, the law that was itself, the mystery of its being, the unfathomable reasons for the comings and goings of the tiny worlds that composed it. Hours drifted by.

Then Tom was awake and they spoke now and then and again there would be silence between them as they listened. Perhaps he had dozed off himself—it seemed sometimes as if Tom had been asleep and awake half a dozen times—and twice they had eaten, content to nibble at the emergency rations, to drink the vacuumed cold water. Ames felt that his eyes were heavy in their sockets and the pain of keeping them open was a fiery ache that numbed his brain. And hours ran together.

What was he searching for What had he expected to find here? Had his myriad, foolish, unimportant little answers arrayed themselves from some malicious, inner intelligence to lead him to a vast and mocking question? Was there some basic antagonism among facts for men who used them? Were they alive and did they resent their captivity? Had there been a time when —long before man, long before an inquisitive intelligence lived — when there were no facts as such, and only the immutable mysteries of creation, content to be, to remain?

He was thinking nonsense now, he knew. He was tired, so tired. Facts, facts, facts . . . like the plucking of strings. What strange things the tired mind was capable of thinking. What were facts? Compact, tiny bundles that tiny intelligences had grasped and formed and fashioned into tools? What could the intelligence do, confronted by this? How could it comfort itself?

"Tom!"

"Huh?" He had been awake then. He grunted, his voice uncertain and anxious, his eyes turned reluctantly to Ames.

"Tom! Watch that small body there—the red one, with the red moss and water! Watch it come out of the pack!"

He knew what it would do. He knew now that he had known for a long time what it would do. He had watched it do the same thing over and over again —how many times. And there it was again!

It was a small asteroid, pale pink and delicate, its surface a compound of of pools like tinted water and crimson, silky moss. It came out of the heart of the Hive. One moment three green balls had swiveled by and then they parted and the red one shot out. It came at breath-taking speed, spinning madly out, to the very edge of the invisible lines that bounded the Hive. And suddenly it slowed and its spinning slowed and it seemed to float by. It hung quite still, its pools unruffled, its moss calm, and it moved by in slow grandeur, traversing an arc that kept it at the edge of the Hive for a long time. Then as quickly as it had come, it was gone. It turned and re-entered the intricate, alive, complex heart of the Hive.

"You saw it Tom?"

The older man nodded.

"How far from us would you say it passed?"

"Three or four hundreths of a point, maybe."

"Tom," Ames said quietly, steadily, "the next time it comes out—it won't be too long returning—we'll land on it."

"What?" The single word was a harsh, grating sound.

"We'll let it take us into the Hive!" There was no recognition of the older man's fear in Ames voice. "I've watched it come out again and again. If we had known about it from the beginning we could have taken it almost immediately. We need never have stopped the tubes until we were on that—"

"On that crazy asteroid?" Tom cried.

"Exactly. On that crazy asteroid. Don't you see? In that case the Berry gauge would have recorded the trip directly to it and. . . ."

"And what?"

"And somewhere inside the Hive—I don't know where but it must be—somewhere inside there is something that is a distance of point three away! We leave the crazy asteroid to make that little point three jump—and then we've arrived!" His weary eyes were alive again. "And coming back it's the same way. That must be the explanation of the point three jump being duplicated! It must be! That crazy asteroid is *the only one* that keeps coming out that way."

TOM had ceased offering resistance. He was too bound up in the mystery, too powerless in the face of Ames' insistence on knowledge, and because he could not oppose. He nodded gloomily, but he had come out of the half trancelike state in which he had spent most of their hours of standing by. Because of this he became aware of a new peculiar restlessness about Ames.

Ames knew that Tom had noticed it. Waiting to test his hypothesis in action, a new anxiety had arisen. He had calculated his factors with mathematical precision and if he was correct so far he could guess something of the outcome. It was like a man adding a string of sums all ending with the digit five: he might not know the total, but he could foretell that it would end with a five. He had foreseen it before—he had earnestly counted on it—and now he became afraid of it. It might not happen after all. It might happen

in an entirely different way. He had not been able to foresee the long hours of waiting here. Was there something else?

"Tom," he said, "I might as well tell you. I've been expecting someone to follow us."

Tom said, "Yeah," in an unquestioning voice. The question followed. "Murchison?"

"Or one of his ambassadors. Still, I don't know. I'm telling you this so's you'll be ready if it comes."

Tom nodded. "I'll be ready." He took out his Foster pistol and examined its chambers. Ames, feeling strangely flushed, followed his example. It was an odd sensation, this handling of a deadly weapon with the expectancy—for deep inside him he knew it was more than merely a possibility—of using it. To an unreal world it added another note of unreality. He had to shake that feeling off, he knew. He had enough to think about, as it was.

And yet, sitting there, waiting for the exact moment to come when the *Rainbow's* now throttled but alive tubes would propel her forward on the investigation of a mathematical decision, it did not seem real. It was still a problem on paper. Fighting the notion brought on a heady exhilaration, a recklessness he had seldom known before. He had never considered himself a man of action—not in terms of violence. The world he knew came into contact with the vast, powerful, subterranean worlds of violence and lawlessness only to punish offenders, to maintain order. For a man who wielded lawbooks to be handling a gun was something that unsteadied him. Had he been foolish? Should he not have called in men equipped to handle such problems? Had he brushed by Judge Averill's counsel too quickly, too thoughtlessly?

The answer lay within the problem. There had been no problem to hand over to anyone else! He had created the problem himself—he was the only one who knew it existed, and he was proving its existence not by reasoning but by acting! And action alone would see it through. He fingered the heavy weapon. His hands felt moist. . . .

AN HOUR and a half later he touched Tom's arm. "Ready," he said through tight lips. The three green asteroids had appeared. They wheeled into view in a triangular arrangement. Some force kept them together but it was not strong enough to keep them in the same order. Always they emerged grouped, but always altered. This time two were close together and the third far back.

The first two began to separate. The third started catching up, then suddenly slowed and held back. The crimson asteroid shot out of the Hive and into the triangle. The green asteroids veered, swung about, came together in a tight little group as if to avoid the wild speed and eccentricity of the flaming body that hounded them. The crazy asteroid flashed out alone, steadied.

"Now!"

The ship leaped forward, her bow swung three points forward of the port beam to intercept the orbit of the asteroid. She came in neat, slackened, straightened out. The asteroid was beginning to gather speed again. The Rainbow started to fall. That small red world below them hardly offered a landing place. Tom's forehead was covered with sweat. His fists knotted but his touch was delicate. The asteroid began to reenter the inner Hive and the Rainbow clung to it, diving at it but losing ground.

The red moss was moving ahead, blurring with speed. If the asteroid once lost the tiny vessel, she would be locked in the Hive, alone amidst hosts of great and small bodies moving at fantastic speeds, with no way to judge their course. Disaster was seconds away and Tom acted.

"Hold on!" he cried.

The Rainbow was three hundred feet above the asteroid. Her bow tilted up sharply and her bow tubes roared in sudden violence. The ship kicked back and she dropped and her stern buried itself in the red moss. Tom's quick maneuver had yanked the ship out of space and stuck it stern first into solidity.

So quickly had it been accomplished that both men were still waiting for the shuddering impact to hit them through the bulkheads when the ship was already fast. There had been hardly any sensation of impact at all. The soft viscous earth and moss had cushioned the ship as she fell and sucked her in.

Ames was about to speak, to congratulate Tom — he understood the maneuver had been imperative and magnificently executed, for it had also preserved the ship's ability to blast out, where a bow-dive might have buried her too deeply—but he could not speak. For the asteroid was now in the Hive and accelerating. It swung about insanely, rushing past body after body, turning and twisting, ever on the point of colliding and just veering off.

The half hour that followed was a nightmare. In the wild images that flashed through Ames mind there was a dim recollection of boyhood terrors on a roller-coaster. Ames kept himself from shouting—he might have screamed—only with the knowledge that the asteroid had come out of the Hive every time. It was only when he remembered that it was the collisions of these bodies that produced the vacuum impacts that made what the miners called "bad weather" that he knew fear. For it was possible, always possible, that they would collide. There would be a vast sound, perhaps flame, then nothing. They would never see it, they would never feel the heat or know the impact. The cataclysm would be entered on weather logs . . . but it is absurd to fear it if this course had been traveled so often, as he thought, before . . . and yet their ship, small as it was, might upset the delicate balance that had preserved this crazy bit of earth and water and moss . . . but then why hadn't other ships done so . . .

GREEN and yellow and gray, balls and slivers, islands of every shape, they bore down on the red traveler to destroy it and lost heart. Immense forms blotted out the sky. Strange shapes danced and lunged and came along and were gone. Then, little by little, they grew less and there was sky again and space again. The asteroid stopped twisting and grew calmer as if from exhaustion.

Not far off—how far away?—lay a quiet asteroid, quite alone. It was mostly brown but spotted with green and blue, and great streaks of black traversed its surface. Black . . . dull, velvety black, as orium was black . . . And the green was vegetation, trees and grass, and the blue was water. This still world, perhaps fifty times the size of the red asteroid, lay tranquil within the heart of the Hive—no, it *was* the heart of the Hive. The mad whirling worlds around it were jealous guards of its peace, sentinels and executioners together, shielding it from possible view. How far had they traveled into the Hive? It was impossible to know. They knew only that it was there.

When the two exhausted, fear-shaken men regarded each other they knew what each thought.

Ames managed to speak. "How far from here is it?"

Tom nodded grimly. "About point three, I reckon."

THERE was no need for further speech. Both knew they could not tell when the red asteroid would swing away again to resume its insane orbit. The method in its madness was plain. Tom touched the controls and the aft tubes and the answering roar shot bits of red moss and earth into space. The *Rainbow* tore herself loose from the embrace of the soft earth and blasted aloft. She soon reached her objective, circled once and settled down to a gentle landing, standing off with her bow pointing up fifteen degrees.

Neither man moved for a few moments. The presence of vegetation, in many places lush and beautiful, generally guaranteed oxygen enough to support human life. Yet the System knew its oddities—and they had not yet identified the vegetation.

They looked out of the bow ports. The *Rainbow* had come to rest on a sandy plain within a shallow valley. The sides of the valley rose leisurely in every direction save one, and that one led to a granitic black-brown series of hills perhaps a mile or so off. A small woods was nearby, and there were winged creatures overhead. Outside, directly ahead of the ship, was a tall, spiny *tono*-grass waving lazily in the wind.

Already there was no sign of the red asteroid; it had gone off to complete its erratic orbit around this haven of quiet. Tom reached for the compartment that housed the sub-atmosphere suits when Ames stayed his hand.

Tom followed the direction of Ames' eyes. There was something moving in the *tono*-grass—moving the spiny laces against the wind. A moment later a shadow appeared among the thick root-stalks and a dark, shaggy head peered out at them. Then slowly, a small black Scotch terrier came walking across the plain towards the ship.

Tom sucked in his breath. "I know that dog," Tom said. "His name's Duke—he belonged to Scotty Purdom."

He got up quickly and led the way to the hatch, opened it and climbed out into the sunlight and the quiet warm wind. Ames followed.

X

A T THE first sign of life aboard the ship, the dog fled headlong to the tall grass. Tom and Ames jumped down to the sandy plain and stood there, searching the grass. After a few moments they saw the little terrier inching forward. Its every movement was quick and nervous, and above all, cautious. It peered at the two men from beneath shaggy brows, its ears cocked, its muscles taut. It looked wild, somehow.

"Here, Duke!" Tom called.

At the first syllable, Duke sprang out of sight. If he still moved in the grass, it was with such practiced care that he remained undetected. Tom turned his puzzled face toward Ames. From the moment he had seen the dog, that expression had settled on him like a mask.

"That's Scotty's dog," he said again. "He was always a friendly little feller . . . not much like . . ." He let his voice die out because his thoughts were obviously elsewhere. Then he said, "You came here expectin' to find Scotty, didn't you?" His hands fumbled with a fieldglass case.

Ames nodded. "Hoping," he said.

"You think he's been hiding here?" He's still somewhere—"

"No," Ames interrupted, sadly. He was still searching for the dog. "If there was a chance that we'd find him here alive— if I ever believed it was possible, and I don't think I did—that dog of his convinced me he's dead." He met Tom's gaze. "Don't you see how that dog acted? It isn't just that he's—well, unfriendly. He's like some animal that never was tamed—and that's because he's been alone for a long time now. If Scotty were still alive somewhere near here, that dog would have run off to him."

"But how would—"

"Look over there," Ames interrupted. The dog had appeared on the edge of the steepest incline from the valley. He sat flattened out against the horizon, watching them. "That dog's learned to fear men," Ames said, watching Tom as the latter trained his fieldglass on Duke.

"You're right," Tom said. He held the glasses in his hand. "Someone shot at him. He's got part of an ear nicked and his left hindquarter's covered with dried blood. But I don't think he's afraid. He looks more to me as if he's waiting to see what we'll do."

"Mmmmm," Ames nodded. "Maybe. Let's follow him."

"You think he'll lead us to Scotty?"

"In spite of himself, yes. I think he'll try to keep between us and Scotty. If he falls back and gets on our flank, that means we're wrong and he's letting us go ahead. But if he runs ahead . . . we'll see."

They began to execute the plan. The moment they started up the long incline, Duke leaped up and was gone. When they reached the summit, the dog was out of sight. Ames led the way towards the woods. They were halfway there when Tom spotted Duke far to the right. He had been hidden behind a small boulder. Abruptly they changed course. Duke ran across a stretch of wild medicine grass on a tangent toward the hills in the distance and disappeared again. They didn't see him again for perhaps five minutes. He had been behind them and to their left, and he was running, not fast and crouching, ahead of them.

"It's the hills," Ames said. "I'm pretty sure now."

THEY set a straight course for the nearest of the hills, and once they did that they had little trouble keeping Duke in sight. He would lie down and hide and wait somewhere along their path, only to get up and run ahead when they were close to him. But each time he ran a bit slower, and waited longer, so that the distance between them decreased steadily as they came to the hills. Now the dog would stand up and let them see him as he faced them.

Tom said, "He knows it's all up with him. He's makin' up his mind whether or not to attack us, poor little feller."

When they reached the first hill, Duke was near enough for them to hear him growl. They paid little attention to him now. The mineral make-up of the hill was testimony enough. The rich chocolate earth was streaked with black veins that were pure surface orium. Behind the first hill rose others, higher, some sheer outcroppings of soil and rock almost entirely black. There above a jagged overhang stood Duke, some twenty feet over them and fifty feet away. He barked loudly and his eyes looked dark and savage. The two men climbed on. Duke hid again.

The hills were great disordered masses of rocky boulders through which Nature's hand had sprinkled powdery orium with a lavish hand. The incredible richness of these often solid boulders was beyond anything Tom had ever heard of. It was scarcely necessary to mine here—all one had to do was take the orium from the surface. Their feet made crunching sounds as they ascended what they soon saw was one of a series of miniature mountains forming a crested semi-circle. Had they been able to perceive this arrangement before, they might have skirted the base of the hills and entered through the open ends of the crescent, but they were already close to the top.

Suddenly they heard Duke barking savagely. The short sharp sound echoed and re-echoed wildly among the boulders, coming from some distance away. Ames ran to the summit as fast as he could.

There, barely visible on the horizon, lay a fairly small space-ship. Below, in the horseshoe-shaped valley formed by the hills, were the shafts and cranes and tunnelers of a mine. Close by the main mine shaft a copter had landed. The barking seemed to be coming out of the large mine shaft. It was followed in a second by a man's hoarse cursing voice, and a second after that by the unmistakable slight, whistling *ping* of a heat pistol, magnified many times by its echo. The dog's barking stopped. A moment afterward its dark, shaggy form came racing out of the mine shaft and a man tumbled out after it.

Ames took all this in in the time it would have taken him to wink an eye. The vessel, the copter, the man—these three discoveries and their meaning were lost on him. He was still standing there, looking down at the inexplicable scene, when Tom, who had climbed up beside him, shouted down: "Throw them hands up—*fast!*"

The man had had his back toward them. He had been holding his right hand stretched out by means of a supporting left hand, and in the evidently crippled right hand he held a Foster pistol. At Tom's voice he wheeled and fired the shot he had been about to send after Duke. He had no surprise on his lean, dark face, and no fear.

Black earth shot up in a cloud at Ames' feet and Ames went down from Tom's shove. The following shot burnt the air where Ames had stood. Tom, flat on his stomach, fired once, twice, three times, his Foster making its tiny clicking release noise. Then he got up on an elbow and swore. "Duck! He's coming up!"

It made no sense to Ames, not until he saw the copter rising in midair. Then he realized that the man had gotten to the waiting copter and was flying up to get at them. In that moment, had Ames gotten up or had he given Tom some sign that he was all right, either man could have fired half a dozen rounds into the momentarily exposed copter. By the time both realized it, the copter had disappeared behind a ridge on their left and almost at their level.

PERILOUS instants ticked by. Ames had taken out his own Foster and opened the safety. He was crawling towards a protecting boulder when the copter shot out horizontally, flying from one ridge to another. Tom sat up and put a hole through its bronzed tail before it disappeared, but from the nose had come a deadly swift succession of tiny gleams of light, the air shimmering all around—the sign of a repeating gun fixed on a bow swivel in the copter. Its beams of heat ate more than halfway through the rock that shielded Tom, forcing him to move.

The copter's game was clear. It could not fire at them openly despite its overwhelming advantage of fire power, but it could keep circling them, flanking their cover, itself covered by one ridge after another. The ridges were like the points of a crown; the copter could shuttle from one to another with a minimum of risk until it caught them between covers. And its machined Foster made all but the heaviest cover untenable.

Again and again the copter darted about the range. Its fire had destroyed most of the upper boulders and Tom and Ames had both been forced to seek cover lower down. The third time the copter appeared, Ames fired and parted a wing strut. He was amazed to hear himself laughing. It didn't sound like him. He dug in and pulled his long legs in behind him. He had lost sight of Tom.

"Tom!" he shouted. "You all right?"

"Fine! Take care of yourself! Keep separated!"

Sure, sure, that was it. They could creep around to outflank the copter . . . if they lasted that long. The next time the copter appeared Ames saw that its occupant had thrown back the glassite hatch to increase his visibility. He was aware of what his opponents were doing. He took new steps. Suddenly the copter swooped up, spun on its side and came down at an angle, sweeping the ridge. He was after Ames. His shots had come so close that they burned away the supporting edges of Ames' rock. The rock moved a bit, loosened, and rolled downhill, leaving Ames out in the open. The copter was wheeling back. Something hit its open hatch cover and made the occupant swerve. Ames, standing up, was following the copter with an outstretched, steady arm. He knew his Foster had cut its mark in the copter. But it was Tom's good shooting that saved him then, giving him time, as the copter swerved, to find new shelter. But he was going lower and lower, and as his own shelter grew less, that of the copter multiplied. It came down after him relentlessly and Tom was forced to come down too.

It was a question of time, nothing more. A strange exhileration had come to Ames, a sort of intense peace. He found himself trying to analyze it and cursed himself for a fool. The copter had dozens of peaks to choose from now. It could move from one to another without being detected half the time, giving it the advantage of surprise when it attacked. And its attacks were more frequent now, and closer. It needed one short burst at close range to end the unequal duel.

The copter slid out from behind a nearby crag and dipped swiftly into the valley, its bow gun flickering. Moments after it was lost from view Ames could still see mad clouds of black dust swirling upward. The copter's persistence could only mean that somewhere below it had caught Tom without protection. Ames pulse was like a hammer as he jumped up to circle around to where he could see the copter, now halfway down the valley and momentarily below him. He forgot his own danger, intent on a glimpse—and then he saw it!

It was less than a hundred feet away, less than thirty feet below his level. Its rotor blades held it in position against the side of a hill that it was eating away. The figure of its driver was low in the seat. Ames raised his gun, and as his arm came up, the dark, quick-moving form of Duke appeared, crawling along the crest of the hill just above the copter. The animal moved with cunning, its form blending into the black hill. It reached a point directly above the driver. A single leap through a few feet of air—it landed within the open hatch of the machine. The dog's snarl mingled with the man's scream as the teeth sank into the back of his neck.

The copter plunged into a neighboring peak, rebounded, hit its rotor blades against rock. The blades splintered off and the copter was lifeless. It crashed over against the hill, dropped twenty feet and kept rolling all the way down into the valley. . . .

CONSCIOUSNESS was returning to the man. Ames laid the man's head on one of the copter's seat cushions and opened his collar. His dark, lean face was turning sallow and bloodless from the draining severed femoral artery which Tom had tourniqueted.

"You're sure?" Ames asked.

"Sure? I've known him since he became Murchison's chauffeur—it's Big Nate Webber, all right."

Ames rose quickly. "Stay with him, Tom. Do what you can and remember this: he mustn't die!" Ames' face was flushed through its weary lines, his eyes looked maddened. "You've got to keep him alive, do you understand?"

He didn't hear what Tom said as he made his way through the tangled wreckage of the copter and began running uphill. A few yards farther up he came upon the mutilated body of the little terrier, where it had fallen, already dead, from the copter during its mad plunge. He kept running as fast as he could, picking his way among the crags, climbing quickly to the summit.

There he made out the *Rainbow* and he plunged downhill toward it. Breathless, his legs like rubber, he ran on. The small ravines and crevices so easily avoided on their upward climb were hidden enemies now and he fell several times. Disheveled, gasping, he reached the plain and kept going without a stop until he came to the ship. He clamored in and quickly gathered up a first aid kit, an electric torch, some sheets of paper and a pen, two canteens of water, and then he was on his way back. Staggering now, he kept his long legs moving, unmindful of the burning dust in his lungs, the stabbing effort to breathe. He climbed the hills again and tumbled, more than ran, down into the valley marked with wrecked machinery. And all the while his brain turned over the unanswered questions, groping for answers. What could he have been thinking of? How this unforeseen thing been possible? *Unforseen!* It was a mockery. It had destroyed his plans . . . *his plans* . . . but not yet, he told himself, not yet . . . not yet. . . .

They worked over Webber half an hour before his breathing had any strength in it, but Ames knew it was close to the end. The strength and vitality that had kept this man alive through a crushing, smashing fall that had completely destroyed a thing of metal was being sapped by internal injuries over which they had no control. Minutes, perhaps a few hours at most, remained to him.

Webber's eyes were open. There was reason in them. He stared at Tom, watching him as fresh bandages were applied. There was hatred and cruelty in those eyes as Ames raised his head to give him more water. This time less of it dribbled down his chin. His lips moved silently, then his voice came, soft, harsh, venomous.

"You'll . . . be . . . paid . . . off . . ."

AMES looked down at him. "Save your strength," he said sharply. "You'll need it. It's a long way back to Mirabello." He caught Tom's surprised glance and frowned a warning.

The bloodless lips curled in a slow sneer "Quit . . . kidding me . . . Jack . . . This . . . is . . . the . . . last . . . stop . . . for . . . me . . ."

Ames met his eyes and laughed quietly. "It is if I want it to be. I haven't made up my mind yet."

A feeble, foul oath dribbled out of the pale lips.

"You're making it up for me," Ames said, matter-of-factly. He paid no more attention to Webber. He capped the canteen and stood up and walked away a few feet. He sank down on a rock and rested, watching Webber, wondering how successfully he had planted the seed. It wasn't until Tom called him a few minutes later that Ames began to hope again. He returned to the dying man, steeling himself for his obnoxious part, hating himself for the bitter deception. When he looked down at Webber and saw the faint light of hope he had brought to life there, it was almost more than he could bear. But there was no time to lose.

"You're . . leveling . . . with . . . me . . . Jack?" Ames nodded and Webber went on. "Really think . . . I'll . . . come . . . out of . . . this . . . okay?"

Ames shrugged then. "If you call twenty years in prison okay," he said, "and if I take you back." He hesitated. "Unless you gave me good reason to take you back."

"Rat . . . on . . . Murchison?"

"That's right."

The sneer returned. "——you," Webber said.

"All right," said Ames. "I'll put it to you this way. If you had a hand in killing Purdom, I'll get you the best deal—"

Webber tried to laugh. His contemptuous eyes closed.

Ames fought despair. He weighed the gamble; if he was wrong he had lost nothing. Webber was too secure, and part of that security lay in his decision that Ames would not let him die there, that he would be taken back anyway. And had there been hope for him, Ames realized, Webber would be right. He could not convince him otherwise. But suppose the rest of his security was taken away—the security that depended on the knowledge that

Murchison was safe? Webber had been Murchison's chauffeur. Was it not possible that the tremendous confidence these men had had in themselves—still evident in Webber's refusal—had that confidence made them commit the error Ames had scarcely hoped to find? To have lost the gamble later would have been a disappointment, but here was a chance to use the possibility that he was right. It was a tiny chance, but it was all he had now.

"Tom," said Ames. "You saw that ship out there? Is that one of Murchison's?"

"Uh-huh. It's his private one."

"Then that's the one he used going to and from the convention at Church's Planet." As Ames spoke, Webber's eyes opened. "That's the one I told Sheriff Kaine about. The Berry gauge in it is what we want." He got up and nodded to Webber. "See what I mean?" he asked softly.

Webber kept staring at him. Presently his lips moved. "What's . . . the . . . deal . . . Jack?" he whispered.

Ames felt his heart throbbing wildly. "Tell us what you know and sign a confession. We'll take you back and do what we can for you." Even then he had been unable to state the cruel lie.

He waited.

After a long pause, Webber said, "You . . . win . . ." He began talking then, in a low, hesitant voice. Ames sat near his head, taking the words down, pausing occasionally to give Webber more water, to raise his head. Tom sat silent, listening. The minutes fled by, each taking a little of Webber's strength with it. His voice grew lower and lower, until Ames finally told him to stop. He had heard the one thing he had not known. He wrote swiftly, putting down the last of it . . .

". . . . Scotty must have seen us coming. We had to follow him down into the mine. He probably didn't know who we were at first, but even after Murchison yelled down to him, he wouldn't come out. Murchison went down. He didn't come up until half an hour later and he told me he had killed Scotty but he couldn't get him out because the gun ate through some shoring and it caved in. Then we went on to Church's. After the convention we came back and took Scotty's and Wylie's ships. We put the bomb Murchison got from Lola into Scotty's ship and waited . . ."

"He's goin' fast," Tom whispered.

AMES stopped writing. He put an arm under Webber and raised him up. "Webber, you've got to sign this now," Ames said. He put the pen in Webber's limp fingers. "Sign it," Ames pleaded.

Webber's eyes were glazed. He gripped the pen feebly and let it go again. "Tired . . . now . . ." he mumbled. "Later . . ." But when Ames put the pen in his hand again, he stared at the paper and began to scrawl a huge N. Ames removed his hand and started him again. He wrote his name in a hopeless tangle of letters.

"You've got to do better than that," Ames insisted desperately.

Something in his voice penetrated the thick fog that now separated Webber from the two men. A strange light flared in those dead eyes and fixed itself on Ames. He kept his head from rolling with the remnants of his control. He wet his lips with a thick tongue. "What's . . . wrong . . ." he asked. His breath was sluggish now but he forced it to form words. "I'm . . . dying . . ." he panted. The realization lit his face with a pallid glow and his lips curled a little to a semblance of a snarl. "You . . . dirty . . . double . . . cross . . . ing . . . son . . . of . . . a . . . bi . . ." His mouth remained open as his head dropped limp against Ames' chest.

Ames laid him down gently and got up. He felt shaken through and through. For many minutes he sat on a rock nearby. He was unaccustomed to violent and ugly death. He sat there until Tom came to him.

"Wasn't pretty," Tom said. "Not even for a human rattler. I feel a lot worse about that little dog. Guess he saved our lives." After a moment he asked, "Reckon that confession's goin' to help Buck any?"

Ames sighed. "I'm not worried about Wylie. I had more evidence than I need to clear him."

"Then what is it?"

"It's still the confession. It did one thing for me—it told me that it was Murchison himself who committed the murder. But it won't convict him. The signature's unrecognizable and our testimony's objectionable because we're prejudiced."

"What about the Berry gauge in his ship?"

Ames shook his head. "It's a magnificent stroke of luck, and even then it's not enough. Proving where his ship was doesn't prove he was aboard it at the time." He thought a moment. "But it's my one crack at nailing him. I've got him tied with a hundred strings and that's the strongest string of all— but it's still string, and you can't generally hang a man with string. We'll see." He shrugged and said, "Let's have a look in the mine. After what Webber said I don't expect much."

They walked along the valley floor to the main shaft. The heavy odor of smouldering wood was testimony to Webber's confession that he had been destroying shoring to hide what remained of Scotty Purdom, when the dog, faithful to the last, had left two potential marauders for an actual one. Gingerly they lowered themselves. It was several minutes before they came to the smoky passage thirty feet below.

They looked at the decaying remains of Purdom, or what little of him showed. For the lower three-fourths of his body lay buried under a huge slab of orium. The solid block was almost pure. In itself it was worth a king's ransom. There was a tragic irony in the death of this little man, imprisoned by his own incredible wealth, entombed in his famous and secret Silver Spoon Mine.

"This is why Scotty's body wasn't aboard his ship when they set it loose with one of Wylie's bombs in it. They couldn't get him out—"

Suddenly the earth trembled. The dank, smoky cavern shivered and columns of dust loosed themselves in a choking, blinding flood from the mine walls and floor and the hollow reverberations of a thunderous explosion filled the mine. A second roar welled up and the world shook. The timbers on all sides groaned and sagged a little and the dust grew thicker. After the first bewildered moment of panic, when Ames looked up he saw that the shaft above them was still clear and unblocked. Light like an opaque haze still streamed down to supplement the illumination provided by his electric torch. Whatever had happened, it had not been in the mine.

They saw what it was a moment after they reached the surface. Murchison's spaceship was gone. In its stead remained a huge, raw crater over which black and brown clouds of fine earth were still settling. Bits of the blasted ship were scattered around for a mile.

The two explosions had completely demolished it.

PRESENTLY, Ames said, quietly, "That's that, I suppose. I didn't give Murchison credit enough. In the end he thought of everything—even of disposing of Webber and the ship—and its Berry gauge. Those bombs were well timed. If Webber had been aboard somewhere in space he'd be floating jelly. And if he were still here, presumably having killed us as he was sent to do, he'd remain here until he starved to death or until Murchison decided to come and kill him."

"Yeah," Tom nodded. "I guess we're goin' to have to be satisfied with just gettin' Buck out. It's hard to beat a man who destroys part of the evidence, impounds the rest, and then goes ahead and manufactures his own evidence to do tricks for him."

They returned to where Webber's body lay only after two fruitless hours of searching for some possible remnant of the blasted vessel's Berry gauge. With spades they took from the mine they began to dig two graves, one for a man, one for a small animal. They hardly spoke at all. Ames worked automatically, glad of the physical exertion to give his mind some reprieve from its tortuous wanderings and explorations. He had given up, but his mind persisted in returning to the cold body of the case, poking the dead carcass. He had to talk to relieve himself.

"This is one instance where the *corpus delicti* is really the corpse," he told Tom. "You know, there's a general misconception that *corpus delicti* refers to a body. It doesn't. It really means the body of the case, of which the corpse is an integral part. Well, here's a dead body of a case. Or is the joke too academic?"

He went on like that until he realized that he was talking nonsense, and when he fell silent again, he kept thinking. There was really nothing to be done. It was just as Tom had put it—Murchison couldn't be beaten because he played according to his own rules. He either hid evidence by impounding it ... *but Ames had gotten around that, hadn't he? ... or he destroyed it ... but sometimes one might resurrect something with circumstantial evidence of its past existence ... or he manufactured his own evidence to do tricks for him ... but that didn't stop the other side from doing the same ... or did it ... and if so, why? ...*

"Why what?" Tom asked.

Ames looked up, startled, and realized he had asked the question in a loud voice. He looked greatly puzzled by what was going on in his own mind, as if he were thinking not merely strange thoughts, but strangely patterned thoughts—thoughts of a nature that had never had a chance to enter his mind and establish some kind of pattern, so that he might recognize them when they returned. No, this was something new. He had never thought of it that way.

"I'm still doing it wrong," he said to Tom, not caring that his meaning was completely beyond Tom. "I listened to everything Averill told me and I thought I'd learned. I lectured him once on going beyond or aside of the law to enforce an essential justice. And what am I still doing? I'm still collecting facts and forgetting people!" He was fairly shouting now. "As far as facts go I've got enough to scare the hell out of him! I've got him even if I can't prove it—but can he be sure of that? Can he possibly be sure when I start throwing facts at him? Will he be able to tell the difference if—"

"Take it easy," Tom gulped, getting hold of Ames' waving arm. "You look like you might blow a valve. Now calm down and let's hear what this thing is that's got you goin' wild."

"I don't know," Ames said, his eyes shining. "I mean I haven't decided on the details yet, but that's the least of it —I'm good at details, you know. I've just got the big idea—*the big idea*—the one that's going to do it." He threw down his shovel. "And the first part of it is this: we're not burying either Webber or Duke."

"No? What are we doin' with them?"

"We're taking them back to Mirabello with us! Don't look at me like that. We'll wrap them in tarpaulin and keep the bodies in the outer chamber where it'll be cold enough to keep them from decomposing. I know it's a messy job but we've got to do it! It's the only—"

"Calm down now, please," Tom begged. "You got me convinced. I ain't sayin' a word, am I? Only get a good grip on yourself."

Ames nodded and sat down. His clothes were wringing with sweat. He couldn't keep his hands still even then. "Whew!" he kept saying . . . .

SOME hours later, when the *Rainbow* had successfully negotiated the return hop to the crazy asteroid when it came around again, Ames and Tom had a chance to check on one of the things Webber had told them. It was almost the only thing Ames hadn't known: that there was a sort of back entrance to the Silver Spoon asteroid. For there was another place on the out-entrance to the Silver Spoon asteroid. emerged long enough to enable a ship to get to it.

They saw the invisible borders of the hive where Webber had come, sneaked in ahead of them, but they remained with the crazy asteroid until it had completed the circuit back to where the

Rainbow had first landed on it, as Ames put it, "to keep the Berry gauge for the return trip as close as possible to a 76 reading—" and winking, "—got to keep the facts straight."

"Calm down," Tom said. "For the luvva Pete, calm down!"

XI

IT WAS late in the afternoon of August 4th when the *Rainbow* settled her battered hulk into the pits of Standish port. The day was hazy and too warm for Spring, the sun overcast, and there were few people about. Perhaps because of this as well as her own monumental unimportance, the *Rainbow's* arrival went almost unnoticed. But two hours later, when her owner's representative came to check on her condition, he found her the center of attraction for a growing crowd of mechanics, miners, field officials and various hangers-on.

On the edge of the field two official cars flanked a truck guarded by deputies. There were more deputies around the *Rainbow,* and inside her, among them the unusual figure of Sheriff Kaine. The cars and the truck had come up unheralded and deputies had carried an open coffin and a basket to the ship. When they emerged, the bare wooden coffin was obviously weighted, and it was sealed. The same was true of the basket. Both were quickly taken to the waiting truck.

There was more than enough fuel there to feed the fires of a dozen wild stories. Tom alone was present, and word came from the port officials— quickly seeping through the throng— that he had left with Terwilliger Ames. No one had seen Ames. There was a coffin. There was also a mysterious basket. It was more than enough, but even more was added when Sheriff

Kaine refused to let the *Rainbow's* representative take charge of her. The unhappy, and quickly branded *ill-fated* vessel was impounded, sealed, and blasted off from Standish on an officially supervised journey, undoubtedly to government sheds at Mayville.

It was all over by the time the *Twin-Sun's* reporters and a photographer arrived. Sheriff Kaine was leaving in one of the cars. He had nothing to say; he would not be quoted. The reporters nosed around and heard a hundred stories—except that to their trained ears it did not sound like a hundred stories, but a hundred variations on one story—and that, that Ames had been killed somehow, or was, at any rate, dead. His body had been carted off together with an important basket of evidence. They discounted the story that Ames' head was in the basket. The rest of it, carefully weighed and pruned and edited, they scribbled in their pads conscientiously.

With the *Rainbow* gone, the newshawks did the best they could: they went to the Standish port registry files and dug up pictures of the *Rainbow* from her halcyon days. They interviewed the port officials, who knew nothing but suspected the worst, and because of their suspicions and earnest desire to avoid undue publicity of such a sort, they talked altogether too much. The photographer also took a dozen shots of Tom as he stood talking with Kaine just before the sheriff left, and when Tom left, they followed him, begging for an interview, offering bribes and inducements for his story of the supposed tragedy.

Tom listened and sighed and reported only that his tongue was in the sheriff's custody. For reasons which he alone knew, he went to Ames' house in Mirabello City, still followed by the reporters, but before he could enter the house he was met by two men who had come from the city as soon as they had heard the *Rainbow* was back. It turned out they knew nothing else of its return. They were regional representatives of System Ethergraph, Ltd.

They carried copies of a graph sent to the Central Office many days before by Terwilliger Ames, notifying S.E. that he was filing suit against them under the Communications Statutory Laws, Section 885, for a branch manager's violation. They had been in Mirabello City for three days waiting for the *Rainbow* to return. System Ethergraph was deeply concerned because the esteemed Mr. Ames had had cause to complain. When Tom reluctantly told them it was impossible for them to see Mr. Ames, the reporters took it upon themselves to explain why. Tom left the enjoyable scene with misunderstood sadness and went into the house.

There he found the remains of an opulent and fantastic omelette, a thing of which Ames had spoken all the way back. He tiptoed upstairs and had a look at Ames as he slept. Of his desire for a long, undisturbed session in bed too, Ames had spoken with some passion. It was as if he had come out of a prison—as indeed, for so many days he had been the prisoner of his thoughts and unceasing work—to return to normality with a vengeance. A third desire, fishing, had also evoked longing from him. The fourth, though Tom was certain it would have been first had Ames been the man to talk of it, had not been mentioned. He had not uttered Sue's name at all.

Tom waited for the deputies to come, left one to guard the house and left with the other to visit Sheriff Kaine. When he returned some two hours later, he carried two interesting objects. One was a bulky jar covered with heavy foil. The second was a special edition of the *Twin-Sun* on which the ink had scarcely dried. He put them both on Ames' dressing table, bade the guarding deputies goodnight and went to sleep. . . .

THE dawn was announced by a series of shouts from Ames' room. He had jumped out of the *Rainbow* a moment after it landed, made his way inconspicuously home, called Sheriff Kaine and had half an hour's talk with him. The sheriff had left for the blast-port and Ames had gone to sleep immediately. The first he knew of his death was when he read about it the next morning.

Pajama-clad but barefoot, he was rushing down the stairs when he was met by the deputies and Tom. He waved the paper at them incoherently and tried to speak, and finally all he managed to get out were the words: "Mystery Surrounds Death Of Ames!" —which was a strict quotation of the headline. Even before he had spoken, Tom and the deputies were weak with laughter. They hung on the stair railing, bracing each other. Ames stared at them until he began to smile helplessly.

Some minutes later, in the kitchen, he heard the story while he had coffee and read the morning edition of the *Twin-Sun* which one of the deputies had brought in.

There were two headlines. The first stated: SHERIFF KAINE REFUSES TO MAKE PUBLIC AUTOPSY VERDICT. The second was in red ink underneath: BUREAU OF CLAIMS BARES SECRET PURDOM-WYLIE PARTNERSHIP. The stories that went with both headlines took up most of the paper and Ames devoured them.

"My God, listen to this," he read. " ' . . . during the night, a story circulated earlier yesterday and generally

discredited gained some credence in view of Sheriff Kaine's unprecedented action in suppressing the coroner's verdict. It was believed possible that the mysterious basket viewed by dozens of witnesses did indeed contain Ames' head, but so badly battered that identification was not immediately possible.' " Ames touched his crown gingerly. " 'Should this prove to be true,' " he read on, " 'the sheriff's action becomes more understandable. It may be that the sheriff will need dental and medical data before the identification is certain. At any rate, Sheriff Kaine's only public statement as to the verdict so far has been: "Gentlemen, the autopsy proves that the corpse is dead" . . . .' "

Ames broke off laughing and went on to the other story. Beside a photo of the *Rainbow*, retouched to make it look grimy with age, was a photo of Colonial Attorney Whitley, under which was his statement: "Naturally I am not free to comment upon matters pertaining to the Wylie trial which begins today, but I can say that the astonishing revelation of the Bureau of Claims is bound to figure prominently in the prosecution's case."

Ames smiled wryly and commented: "To say nothing of the case for the defense once a certain material witness testifies." He sighed and turned a page. "Be a good fellow and make me an omelette, Tom? I want to read some of these touching tributes to me by fellow citizens."

"Ordinary omelette or special?"

"Super. And don't spare the Uranian onions or garlic. I don't want anybody to have any doubts about my being alive." He added, "Does Judge Averill know the truth?"

"Uh-huh. Kaine told him." He went on, with careless emphasis: "Anybody else who might like you still thinks you're dead but not buried."

Ames glanced at him. Presently he put the paper down with a thoughtful smile. "What a wonderful morning this must be for Murchison."

Tom nodded, cracking eggs. "I'm thinkin' you ought to wear a lily in your lapel. I just can't wait for that blessed moment when you march into that courtroom." He sighed. "Soon's you're through eatin' we got a date upstairs with that jar. Remember?"

"Mmmmmm," was Ames' comment. He was lost in thought.

IT WAS almost ten o'clock when the blessed moment for which Tom waited arrived, except that it was more than an affair of a moment. It began almost immediately after Ames left his house. As he rode through the streets of the town in an official car he was seen, and the news spread almost as fast as the car traveled. When the car stopped briefly in the town square before a florist's, Ames was seen going into the shop and coming out. The excitement caught up with him and beat him to the courthouse. By the time he alighted there, a police escort was necessary to get him into the building.

But even Ames had under-estimated what was happening. The halls were crowded beyond Mirabello City's power to crowd them. There were more photographers and reporters than a dozen newspapers could have provided. Flash bulbs popped on every hand and people tried to break through the cordon around him. Blinded and bewildered, he was pushed through a mobbed court-room into the inner well before the bench. There he was besieged, and presently he began to understand, from what the numerous howling newspapermen were saying, precisely what had happened.

Newspapers from the Group around and from far beyond it had begun to pour their men into Mirabello since the afternoon of the day before. They had come from everywhere by special ship, by chartered clippers, to get in on the case, and more were arriving hourly. The *Twin-Sun's* syndicated scoop of Ames' death had been graphed throughout the System, and the *Twin-Sun* had been even more lurid in its graphed accounts of developments than it had been at home. Stories carried implied tie-ups of his mysterious death and the trial, and of both of these with the news of the Bureau of Claims revelation.

But even this had not quite explained the mass immigration, and certainly not to the equally bewildered newsmen of the *Twin-Sun*. There was more to it. Ames, a brilliant and famous New York lawyer, had disappeared some four months before. The first word of his whereabouts had come when he had ethergraphed for credentials to friends, and then it was known he was in Mirabello. In Mirabello! And what was he doing there? Why had he gone? What lay behind it? And then System Ethergraph's news release that a certain T. Ames had filed, or intended to file, suit for criminal action. And then, filtering through, accounts of his being involved in a murder trial—and finally, his mysterious death on the eve before he was due in court as a material witness, a status he had achieved through an unbelievable series of accusations. What did it mean? What did it add up to?

It added up to what Ames saw, heard and felt all around him—a jammed courtroom, newspapermen, specially leased graph wires in the courthouse, vast noise and excitement, and a police problem. He retreated, muttering, to a chair near the bench and mopped his brow and caught his breath. He straightened out his neat blue suit and adjusted the wild cowlicks of his hair. He sprinkled a dab of water on the lily he had gotten at the florist's, which he wore in his lapel. Finally, when some order had been restored by courtroom attendants, he turned in his seat and glanced around.

CLOSEST to him was the table reserved for the prosecution. Colonial Attorney Whitley and the seven or eight men of his staff were in huddled consultation around it, and as Ames glanced at them, Whitley got up and came toward him. Farther over, at the table for the defense, sat Farley and Buck Wylie, with Lola Marannes between them. Several people, among whom Ames recognized witnesses from the indictment proceedings, sat in the first row of seats, near the jury box. As Whitley neared Ames the jury started filing in from its room.

At the same moment, Ames spotted Tom in the third row. He was sitting beside Sue Wylie. Ames saw that the girl had been looking at him from the start; his eyes met hers and locked. Whitley was beside him now, and Ames murmured, "Excuse me," got up, walked to the railing and gave the lily to a court attendant with whispered instructions. The attendant smiled and delivered the lily to Sue Wylie. The delivery, her hesitant smile, and Tom's broad grin were immediately recorded by a dozen popping flashbulbs. Immediately attendants descended on the owners of the forbidden and hitherto secreted cameras, causing a new uproar.

Whitley was saying, " . . . our congratulations on your being here."

Ames grinned at him. "I couldn't afford not to be here," he told Whitley. "I'm out on five dollars' bail, and the way business has been, I need it."

"Yes, of course," Whitley coughed. "Just the same, I felt—"

He didn't get a chance to finish because Judge Averill's chamber door opened and the judge came out in his robes. The clerk intoned his ancient cry and the quieting courtroom stood until the judge was seated.

The formalities took a few minutes. Averill noted the presence of the C.A. and Farley, attorney of record for the defendant, consulted with both, as well as with members of Whitley's staff and late additions to Farley's. Once glances were directed at Ames. The judge frowned, made a notation and said something that ended the consultation. As the men returned to their tables a hush fell over the courtroom. For the first time the judge looked toward Ames and inclined his head.

The trial began.

Whitley addressed the jury in a quiet, studious manner. He outlined the nature of the case, the prosecution's intentions and touched on witnessed and circumstantial evidence, motivation and penalties. When he sat down, Ames followed his confident gaze to where Murchison was sitting in the second row, directly behind Ames.

By comparison, Farley was ill at ease. He expressed confidence in the jury's ability to decide on evidence and to take the law as directed by the judge. There was a cloying quality in his unsubtle wooing.

One of Whitley's staff, a heavy-set young man named Tisdale took over. He summoned, in order, Harvey Franshaw and Timothy Saunders and led them patiently. It was established that Scotty Purdom had, during the evening of July 9th, phoned Buck Wylie from the Rocketeer's Cafe and made an appointment with him for the following morning. On the morning of the 10th, Purdom and Wylie were seen together at the Standish blast-port, engaged in conversation. Each then left in his own ship and both headed east together. Both men were seen together later that day. They had returned to Standish port where Purdom fuelled his vessel and again they left together in the two ships, heading northwest.

Franshaw went unchallenged. Saunders was asked by Farley: "Can you, sitting here, tell me which direction is northwest?" Saunders consulted a watch, looked at a window and pointed accurately to northwest.

Tisdale then called a traffic manager from the Standish port. The manager, from ledgers, testified that he had records of two arrivals and departures on July 10th for vessels named *Spoon Special* and *Hellcat,* and that these arrivals and departures had taken place a minute or two apart. The testimony was interrupted by Farley, who objected to a waste of time and conceded that the two ships had come in and left together.

Tisdale smiled, ignored him, and went on with the prosecution's evidently painstaking case. Two Standish attendants testified to fueling the *Spoon Special* on the 10th. Then Tisdale called Larry Mason.

Mason, a middle-aged man, was identified as an employee at the Wylie *arrando* for five months previous, and still employed there. He testified that on the morning of the 10th, he had fuelled the *Hellcat* while Purdom and Wylie waited. Again Farley objected to a waste of time and offered to concede.

WHITLEY got up. "Your Honor, unless defendant's attorney is also willing to concede defendant's guilt and so plead, I must ask that he be restrained from further interruptions."

Judge Averill said: "The court advises Mr. Farley to examine more carefully what he concedes. The defendant's life in his hands. It may be that the prosecution is establishing a point which defense may not be willing to concede after all."

As if to prove the value of Judge Averill's advice, Tisdale then took a new line. He asked Mason: "Was there enough fuel at Wylie's own port to have fuelled the *Spoon Special* too?

"Yes, sir. Enough to have fuelled twenty ships like her."

"But you did not fuel the *Spoon Special?*"

"No, sir."

"In other words, you fuelled only the *Hellcat,* but the *Spoon Special* was then sent on to Standish port to fuel there?"

"Yes, sir."

Farley was on his feet. "Objection. The witness did not see the *Spoon Special* being fuelled at Standish."

Judge Averill directed: "Strike the question and answer from the record." To Farley he said: "Mr. Farley, you did not previously contest testimony to the effect that the *Spoon Special* was fuelled at the Standish port. Unless you desire, at some point, to offer contradictory evidence, the Court does not understand your correct, though useless, objection."

Farley flushed. "The law is the law," he stated with pettish arrogance. "He had no right to ask that question."

Averill frowned at him, then looked away. "Proceed, Mr. Tisdale."

Tisdale asked: "Do you know why . . . Strike that out, please. Did you hear anything that might have explained why the *Spoon Special* was not fuelled at the Wylie port?"

Farley was up again. "Object to 'might have explained'."

"Sustained. Witness is not here to venture guesses."

Tisdale asked: "Did you, Mr. Mason, at any time during the fueling, hear anything said by either Wylie or Purdom?"

"Yes, sir. I heard a few things."

"Anything about the fuelling?"

"Yes, sir. Scotty told Mr. Wylie that if he could fuel the *Special* right then and there, he'd save time and wouldn't have to go to Standish. Also, I heard him say, 'It's the same money, ain't it?'"

"What did Wylie say to that?"

"He said it would look better if Scotty went to Standish for his fuel. He said there were too many people wondering about them already, and he mentioned that the whole idea annoyed him from the start."

Ames glanced around at the courtroom, partly because he was a little bored with the prosecution's slow development of a theme to prove Wylie's partnership with Scotty, partly from interest in what he saw on the faces he regarded. Buck Wylie looked grim but patient, his hand resting on those of the girl beside him. Tom and Sue were attentive, and Murchison, who saw Ames turn toward him, had a benign expression which he did not change for Ames. The lawyers for both sides were engaged in furious scribbling and note-passing. He swallowed a yawn.

"To your knowledge, Mr. Mason," Tisdale had asked, "was there ever an occasion on which Wylie did fuel a vessel for Scotty?"

"Yes, sir. About six weeks before that time, Mr. Wylie fuelled the *Hellcat* and let Scotty Purdom take her. I wasn't supposed to know—"

Tisdale stopped him, anticipating Farley as he rose to object, and the latter part of the answer was deleted. Buck Wylie's face showed open rage as he bent to listen to Farley. A murmur had run through the courtroom. Farley

got up before Tisdale could resume.

"If the court please, defense agrees and admits the point Mr. Tisdale is so laboriously making. Mr. Wylie admits he was engaged in a partnership with Purdom for several months before Purdom's disappearance."

"Order!" Judge Averill rapped sharply. To Tisdale he said dryly: "Counsel for defense seems impatient, Mr. Tisdale. If the State agrees, Mr. Farley's statement will be entered in the testimony."

WHITLEY expansively signified agreement and Tisdale offered in evidence a certified duplicate of the file claim that day made public by the Bureau of Claims. It was accepted and entered. Tisdale resumed.

"Mr. Mason, what did you do after you fuelled the *Hellcat?*"

"Mr. Wylie and Scotty left, then I fuelled the *Gaucho* like Mr. Wylie told me. Then, it being a Saturday, I went to town."

"Did you see Wylie—"

"That's a lie!" Buck Wylie cried. For a moment no one knew what he meant, because he had reacted so slowly to Mason's previous answer. He was standing now, shouting, "I never told him to fuel the *Gaucho!*" He was livid with fury, and only Lola Morales' entreaties finally quieted him down; he paid no attention to Averill's orders. He sat there looking at Mason, lips tightened to a line, dangerous and ugly.

"Mr. Mason, do you remember the day of July 24th?"

"Yes, sir, I do. I have special reasons, of course, what with Scotty's ship being found that day. That was a Saturday and I'd gone to town the night before with the boys, but that morning, about eleven, I came back to the *arrando*. I had a special date in town for the night and I wanted to be dressed up special. About noon, before I left, I saw the *Gaucho* come into our port. Mr. Wylie'd left in her the Sunday before. With him coming back after a long trip I knew that if he or the foreman spotted me, they'd put me to work on her, so I beat it good and fast. I went back to town and that night I heard about Scotty's ship being found adrift over at Grey Mountain."

"And when was the next time you saw the *Hellcat?*"

"The next morning, Sunday, about eleven. She was back at our port. I'd gone back to the *arrando* early because I heard the Sheriff was coming up there with Mr. Whitley and I wanted to be there too."

Tisdale thanked Mason and turned him over to Farley. Farley got up quickly and fixed Mason with a belligerent look.

"On July 10th, the day you fuelled the *Hellcat*, you left shortly thereafter and did not return to the *arrando* until early Monday morning?"

"Yes, sir, that was the custom. We all got back together."

"Then, as far as you know, it is entirely possible that Mr. Wylie returned to his arrando shortly after you left and was there all the time until you yourself returned. Is that right?"

"It was possible."

"That's all," said Farley, looking satisfied.

His satisfaction was not mirrored in Buck Wylie's dark, angry face, nor did it last long. Tisdale then introduced three witnesses who were employed by Wylie and who substantiated various parts of Mason's evidence. They did not substantiate his statement that Wylie had ordered him to fuel the *Gaucho* the day Purdom left, not having been there. None was cross-questioned by Farley. The prosecution then called a Dr. Ballister, expert on explosives, and Whitley himself took over.

As Exhibit A, Whitley submitted to the Doctor's examination the fairly small but extremely heavy and powerful demolition bomb found in the *Spoon Special*. Printing, serial numbers and manufacturer's trademark identified it as one of a large shipment Wylie had bought some time before. The expert offered his opinion that it was likely, had the bomb gone off, that it would have been difficult to trace its ownership.

On this point, Farley, in his questioning, got Dr. Ballister to admit that it was *possible* that the ownership of the bomb *could* have been traced even from fragments the size of a pinhead. The expert left the stand a good deal unhappier than he had taken it.

Whitley then called Harry Reichard. Reichard had seen the *Hellcat* towing the *Spoon Special* off Grey Mountain on the afternoon of the 24th. Farley got Reichard to admit he had not seen who was at the helm of the *Hellcat*.

WHEN old Bob Halloway took the stand, there was an outbreak of scattered applause and a warning from the judge. Whitley had trouble confining his witness to legal evidence, but his story was the same one he had told at the indictment proceedings. He had seen the *Spoon Special* on the evening of the 24th, moving in a slow circle over Grey Mountain. She did not respond to AV signals. He grappled and boarded her, put out a live fuse in a bomb. He identified the bomb. There had been no one aboard the ship. He had called Standish and taken both ships in to port.

Throughout his testimony he kept trying unsuccessfully to tell the crowded courtroom of his personal danger and the injury to his hands. When

Hadden

Outlined in light were Tom's head and both his arms

Farley waived examination and the old man left the stand, new applause broke out. The old man reacted and in a fit of enthusiasm shook a fist at Buck Wylie and shouted: "Damn your hide, if I wuz a younger man I'd a paid you off fer my hands myself! In my day—"

The rest of it was lost in the uproar. Farley had instantly jumped up and heatedly demanded a mistrial. He was still the last one speaking when order was finally restored.

Judge Averill fixed a stern, inquisitive gaze at him. Curtly, he said: "You know very well, Mr. Farley, that no grounds for a ruling of mistrial exist. Motion denied. The jury will disregard Mr. Halloway's additional remarks.

Proceed, Mr. Whitley."

But the even tenor of the trial had been broken. Until that moment it had developed along slow, routine lines, with the prosecution methodically fashioning a noose around Buck Wylie's neck. It had borne out none of the drama it promised; several reporters had sauntered out and others stopped taking notes. Halloway's outburst had charged the room momentarily, and

now something occurred to increase the tenseness.

Whitley called John Murchison to the stand and announced him as the last State's witness. Until then Ames, constantly under observation, had shown small interest in the trial. Even Halloway's outbreak had not ruffled his calm. But now he leaned forward in his chair, elbows on the table and his earnest face cupped in his hands,

watching Murchison. The courtroom seemed to lean forward with him.

And then Murchison's evidence took a brief three or four minutes. He avowed his partnership with Purdom, sketched in the man's known background. He then reported on Purdom's unfailingly regular habits. That was the point Farley attacked with helpless savagery.

"Will you not admit, Mr. Murchison, that there is a distinct possibility that Scotty Purdom merely wandered off somewhere alone?"

"In what? You mean he sent his ship back magically—"

The answer was stricken out. Answering again, Murchison said, "In my opinion, there is no such possibility. In the years I knew him he never once deviated from habit. Why should a man of such great wealth 'merely wander off'? Unless you can produce testimony that he was insane, and I defy you—"

"That will be all, Mr. Murchison," Judge Averill broke in. "Mr. Farley, the Court expects you to confine the State's witnesses to testimony, not to conjectures and challenges, which, if allowed to continue, might very definitely damage the defense of this case. It should not be necessary for the Court to undertake your functions."

Farley, deeply flushed, seemed unable to go on. After a moment he dismissed Murchison. As he walked back to his table and Ames leaned back in his chair with a grin on his face, a loud buzz swept the courtroom. Every eye was fixed on Farley as he sat down. Buck Wylie's head was down. He did not seem to be listening to the lawyer on his right who was whispering to him.

Whitley's voice was satisfied. "The State rests, your Honor."

JUDGE AVERILL nodded and consulted his watch. The prosecution had presented its tight case in a little over two hours, an astonishing feat. It was a quarter past twelve. After a momentary hesitation, the judge asked if there were any witnesses for the defense.

Farley spoke to the lawyer who had been talking to Wylie and that young man, named Brent, rose and gave a name to the clerk. The name, Godfrey Loomis, was called and a tall, well-dressed man came to the stand. He was sworn in and Brent quickly established him as an official of the Bureau of Claims.

"Precisely what do you do for the Bureau, Mr. Loomis?"

"I am an investigator for the Commerce Division. My work consists of checking all filed claims to see that the claimed locations exist, that they have been properly marked, and do not infringe on other claims which may be in the vicinity."

"In other words, you are a sort of detective?"

"Well, yes, you might say so."

"And you have had long experience and are skilled in your work?"

"I think I can safely say so."

"Mr. Loomis, will you describe to the jury the nature and findings of your work from July 29th to August 3rd?"

"I came here to Mirabello City on July 29th at Mr. Farley's request to undertake an examination of certain areas. In all, I visited six places named and located by Mr. Wylie, covering millions of miles. I found at each of these places the official markers of the Bureau for a preliminary claim. Each of them was signed with Mr. Wylie's name and with dates ranging from July 14th to July 23rd. There were also unmistakable evidences of recent habitation at each of these places."

"What would you call evidence of such habitation?"

"The markers were all new and unaffected by weather. Also there were fireplaces with the ashes still intact in several instances."

"Would you, Mr. Loomis, say from these evidences that Mr. Wylie had been at these places——"

"Objection!" Tisdale called. "Witness is being asked a question he cannot possibly answer unless he saw Mr.

Wylie there with his own eyes."

"Sustained."

Brent nodded and asked: "Did any of the places you visited take you within fifteen million miles of the Lydonna Group?"

"No, they did not."

Brent then offered in evidence a sworn deposition, concurred in by two accompanying witnesses, enumerating the places visited and their relative distances from the Lydonna Group and Mirabello. After that Tisdale took the witness.

"You are a detective, Mr. Loomis?"

"Well, sort of."

"What is your official classification?"

"Claim adjuster."

"Have you ever performed duties which you could call detective work and has the Bureau ever used your services in such a capacity?"

"Well, that depends on what you call detective work."

"Have you ever been called on to testify in any criminal action by the Bureau which involved your own special findings?"

"Only insofar as they pertained to claim infringement."

"Were professional detectives also called on in these actions?"

"Yes."

"Then it would appear that the Bureau does not consider you a competent substitute for such professional detective work?"

"I . . . ah . . . well, you might say so."

"Could you swear that the fireplaces and ashes were not a week or two or possibly even three weeks older than you guessed they were?"

"Well, I don't know if I'd swear to it. After all, I'm not a—"

"A professional detective, you mean? We've already established that, Mr. Loomis," said Tisdale with a warm smile. "Now, would you be willing to swear that it was Mr. Wylie who put up those markers *himself?*"

"I don't see how I could."

"Neither do I," Tisdale smiled again. "One more question. As far as you know, *couldn't* someone else have put those markers?"

"Well, yes . . . certainly it's possible."

STILL smiling, Tisdale excused the distressed witness and sat down. There was a pause before Farley got up. He seemed only partially recovered from his earlier discomfiture. He turned toward Lola Morales and motioned her to the stand. She was waiting. She squeezed Wylie's hand and walked up confidently. Her sultry beauty had its effect on the spectators and she acknowledged their murmurs from under shaded lashes.

Farley proceeded cautiously with her. His chief difficulty seemed to be concerned with her residence at the Wylie *arrando*. He finally established that she was a "friend" of Wylie's who had been staying at the *arrando* on an extended visit. Farley went on.

"Miss Morales, tell us what you remember of the events of July 10th. You recall the day, I assume?"

"Perfectly. He left the *arrando* early that morning and returned before noon with Mr. Purdom. Then both of them left. About two o'clock I saw the *Hellcat* come in. Mr. Wylie came to the house and the *Hellcat* took off again. Mr. Wylie told me that Mr. Purdom was using his ship."

"How long did Mr. Wylie stay home?"

"Until Sunday, July 18th, eight days later, when he left in the *Gaucho* on his usual prospecting trip. He always went the third week of every month."

"When did you see him again?"

"Just before noon on the 24th. He

returned in the *Gaucho.*"

"Now, Miss Morales, I want you to be very careful in answering my next question: Did he go out again that day, the 24th?"

"He definitely did not."

"You were in a position to have known had he gone out?"

"Most certainly. We were together all that afternoon and evening until quite late that night." Gratuitously she added, "We spent the afternoon listening to a concert."

Her last remark elicited a ripple of laughter that brought her up defiantly in her chair. Farley blushed, cleared his throat and went on, speaking loudly and carefully. "In other words, Miss Morales, you know that Mr. Wylie was home by noon of the 24th and stayed there?"

"Most certainly."

Farley indicated he was through and Tisdale advanced to the girl with a serene and polite expression.

"Miss Morales, how long have you been staying at the *arrando?*"

"I'm not sure."

Tisdale smiled. "You seemed quite sure about dates a minute ago, Miss Morales. A month? Six months? A year? How long?"

"A little over six months."

"Rather a long visit, isn't it?"

Over a few titters from spectators, the girl raised her voice harshly. "What if it is? What's that to you?"

"Nothing, I'm sure," Tisdale said quickly. "Do you have any other address, Miss Morales?"

"Not at present."

"Are you related to Mr. Wylie in any way?"

"We're good friends," the girl said, growing angry again.

"May I ask whether you have ever been engaged in any occupation?"

"I have never had a job, if that's what you mean. Is all this necess——?"

"May I inquire as to the source of your income?"

Through clenched teeth the girl answered in a level voice: "I inherited a million dollars from a dead lawyer. Cold cash."

Tisdale's smile flashed again, briefly. "Miss Morales, you say you're a good friend of Wylie's. With no offense meant, and taking into consideration that you are testifying under oath, may I ask whether you might consider—ah —fibbing, to protect him?"

"Objection!" Farley cried. "Witness is under oath."

"Strike out the question," the Judge ordered. "Mr. Tisdale, the Court will not allow you to address insinuations to the jury under guise of examining a witness. The jury will disregard the question."

Tisdale looked humbled. He hesitated a moment, then looked up at the girl and shot at her: "Isn't it true that Buck Wylie has been keeping you? Isn't it true that he pays all your bills, buys your clothes, gives you money? Aren't you Buck Wylie's mistress?"

LOLA MORALES jumped off the chair and swung a resounding smash into Tisdale's face. She was restrained from following it up only by the quick action of a court attendant. Wylie was standing, trembling with poorly controlled rage, while two lawyers held him. Judge Averill rapped his gavel and threatened to clear the courtroom if there was another outburst from the spectators.

Tisdale, safely across the inner well, demanded: "What about an answer to that question, Miss Morales? Isn't it true?"

Lola Morales stood up and said in a loud voice: "No, it isn't, you damned, dirty, lying lawyer! It isn't true!"

It took another five minutes to quiet the courtroom again. Tisdale had signified he was through with the witness and the prosecution's table looked expectantly from Farley to Judge Averill. Quiet was finally restored only because Farley made an announcement that astonished the courtroom.

"The defense has no more witnesses to call, Your Honor."

The judge shook his head. "It's just as well. I was about to declare a recess. This afternoon, when Court reconvenes, the State will summarize—— You're out of order, Mr. Ames! Sit down, please!"

Ames remained standing. He had gotten up a moment after Farley closed the case for the defense. "Your Honor, if you adjourn this session now and begin the next one with the State's summary of the case, I won't have had my chance to speak here. Therefore, I must risk—"

"Your Honor, I object!" Whitley thundered. "Mr. Ames has no—"

"He has no right to volunteer evidence!" Farley cried.

"——I must risk," Ames continued, "the Court's displeasure by now speaking out of order. I petition your Honor that I be heard."

All through this triple exchange and shouting, the courtroom had been hushed. The silence now offered a tense, very dramatic contrast to the previous behavior of the audience. Not a man or a woman there but was on the edge of a seat, waiting to hear Judge Averill.

"Mr. Ames, the Court is aware that you are here as a material witness, both on the application of the State as well as the defense. However, at the beginning of this trial, the Colonial Attorney and counsel for defense notified the Court that in view of later findings, you would not be called for testimony by either side. The Court acknowledges that it is highly unusual for defense counsel, especially, to spurn examination of any testimony that might help his client, or, if he fears damage to his client as a result of such testimony, for the Colonial Attorney to refuse to take advantage of the possibility. However, the Court is bound in this instance and finds it impossible to grant your petition."

"If the Court please," said Ames quietly, "may I respectfully submit contrary finding on appeal to the Colonial Supreme Court, in the case of Ajax Vessels vs. Grant, Volume 12. Also the case of Farwell, Vosseler vs. Mercurian Commonwealth, Volumes 21, 26 and 27. Also the case of Grimes, Grimes and Thackeray vs. Jones, Tyuio Superior Court, Volume 6. Also the special appendix, part 3, of *MacDougal's Interplanetary Torts and Laws*, relative to appeals from a material witness. Also—"

"One moment, Mr. Ames," Judge Averill interrupted, looking up from the rapid notes he had been taking. "Was that part 3 of the special appendix you mentioned?"

"Yes, Your Honor."

His Honor wrote again, put down his pen and looked down at Ames with a pleasant smile. "The Court will take your petition under advisement and render a decision as soon as Court reconvenes. Decision therefore is reserved. This Court stands adjourned until two o'clock."

It was not a moment too soon, for during Ames' listing of references the courtroom had gotten to its feet, biding its time for an outburst. It came before the Judge had taken his smile with him to his chambers. Reporters swarmed around Ames, hurling questions at him, asking his opinion, pushing him back against the wall.

He was saved only by Sheriff Kaine's quick action and his announcement of a small luncheon for the visiting newspaper people, who numbered a mere fifty or so. Sue Wylie and Tom were among those present, but they were at the other end of the table. And as Ames parried questions and kept looking toward them, his expression was, in the words of one astute reporter, "—he looks at that dame as if he wanted to eat her instead of that omelette he ordered."

XII

PRECISELY at two o'clock, in an atmosphere as hushed and funereal as a tomb, Judge Averill declared the Court in session. He had been preceded by an attendant who carried an armload of books. The judge referred to two of these books, added a note, then looked up. His eyes traveled from Whitley to Farley and rested on Ames.

"After careful consideration of Mr. Ames' petition, it is the decision of this Court that he may be heard. There are, however, reservations. Anything Mr. Ames says here in open court does not provide him immunity to civil action for slander or libel, nor from criminal action proceedings by the State. Mr. Ames may submit documentary evidence but he cannot summon witnesses to testify. Such summons may, however, be ordered by the Court, with or without such application from Mr. Ames, as the Court sees fit.

"Mr. Ames, do you still want to testify?"

"I do, Your Honor."

Both Farley and Whitley quietly entered their "Exception" to the Judge's decision and a few moments later the judge said, "Proceed, Mr. Ames," in a soft voice that carried clearly to every corner of the room.

In complete silence, Ames crossed the well to Sheriff Kaine and took from him a locked, heavy leather bag. He opened the bag and began to empty it of its many papers. Included were official graphs, newspaper clippings, letters, and odd sheets of paper. Ames offered them piece by piece as documentary evidence. As the clerks stamped each piece, Whitley and Farley stood by close at hand. Once or twice there were whispered conferences among them and Ames and Judge Averill. When all the evidence had been entered, Ames stood alone in the center of the well.

"Ladies and gentlemen of the jury, you have heard His Honor declare the bounds within which I must testify. Since I cannot call back many of the witnesses you have heard without the Court's consent, I must first show cause to recall these witnesses. This I intend to do. I intend first, however, to tell you what I know they could— and might—have told you, had they been properly questioned, and had their testimony been related.

"I intend also to prove that the State's case against Mr. Wylie is a deliberate fraud, entered into knowingly, in secret conspiracy, by the Colonial Attorney and counsel for the defense."

Ames expected the reception this declaration drew from the courtroom and he waited until the storm subsided in a sea of sighs. His eyes roamed the room. He saw Sue Wylie's drawn face beside Tom's study in confidence. He saw the dark, unbelieving, bewildered hope in Buck Wylie's fear-ridden eyes, for Wylie knew as well as everyone there that he had been doomed. And he studied the lawyers, the general disbelief and outrage of the staffs, though Whitley looked fierce and stolid and Farley sat in sweating expectancy. He did not look toward Murchison.

"Moreover," Ames resumed, "by documenting the instances in which Mr. Wylie has been left helpless by a combination of circumstance, false testimony, planted evidence and deliberately inadequate defense, I intend also to place before you a clear case indicting the real murderer of Mr. Purdom. To do this I shall have to make statements which will remain hypothetical until the Court, by calling witnesses for me, transforms theory to fact. I ask your patience, please."

HE SAT down carelessly on the edge of his table so that he faced the jury and the courtroom. "First, what is the State's case? They have shown that Purdom, a man of unfailing habit, is missing, and that it is reasonable to assume he is missing because he is dead. They have shown that Wylie and Purdom were secret partners in a claim. They have shown that Purdom met Wylie on the 10th, borrowed the *Hellcat* from him for a second time, and then left for an unknown destination with both his ship and Wylie's. It is the State's contention that Purdom borrowed the *Hellcat* to bring back a double load of orium, as Wylie's partner.

"The State has also, with the services of a perjured witness, Mason, indicated that it may claim that Wylie later followed Purdom in his *Gaucho*. This is refuted by the testimony of Miss Morales alone, who declares he returned that day and stayed home. But the State does not need this line of attack, because it can claim that Wylie knew where Purdom was going anyway. So, using one line or the other, it will claim that Wylie left

Mirabello on the 18th, proceeded to where he knew he would find Purdom, and killed him. He then took the *Hellcat* and *Spoon Special* in tow behind his *Gaucho,* came back to Mirabello.

"He landed all three ships in an inconspicuous place, brought the *Gaucho* alone home, then returned, took up the *Hellcat* and *Special* again and went to Grey Mountain. There he planted one of his bombs in the *Special,* set it in a circular course, and returned home with the *Hellcat,* in the expectation that the *Special* would blow up so completely that it would be assumed no trace had been left of Purdom. The murder would be called an accident, cause unknown.

"The motive is self-evident: complete possession of a claim soon to be made public, and presumably very valuable. This value has been indicated by Mr. Murchison not on a basis of fact—for no one seems to have tried to visit this claim—but by pointing out that Purdom was for ten years content to mine his fabulously rich Silver Spoon Mine. It then follows that if he finally did pay attention to another mine, that it must be another bonanza. I do not deny this, and I think it is probably true; the mine must be valuable.

"But it is one thing to establish a motive and another to prove that a man would be willing to kill. I dare say we in this courtroom all have had sufficient motive to contemplate murder at one time or another, without actually murdering. That is because we are not psychologically constituted so as to be able to murder. So the State also had to prove that Wylie is a man so psychologically constituted that he can murder when provided with a powerful motive.

"The point is a very necessary one.

Wylie is in his own right an extremely wealthy man. Ordinarily one might question whether a man of such wealth would kill to obtain full ownership of something which was already half his. But the State did not touch upon this vital point at all. Why? Isn't it a remarkable omission? Buck Wylie is a man with a criminal record—"

Farley fairly shouted: "Your Honor, I move for a mistrial!"

Judge Averill paused, then said: "Decision reserved."

Ames nodded and went on. "I was about to point out that the State could not bring out Wylie's criminal record without running the risk of a mistrial. But it did not have to think about the problem at all—it was well taken care of for them by Mr. Murchison. The *Twin-Sun* spread the news ably, going so far as to editorialize on Wylie's criminal record. There was no doubt in Mr. Whitley's mind that any jury that might serve in this case would have full knowledge of Wylie's background, including the fact that he was once a gunfighter. And, ladies and gentlemen, if you will search your minds even perfunctorily, you will probably realize how correct Mr. Whitley was.

"But if the job was done for the State by the *Twin-Sun*, why didn't Mr. Farley try to undo it? He knew that Wylie's record was known, that it would mitigate against him. Why didn't he make the effort to show that there was a *reasonable doubt* that a one-time gunfighter, now a wealthy and respectable miner, might not kill for half a claim? That he made no such effort seems to me to be evidence of incompetence or—as I say—of sabotage!"

AMES rubbed his chin reflectively. "But to return. The only proof

that Wylie was able to offer *that he was home at noon of the 24th and stayed there* was again Miss Morales. If he was home from noon on, *he could not have been* the man at the helm of the *Hellcat* when it was seen towing the *Special* that afternoon. Miss Morales says so, and if you are to believe her, then you cannot believe the State's case, unless the State produces proof that someone else, at Wylie's behest, did the trick for him. The State has not shown this, since it believes—" and Ames allowed himself to smile, "—that Miss Morales' testimony is worthless."

He got up and paced three feet back and forth, hands behind his back, speaking as he walked. "Skipping lightly over several other facts for the moment—I'll come back to them— let's take a quick look at Wylie's case.

"He was a partner of Purdom's. They filed a mutual claim on February 5th in the Lydonna Group. Probably they had some arrangement for working it—only Wylie's subsequent testimony will establish this. But my guess, based on other things I know, is that Wylie provided the money and machinery—the active management— though Purdom may have been the original discoverer. This would indicate Purdom's trust in Wylie. I think he did trust him, at least in the beginning. Another indication of his trust is a clause in Purdom's partnership agreement with Murchison. I have entered that agreement, seized by Sheriff Kaine, in evidence.

"The agreement has a clause, dated March 2nd, which states that the Purdom-Murchison partnership is confined to the Silver Spoon Mine and has no bearing on any other interest of Purdom's. This means that if Purdom died, Wylie would inherit the other half of their joint claim. We all know how careful and suspicious a man Purdom was. It is hard to believe he would enter into that kind of a partnership with Wylie *unless he trusted him,* since it gave Wylie an obvious interest in Purdom's death." Ames stopped pacing to add, "And I believe that Wylie had full confidence in Purdom.

"He did not question Purdom when he was asked for a loan of the *Hellcat* either the first or the second time. He was, however, careful about it because their partnership was a secret. Open lending of his best ship to Purdom would point suspicion at both of them, so the second time he asked Purdom to go through the motions of fueling the *Hellcat* at Standish, at least in that way making their connection less obvious. I imagine that he was puzzled by Purdom's carelessness that second time, for the first time he lent him the *Hellcat,* it seems both men were very wary.

"And the second time, July 10th, put an extra burden on Wylie because it left him without an available ship. Mason has testified that Wylie ordered him to fuel the *Gaucho* that day. However, from records seized at the Miller Sheds, I can prove that the *Gaucho* was laid up for repairs that day and for some time following—proving Mr. Mason a perjurer of the first order."

HE PAUSED again because of the noise that greeted his last statement, but as soon as he stopped speaking the courtroom grew quiet. At that moment, Farley got up and started out of the courtroom. Two of the sheriff's men unobtrusively accompanied him from the rear of the room.

Ames said: "Here again I pause to ask why the defense made no attempt to gather available documentary proof. These records were at Miller's Sheds until Sheriff Kaine impounded them, but they were always available.

The fact remains no one asked to see them.

"On July 18th, Wylie left in the *Gaucho* on a prospecting trip. This was a long established custom of his; he always went out the third week of every month, as everyone knew. The State carefully inquired as to Purdom's regular habits, but the defense did not show any interest in Wylie's habits. The defense did, however, employ Mr. Loomis and two men to go to the places Wylie claims he visited on that trip.

"Of course, the State could easily claim that Wylie had killed Purdom at any one of those places or at another, unvisited, place, either near there or en route. The State thus assumes that Wylie knew where his partner, Purdom, was going, and asks you to accept that reasonable assumption. The defense merely lists some six places, pointing out that all were far from the Lydonna claim. It does not attempt to prove, for instance, that Purdom definitely went to the Lydonna claim. It merely hopes you will think so, but perhaps that is because Wylie himself has no idea where Purdom went.

"But let us make our own assumption and let us make it a wild one. Let us assume that Purdom went to none of the six places marked by Wylie, that Wylie met him somewhere else and killed him. If the defense was interested in building up even this poor alibi, why didn't it hire a crack detective to send off on a wild goose chase? First the defense sends a man on a useless errand, and second, it picks a useless man.

"I submit that Mr. Farley knew any testimony offered by Loomis would be worthless, not only because it proved nothing, but because even *if* there was anything to prove, Loomis was *not* the man to do it, as you have seen!"

Ames smiled again and made a little gesture with his hands as he asked the jury: "Who is Loomis? A claim adjuster! Is there anything more futile than sending a paper clerk on a worthless errand? I hardly think so. And you yourselves, ladies and gentlemen, were witnesses to the ease with which the State discredited an eminently discredible witness. Duck soup, from start to finish."

An edge of irony was beginning to form under Ames' words. He had started calmly, speaking in a soft voice and unhurried manner. Now he was sharp, inquisitive, given to gestures. After his last remark he turned to Tisdale with a low bow and murmured, "With no offense to you, Mr. Tisdale. You were brilliant."

Then he clasped his hands and said, "Wylie came back at noon of the 24th. Even Mason does not dispute the time of arrival, but he would if it was necessary. Mason is on somebody's payroll. His testimony still helps the State, because it points out that Wylie was around in time to have left and gotten the *Hellcat* and *Special* if he had left them somewhere. The fact is that Wylie stayed home from that noon until he was arrested the next day by Mr. Whitley—*but can he prove it?*

"Yes," Ames laughed openly, "he can, with the testimony of Miss Morales, *if* you believe her. Can you? Do you?" he demanded. "Look at the way this thing was arranged. Everything questionable happened on a Saturday afternoon, when everyone at the Wylie *arrando* who might be able to testify for him would be sure to be in town. Purdom left the 10th and was due back the 18th—but his ship was not discovered until it coincided with Wylie's return on the 24th. There were people who knew Wylie

would leave on or about the 18th—and they knew he would be back on the 24th—*so they held back the discovery of Purdom's ship which they had planted some time before.*

"Meanwhile," he held up a hand to stop the noise, "Wylie was left at the mercy of one witness on two occasions—Miss Morales! I submit that had it been deemed necessary, Miss Morales would have testified that Wylie *did* leave on the afternoon of the 24th! That—"

"That's a damn filthy—" Lola Morales screamed, standing up, when Buck Wylie's hand closed on her wrist and yanked her down to her chair. His face was black as a thundercloud. The girl gasped something and started to sob, but Wylie muttered something to her that stopped her immediately.

A T THAT moment Farley returned to the courtroom. The deputies left him at the head of the aisle and he went alone to his table. But he did not sit down in the chair he had vacated. He took a seat farthest from Wylie and sat with his hands limp in his lap. He looked quite sick.

"I was saying," Ames resumed, "that Miss Morales testified for the defendant, and that she was allowed to do so because the conspirators knew how worthless her testimony was. I submit, and stand ready to prove when Mr. Wylie takes the stand, that Miss Morales has been Mr. Wylie's mistress for some time. But the fact is well known, and though the State did not *prove* it, it did not really require proof more than was offered that Miss Morales was beholden to Wylie, and might be presumed to perjure herself to help him. Thus, she is allowed to give testimony that will not be accepted.

"But. even then, you will notice, she did not—and the defense did not—really try to build up her case. Mr. Farley left her status as a *friend* clearly open to attack. Had Miss Morales been willing to perjure herself to help Wylie, why did she not, for instance, claim that she was a distant relative—*anything*—rather than let the jury assume what was otherwise almost an open admission that she was prejudiced toward Wylie's favor? Why should a witness who wanted to help Wylie give Mr. Tisdale such contemptuous and meaningless answers? No, she was well chosen for her job, which probably included other minor duties, as I shall presently enumerate.

"And here again," Ames bowed, "Mr. Tisdale shone." He added, more seriously, "I do not mean to impugn Mr. Tisdale, who, I think, is moderately proud of doing an assigned work. That his brilliance resembles paste jewelry is the fault of a paste case. Nor do I say that every witness for the State is guilty of perjury. Not at all.

"Franshaw, Saunders, the Standish traffic managers, the various attendants, all told the truth. They heard the appointment made, they saw the men together. *But they were meant to see and hear!* Mason is a liar, but not entirely. We know he lied about the *Gaucho*, and we may be quite sure he did not overhear Wylie and Purdom discussing their partnership. Both men were much too cautious for that. Mason might have lied about the 24th, however. He might have said that he came to the *arrando* at two o'clock and saw Wylie leaving. That would kill Wylie's story, so why didn't Mason say so?

"Because that would have refuted Miss Morales too directly! It was decided not to build too airtight a case

against Wylie. It might begin to smell a little. Leaving him with worthless alibis was good enough and shrewd planning. All this, of course, presupposes a central intelligence, and thus is my central theme.

"Whether Reichard actually saw the *Hellcat* towing the *Special* is for you to decide. Possibly he did, and the conspirators let him live because they were sure he hadn't seen who was at the helm of the *Hellcat*. Possibly then they decided his honest evidence was valuable. Or, he may be a witness along the Mason lines—I cannot say.

"As for Mr. Halliday, no one doubts his story. That he happened along is one of the few genuine accidents in this intrigue, and his brave action serves to throw a penetrating light on the case.

"Halliday prevented the bomb from going off. What if he hadn't prevented it? To be sure, his action preserved a bomb which is a very damaging bit of evidence against Wylie, on the face of it. But Dr. Ballister has admitted that the bomb could have been traced and its ownership established even if it had been blown to infinitesimal fragments. Had he not admitted it, I could provide six dozen assorted experts who would—"

There was general laughter and Ames himself smiled at his own unconsciously extravagant image. "I submit," he went on, "that the conspirators expected an explosion, and expected to be able to prove, with the help of experts, that the bomb had belonged to Wylie. Halliday left them with the bomb intact, which was just as good or better.

"But look at it from Wylie's point of view. Suppose he actually had wanted to blow the *Special*, after doing what the State says he did. Wylie has been a miner for some time. He knows bombs and knows they can be traced. Why should he have used one of his own bombs? The State had Dr. Ballister say it would *likely* have been impossible, a statement he later swallowed. But why should Wylie take that chance? Why not get a bomb, somewhere, anywhere—it isn't difficult for a miner—which could *never* be traced to him?"

AMES stroked his face reflectively and said, "No, the plant is too obvious. It fairly shrieks Wylie's innocence. But it does more than that. It asks two important questions.

"First, what happened to Purdom's body? If Purdom was murdered, why not put his body in the *Special* and have the investigation assume he was killed in the explosion? Had there been an explosion we might never have known whether or not Purdom or his body was in the ship. Now we know Purdom wasn't in it.

"Second, what about the bomb itself? The Wylie *arrando* employs many people. How many of these people had access to the underground bomb shed? I do not pretend to know, but I do know that *at least one* person besides Wylie had access to it, because Wylie didn't take that bomb—so who did? Possibly Mason? Possibly Miss Morales helped him? She has complete run of the place. At any rate, this line of questioning was never attempted by the defense, elementary though it appears. Why?

"Why?" Ames asked again. "When I first became interested in the case professionally, I was struck by the number of times I had to ask myself *why*. The question of Purdom's body convinced me that something was wrong, and various other circumstances increased that conviction. I was running down some of my suspi-

cions when I was fired by Wylie, but since I knew who was behind that advised action, I realized I was proceeding correctly. As a material witness—"

He paused, grinning. "At this point I should like to insert, purely for the record, that I was drunk because I had to be; it was my one chance to re-enter the case with some authority, and it enabled me to get the records, documents, etcetera, which I needed." He paused again and studied first Whitley, then Farley. He did look toward Murchison; he had once glanced at him. His grin was gone when he spoke again.

"I think I have indicated sufficiently the lines along which Wylie's innocence can be proven. They seem to me much better than the defense's obvious intention to cling to the assertion that Purdom is not dead, but has disappeared—a curious defense in the face of so many curious incriminating facts. But the best proof of Wylie's innocence is proof of another's guilt. From here on my testimony is concerned with lodging the guilt where it belongs.

"If I am correct in what I have said so far, it is apparent that Wylie is the victim of a concerted plot, and that the plotters are people who knew his habits, his business, his background. I submit, and will prove, that these plotters include at least Mr. John Murchison, Miss Lola Morales, one Jake Webber, not present, and to some extent, the Colonial Attorney, Mr. Whitley and counsel for the defense, Mr. Farley. . . ."

AGAIN it was necessary to halt the trial while Judge Averill gave final warning that the next outbreak would be the last before the courtroom was cleared. Ames scarcely paid any attention to the vast outpouring of shouts, screams, cries, applause, moans, sobs and sighs. He measured off his three feet of floor and paced them, and when it was quiet again, some minutes later, he spoke.

"Such a conspiracy could only be fathered by the possibility of great profit to all involved. I submit that such profit did, and does today exist, and that the stakes of the game was not only the Silver Spoon Mine, but all of Wylie's vast holdings to the last red cent, and also the new claim in which Wylie and Purdom were partners.

"On February 5th, Wylie and Purdom became partners. Murchison knew something of the sort had happened by March 2nd, for on that day Purdom entered the limiting clause in his partnership agreement with Murchison. Until that time Purdom had had no other interests but the Silver Spoon—so the moment he confined his Murchison partnership to the Silver Spoon, Murchison knew other interests had come into existence.

"It took him six days to find out, by one means or another, that Wylie was involved, for on March 8th, Murchison graphed the I. P. Regional Headquarters and made inquiries on Wylie's criminal record. He had known about it before; now he wanted the complete dope. On March 11th the I. P. furnished the dope, and Murchison carefully filed it away for future reference. He subsequently used it the day Wylie was arrested, and thus performed a public service—after keeping it more than four months! But he also used it in another way. I'll come to that soon.

"On April 15th Murchison became the possessor of information that provided additional power to his motive. Before that he had already decided to operate on Wylie, but April 15th

clinched it. For on that day the Interplanetary Colonial Council passed an amendment to the Criminal Code which applied to the colonies here, and which suited him perfectly. That amendment was Section—ah—Section 4551.

"That amendment stated that in the event of a criminal act, any person injured by that act, even indirectly, could not only sue for damages, but could claim a penalty judgment against the criminal's entire possessions. For instance, a man is killed by a pirate, and the man's wife is his legal heiress. Under the new Section the wife's claim does not end with the State's—which is to exact the penalty for murder—but also gives her legal claim to everything the pirate owned. That claim is a penalty judgment, and supersedes all other claims, those of the State included.

"It applied to Murchison as well. He and Purdom were mutually each other's heir in their partnership. If Purdom were murdered — say, by Wylie, then Murchison would not only inherit the Silver Spoon *but he could claim and get everything Wylie owned!* What could be sweeter? He had been thinking of killing Purdom and framing Wylie before, but now he began to act. The first thing he did was to violate the ordinance that compelled the *Twin-Sun* to publish the *new* law. He didn't publish it. It was hardly worth hiding—who would have paid much attention to it?—but he was covering every trail from then on.

"Two obstacles lay in his way, however. The first was that he didn't know where the Silver Spoon Mine was. He might inherit it, but it would remain an inheritance on paper. Probably he had many times thought over ways and means of doing away with Purdom, but he hadn't hit on a way that would also reveal the mine's location. That thought must have occurred to Purdom too, for he guarded his secret as if his life depended on it, which it did. As long as Murchison didn't know where the mine was, he had an interest in keeping Purdom alive, and he drew his share of the enormous profits.

"The second obstacle was finding a way to frame Wylie. As it subsequently turned out, the answer to one led to the answer of the second. He devised an extremely clever way of doing both. . . ."

AMES let his voice down and for the first time he faced Murchison directly. Not a sound came from the rapt audience. Murchison returned his gaze tolerantly and then a slow, pleasant smile broke on his face. "Please go on," he said. He folded his arms across his chest.

Ames nodded complaisantly.

"Murchison began to work on Purdom. Through hints and sly insinuations he began building up Purdom's latest mistrust of everyone until it included the one man, Wylie, he had trusted. And then he focused his attention on Wylie, convincing Purdom that he had ways of knowing that Wylie was shadowing him, or attempting to. Murchison pretended to be concerned only with protecting the Silver Spoon. Purdom didn't know that Murchison knew about his partnership with Wylie, so when he received repeated warnings about Wylie, it meant only one thing to him —that Wylie was using their partnership to get at the Silver Spoon. By June he had Purdom jittery, and then he suggested ways and means of keeping Wylie off his trail.

"By then too, of course, he had arranged his alliance with Mr. Whitley and Miss Morales. They were ready to play their parts.

"Sometime early in June, before Purdom left on one of his trips to the Silver Spoon, he asked Wylie to lend him the *Hellcat* to take with him. He did this to make sure that Wylie wouldn't follow him, because the only other ship Wylie owned that was fast enough to keep the *Special* in sight was the *Gaucho,* and she was in the Miller Sheds for one of her numerous overhaulings. If he had the *Hellcat,* he could be reasonably sure that Wylie couldn't follow him to the Silver Spoon.

"He told Wylie he wanted it because he was expecting a storm in his mining area and wanted to pull a double load before the storm broke. Wylie probably didn't believe him but asked no questions. Purdom had never used this common custom before, but he also had not had a partner before, and maybe he was taking advantage of the partnership by getting free use of a ship. It didn't bother Wylie except that it meant they had to do the whole thing secretly.

"But now Murchison knew that Purdom was going to the Silver Spoon with two vessels. That gave him his chance. He knew Purdom's habits and got around them. He knew that whenever Purdom returned from a trip to the Silver Spoon the first thing he did was to take the *Special* to Miller and have the Berry gauge moved back to zero. Miller had to take his glasses off before Purdom would allow him to get near the gauge—to illustrate Purdom's extreme caution. Because of this, and because he knew too well how miserly Purdom was, Murchison correctly assumed that Purdom wasted no fuel going to and from the Silver Spoon, and that if he could get at the figures on the gauge, that they would reveal almost to a certainty where the Silver

Spoon was—a fact he had to know.

"He couldn't get at the *Special's* gauge, but he had worked out a way to get at the *Hellcat's*. And since he knew both ships were going to the same place that time, one was as good as the other. So, on June 12th Murchison went to Miller and asked him to get the figures on the *Hellcat's* gauge. His pretext was an investigation for the *Twin-Sun* on something concerning Wylie, and to back it up he showed Miller the criminal record he had received from the I. P. months before.

"The *Hellcat* wasn't in the sheds then and Miller wasn't expecting her— actually she was out with Purdom, and Murchison expected her back soon— but Miller refused out of loyalty to Wylie. The next day, June 13th, according to a copy seized by Sheriff Kaine, Murchinson came back and presented Miller with an authorization to surrender the data. It was signed by the Colonial Attorney, Mr. Whitley. But the *Hellcat* wasn't there, not yet. It came in, according to Miller's records, on June 16th, brought in by Wylie himself. And Purdom arrived at the same time with the *Special*.

"What had happened was that Purdom brought the *Hellcat* back to Wylie, who then immediately took it to Miller, with Purdom right behind him. When they arrived together, to Miller it appeared to be nothing more than a coincidence—he had no way of knowing that both ships had been to the same place and had just returned. He was surprised that Wylie also wanted his Berry gauge zeroed, but he did it. While Purdom's main concern was keeping Wylie busy, he kept an eye on Miller to make sure that Miller was working on the *Special* without his glasses.

"But then his vigilance relaxed a little. When Miller went to the *Hell-*

cat's gauge, he copied down the readings he found there. After both men left, Miller called Murchison in obedience to the C. A.'s authorization and turned over the readings to him.

"And that told Murchison where the Silver Spoon was."

AMES stopped, blew his breath out noisily and returned to sit on an edge of his table. He seemed wearied by the length of his address to the jury, but the knowledge that he was nearing the climax gave him new energy. He wondered how close to the end Murchison's calm would last.

"I said," he resumed, "that Murchison found out where the Silver Spoon was. The task might have been difficult, but the fact is that the mine was so located that a Berry gauge reading was a dead giveaway. I will presently go into this in some detail, but in part it explains Purdom's concern for the gauge.

"After Murchison's exploratory trip to the Silver Spoon, taken with his chauffeur, Jake Webber, he waited for his chance. He let Purdom make another trip in the latter part of June, unmolested, because Wylie was off prospecting and Purdom had gone in his *Special* alone. On the 10th of July, however, he asked Wylie for the *Hellcat* again. Possibly he meant that to be the last time, since by today, August 5th, their partnership would be made public.

"Again Wylie consented, *but*—notice how Purdom went about making himself safe! He called Wylie from the Rocketeer's Cafe and used the phone *at the bar!* He made an appointment at Standish port and twice that day was seen with Wylie. He was plainly hoping that any hostile notions Wylie might have been nursing would be deterred by such publicity. At any rate, after fuelling his ship at Standish, he and Wylie left together. Some fifty miles out they space-anchored. Purdom took Wylie back to the *arrando* in his own ship, returned to the *Hellcat*, took her in tow and went on to the Silver Spoon.

"Coincidentially enough," Ames cocked his brows, "Murchison left Mirabello on July 16th to attend a newspaper convention at Church's. Had there not been a convention, Murchison would have found another excuse to be away. He attended that convention, all right, and the *Twin-Sun* ran a photo of him there on the 19th.

"The *Twin-Sun's* society notes did not, however, mention the fact that on the way to Church's, Murchison and Webber stopped at the Silver Spoon and murdered Purdom before they continued their merry trip.

"The convention ended on the 21st. Murchison's ship was fast enough to have made that trip in forty hours. But it took him three days to go there and three to come back, so that he returned, according to his own admission, on the evening of the fateful 24th. Why? Because when he left Church's he came back to the Silver Spoon to bring back the *Hellcat* and the *Special!*

"He had one poor stroke of luck, though. He had meant to bring back Purdom's body and have it blown up in the *Special's* explosion, to do it up brown. But he had killed Purdom in one of the mine shafts, and Purdom had been effectively buried under an enormous orium deposit. He couldn't get Purdom out quickly, so he had to leave him in the mine.

"The rest worked out on schedule. He already had one of Wylie's demolition bombs, supplied by Mason or Miss Morales, and it was planted in the *Special*. Murchison and Webber waited somewhere off Mirabello with the *Hellcat* and *Special* in tow, and when Wylie returned at noon of the 24th, Miss Morales signalled the tidings from an AV transmitter in the living room of Wylie's own home. Webber got into the *Hellcat* and towed in the *Special*. If Reichard told the truth, that was what he saw. No wonder the *Hellcat* wouldn't return his signals, if he signalled. Over Grey Mountain, Webber went aboard the *Special*, put her into a slow circle, lit the fuse and got out.

"He knew there was no one at the Wylie *arrando* on a Saturday afternoon, so he brought the *Hellcat* in to the Wylie blastport. Then he made his way back to town unseen. Some hours later, Murchison, alone in his ship, elected to come home. It was a quiet return, and no one seems to have noticed whether or not Webber was with him. The *Twin-Sun*, so eager to report Murchison's departure and arrival at Church's, did not see fit to mention his return.

"The next morning Murchison composed his editorial denouncing Wylie and exposing his criminal record."

THE stillness of the courtroom was faintly oppressive now. It measured and emphasized Ames' occasional pauses for breath. Murchison no longer smiled, but there was no suspicion of trouble on his face. He seemed deeply interested and attentive, nothing more.

Now Ames took out several sheets of paper from among those submitted in evidence. "These," he explained, "are copies of the readings from the Berry gauges of the *Hellcat*, the *Spoon Special* and the *Gaucho*. They have been certified and the unsealing process photographed. I am aware of the fact that such readings are apt to be worthless, but in this instance, as I will prove, they actually proved to be the key . . ."

He went on for some ten minutes, explaining the notations, dwelling in particular upon the point 3 reading, and gradually, without emphasizing the point, he slipped into an account of his voyage to the Silver Spoon within the Hive. He recounted the almost incredible details, the appearance of the crazy asteroid, the mine itself, Webber's appearance and the duel in the hills. He ended by mentioning the explosion of Murchison's ship and Webber's confession.

"The confession," he admitted, "is unfortunately not much good because Webber was too far gone when he signed it. But every statement I have made is substantiated by one or another of the facts I have submitted in evidence. Together they make up a case that is, considering the circumstances, amazing clear, and they point to John Murchison as the man responsible for the murder of Scotty Purdom. . . ."

In the silence, Judge Averill said, "Mr. Ames, do you wish to call any witnesses or to cross-question any previously offered testimony?"

"If it please the Court, I should like to question Mr. Murchison."

"Mr. John Murchison will take the stand."

Murchison rose unhurriedly, walked down the aisle into the well and stood before the bench. "Your Honor," he said quietly, "I have nothing to hide. Under ordinary circumstances, I would welcome—I would insist—on being allowed the privilege of answering the fantastic charges made by Mr. Ames. However, I am so stunned and so . . . so completely shocked by these cunning and malicious perversions of the truth that I cannot, in fairness to myself, take the stand at this time. I state my innocence unequivocally and completely, but it nevertheless behooves me to stand on my constitutional rights, and to refuse to testify on the grounds that my testimony may tend to incriminate and degrade me."

Judge Averill was silent for a moment. He studied Murchison in a strangely preoccupied way, then sighed and said, "Mr. Murchison, you are not on trial here, and you do not have the rights of the accused in refusing the stand. Moreover, you have already, of your own free will, testified in this court. As a witness, your testimony is open to cross-examination. This Court has granted Mr. Ames the right of summoning witnesses, and it orders you to take the stand."

Murchison hesitated. "And if I refuse, Your Honor?"

"You will be held in contempt of court," the Judge answered gravely. "And I will immediately summon the grand jury to undertake indictment proceedings against you. Surely such a course is ill-advised for an innocent man?"

Again Murchison hesitated. Presently he shrugged and walked to the witness box. He faced Ames calmly enough, but with an expression that was at once patient and suggestive of restrained fury. It was as if he were saying, "I'll do what I must, now, but I will straighten our account in the future for this hopeless and baseless inquisition." But all he said was, "Yes, Mr. Ames?"

Ames said, "Do you deny Webber's story—that you stopped him from trying to kill me after that day he took a shot at me—that you—"

"I'll make it easier for you, Mr. Ames. I deny everything. I deny every last word that tries to implicate me in any way."

Ames nodded but asked: "You deny ever having been on the asteroid where the Silver Spoon Mine is?"

"Suppose I ask you, Mr. Ames, to

produce the slightest shred of evidence
that I ever was there—if indeed you do
know where it is—instead of building
up your fantastic case by repeating false
allegations. What proof have you aside
from a supposed confession which you
yourself have declared worthless?"

"You haven't answered my question."

"That I deny having been to the secret Silver Spoon? Of course I deny
it."

"Because if you admitted it, you
would be admitting that my fantastic
case was not without basis?"

"Rather," said Murchison, "because
if you prove it, you will prove your case.
And unless you do offer proof instead of
involved speeches, I am afraid I can't
help you, my insane young friend."

Ames nodded again. "I agree with
you, Mr. Murchison. If you'll bear
with me, I will furnish the jury with the
proof—or, at least, with what I consider
the beginning of irrefutable proof.
Keep your seat, Mr. Murchison, I won't
be long."

Ames turned to the jury. "I did not
mention, in my summation, that Tom
Blake and I brought back the body of
the late Jake Webber. In addition, we
brought back Purdom's dog, Duke. We
did this because of a curious physical
phenomenon that seems to be endemic
on the asteroid where the Silver Spoon
is. Rather than contenting myself with
describing it, I will demonstrate it and
let you judge for yourselves."

AFTER a brief consultation with
Sheriff Kaine, attendants brought in
a large screen, oval-shaped and mounted
on a stand that brought it to a height
of seven feet, and a white cabinet.
When the cabinet was opened, it revealed an inner board studded with
dials and switches, and from which a
conic projector, somewhat like a small
searchlight, was brought out. A man,

identified as a laboratory expert attached to Kaine's staff, came forward in
a white coat. He flicked on a switch
and a scarcely visible beam of light
played on the screen. He twiddled dials
until the light vanished altogether.

"This cabinet," Ames explained,
"houses a miniature radium detector.
By utilizing an invisible light wave-
length it picks up traces of a rare radium-like substance. Dr. Lowell here
will explain it more fully later. It has,
however, an immediate application."

Ames then called Tom Blake. Sour
Tom made his way into the well with
his usual acid expression. Ames asked
him to stand behind the screen, which
was backed by a window on which the
shades had been drawn. Tom walked
behind the screen. Only his legs showed
under it. Dr. Lowell fussed with the
dials again. Slowly, a light appeared
behind the screen. It grew brighter and
took form. Within fifteen seconds it
had outlined in light the mass of Tom's
head and both his hands.

"Leave the cabinet now, please, Doctor," Ames instructed. To the jury he
then said, "It appears that the asteroid
on which the Silver Spoon is located is
one of those System rarities which contains in its atmosphere a huge mass of
these suspended radium-like particles.
Anyone setting foot on that asteroid,
even for a moment, would pick up
enough of those particles on his exposed
skin to show up easily on this screen.
This effect lasts no longer than a month
at most. In other words, such a result
—this bright outline—could not be gotten from anyone who had not been on
that asteroid within the past month.

"The nearest known System body
which might produce this result is in the
Mercurian Innesta Group, and in that
case the particles could be subjected to
laboratory tests, since they differ."

He then asked Tom to sit down again

and Dr. Lowell himself went behind the screen. Nothing happened; he remained hidden. After him the Sheriff and two more men went behind the screen with the same negative results. Then Ames regarded Murchison.

Murchison was sitting with his hands folded across his chest, a supercilious, saddened smile on his face.

Ames said nothing and walked behind the screen. Those on the other side could see his head and hands appear. Then they watched his hands open his collar and part of his neck appeared. A minute later he came out, buttoning his shirt.

To the jury he said: "I think my point is apparent now. I have had the body of Jake Webber subjected to this test. Dr. Lowell has also tested the body of Purdom's dog. When Purdom's body is brought back, the same tests can be applied." He turned to Murchison and walked to him. "Mr. Murchison, will you be so good as to step behind that screen?"

Murchison made no answer. His eyes seemed half closed but he did not move. His smile persisted and he said nothing. His attitude, with his folded arms, seemed faintly defiant.

"Well, Mr. Murchison?" Ames asked.

When Murchison still made no move, Judge Averill said sharply: "Need I remind you, Mr. Murchison, that your—"

He did not finish what he was saying, for suddenly Sheriff Kaine came forward swiftly. He walked directly to Murchison and touched his arm. The touch was enough to unbalance the sitting body. For it was no more than a body. As it sprawled forward into the sheriff's arms, its folded arms came apart, and as the right hand fell, a small-barreled Foster gun rolled out of the relaxed grip and clattered to the floor. Only then did they see the shoulder holster that had held it concealed. Below the holster a small hole had burned through Murchison's heart. The heat ray had passed through his body and touched the chair, and it was the tiny wisp of smoke behind the chair that Kaine had seen.

Murchison had held on to the end. . . .

IT WAS some four days before the wearied reporters finally found Ames, an accomplishment made possible only by their shrewd, desperate bribe to a small boy named Willy, who said he thought Ames was fishing, and who said he thought he knew where. And laden with enough candy to open his own shop, Willy led them through tall grass to the edge of a stream where Ames was, indeed, fishing.

Beside him sat Tom, and a little further off, unpacking a picnic basket, was Sue Wylie. Ames spoke to the reporters only because, as he told them, he was in a hurry to get on with the picnic. He parried all questions about the disposition of Whitley, Farley, Lola Morales and the others on the grounds that he was to be called as a witness against them, and consequently could not discuss the case.

"Hah!" one bitter reporter laughed. "Now you're extra-legal again, eh? What about commenting on that story Sheriff Kaine out—the one about that test being a fake?"

"A fake?" Ames inquired mildly. "It did the job, I thought."

"Yeah, but you and this fellow Tom Blake rubbed a kind of ointment on your face and hands, didn't you? You got that stuff in a jar in a drugstore in town, didn't you?"

"Mmmmm," was Ames' nodded agreement.

(Concluded on page 121)

I, ROCKET

By RAY BRADBURY

AT THE rate things are coming and going it'll take a few hundred years to break me down into rust and corrosion. Maybe longer. In the meantime I'll have many days and nights to think it all over. You can't stop atoms from revolving and humming their life-orbits inside metal. That's how metal lives its own special life. That's how metal thinks.

Where I lie is a barren, pebbled plateau, touched here and there with pale weedy growths, a few hunched trees coming up out of planetoid rock.

There's a wind comes over the plateau every morning. There's rain comes in the twilight, and silence comes down even closer in the night. That's my whole life now, lying here with my jets twisted and my fore-plates bashed.

Somehow I feel I haven't fulfilled my destiny *in toto*. A rocket ship isn't built to lie on a hard gray plateau in the wind and rain—alone. After those trips through space it's almost too much to believe, that the rest of my days will be wasted here——

But while I'm rusting and wonder-

A thing of steel and alloy—a rocket ship. Yet it claimed respect and gave a great enduring loyalty

Gushing oil followed the flying length of pipe as Belloc reeled back

ing, I can think it all over. How I came to be here, how I came to be built. . . .

I've taken them all in their time, the crew; seen them wounded, crushed by centrifuge, or shattered by space-bombs; and once or twice I've had my rear-jets pounded off in a double-fisted foray: there's hardly a plate in my hull hasn't been welded again and again, not a chronometer in my control console hasn't been blasted and replaced.

But the hardest thing of all was replacing the men inside me. The little guys who ran around with greasy faces, yelling and fighting for air, and getting their guts frozen to their peritoneum every time I swung into an unexpected arc during the days when free gravity was experimental.

The little guys were hard to find, harder to replace after a particularly violent thrust between worlds. I loved the little guys, the little guys loved me. They kept me shining like a nickel moon, nursed me, petted me, and beat me when I deserved it.

From the very first I wanted to be of some help in the wild excursions from Earth to Deimos-Phobos co-ordinate Bases, the war moons held by Earth to strike against the Martians.

My birth-period, and the Base where I was integrated, skeleton, skin and innards, went through the usual birth-pains. It is a dim portion in my *memory*, but when the final hull was melted to me, the last rungway and console fitted to my hulk, the aware-ness was there. A metal awareness The free electrical atom flow of metal come aware.

I could think and could tell no-body that I thought.

I was a war rocket. Fore and aft they placed their space-artillery noz-zles, and weighted me with scarlet am-munition. I began to feel my purpose,

expectantly, perhaps a bit impatiently.

I wasn't really alive yet. I was like a child half out of the womb, but not yet breathing or making any sound or making any movement. I was wait-ing for the slap on the back to give me strength and directed purpose.

"Hurry it up, hurry it up! Skip!" directed the munitions-lieutenant, standing by my opened air-locks that day so many years ago. Sunlight baked my metal as men hustled in and out with small rubber-tired trucks bearing the tetron space explosives. "We've got a war to meet!" cried the lieuten-ant.

The men hurried.

There was some fancy bit of busi-ness about a christening going on si-multaneously with this scurrying about in my cargo cubicles. Some mayor from some city crashed a bottle of foaming liquor on my prow. A few reporters flicked their cameras and a small crowd put up their hands, waved them a fraction and put them down again, as if they realized how stupid it really was, wasting that fine cham-pagne.

IT WAS then and there I saw the captain, Metal bless him, for the first time. He came running across the field. The Master of my Fate, the Captain of my Soul. I liked him right off. He was short and whipped out of wrinkled hard brown leather, with green, implacable diamond eyes set in that hard leather, and a slit of white uneven teeth to show to anybody who disobeyed. He stomped into the air-lock and set his clipping boots down and I knew I had my master. Small tight knuckle bones and wrists told that, and the way he made fists and the quick, smooth manner in which he cracked out the orders of the day:

"Snap it!" he said. "Get rid of that

damned mayor out there! Clear apron! seal the locks, clamp ports and we'll push the hell out of here!"

Yes, I liked him. His name was Lamb; ironic for a man lacking lamb-like qualities. Captain Lamb, who threw his voice around inside me and made me like the steel edge to it. It was a voice like silk-covered brass knucks. It flowed like water, but burned like acid.

They rapped me tight. They expelled the mayor and his splintered champagne bottle, which by now now seemed childish. Sirens shouted across the base apron. The crew did things to my alimentary canal. Twenty-seven of them.

Captain Lamb shouted.

That was the slap on the back that brought me my first breath, my first sound, my first movement. Lamb pounded me into living.

I threw out wings of fire and powder and air. The captain was yelling, snuggled in his crash-hammock, zippered up to his sharp chin; men were swaying, sweating in all their suspensory control hammocks. Quite suddenly I wasn't just metal lying in the sun any more. I was the damnedest biggest bird that ever sang into the sky. Maybe my voice wasn't anything but thunder, but it was still singing to me. I sang loud and I sang long.

This was the first time I had been outside the hangar and the base to see the world.

I was surprised to find that it was round.

A S ADOLESCENCE is to man, his days from thirteen to eighteen when overnight his viewpoints are radically reformed, so it was with my first plunge into space. Life was thrown at me in one solid piece. All of the life I would ever know was given to me without apprenticeship, suckling or consideration. I had growing pains. There were stresses, forces attacking me from all sides simultaneously, feelings, impressions I had never considered possible. The solid understandable gravity of Earth was suddenly taken away and the competition of space gravities each tried their luck with me.

The moon, and after the moon a thousand dark meteors crashing by, silent. Tides of space itself, indescribable, and the urge of stars and planets. And then a thing called momentum when my jets were cut and I moved without breathing or trying to move.

Captain Lamb sat in the control room, cracking his knuckles. "She's a good ship. A fine ship. We'll pound the holy marrow out of those Martians."

The young man by the name of Conrad sat beside the captain at the duo-control. "We'd better," he said anxiously. "There's a girl waiting in York Port for us to come back."

The captain scowled. "Both of you? You *and* Hillary?"

Conrad laughed. "The two of us. Both on the same war-rocket, going to the fray. At least I can keep my eye on that drunkard this way. I'll know he's not down in York Port scudding along on *my* acceleration. . ."

Captain Lamb usually said all his words quick, fast, like lines of mercury. "Space is a funny place to talk about love. Funny place to talk about anything. It's like laughing out loud in a big cathedral, or trying to make a waltz out of a hymn."

"Lo, the sentimentalist," remarked Conrad.

Lamb jerked. He scowled at himself. "Lo, the damned fool," he said, and got up to measure the control room with his little strides.

They were part of me. Lamb, Conrad and the crew. Like blood pulsing in the arteries of a warm body, like leucocytes and bacteria and the fluid that sustains them—air—locomoting through my chambers into my heart, my driving engines, feeding my livened appetites, never knowing that they were only units of energy like corpuscles giving a greater mass—myself—nourishment, life, and drive.

Like any body—there were microbes. Destroying elements. Disease, as well as the sentinal leucocytes.

We had one job to do. I knew of this. To fend off the ever increasing attacks against earth's Phobos-Deimos citadels. I felt tension spreading, growing as each day went by. There was too much cigarette smoking, lip biting, swearing among the crew-members. Big things lay ahead.

THE microbes within my body were in a small dosage; but virulent because they moved free, unchecked, unsuspected. Their names were Anton Larion and Leigh Belloc. I refer to them as bacteria simply because, like microscopic forms in a large body, their function was to poison and destroy me. And the best way to render me inactive would be the destruction of part of my red-blood. That meant Captain Lamb. Or part of his technical war-staff. Larion and Belloc planned for their poisoning, quietly, carefully.

Self-preservation is an eternal, all-encompassing thing. You find it in metal as you find it in amoebas; you find it in metal as you find it in men. My body would be attacked. From outside I feared nothing. From inside I was uncertain. Coming from an unexpected quarter that attack might kill

me so very soon after my birth. I didn't approve of the idea.

I went through space toward Mars. I couldn't speak.

I could only feel voice-vibrations throughout my length. The voices of Hillary and Conrad arguing about their woman named Alice in York Port, and the captain snapping at the heels of his crew when we hit the asteroid-skirt, and then the subtle undercurrent of poison stirring in the midst of this—Larion and Belloc—their voices touched my hull:

"You're familiar with the plan, Belloc; I don't want you turning silly at the crisis."

"I know what to do. Don't worry. What the hell."

"All right, I'm just explaining. Now —as far as killing Captain Lamb, that's out. We're only two against twenty-four others. I want to be alive to collect that money we're guaranteed for this—work."

"Logically, then—the engines. . . ."

"I'm in favor of it, if you are. This is a war-rocket; spare parts, excess cargo, all that's eliminated for speed. Timebombs should work miracles with the main jet-engines. And when it happens we can be out and away in space in plenty of time?"

"When?"

"During the next shift of crew relief. There's a certain amount of inescapable confusion then. Half the crew's too tired to worry, the other half is just turning out, groggy."

"Sounds okay. Huh. It seems a damn shame though, in a way."

"What?"

"Nice new rocket, never tested before. Revolutionary design. I never enjoyed working on engines before, until I got my station with this jalopy. She's sweet. Those engines—sweet as the guts of a flower. And it all goes to hell before it has a chance to prove itself."

"You'll get paid for it. What else do you want?"

"Yeah, I'll get paid, won't I? Yeah."

"Shut up, then. Come on."

The routine circulation of crew-blood through the arteries of the ship took Larien and Belloc below to their stations in the fuel and engine cubicles. The poison was in my heart, waiting.

What went on inside my metal is not to be described. There are no similes, comparatives for the hard, imprisoned, frustrated vibrations that surge through tongueless *durasteel*. The rest of the blood in me was still good, still untouched and untainted and tireless.

"Captain." A salute.

"Belloc." Lamb returned the salute. "Larion."

"Captain."

"Going below?" said the captain.

"Yes, sir."

"I'll be down in——" Lamb eyed his wrist watch. "Make it thirty minutes. We'll check the auxiliaries together, Belloc."

"Right, sir."

"Go on down, then."

Belloc and Larion descended.

LAMB walked quickly into the computation cube and struck up a rapid word exchange with young Ayres. Ayres, who looked like he was barely out of blushing and floppy hair and semantics school, and still not shaving as often as the others. His pink face glowed when the captain was around. They got on like grandfather and grandson.

They probed charts together. When they finished, Lamb walked off the yardage in the computation room, scowling, examining his boots. Ayres computated.

Lamb paused, looked out the visual-port concernedly. After a moment he said, "When I was a very little kid I stood on the edge of the Grand Canyon, and I thought I'd seen everything there was to see——" A pause. "And now I've got my first captaincy, and——" he patted the hull of my body quietly "——a fine first rate lady of a ship." Quick, to Ayres: "What are you, Ayres?"

Startled, Ayres blinked. "Me, sir?"

The captain stood with his strong, small back to Ayres, inspecting the stars as if they were a celestial regiment under his personal say-so. "Yes. I mean religion," he explained.

"Oh." Ayres pulled his right earlobe with finger and thumb, musing. "I *was* a first class agnostic. Graduated, or should I say demoted? From an Atheist academy."

The captain kept looking at the stars. "You use the word 'was,' Ayres. You emphasize that word."

Ayres half-smiled. "Sure. I mean—— yes, sir. But this is my first trip, sir, so that changes things."

"Does it?"

"Yes it does, sir."

The captain rocked casually on his heels. "How's that, Ayres?"

"You know the tale as well as I, sir. It's an old tale. And a good one, I might add. To put it one way: 'A Baptist is an atheist who took a trip to the Moon.'"

"That holds true for Methodists, Episcopalians and Holy Rollers, doesn't it?"

"It does, sir."

The captain made a noise that sounded like laughter. "We're all the same. Every damned one of us, Ayres. Hard-shelled God-fighters, good and true, when we're home in Brooklyn and Waushawkee. Take away land and gravity, though, and we're babes, undiapered and crying in a long dark night. Hell, there's not a man rocketing today who isn't religious, Ayres!"

"Are you religious, Captain?"

Lamb closed his mouth, looked out the port straight ahead. He raised one small-boned hand, spreading it in a measured movement. "It's always the same, Ayres. The first trip converts us. The very first trip. All you have to do is stand here for fifteen minutes or half an hour looking at space, feeling how insignificant you are flying around like a gnat in the middle of it, looking at those damned wonderful stars, and first thing you know you're down on your knees, crying your eyes out, with a hot stomach, a wild head and a humble attitude forever after."

Lamb pulled back from himself suddenly, snapped around, stalked to a down-ladder, grabbed a rung and glared at Ayres. "And so," he pointed out, "you'll notice that I never look at the stars too long! I've a ship to run—no time for it. And in case you believe all I tell you—go to hell! I should demerit you for questioning a superior!"

Lamb dropped down the rungs like a weight.

AYRES sat there a moment, trying to computate. After a while he looked up at the star-port. His eyes dilated very dark and wide. He stood up. He walked across the computation room and stood there, staring out. He looked like he was listening to music. His lips moved.

"What did the Cap say? Stand here fifteen minutes or half an hour? Why, hell—" He bent his knees until they touched the deck. "I got the Cap's time beat all hollow!"

Good blood. Good leucocyte. Good Ayres.

Mars come up ahead, the first really intense gravity I had felt since leaving earth and moon behind. It came up like a ruddy drop of dried blood on the void. Mass is the sexual drive of space, and gravity the intensified yearning of that mass, the gravitic libido of one tremendous body for the love, the following of any and all smaller bodies who transgress its void boundaries. I have heard the simple men within me speak of a planet as one speaks of a queen bee. The ultimate gravity toward which all smaller gravities and bodies yearn. Merciless harlot, mating with all, leading all on to destruction. Queen bee followed by the swarms. And now I was part of a swarm, the first of many yet to follow, answering the urge of one gravity, refusing another.

But still the poison was in me. And no way possible for Captain Lamb's crew to know of it. Time ticked on my console-chronometers and swung by, imperceptibly majestic in the moves of stars.

Captain Lamb went down to the engine rooms, examined my heart and my auxiliaries. Bitingly, he commented and instructed, interspersing that with vituperative barks. Then he hopped up the rungs to the galley for something to eat.

Belloc and Larian stayed below.

"First now, Belloc, you checked the life-boats?"

"I did. Number Three boat's ready. I fixed it an hour ago."

"Good. Now. . . ."

THE Slop put out a bowl of soup for Captain Lamb. Lamb pursed his lips to a spoon of it, and smacked them in appreciation. "Slop?"

"Yes, sir?" Slop wiped greasy hands on a large towel.

"Did you invent the gravity soupbowl and gravity spoon?"

Slop looked at his feet. "I did, sir."

"An admirable invention, Slop. I recall the day when all rocket liquids were swilled by suction from a nippled bottle. Made me feel like a god-damned baby doing it."

Slop chuckled deep, as he returned to cleaning the mess-plates. "Ship gravity wasn't strong enough to hold soup down, so I thunk up the gravity spoon in my spare time. It helped."

The captain ate in silence. After a moment he said, "I must be getting old, Slop. I think I'm sick."

"Captain!"

Lamb waved his spoon, irritated. "Oh, nothing as bad as all that. I mean I'm getting soft-headed. Today, I feel—how should I put it? Dammit to hell, it's hard finding words. Why did you come along on this war-rocket, Slop?"

Slop twisted his towel tight. "I had a little job to do with some Martians who killed my parents three years ago."

"Yes," said the captain.

Belloc and Larian were down below. Slop looked at his chief. At the tight little brown face that could have been thirty-five as easily as forty or fifty.

Lamb glared up at him, quick. Slop gulped. "Pardon me."

"Uh?"

"I was just wondering. . ."

"About. . . ?"

Belloc. Larian. Belloc down below. Larian climbing rungs, on his way to get the time-bombs. Mars looming ahead. Time getting shorter, shorter.

In a dozen parts of my body things were going on at an oblivious, unsuspecting norm. Computators, gunners, enginers, pilots performed their duties as Lamb and Slop talked casual talk in the galley. While Larian muscled it up the rungs toward his secreted time-explosives.

Slop said, "About why you became captain on a war-rocket, yourself, sir?"

"Me?" Lamb snorted, filled his mouth half a dozen times before answering very slowly. "Five years ago I was in a Blue Canal liquor dive on Mars. I met a Martian girl there. . ."

"Oh, yes. . ."

"Yes, *nothing*, you biscuit-burner! Damn but she was sweet. With a temper like a very fine cat-animal, and morals to match. Hair like glossy black spider-silk, eyes like that deep cold blue canal water. I wanted to bring her back to Earth with me. The war came, I was recalled and—-"

"And someday," finished Slop, "when you've helped get the war over, you'll go looking for her. And being at Deimos-Phobos Base, maybe you can sneak down and kidnap her sometime."

Lamb ate awhile, making motions. "Pretty childish, isn't it?"

"No, I guess it's all right if she's still waiting."

"She is—if I know Yrela, she is."

Ayres in Computation.

Mars off in space, blood-red and growing.

Lamb in the galley.

Hillary and Conrad in control room One!

And down below, where all of my power grew and expanded and burst out into space, I felt the vibration of Belloc. And coming up the ladder to the supply room—Larian.

Larian passed through the galley. "Sir."

Lamb nodded without looking up from his meal.

Larian proceeded up to Computation, passed through Computation, whistling, and lingered in Supply AC.

Space vibrated with my message.

MY GUNS were being trimmed, oiled and ready. Ammunition passed up long powered tracks from Locker

Five to Blister Fourteen. Scarlet ammunition. Men sweated and showed their teeth and swore. Belloc waited down below, his face twitching its nerves, in the engine room. The captain ate his meal. I drove through space, Ayres computated. Belloc waited. Captain, eating. Space. Larian. Time-bombs. Captain. Belloc. Guns. Waiting. Waiting. Driving.

The metal of my structure was sickened, stressing, striving inward, trying to shout, trying to tell all that I knew in my positive-negative poles, in my sub-atomic awareness, in my neutronic vibrations

But the blood of my body moved with a mind of its own, pulsing from chamber to chamber in their sweating, greasy togs, with their waiting, tightened faces. Pulsing nervously. Pulsing, pulsing, pulsing, not knowing that soon poison might spread through every and all of my compartments.

And there was a girl named Alice waiting in York Port. And the memory of two parents dead. And on Mars a cool-eyed Martian dancing girl, still dancing, perhaps, with silver bells on her thumbs, tinkling. Mars was close. I made an angry jolt and swerve in space. I leaped with metal frustration!

Around and around and around went my coggery, the flashing, glinting muscles of my soul's heart. Oil surged through my metal veins. And Belloc was down below, smoking one cigarette after another.

I thought about Ayres, about Captain Lamb and the way he barked, about Ayres and the way he kneeled and felt what he had to feel. About Hillary and Conrad thinking about a woman's lips. About The Slop troubling to invent a gravity soup plate.

I thought about Belloc waiting.

And Mars getting near. And about the war I had never seen but always

heard about. I wanted to be part of it. I wanted to get there with Lamb and Hillary and The Slop!

The Slop took away the plate the captain had cleansed with his spoon. "More?"

Lamb shook his head. "No. Just a hunk of fruit now. An apple or something." He wiped his small mouth with the back of his hand.

"Okay," said The Slop.

At that moment there was a hiss, an explosion.

Somebody screamed, somewhere.

I knew who it was and where it was. The captain didn't. "Dammit to hell!" he barked, and was out of the galley in three bounds. Slop dropped a soup kettle, following.

WARNING bells clamored through me. Ayres, in Computation, grinding out a parabolic problem, jerked his young, pink face and fear came into it instantly. He arose and tried walking toward the drop-rungs, but he couldn't do it. He didn't have legs for the job.

Conrad scuttled down the rungs, yelling. He vanished toward the engine room; the floor ate him up.

Hillary grabbed the ship-controls and froze to them, listening and waiting. He said one word. "Alice——"

Slop and the captain got there first in Section C.

"Cut that feed valve!" yelled Lamb. The Slop grasped a valve-wheel glinting on the wall in chubby fingers, twisted it, grunting.

The loud, gushing noise stopped. Steam-clouds billowed in my heart, wrapping Captain Lamb and The Slop tight and coughing. Conrad fell the rest of the way down the ladder into my heart, and the steam began to clear away as my vacuum ventilators began humming.

When the steam cleared they saw Belloc.

The Slop said, "Gahh. That's bad. That's *very* bad."

Conrad said, "How'd it happen? Looks like he died quick."

Lamb's leather-brown face scowled. "Quick is the word. That oil-tube burst, caught him like a steel whip across the bridge of his nose. If that hadn't killed him, scalding oil would have."

Crumpled there, Belloc said not a word to anybody. He just bled where the oil pipe had caught him on the nose and cheek and plunged on back into his subconscious. That was all there was to him now.

Captain Lamb cursed. Conrad rubbed his cheek with the trembling flat of his hand. "I checked those oil-lines this morning. They were okay. I don't see—"

Footsteps on the rungs. Larian came down, feet first, quick, and turned to face them. "What happened . . . ?" He looked as if somebody had kicked him in the stomach when he saw Belloc lying there. His face sucked bone-white, staring. His jaw dropped down and he said, emptily, "You—killed him. You—found out what we were going to do—and you killed him . . ."

The Slop's voice was blank. "What?"

"You killed him," repeated Larian. He began to laugh. He opened his mouth and let the laughter come out in the steam-laden room. He darted about suddenly and leaped up the rungs. "I'll show you!"

"Stop him!" said Lamb.

Conrad scuttled up at Larian's heels. Larian stopped and kicked. Conrad fell, heavy, roaring. Larian vanished. Conrad got up, yelling, and pursued. Captain Lamb watched him go, not doing anything himself, just watching. He just listened to the fading feet on the rungs, going up and up.

The deck and hull quivered under Lamb's feet.

Somebody shouted.

Conrad cried, from far off, "Watch it!"

There was a thumping noise.

Five minutes later Conrad came down the ladder lugging a time-bomb. "It's a good thing that oil-pipe burst, Cap. I found this in Supply AC. That's where Larian was hiding it. Him and Belloc—"

"What about Larian?"

"He tried to escape through an emergency life-boat air-lock. He opened the inner door, slammed it, and a moment later when I opened that same inner door, I almost got killed the same way—"

"Killed?"

"Yeah. The damned fool must have opened the outer door while he was still standing in the middle of the air-lock. Space suction yanked him right outside. He's gone for good."

The Slop swallowed thickly. "That's funny, he'd do that. He knew how those air-locks work, how dangerous they are. Must've been some mistake, an accident, or something . . ."

"Yeah," said Captain Lamb. "Yeah."

They held Belloc's funeral a few hours later. They thrust him overboard, following Larian into space.

My body was cleansed. The organic poison was eliminated.

Mars was very close now. Red. Bright red.

In another six hours we would be engaged in conflict.

I HAD my taste of war. We drove down, Captain Lamb and his men inside me, and I put out my arms for the first time, and I closed fingers of power around Martian ships and tore them apart, fifteen of them—who tried to prevent our landing at Deimos-

Phobos Base. I received only minor damage to my section F. Plates.

Scarlet ammunition went across space, born out of myself. Child out of metal and exploding with blazing force, wounding the stratas of emptiness in the void. I exhilarated in my new found arms of strength. I screamed with it. I talked rocket talk to the stars. I shook Deimos Base with my ambitious drive. I dissected Martian ships with quick calm strokes of my ray-arms, and spunky little Cap Lamb guided my vitals, swearing at the top of his lungs!

I had come into my own. I was fully grown, fully matured. War and more war, plunging on for month after month.

And young Ayres collapsed upon the computation deck one day, just like he was going to say a prayer, with a shard of shrapnel webbed in his lungs, blood dropping from his parted lips instead of a prayer. It reminded me of that day when first he had kneeled there and whispered, "Hell, I got the captain's time beat all hollow!"

Ayres died.

They killed Conrad, too. And it was Hillary who took the news back to York Port to the girl they had both loved.

After fourteen months we headed home. We landed in York Port, recruited men to fill our vacancies, and shot out again. We knocked holes in vacuum. We got what we wanted out of war, and then, quite suddenly one day space was silent. The Martians retreated, Captain Lamb shrugged his fine-boned little shoulders and commanded his men down to the computation room:

"Well, men, it's all over. The war's over. This is your last trip in this damned nice little war-rocket. You'll have your release as soon as we take

gravity in York Port. Any of you want to stay on—this ship is being converted into cargo-freighting. You'll have good berths."

The crew muttered, shifting their feet, blinking their eyes. Cap said:

"It's been good. I won't deny it. I had a fine crew and a sweet ship. We worked hard, we did what we had to do. And now it's all over and we have peace. Peace."

The way he said that word it meant something.

"Know what that means?" said Lamb. "It means getting drunk again, as often as you like; it means living on earth again, forgetting how religious you ever were out in space, how you were converted the first trip out. It means forgetting how non-gravity feels on your guts. It means a lot. It means losing friends, and the hard good times brawling at Phobos-Deimos Base.

"It means leaving this rocket."

The men were silent.

"I want to thank you. You, Hillary. And you, Slop. And you, Ayres, for signing on after your brother died. And you, Thompson, and McDonald and Priory. And that's about all. Stand by to land!"

WE LANDED without fanfare. The crew packed their duffles and left ship. Cap lingered behind awhile, walking through me with his short, brisk strides. He swore under his breath, twisted his small brown face. After awhile he walked away, too.

I wasn't a war-rocket anymore.

They crammed me with cargo and shipped me back and forth to Mars and Venus for the next five years. Five long years of nothing but spider-silk, hemp and mineral-ore, a skeleton crew and a quiet voyage with nothing happening. Five years.

I had a new captain, a new, strange

crew, and a strange peaceful routine going and coming across the stars.

Nothing important happened until July 17th, 2243.

That was the day I cracked up on this wild pebbled little planetoid where the wind whined and the rain poured and the silence was too damned silent.

The crew was crushed to death inside me, and I just lay here in the hot sun and the cold night wind, waiting for rescue that never seemed to come.

My life blood was gone, dead, crushed, killed. A rocket thinks in itself, but it lives through its crew and its captain. I had been living on borrowed time since Captain Lamb went away and never came back.

I lay here, thinking about it all. Glorious months of war, savage force and power of it. The wild insanity of it. I waited. I realized how out of place I was here, how helpless, like a gigantic metal child, an idiot who needs control, who needs pulsing human life blood.

Until very early one morning after the rain I saw a silver speck on the sky. It came down fast—a one-man Patrol inspector, used for darting about in the asteroid belt.

The ship came down, landing about one hundred yards away from my silent hulk. A small man climbed out of it.

He came walking up the pebbled hill very slowly, almost like a blind man.

He stood at my air-lock door. I heard him say, "Hello—"

AND I knew who it was. Standing there, not looking much older than when first he had clipped aboard me, little and lean and made of copper wire and brown leather.

Captain Lamb.

After all these years. Dressed in a black patrol uniform. An inspector of asteroids. No cargo job for him. A dangerous one instead. Inspector.

His lips moved.

"I heard you were lost four months ago," he said to me, quiet-like. "I asked for an appointment to Inspector. I thought—I thought I'd like to hunt for you myself. Just—just for old times sake." His wiry neck muscles stood out, and tightened. He made his little hands into fists.

He opened my air-lock, laughing quietly, and walked inside me with his quick, short strides. It felt good to have him touch me again, to hear his clipped voice ring against my hull again. He climbed the rungs to my control room and stood there, swaying, remembering all the old times we had fought together.

"Ayres!"

"Aye, sir!"

"Hillary!"

"Aye, sir!"

"Slop!"

"Aye, sir!"

"Conrad!"

"Aye, sir!"

"Where in hell is everybody? Where in hell is everybody?" raged Lamb, staring about the control room. "Where in the God-blamed hell—!"

Silence. He quit yelling for people who couldn't answer him, who would never answer him again, and he sat down in the control chair and talked to me. He told me what he'd been doing all these years. Hard work, long hours, good pay.

"But it's not like it used to be," he told me. "Not by a stretched length. I think though—I think there'll be another war soon. Yes, I do." He nodded briskly. "And how'd you like to be in on it, huh? You can, you know."

I said nothing. My beams stretched and whined in the hot sun. That was all. I waited.

"Things are turning bad on Venus.

Colonials revolting. You're old-fashioned, but you're proud and tall, and a fighter. You can fight again."

He didn't stay much longer, except to tell me what would happen. "I have to go back to Earth, get a rescue crew and try to lift you under your own power next week. And so help me God, I'll be captain of you again and we'll beat the bloody marrow out of those Venerians!"

He walked back through my compartments, climbed down into my heart. The galley. The computation. The Slop. Ayres. Larian. Belloc. Memories. And he walked out of the airlock with eyes that were anything but dry. He patted my hull.

"After all, now—I guess you were the only thing I ever really loved . . ."

He went away into the sky, then.

And so I'm lying here for a few more days, waiting with a stirring of my old anticipation and wonder and excitment. I've been dead a while. And Cap has showed up again to slap me back to life. Next week he'll be here with the repair crew and I'll sail home to Earth and they'll go over me from seam to seam, from dorsal to ventral.

And someday soon Cap Lamb'll stomp into my air-lock, cry, "Rap her tight!" and we'll be off to war again! Off to war! Living and breathing and moving again. Captain Lamb and I and may be Hillary and Slop if we can find them after all this time. Next week. In the meantime I can think.

I've often wondered about that blue-eyed Martian dancing girl with the silver bells on her fingers.

I guess I could read it in Captain Lamb's eyes, how that turned out.

I wish I could ask him.

But at least I won't have to lie here forever. *I'll be moving on—next week!*

MURDER IN SPACE
(Concluded from page 107)

"Well?" fifteen voices demanded, pencils poised.

Ames scratched his head. "If you gentlemen will look through the testimony I gave, you may notice that I did not specify that either Webber's body, or the dog's—or, for that matter, Purdom's, or even Murchison's, would react the same way. I merely said the tests had been applied to the dog and Webber. I did not say whether the results were the same. As a matter of fact, they weren't. There's a law against tampering with evidence, you know."

"What about you and Blake being evidence? What about that?"

Ames nodded. "I don't pretend I didn't know what I was doing," he said. "Tom and I were free to use any ointment we wanted, and to use any kind of screen—the screen was an ordinary linen and there was no light, you might care to know. But had Murchison dared, he could have brazened it out, and cross-examination, or questioning of Dr. Lowell, would have brought out the truth. I just didn't think Murchison would go behind the screen."

"But what if he had?"

"No," Ames said, and shook his head. "You see—" He broke off and began playing his line carefully. A moment later he yanked out a small, lustrous blue fish. It landed struggling on the grass, and then began to change color. It turned dead white, then pink, then redder and redder, and all the while it was blowing itself up until it was several times its previous size. Suddenly it exploded and only its lips were left. The astonished gallery watched Ames use the lips for bait and he casted out easily and relaxed.

"That was a crazy-baiter," Ames observed. "Astonished you, but not me. Reason: I'm an experienced fisherman. It's the same in law and in life. You have to know what you're fishing for. You see, there are some fish that just *won't* be caught. If you catch them, they either break away and confess, or they explode . . . or they kill themselves. . . ." He sighed. "I didn't expect anything as dramatic as a courtroom suicide, but I knew my fish. I knew he wouldn't step behind the screen. And when I yanked him out there for everyone to have a look . . . he exploded, that's all. . . ."

"And," said Sue Wylie, coming up, "if you people don't leave Ames to his lunch now, there'll be another explosion in about a minute."

"You, dear?" Ames asked.

"Me, dear," Sue said.

"Then there'd be nothing left but your beautiful lips."

"Yes, dear."

Sour Tom got up with a groan. "This, folks," he announced acidly, "goes on all day. Any wonder them durn fish get apoplexy?"

He had to run to catch up to the quickly retreating newspapermen.

THE END

THE FREE-LANCE
OF SPACE

**All that stood between mankind
and the loss of a life-saving drug was
Rake Allan — who hated humanity**

By EDMOND HAMILTON

ILLUSTRATED BY JULIAN S. KRUPA

THE room was a badly lighted, metal-walled cubicle in a disreputable vibration-joint near the great Uranus spaceport. Into it penetrated whispered sobs of frenzy or delight from other rooms where men lay beneath the drugging, intoxicating influence of the forbidden blue vibrations. But neither of the two men in this room was indulging in the narcotic force.

One of the two, the one who bent across the little table and talked so earnestly, had the stringy figure and pale blue skin and huge-pupiled eyes which identify the Saturnian the solar system over. The other man was as obviously an Earthman, a tall, rangy, sleepily smiling fellow who lounged back and listened with a half-veiled mockery in his lazy black eyes.

"There's five hundred thousand Earth dollars in it for you!" the Saturnian was telling him tensely. "A half million—isn't that high enough pay for even the Free-Lance?"

The Earthman shrugged. "Perhaps. But you haven't told me yet what this secret is that you want me to get for you, Brun Abo."

"Nobody knows the exact details of it—nobody but Doctor Su himself," said the other vehemently. "All we know is that it's something that can bring dead men back to life."

He bent forward, gesturing jerkily with his thin blue hands. "Doctor Su himself is nobody—a pedantic old fool of a Martian biologist who came here to Uranus six months ago. But somewhere on this planet's wild moons, he found the drug or chemical he was seeking.

"For when he first got back here to Uranopolis from the moons, he talked a little about it. Bragged that he'd perfected a formula which could revivify any man who had been killed by space-shock—that is, by sudden asphyxiation in the cold vacuum of space.

"Of course, we were immediately interested in securing that formula for the exclusive use of the Saturnian Space-Navy. In case of another interplanetary war, it would be priceless to us. You see that?"

"Of course," nodded the Free-Lance. "In times of war, a space-navy can lose half its highly-trained men in a few battles. Most of them die from space-shock, and if they could be revived——"

"—that navy that could do that would soon get the upper hand of its enemy," finished the nervous Saturnian. "We offered Doctor Su a fortune for his formula. Other planetary agents made offers to him also, we're sure. But he refused them all. He denied even having such a formula. And he's returning to Mars on the *Draco* tonight."

Brun Abo leaned forward. "We resolved to get that formula from him before some other planet secures it. We were going to send one of our own men along on that ship, until we learned that you were hiding here on Uranus. At once, we decided to hire you as our agent.

"If anybody can get that formula for us, you can! You're famous throughout the system—Rake Allan, the Earthman, the notorious Free-Lance who owns allegiance to no world. Everyone knows your exploits, how you once joined the Jovian secret service and helped hunt for yourself, how you impersonated the Neptunian governor of the moon Triton, and so on.

"You can board the *Draco* tonight and have Doctor Su's formula before the ship reaches Mars. We don't care how you get it. The half-million is yours when you deliver the secret to us."

THE Free-Lance asked mildly. "You aren't afraid that I might secure the formula and then not turn it over to you Saturnians?"

"No, we're not afraid of that," smiled Brun Abo. "You're an Earthman, but Earth means no more than any other planet to you since they kicked you out of their diplomatic service and outlawed you. It's well known that the Free-Lance sells to the highest bidder."

Rake Allan said softly, "That is correct, Brun Abo. But how am I to know who is the highest bidder unless

I first secure the formula and then offer it to whoever gives the highest price?"

Brun Abo jumped to his feet, his blue face livid. "You're joking! You wouldn't do that, after it was I who disclosed the whole thing to you?"

"Did I ask you to tell me about it?" said Rake Allan in mild reproach. "No, *don't* try to shout," he added swiftly, and leaped.

There was a quick, silent tussle in the little room. The Saturnian was trying to cry out, but Rake Allan's strong hand across his mouth prevented him. The man from the ringed planet was like a child in the rangy Earthman's grasp.

Deftly, Rake Allan bound and gagged the Saturnian. Then he dumped him on one of the bunks at the side of the little room, and looked down at him with the mocking humor deepening in his lazy eyes.

"This will be a lesson to you, Brun Abo," he told the helpless man. "A lesson that the Free-Lance *always* works alone."

He detected the thought behind Brun Abo's raging eyes, and shook his head reprovingly. "No, you're not going to twist free and call the police when I leave here. The Uranian police are capital fellows but I've no desire to meet them tonight—they have some old scores against the Free-Lance which I've no time to discuss with them now."

He reached up and snapped the switch of the vibration-projector over the bunk. A blue beam streamed down from the projector onto Brun Abo's bound form, a cascade of light that deepened to purple as the Earthman turned the switch to the "Full" notch.

It was the narcotic force, the insidious, brain-stupefying, intoxicating vibration which had been banned by every planet but which still flourished as a secret vice in every shady corner of the solar system. Under its potent influence, in a few moments the Saturnian's raging eyes began to glaze, his face to grow lax and foolish.

Rake Allan waited until Brun Abo's face was a stiff, drugged mask, until he was whispering meaningless words in a drunken delirium. Then he unbound the man and turned off the projector. And then the Free-Lance walked calmly out of the little room.

He went across the dimly lit main room of the disreputable resort, between tables crowded with noisy spacemen and hangers-on, to the desk where sat the brutal-faced Uranian proprietor of the place.

Rake Allan tossed down a square platinum coin and said, "My friend in there has had more vibrations than he can stand—just let him sleep it off till morning without disturbing him."

The Uranian nodded and growled: "Those Saturnians are all alike—never saw one yet who could handle his vibrations."

The Free-Lance laughed, and without appearing to hurry, went out of the dive into the velvet softness of the Uranian night.

Under two bright moons, the dark towers of Uranopolis stretched north and west. Only a mile away blazed the blue-white lights of the great spaceport, on whose outskirts sprawled this slum of metal shacks whose dingy resorts were popular with interplanetary sailors.

Rake Allan hastened through the dark, alley-like streets with long, swift strides. He reached the wretched tenement that had been his hiding-place for two weeks, and raced up to his room. There he rapidly fished small, gleaming instruments from his space-bag and fitted them into a soft, flat leather belt he wore inside his jacket.

THE Uranopolis spaceport, when he entered it a half-hour later, was a noisy, bustling confusion of spacemen, passengers, porters and stevedores of all planetary races, eddying amid the towering ships.

"You're sure I'm in time to catch the *Draco?*" the Free-Lance asked the yellow Uranian porter who lugged his bag.

The porter nodded. "Lots of time— the *Draco* will take off two hours late because half its crew got drunk and deserted here."

That, Rake Allan thought, was a break for him. It would give him an even chance to put into effect the stratagem by which he hoped to gain possession of Doctor Su's secret.

He went up the gangway to the towering, torpedo-shaped bulk of the liner, and was halted by the harassed-looking young Uranian deck-officer who stood there checking the passengers.

"Francis Leigh, Earth businessman," the Free-Lance answered, handing over his forged passport. "I have no ticket —just got a hurry call back home a few hours ago, and hoped I could make your ship."

"You wouldn't have made it if we hadn't had to delay to replace our blasted deserters," the officer told him. "See the purser about a cabin."

That was exactly what Rake Allan wished to do. He found the fussy little purser in his office.

"Yes, we can let you have a single cabin to Earth, Mr. Leigh," he assured. "How about one on Number Three deck?"

"Let me see the deck-plan, please," the Free-Lance requested.

The purser handed over the big diagram upon which each cabin was marked with the name of its occupant. Rake Allan's eyes flew over it, and he quickly located that for which he searched.

Cabin Forty-four, on Number Four deck, was marked with the name of Doctor Quil Su, Syrtis, Mars. Number Forty-six, the only cabin immediately adjoining the Martian's, was marked with the name of "Miss Christine Willets, New York, Earth."

Rake Allan had hardly hoped to be lucky enough to get a cabin immediately beside the Martian's. But it made things harder.

"Yes, a room on Three deck will be all right," he said casually. "Will you have my bag sent down to it?"

He paid for his ticket and then strolled apparently aimlessly through the promenade decks and corridors.

"Take-off in five minutes!" the loudspeakers were blaring now.

Excited passengers were waving last farewells to the crowd down in the spaceport lights. Crewmen in gray uniforms, Jovians, Martians, Venusians, were being prodded to their stations by the sharp voices of harassed officers.

The gangway was withdrawn. The big space-doors, controlled from the bridge of the liner, began to grind shut. Signal bells rang.

The Free-Lance unobtrusively made his way down to Number Four deck. He paused, listening, outside the door of Cabin Forty-four.

There was no sound from inside. Doctor Su had not, then, come down yet to his cabin.

"We're about to take off, aren't we?" a bass voice asked.

Rake Allan turned quickly. A fat, friendly-looking green Jovian had come out of the cabin across the corridor.

"Yes, in just a few minutes," smiled the Free-Lance. "If you want to wave goodbye to friends, you'd better hurry."

The Jovian waddled hastily away. The Free-Lance went swiftly to the door of the cabin adjoining that of the

Martian scientist and bent to listen.

He heard sounds from within it, as of unpacking. "So Miss Christine Willetts, New York, is already down here," he muttered.

He had hoped to get into her cabin before she came. Now there was only one thing to do. He had but a few moments in which to work.

From a pocket of his belt, he swiftly brought out a tiny, shining cylinder with a little nozzle at its end. The nozzle he fitted rapidly into the keyhole of the girl's cabin-door. Then he turned the tap, and heard the highly-compressed anaesthetic gas inside the cylinder hiss into the room.

AN INSTANT later came a low, choking sound and then the thud of a falling body. The Free-Lance hastily withdrew the nozzle, thrust a skeleton key in its place, and unlocked the door.

He stepped swiftly inside, holding his nose for a few seconds until the ventilating-system carried away the anaesthetic fumes. Then he closed and locked the door, and bent rapidly over the girl.

She had fallen upon her face, a slim figure in blue with honey-colored shoulder-length hair. He turned her over. Her unconscious, lovely face hit him like a blow.

"Jean!" he exclaimed. "Jean King! So *that's* the game—"

The Free-Lance was startled, his thoughts and emotions whirling. He knew this girl.

When he had been Rake Allan of the Earth diplomatic service, Jean King had been his fellow-worker—and more. But he had not seen her since the Earth government had disowned and disgraced him.

His face hardened. "I might have known I wouldn't be the only one after

Doctor Su's formula."

He tore strips from the bedding and efficiently bound the girl's wrists and ankles. As he was fitting a gag for her mouth, her eyes opened. She looked up with dazed unbelief into his brown face.

"Rake Allan!" she whispered. "But what are you doing here?"

"Just what you're doing, Jean," he answered ironically. "The only difference is that you want Doctor Su's secret for your government, whereas I want it for myself."

Understanding flashed into her blue eyes. "Rake, listen! I *was* ordered by New York to take this ship and stay close to Doctor Su. But not to take his formula from him, but to help guard against other planets' agents taking it."

The Free-Lance laughed. "I think that as a secret agent you're deteriorating, Jean. You used to tell more plausible stories when we worked together."

"Rake, it's true!" she insisted desperately. "Doctor Su intends to give his formula to the whole system when he's fully tested it. It would save thousands of lives every year by making it possible to revive dead of space-shock.

"But if some single planet gets sole possession of the formula, it'll be hoarded for use in possible future wars. That's why Earth doesn't want to see any other planet get it. Jupiter, Saturn —all of them would give anything for it, we know."

The Free-Lance shook his head. His tone was bitter. "I am not so ready to believe in the kindly benevolence of Earth Government."

Jean's blue eyes clung to his face. "You're still angry because our government disowned you when you were arrested on Venus?"

"Haven't I a right to be angry?" he

rasped. "Wasn't I following my superior's orders in helping those swampmen rebel? And didn't my saintly superiors let me rot in a Venusian prison two years for it?"

"Rake, they didn't dare admit that you were obeying their orders!" she protested. "It would have meant war between the planets."

He shrugged. "I'm not complaining, at this late date. I've enjoyed life more as the Free-Lance than as a diplomatic official. And when I sell this space-shock formula to the highest bidder, I'll be able to enjoy life even more fully."

"Rake, you can't do it——"

Her pleading words were cut off by the gag he slipped deftly into place across her lips.

Then he went to the chromaloy wall that seperated this room from the Martian scientist's cabin. He fitted a little stethoscopic "eavesdropper" to his ear and listened at the wall.

THERE were sounds of movement in the adjoining cabin. Doctor Su had arrived. The faint creak of springs meant that the Martian was lying down in his bunk for the take-off.

The Free-Lance brought out of his kit a compact atomic cutting-torch. He held it against the wall, waiting with his finger on its switch.

The take-off alarm rang loudly through the ship. Next moment came a lurch and deafening roar of rocket-tubes as the *Draco* rose from its dock for the long voyage into space.

Rake Allan released the tiny, needle-like white flame of the atomic torch. The crackling hiss of the tool was smothered by the continuous roar of rockets. He braced himself against the pressure.

The tiny flame quickly cut a half-inch hole through the metal wall. He snapped off the instrument, and peered through the aperture.

Doctor Quil Su, an elderly, little Martian with a wrinkled red-skinned face and very thick spectacles, lay upon his bunk. He had not noticed the piercing of the wall.

Rocket-thunder was still steadily shaking the ship as it roared out of Uranus' atmosphere into clear space. The Free-Lance had to work rapidly while he had that steady roar to mask his activities.

"There *should* be enough of the somnite gas left in this," he muttered, as he brought out the shiny little cylinder again.

He placed its nozzle in the tiny hole in the wall, and then released the remaining anaesthetic gas into the Martian's cabin.

There was a smothered exclamation from Doctor Su, inaudible almost even to his ears.

The Free-Lance waited tensely the few minutes required for the ventilating system to carry off the anaesthetic gas in the next room.

"Now!" he told himself, and set hastily to work once more with the tiny atomic cutting-torch.

He used its needle-like white flame to cut a section out of the chromaloy wall, as big as a window. Then he stepped through into the Martian scientist's cabin.

Doctor Su lay unconscious in the bunk. Rake Allan ignored him for a moment, and began a rapid search of his baggage.

A square black bag that the little scientist had kept close to his hand looked the most promising. It proved to contain a large glassite flask that held several pints of dark brown liquid. There was also a complete self-sterilizing hypodermic outfit.

"Looks like the stuff," the Free-

Lance muttered. "But where's the formula for it?"

He could not find any written formula. Then, as the rocket-blasts died away to a low drone, he heard the little Martian stirring.

Rake Allan turned rapidly, drawing his atom-pistol. Doctor Su was sitting up, bewilderment on his spectacled face. Then alarm froze his wrinkled face as he saw the flask of brown liquid Rake held.

"You're stealing my elixir!" stammered the scientist. "You're going to kill me for it!"

"I never kill, Doctor Su," said the Free-Lance calmly. "I take it that this is the space-shock cure, then. That's good. I want the formula, too."

The Martian instinctively clutched his pocket. Rake Allan grinned. "Thanks for telling me where it is."

He reached forward and dipped the folded paper from the other's pocket. A glance disclosed it to be a chemical formula of incredible complexity.

"Don't take that too!" begged the Martian frantically. "It's the result of years of work—I can never reproduce it from memory."

"That fact will make it all the more valuable when I offer it for sale," replied the Free-Lance coolly.

Doctor Su's thin shoulders sagged. "I see. You're going to sell it to some planet to be kept as a secret war weapon. That's what I was afraid of, when they all tried to buy it from me."

There was misery in his blinking eyes. "And I wanted to give it to the whole system. All the thousands who die from space-shock in wrecks and disasters—it would have saved them."

RAKE ALLAN grimly subdued the pricking of his conscience. "You should have published the formula to the system at once, if that was your in-

tention. Why didn't you?"

"It hasn't been tested on a human being," Doctor Su said dully. "It works perfectly on animals, and I'm absolutely certain it will work on humans in the same way. But I couldn't ethically publish it until I had returned to Mars and made my test of it."

"You mean—you've got a space-shock victim on Mars whom you meant to try the stuff on?" the Free-Lance asked curiously.

Doctor Su nodded heavily. "Yes. My son. He was frozen by space-shock when his ship was wrecked off Mars two years ago. That's what started me searching for a cure. I've kept his body in a refrigerated vault ever since, hoping and hoping."

He looked up appealingly at the Free-Lance. "Two cubic centimeters of that elixir, injected hypodermically into my son's veins, would revive him. Can't you leave me that much, even if you take the rest of it and the formula?"

Rake Allan's throat tightened at that pathetic plea. He stood for a moment, his face unreadable. Then he put away his pistol.

He went back through the gap in the wall, and released Jean King from her bonds. He told her and the wondering little Martian:

"You two win. I can't take the damned thing if that's how things are. Go ahead and give it to the System."

Jean's blue eyes were bright with unshed tears. "Rake, I knew you couldn't do it. I know you too well—"

He interrupted roughly. "I'm getting off this craft, by borrowing one of its life-boats, as I intended to do. I advise you and Doctor Su to publish that formula the moment you've made the test—"

The wild shrilling of an alarm bell cut across his words. With it came the dim echo of crashing atom-guns, of shrieks and yells and curses.

"What the devil!" blazed the Free-Lance, leaping to the door.

He flung it open—and in the corridor outside stood the fat, genial green Jovian whose cabin was across the passage. The Jovian had a heavy atom-gun in his hands, and two others of his race stood beside him, similarly armed.

"Don't try it, Free-Lance!" cried the Jovian as Rake Allan's hand darted toward his jacket, for his own pistol. "I don't want to kill everybody in this room!"

Slowly, the Free-Lance raised his hands. The Jovian deftly fished his gun from his pocket. Then he pushed them back into the cabin.

"Jovian secret service," spat Rake Allan. "Of course—what a fool I was not to guess it."

The Jovian grinned. "I'm Stakan Awl, and I do represent my government. Just as the girl represents Earth and you represent—yourself."

Rake Allan's eyes were pinpoints of suppressed rage. He heard the babble of uproar elsewhere in the ship dying down. A breathless Jovian in gray spaceman's uniform came running into the cabin.

"Ship's all taken over, sir!" he reported to Stakan Awl. "We only had to kill two officers and one cyc-man. The rest, and the passengers, are all locked up under guard."

"Tell Lorgor to maintain the present course for the time being," snapped Stakan Awl, and the man sped away.

Rake Allan raged. "Nice fifth column work! You got half the *Draco's* crew drunk in Uranopolis, spirited them away, and had your own men hired in their place!"

The Jovian grinned again. "When Jupiter wants anything, it doesn't use half-measures. And we want Doctor Su's discovery very much."

His eyes flickered to the big brown liquid. "I presume that is the space-shock cure. Has it been tested?"

DOCTOR SU, seeming stunned by this sudden reversal of fortune, answered falteringly. "No, not on human beings. Yet it's certain that it will work on humans just as it did on space-shocked animals."

"Nevertheless, we'll make doubly certain by testing it," Stakan Awl declared. "Of course, we'll need a subject. Will you volunteer, Free-Lance? Or would you rather we used the girl?"

Horror came into Jean King's white face. "You're going to kill him—"

"Only temporarily, if Doctor Su's cure is as certain as he says," answered the Jovian. "We shall simply put the Free-Lance out into space for a few moments, and then bring him back inside and revive him with the formula."

"And then kill me again, and everyone else aboard this liner, so there'll be no tales told," gritted Rake Allan.

Staken Awl shrugged. "As to that, I make no promises."

He motioned with his atom-gun toward the door. The Free-Lance strode grimly toward it.

He had to lower his hands to pass through the door. As he did so, the expedient he had germinated in his brain had its chance.

Rake's lowered hand dived suddenly into his pocket, snatched out the little atomic cutting-torch, and flung it behind him. As he hurled it, he snapped its switch open.

The hissing, flaming little instrument, whirling through the air, so startled the Jovians that they recoiled from it before trying to bring their weapons to bear on the Free-Lance.

In that moment, Rake Allan was out the door and plunging down the corridor as fast as his long legs could carry him. His rapid steps echoed against the metal walls.

Yells rose behind him. As he rounded a turn in the corridor he collided squarely with a squat, armed Jovian running in answer to the cries. Rake's fist smashed the man's green face, and he snatched the atom-gun from his nerveless hands as he toppled.

He turned instantly and loosed a crashing bolt from the atomic gun, down the corridor. Stakan Awl and the others back there darted hastily back into the cabin.

"Get him!" Stakan Awl was bawling to his two companions. "After him, you fools!"

But the Free-Lance was already plunging up onto the promenade deck. If he could get to the bridge, and bring the *Draco* back around toward Uranus—

The promenade deck looked deserted, now that all passengers were locked below. But two Jovian spies running down the companionway from the bridge saw him coming and raised their guns.

They toppled in stunned heaps as the Free-Lance sent a bolt of blazing energy at them. He raced over their senseless bodies, up the stair into the big bridge-room.

The Jovian at the controls there turned startledly, and the other man who was poring over the navigation dials reached for his atom-pistol.

The Free-Lance dropped the second man with a quick shot, and clubbed the pilot before he could rise from his chair. Then he hastily slammed shut and bolted the crystal door of the bridgeroom

He jumped to the controls. "If I can turn her before they cut the cycs—"

Already, there was a thunderous hammering of Jovians outside the bridge-room door.   .

RAKE frantically fumbled at the super-complex controls of the great liner. He was used only to piloting small space-cruisers—he couldn't identify the proper rocket-throttles.

Then he found them. His hands hastily opened them. Once he had the *Draco* turned back to Uranus, the Jovians would see that their game was up, for Uranus patrol-cruisers would swiftly investigate anything so unusual as the return of an express-liner.

No roar of rockets followed his opening of the throttles! Furiously, he shoved the throttles in and out. But no response came.

"Hell, Stakan Awl has already ordered them to cut all the cycs!" he gritted, cursing the Jovian spy's presence of mind.

The hammering on the door was getting louder, and now he heard the hoarse voice of Stakan Awl out there bawling orders.

"Cutting-torches! Get them from the tool-room and burn through the door!"

The Free-Lance looked around. He could kill some of them when they broke in, but the end was certain.

Then as his blind gaze fell upon one of the big banks of controls, his lean body stiffened. He was looking at the panel on which were the oxygenator, ventilator and space-door controls.

"Good God!" he whispered. "It's one way—"

A terrible stratagem had entered his mind. Sweat beaded his forehead as he considered all its implications.

He looked wildly around. There should be space-suits somewhere in the bridge, for emergency-escape use—

He found the suits, in a locker at the end of the room. As he donned one of them and a helmet, a white flame began to eat through the door from outside. He had only seconds.

Clumsy in his space-suit, the Free-Lance ran back to that control-panel upon which his stratagem centered. He raised his hand toward one of the big copper levers at the top of the panel.

He was trembling, inside his suit. He *couldn't* do this! For if he did, he was gambling the lives of a hundred innocent passengers, he was gambling Jean's life, upon the assertion of a single man.

Yet Jean and everyone else upon the ship would die if he *didn't* do it! The Jovians would leave no witnesses—

The torch-flame was now burning a whole section out of the door. Convulsively, Rake Allan pulled down the copper lever.

There was a strange whistling, sighing sound all through the ship. With it came shrill cries of terror, suddenly cut off.

Then silence. Silence, and cold. The air inside the bridgeroom had whistled out through the half-burned hole in the door, and the Free-Lance was standing in the icy vacuum of space.

He had opened the space-doors of the Draco! And every person in the liner but himself was now a stiff, frozen corpse.

He stumbled to the door, and unlocked and opened it. Outside it lay Staken Awl and the other Jovians, their faces blue and rigid, their bodies frozen to the hardness of diamond by the awful cold.

Rake Allan again operated the remote control, this time to close the space-doors. He started the oxygenating system going again. As air flooded from the tubes, he took off the space-suit and helmet.

Then he stumbled over the stiff bodies of the Jovians, and made his way down to Deck Four. In the cabin there, old Doctor Su and Jean King were lying

like all others on the ship, motionless, dead.

Dead? Were people who died from space-shock really dead? It had long been debated by the system's scientists. Many had held that one who died from the vacuum of space really suffered only a form of suspended animation, that no vital organ or tissues were damaged by the sudden terrible freezing, and that someday a stimulant might be found which would start life going again in the frozen body.

Doctor Su claimed to have found such a stimulant. That big flask of brown liquid was it. But it had only been tested on animals. If it didn't work on humans—if it didn't work——

THERE was a prayer in the Free-Lance's heart as he filled the hypodermic with two cubic centimeters of the elixir, and bent over Jean King's frozen form, and injected it into her veins.

The few minutes that followed were an eternity he would never forget. He told himself that the girl's white face was softening and flushing, and then he told himself it was only wishful thinking—

Her eyelids fluttered. And then she was looking up at him. Surprise, gladness—and something more—in her blue eyes.

"Rake, what happened? Did I faint? Stakan Awl——"

He put his arms around her and told her. She shuddered violently.

"I was *dead?*"

"Not really dead, Jean, though the system for years believed it to be a state of death."

She clung to him, crying. "Rake——"

It was some minutes before she was calm enough to let him inject the elixir into Doctor Su himself.

The old scientist, at first dazed, was

soon wild with elation. "It means my son will live again, then!"

"There are all the passengers and officers on this ship to revive," Rake Allan reminded him. "And the Jovians, too, though not till they're disarmed. There's enough of the elixir for all?"

Doctor Su nodded, too choked with emotion to speak.

"Then I would suggest," the Free-Lance added, "that you broadcast your formula at once to the system and end all possibility of its being stolen and kept secret. You can publish it now that it's been tested."

The little Martian excitedly started off on the task of bringing more than a hundred people back from pseudo-death to dazed life.

But Jean still clung to Rake Allan. "Rake, you'll go back to Earth with me, now? Earth Government will be only too glad to retrieve that old wrong it did you, for this achievement."

His lean brown face softened. "Jean, I've never stopped thinking of you. If I go back, will you——"

"Yes!" she cried. "Yes!"

Minutes later, Rake Allan raised his head and laughed. "I'll bet we get wedding presents from the police of nine planets, when they hear that the Free-Lance is finally settling down!"

WRITTEN ENTIRELY BY FIGHTING MEN!
The Sensational July Issue of Amazing Stories

Every story, every article, every letter! Here is a collection of truly superior, truly inspired stories written by our fighting authors on their precious few free hours! Read this gallant issue and be convinced. These soldier writers are GREAT writers!

This is their salute to the way of life they are fighting for!

DON'T MISS IT! ON SALE AT ALL NEWSSTANDS MAY 9

The HEADLESS HORROR

By HELMAR LEWIS

ILLUSTRATED BY MALCOLM SMITH

YOU would have thought there was a madman in the airport phone-booth. Jimmy Hart was hanging on to the receiver with his right hand, dancing impatiently, opening the glass door at second intervals to look out into the airport waiting-room, drumming nervously against the pay-box and mumbling almost incoherently.

"Ryan! Ryan!" he wailed. "For gosh sakes, answer your phone!"

Suddenly, he heard a click through the receiver. His eyes widened with joy. He grabbed hold of the mouth-piece and yelled into it, "Ryan, you old buzzard, I've got a story for you that'll frizzle the two hairs on your head!"

"Give!" came from the receiver.

"I came down to the air-port to interview a couple of movie-stars, you remember," Jimmy began.

"So what?" Ryan roared back.

"So this," Jimmy continued, "just before the West Coast plane pulls in, a funny looking plane comes zooming up over the airport, hangs around like a

helicopter for a couple of minutes until it got the O.K. for the runway, and then comes taxiing in."

"So what?" Ryan demanded again.

"So this," Jimmy continued, almost breathlessly, "what do you think steps out of this plane?"

"Santa Claus!"

"Nope!"

"The little man who wasn't there."

"Nope!"

"The leg-man who's going to take your place after I throw you out on your ear," Ryan barked exasperatedly, "unless you stop asking me riddles!"

"It'll kill you! It's the biggest story of the year," Jimmy chortled, "and, what's more, I've got it to myself. I'm the only news-hawk at the airport!"

"Are you drunk?" Ryan demanded.

"I wish I were!" Jimmy replied, "and so does everyone else who's seen this thing walk out of that plane!"

"What thing?"

Jimmy gasped for breath. "Grab ahold of your desk, chief," he managed

Every beautiful girl in America vied
for the honor of winning a wierd necklace
to be presented by a man who had no head

135

to get out, "on account of you're going to need some support. It was a man without a head!"

Jimmy heard an enraged snort through the receiver. Then he heard Ryan bark out, "You *are* drunk! And, what's more, you're fired!"

Jimmy laughed. "O.K. If I'm fired, then I'm going to phone the *Record* right now and turn over this story to Danny Golen exclusively!"

"Wait a minute!" the city-editor protested. "How the hell do you expect me to believe that you just saw a man without a head getting out of a strange airplane—in this day and age?"

"It's true!" Jimmy said, "I saw the guy with my own eyes. He hopped out of the plane and, so help me Hannah, where there was supposed to be a head on top of his shoulders, there was nothing, not a damned thing!"

"Are you nuts?"

"I thought I was going screwy when I saw it," Jimmy explained. "But I rushed up to where he was standing near the plane and took a good look at him and, I'll be a monkey's avuncular relation if the guy wasn't lacking a head!"

"Where is he now?"

"Being examined by the airport officials," Jimmy said. "I thought I'd take the time to get this call in so's to warn you of what's happening. You'd better hold a couple of columns for me on the front page on account of I'm going to have a story for you that'll——"

HE BROKE off suddenly when he caught sight of the door to the airport manager's office as it opened slowly. "Got to hang up, chief!" he cried. "It's coming out! I'll get the story and the interview and phone it in later." Just as he was about to hang up, he hollered into the phone, as an afterthought, "and remember, chief, I ain't drunk!"

He ducked out of the phone booth and rushed over to the airport manager's office just as a number of people walked out. In their center, Jimmy saw the man without a head. He rubbed his eyes, shook his head as though he were coming out of a knockout punch and then looked again. He still saw what he had seen before—a man without a head, walking about as if he were alive. But how the heck could a man be alive, Jimmy thought, without a head? He pushed his way into the group of people.

"I'm Jimmy Hart of the *Globe!*" he said, "and I'd like to get an interview with you and the story of your trip."

The officials began to give Jimmy the brush-off but, suddenly, they stopped pushing him. Not a word had been spoken but, somehow, they had received some sort of message from the man without the head because the airport manager said something which was an obvious reply to a statement made by the headless man.

"Very well," he said, "if it's O.K. with you, we'll let him ask you a few questions.

Jimmy gulped. Then he stuttered out, "Look! can I believe my eyes when they tell me that I'm now looking at a man without a head?"

He waited readying himself for a verbal answer. But he heard no sound. Instead, he felt an answer insinuating itself into his brain—without words. He felt himself being told—soundlessly, "Yes! As you can readily see, I have no head."

Jimmy's jaw dropped. "I know what you're trying to tell me," he said, his voice dripping with awe, "but I'll be damned if I can hear a sound. How do you do it?"

Again—without the vehicle of vocal sounds—he felt an answer being conveyed to him. "It is simple," the message ran. "I use the extra-sensory faculty of thought transference. In other words, I can convey my thoughts to you simply by adjusting our wave-lengths so that they are in complete accord. It is much like the old fashioned radio set where you were able to tune in on the *radio* wave-length of a broadcasting station. In my case, however," the headless man continued, "I am able to tune in on your thought wave-length and convey my own thoughts to you without resorting to the crutch of speech."

"How? Jimmy demanded, goggle-eyed.

THE headless man raised his hands. Instead of ordinary fingers, Jimmy saw five elongated, octupus-like appendages waving nervously in the air, almost a foot long. The tips of the fingers seemed to glow with an inner light and there was a sensitivity along their entire length that made them appear almost fragile.

"With these," the headless man replied. He lowered all the appendages except the fore-finger of his right hand. "This is the one I use as a sort of radio aerial. It is sensitive to sound and, with it, I pick up the sound-waves of your speech and of all the other sounds around me, in the same manner as do your own ears, which I, as you observe, lack."

"How about broadcasting?" Jimmy asked.

The headless man raised the forefinger of his left hand. "It is with this that I send out my thought-waves to you. There is a gland in my body—which the scientists of Haar, my native country, have called the *adripat* gland —with which I am able to adjust the wave-length automatically so that I can make contact with your own psychical wave-length."

"How about the other fingers?"

"They serve various purposes," the headless man replied, "purposes which are too involved for the short time I have to spend with you. And now, if you will excuse me . . ."

"Just one more question," Jimmy insisted.

"Yes?"

"What's the purpose of your visit here?"

There was a long pause in Jimmy's consciousness. Then he heard, or rather felt, the reply, "Strangely enough, I have come from my native country to conduct a search for 'the body beautiful,' for the most perfectly formed body of the most beautiful girl here."

"But why?" Jimmy demanded.

He got no answer. Instead, the headless man turned on his heel and, with the airport officials in tow, "I shall be at the Hamilton Arms Hotel," Jimmy felt the headless man telling him, "where I shall make myself available to you and to your fellow journalists after I have rested."

FORTUNATELY, Jimmy's story on the arrival of the headless man caught the early editions of his paper. Only after he had been convinced that Jimmy was telling the truth, and that his story was not a hoax, did Ryan, his city-editor, agree to telephone the airport officials for a confirmation.

"The biggest story of the year!" he gulped out after he had hung up the receiver, "we'll scoop the country on this!"

"What did I tell you, chief!" Jimmy crowed.

"We'll need a daily followup," Ryan mused aloud, "and I'm putting you on them alone at first. We'll get a sob-sister on with you for the woman's angle of the 'body beautiful' contest," he added. "And we've got to get some pics, so grab ahold of any photog who's got a box handy and get over to the Hamilton Arms Hotel. I want to spread this story over the whole front page!"

From then on, in the company of a photographer, Jimmy shadowed the headless man wherever he went. He camped in the lobby of the Hamilton Arms Hotel. By that time, with the publication of his opening story, all the other New York newspapers and press associations had already assigned their top-flight men to the story of the headless man.

Of Jimmy's scoop, Life magazine wrote in its "Press" section, "Last week, Jimmy Hart, ace leg-man on the New York *Globe*, scooped the entire world with a strange and startling news story." Then it went on to quote from Jimmy's story using practically everything he had written. "This *rara avis* in modern news-reporting, a world scoop, should earn for Pressman Hart the coveted Pulitzer Prize," it concluded.

For Jimmy, the assignment was a reporter's dream. His expense account was unlimited. And, what was more, it took him practically across the entire country. He was present, for instance, when the headless man was examined by the immigration officials in Washington. Standing in front of dozens of news-camera klieg lights and with a paper in his extended hand, the headless man explained, solely by thought transference, the legality of his visit to America.

"This visa," he said, "is a legitimate one given to me personally by my monarch, Queen Viir."

"How about the quota?" one of the minor officials asked, his eyes agoggle from the fact that he was actually talking to a man without a head.

"There is no quota from my country of Haar," the headless man replied. "And besides, I am here in the capac-

ity of ambassador, which means that I am not subject to any quota which your country may set up. Also, I am here only on a short visit."

At another time, Jimmy was in the crowd of reporters present at the examination of the headless man by a group of scientists. The headless man had amiably agreed to the scientific examination and seemingly answered their questions with a candor that put them at their ease.

And as the photographer's bulbs flashed and the klieg lights for the news-reel camera's flared, the headless man demonstrated to the group gathered around him, the manner in which he was able to use his elongated fingers for sight, hearing, smell and thought transference. He wound up the demonstration by showing them how he ate his food. Solemnly, he cut a piece from a steak, salted it and dropped it into the hole in the middle of his shoulders where his head would ordinarily have been. Then, taking a cup of coffee in his right hand, he poured its contents into the shoulder hole as well.

"Down the hatch!" Jimmy whispered to his photog.

WHEN word got out that the headless man was going to make a tour of the Fifth Avenue shops, to purchase a vast amount of things for his queen, the entire street was lined with a crush of curious people that made it necessary for the police to call out the riot squad. They were lined up and down Fifth Avenue in droves. And when finally the headless man alighted from his automobile to enter one of the exclusive stores, the press of people almost burst through the cordon of police detailed to protect him. Women fainted by the score, not only because of the mob but because of what they saw.

It was one thing to see a photograph of a headless man. There was always the possibility that it was retouch job. There was always the possibility that the camera lied. But when these same people were confronted with the actuality of a man without a head walking sedately in front of their very eyes, "I tell you I saw him with my own eyes!" they all protested to unbelieving friends afterwards. "It isn't a fake."

"It's a press-agent stunt!" was the general tenor of cynics' and doubters' objections. "Pretty soon, we'll be told that we'll be able to see the headless man in Barnum & Bailey's Circus or something."

It was to offset this wave of doubt that the headless man agreed to appear in a radio interview on a national hook-up that was broadcast over every major chain.

There was doubt, at first, as to whether he would be able to broadcast over ordinarily radio waves without the use of sound waves to activate the microphones. But the headless man had airily waved aside their doubts.

"Thought transference," he explained, "is possible, not only by means of thought waves but also by radio waves."

The hour for the radio interview found the headless man in a studio without benefit of script. Harris Hymes, who had interviewed practically every important personage in the world, stood across from him. The prepared script in his hand quivered like a leaf in the wind. His first case of mike-fright was brought about by the fact that, across from him, stood a man without a head, a man without a tongue and mouth, who was going to broadcast a message to millions and millions of eager-eared listeners.

When Harris finally got the red-light to go ahead, he cleared his throat. He was certain he would be unable to speak. Words finally came and soon he found himself reading,

"Ladies and gentlemen of this vast radio audience. Standing before me at this microphone is a man of whom you have heard much for these past three weeks but whose voice few have been fortunate enough to hear. Now, in answer to my questions, you will be privileged to hear the actual voice of a man without a head. Ladies and gentlemen, the next voice you will hear— or, rather, feel—will be that of the headless man of Haar."

Millions of ears unconsciously edged closer to the loudspeakers of radios. In the radio studio, the studio audience comprised of celebrities and newspaper men leaned forward to catch every word. But they were surprised to discover that it wasn't necessary. They could hear no sound coming from him. Nor could the millions of radio listeners hear a solitary sound issuing from the loudspeakers of their radio sets.

THOSE in the studio simply saw the headless man raise the forefinger of his left hand to a point about a foot from the microphone. They saw the tip of the finger quiver sensitively, like the antennae of a great moth. Then, although no sound issued from the man's body nor from the radio sets, the millions of radio listeners, and those in the studio audience, were able to *feel*, to *sense*, in some strange way, as though the message were being incised subtly into their brains without the activating medium of sound, the thoughts of the headless man.

"Ladies and gentlemen of America," they felt him convey to them. "I represent Queen Viir, ruler of the country of Haar."

"Where is your country of Haar?" Harris asked.

There was a slight pause. Then came the answer, "I cannot tell you exactly. But I can say that it is a small kingdom located in the impenetrable fastnesses of the Central American jungles and mountains. I am the first Haarian to come into your world. I hope I shall not be the last. I hope that soon, as the Ambassador of Haar, I shall begin negotiations to cement our two countries in mutually beneficial relations."

The intervening announcer cleared his throat before asking the next question. "Are all the inhabitants of your country er . . . ah . . . similarly afflicted?"

The response was direct and had the suggestion of a mocking sneer in it. "Our affliction, as you call it," was the reply, "is, to us, a boon. Among a number of virtues in being headless, for example, is the fact that we are not afflicted with baldness. But I can tell you that all of my countrymen are headless, like myself. Our historians have traced the ancestry of our race to a man and woman—Haar and Heer —who were, thousands of years ago, mutations, as you might say, of the original human race. In some strange way this pair of people had been born, in the remote fastness of my country, without heads. And in still another strange way—strange to you, not to us —they discovered that they had no use for the ordinary human head. Certain compensations had been set up in their bodies to make up for the obvious lack of sight, hearing and speaking. Certain extra-sensory powers were given to organs which, ordinarily, in normal human beings do not have those powers. The powers of sight, hearing and speech are furnished by our sensitive fingertips. I am not a scientist so I cannot go into more detail about these various phenomena."

"Now, what is the purpose of your visit to America?" the announcer asked.

"As is obvious," the headless man replied, "we Haarians—and especially our ruler, Queen Viir—are lovers of the beauty of the body rather than of the face. I have come here, as a representative of my queen, to choose the girl who possesses the most beautiful body in your country. This will be done by means of a 'body beautiful' contest which will be conducted in every city and in every state until we have discovered the girl who, in the opinion of your judges and myself, possesses the 'body beautiful.'"

"And the prize to the winner?"

"The winner of the 'body beautiful' contest will receive from me the beautiful Queen Viir diamond and sapphire necklace, such as can be seen around my own neck, but much more valuable. To Haarians, this necklace is a badge of Haarian nobility. Ordinary Haarians wear inferior necklaces but only a few possess such as the one I shall present to the winner. I trust that, from now on, the girls of America—whose reputation for bodily beauty is unexcelled in the world—will come forward and enter this contest which should net the winner, in addition to the Queen Viir necklace, fame and fortune over the entire world!"

JIMMY HART was seated in a restaurant booth around the corner from the broadcasting studio. With him were his fiancee, Aline McDonald, and her brother Frank. The three of them had just left the studio from which they had heard and seen the headless man broadcast.

"What do you make of this guy?" Frank asked.

Jimmy munched a breadstick thoughtfully. Then he said, "I don't know, Frank. I don't know what to say. The idea of a man walking around without a head — in fact, of a whole country of people walking around without heads — is flabbergasting enough without wondering about what it all means. I just have a hunch, that's all."

"You and your hunches!" Aline laughed.

"What is your hunch," Frank asked.

"He ain't kosher, on the up-and-up."

"The 'body beautiful' contest, too?" Aline asked.

"That's what I'm talking about," Jimmy replied. "I just don't get the idea of this headless guy suddenly coming into a world of normal human beings after having been hidden away in some unknown country for thousands of years, and for the crazy reason of conducting a 'body beautiful' contest. It just don't make sense to me. There's something behind it all."

"I saw the picture of the Queen Viir necklace in the *Globe*," Aline said. "It's beautiful!"

"Sis could win it hands running, with her figure," Frank said.

"Who said I wanted it?"

"Aline isn't going to enter any 'body beautiful' contest!" Jimmy said. "Not if I can help it!"

Aline was piqued. "Maybe you think I couldn't win it?"

Jimmy began to attack the order of spaghetti the waiter had placed before him. "Let's not talk about it," he said. "I've got enough trouble shadowing this headless guy for the paper without having to worry about my girl-friend."

JIMMY saw little of Aline after that. His time was taken up entirely as part of the reportorial entourage that followed the 'body beautiful' tour of the headless man over the entire country. Full-page ads in newspapers and magazines, and dozens of daily recorded minute broadcasts on the large radio stations, brought news of the contest to the entire country. A few disgruntled cynics wondered where all the money was coming from and why it was being spent so prodigiously. But these solitary voices of dissent were shouted down by the multitude.

"We should be proud that the people of other countries appreciate the charm and beauty of our fair sex!" was the constant reply to the critics.

And the general public agreed and went over the contest and the appearance of the headless man as he traveled from city to city drumming up the contest. In Chicago, a "Body Beautiful Club" had been organized by a group of business women. And its entire membership of 1500 greeted the arrival of the headless man at the Union Station. Thousands of other curious people were there also and they milled around the headless man and his group until a squad of policemen were forced to rescue him from their midst. Ten women in Chicago offered themselves in matrimony with the headless man.

"Why should you want to marry a man without a head?" Jimmy asked one of them during an interview with her for his paper.

The woman showed him a newspaper clipping of a photograph of the headless man which she had framed in gold. "There's something about him!" she replied, with almost breathless awe," "something that attracts me physically."

Others were not so attracted. Many women, and men too, when they finally found themselves looking at the headless monstrosity, swooned away out of sheer fright. In Hollywood, at an enormous "body beautiful" contest that was run off in the Rose Bowl to accommodate the hundreds of thousands who demanded entrance, two movie stars succumbed to the horror of what they were looking at as they stood close by the headless man and stared in terror at his headless shoulders. And when Lola Andrews, the girl who won the California state contest, was lead to the headless man to receive his congratulations, she was forced to stifle a scream of terror that pushed its way into her throat.

There was no doubt about it. The "body beautiful" contest had become a countrywide sensation. The headless man had accomplished his purpose. And, as he and his entourage of reporters and press-agents were on the train, returning to New York for the contest finals, he told the men and women grouped around him that he was looking forward to the finals.

"From what I have seen, the girl who is going to win the contest will have to possess a glorious body!"

Off to one side in the train, Jimmy sat hunched up in his seat and moodily contemplated the landscape sliding past the window. Somehow, he had become fed up with the whole thing. At first, his instinctive, reporter's nose for news had given the affair the savor of the news chase that had always been attractive to him. But, now, the savor had given way to a bitter taste in his mouth. It was all old stuff. The gullible American public had fallen for the guff hook, line and sinker. But it was more than that that bothered Jimmy. Something, some vague, indefinable something burrowed in Jimmy's brain like a worm. It was a premonition, a fear that seemed to warn him of something horrible impending.

THE feeling of impending doom still hovered over Jimmy as he walked up the stairs of the brown-stone house where Aline and Frank McDonald lived. He was greeted by Aline with a question instead of the customary kiss.

"Guess what, Jimmy?" Aline flung at him.

"What?" Jimmy asked moodily.

"I just got a call from the 'body beautiful' committee and they've . . ."

"What?" Jimmy roared slamming the door behind him.

Frank came running up to them. "Yeah!" he cried, "Sis just got a phone call from the committee telling her she's been chosen to represent New York in the 'body beautiful' contest!"

"Aline!" Jimmy cried, almost in despair, "you shouldn't have sent in your photograph!"

Frank slapped Jimmy on the back. "She didn't!" he chortled, "I did!"

"I didn't know anything about it!" Aline protested.

"She's got a figure that'll grab off all honors!" Frank insisted. "Sure I sent in her photograph. She wouldn't do it herself. And look what it's got her —a chance to win the 'body beautiful' contest of America!"

"No go!" Jimmy said. "You're going to turn the bid down!"

Something in Aline bridled at the command. Actually, her reaction to the news was half-hearted. She had felt flattered by the choice of the committee but her heart had been set too long on getting married to Jimmy, when they were able to, and settling down with him in a cozy little flat to have kids. But Jimmy's peremptory bossiness stiffened her determination.

"That's not fair!" she retorted to his command.

Jimmy jumped up from the chair. "I'm not going to allow my future wife to go running around almost naked in front of a bunch of goggle-eyed, old futsy-dutses and a guy who hasn't even got a head!" he complained bitterly.

"But she may win the contest!" Aline's brother threw in, "and that'd bring in enough dough so's you and her could get married right away, like you always wanted to!"

Jimmy snorted. "That's a helluva way for a guy to get married!" he cried. "There's another name for that kind of thing and I'm not fixing for anyone to throw it at me!"

"You're being silly!" Aline said angrily, "after all, what can I lose?"

"Me!" Jimmy replied.

They stood there for almost half a minute staring angrily at each other, their nerves taut and tense, their bodies stiffened with rage. Finally Jimmy gave way. "Look, hon!" he said pleadingly, "just do this one favor for me, huh?"

"I may not even win the contest!" Aline replied.

Jimmy shook his head. "I don't know about that," he said, as he took her in his arms lovingly. "Only a bunch of headless guys without eyes could pass you up as the winner!"

Aline laughed. "Then you admit, Jimmy, that I might win the contest!"

Jimmy gloomily agreed. "Yeah!" he said, "then what'll happen? You'll go to Hollywood like the thousand and one other gals who have won beauty contests. You'll forget all about us. You'll have your day as a beauty contest winner. Everyone'll throw flowers at you and compliments. You'll be this hour's toast. But, tomorrow, they'll forget all about you. You'll be a has-been, a wash-out. And then where'll you be?"

Aline threw her arms around Jimmy. "We'll be exactly where we are now, Jimmy!"

He felt the warmth of her arms around him, saw the glow of love in her eyes and sighed. "O.K.," he said, "If that's the way you want it, then it's O.K. with me!"

A MONTH later, Jimmy Hart and Aline's brother, Frank, stood in the wings of the Gayety Theater and watched the procession of beautiful girls parade across the stage. The committee of judges, centered around the headless man, sat in the front rows of the audience with notebooks in hand. When the state winner of Washington walked across the stage, there was a lull in the audience's whispers. The judges would soon hand in their decisions. Aline was seated in the rear of the stage, together with the rest of the contestants. Jimmy looked across to her constantly, wondering where it was all going to lead.

"I don't like it, Frank!" he insisted, "I just don't like it!"

"I know which one you do like."

"All kidding aside," Jimmy gloomed, "there's something about this whole setup that doesn't smell kosher to me!"

"Like what?"

"Like that headless guy sitting down there. I just don't get it. What the hell is he doing being alive in the first place. Take a look at him sitting there in the first row."

Frank looked. "So what? So he hasn't got a head! There's a lot of guys I know who have heads which they use only for hat-racks. This guy seems to have a helluva lot on the ball if you ask me."

"That's just it!" Jimmy said. "He's one smart cookie, a brain, even if he hasn't got a head. And I don't see what the hell a brain like that is doing here running a contest for the 'body beautiful.' It just don't make sense to me!"

"Wait a minute!" Frank plucked at Jimmy's sleeve. "There's the guy coming out to make an announcement. They've got the judges' votes all tabulated!"

They watched an important-looking little fat man waddle to the center of the stage, simper back at the 48 girls seated cross-legged behind him, and then raise his hands for silence.

"It's it!" Jimmy said.

"Ladies and gentlemen!" the little fat guy began to spout, "I have the honor and distinction of presenting the sponsor of this 'body beautiful' contest, who will announce the name of the winner and make the presentation . . . the Headless Man from Haar!"

There was a round of applause as the headless man threaded his way down the first aisle ascended the stairs leading up to the stage and took a sheet of paper from the little fat guy. He looked down at it and then went over to a small table on which there was a large box. He took up the box and returned to the center of the stage.

The amazing phenomenon happened again. Without saying a vocal word, he was able to convey to the entire audience, through the means of thought transference, the following message:

"Ladies and gentlemen. I have the great honor to announce that, after considerable deliberation, the judges have come to the conclusion that the possessor of the most beautiful body in America belongs to . . . " He hesitated dramatically before announcing the name. ". . . to Miss Aline McDonald!"

THERE was a deafening burst of applause from the audience as the headless man opened the box in his hand and withdrew an enormous necklace from it that glinted in the spotlight like an acre of diamonds in the sun. Then he walked over to where Aline was standing, took her hand and brought her to the front, center of the stage.

"May I have the honor," she and the audience felt him say, "to present you with this diamond necklace, symbolic of the possession of the most beautiful body in all of America!"

With those words, he placed the heavily encrusted necklace around Aline's lovely neck. Watching from the wings, Jimmy could not prevent a snort of disgust from issuing from his lips.

"Damn futsy-dutsy horse-feathers!" he growled. But, in the next moment, he rushed over to where Aline was standing and blushing prettily, followed by Aline's brother. "Darling!" he said, "I knew you'd do it! I knew you had it on you!"

But instead of responding to his enthusiasm, Aline silently pushed his arms from around her. "Not here, Jimmy!" she said coldly, "in front of all these people." Then she turned away from him, took the proferred arm of the headless man and walked off the stage with him into the opposite wings.

Jimmy stood frozen to his tracks. His cheeks tingled as though he had received a slap in the face. His mouth fell open slightly.

Behind him, Frank whistled unbelievingly. "That ain't like Aline!" he said. "Why, she'd be the last one to go high-hat on a guy!" And then, remembering that he too had been snubbed, he added, "And on her own brother too!"

Jimmy scratched his head in puzzlement. When he eventually recovered from his outraged surprise, he turned and started to leave the stage and the theater.

"I knew there was something screwy about this whole business!" he said bitterly. "I don't like it, Frank! Something's going on that I don't understand! Something dirty and underhanded! Something that don't look good for Aline!"

IN HER sumptous suite in the Hamilton Arms Hotel, Aline also sensed that something was happening to her.

Seated in a flimsy negligee she had found among the complete wardrobe furnished her at the expense of the headless man, she looked into the mirror of the dressing-table and contemplated the amazing events that had suddenly changed the entire course of her life.

"Why did I do that to Jimmy?" she asked her reflection in the mirror. "I love Jimmy and I'm going to marry him. Why did I turn away from him? He looked so hurt standing there, as if I had slapped him on the face."

But she could find no answer to what had happened. Something within her had burrowed into her brain like a worm, and had forced her to say and do what she had said and done. Something uncontrollable that took hold of her, in spite of her real feelings, and forced her to do things against her will. She tried to think back to the recent events. Just before the winner had been announced, she had been thinking how nice it would be if she won the contest. Then she could marry Jimmy, as they had been planning all these years. Then they had announced her as the winner. Of course, she had been proud and felt flattered. But behind it all, she knew that she loved Jimmy and was going to marry him. Then the headless man had placed the Queen Viir necklace around her throat. Something sharp had penetrated her, at the time, she remembered. Something that was as cold as an icicle and seemed to bury its point deep into the innermost recesses of her heart.

She leaped up from the stool. Yes, she decided, it had been the necklace. But the headless man had warned her to keep it on all the time.

"It would anger the Queen Viir, if you took it off," he had said.

Aline looked into the mirror and saw the jewels of the necklace glinting coldly in the light. She tried to raise her hands to tear it away. But to her horror she discovered that she was unable to do it. And at the same time, she experienced a desire to allow it to remain. Some hidden force within her had rapidly taken hold of her slipping subconscious and was pulling up the distaste that had swept over her momentarily.

"No!" she said aloud, "I'm going to wear it. I'm proud of it!"

Her reverie was broken into by the sharp, incisive sound of the door-buzzer in the next room. Gathering the flowing hems of the dressing-gown around her, she opened the door of the boudoir and swept imperiously into the gorgeously decorated living room of the suite. When she opened the hall-door, she saw Jimmy and her brother Frank standing in the hall-way. Jimmy fiddled embarrassedly with his hat. Frank was puzzled.

"I told you I did not care to see you," she said. "And I don't want you to telephone me any more!" She tried to close the door on them but Jimmy shoved his foot into the doorway.

"Not so fast, hon!" he cried. He pushed the door open wider and, followed by Frank, entered the room. He looked around at the costly furnishings with a sinking heart. Aline wasn't the kind that fell for this kind of stuff, he thought. Something had happened to her. He looked into her cold face as though trying to uncover some sign of the girl who had been in love with him only a few days ago.

"What's come over you, Aline?" he asked.

"Nothing!" she retorted.

FRANK came to life. "What's the idea of pulling this high-hat stuff on your own brother and the guy you're going to marry?" he demanded.

"*Was* going to marry!" Aline interposed.

Jimmy stiffened. "What?" he demanded. "So it's come to this, huh?"

"Yes."

Jimmy was on the point of throwing an angry, bitter retort. But he remembered suddenly that he was confronted not with Aline, with the girl he loved and who loved him, but with someone else, with someone whose brain seemed to have been overcome by a foreign influence.

"What are you going to do, Aline?" he asked softly.

The answer to his question was given to him without a word being spoken. Subtly, he felt, incised into his subconscious, "She is going to leave with me for Haar."

Jimmy and Frank turned quickly. They saw, standing in the doorway leading to the adjoining suite, the figure of the headless man. There was a fearful air about the tableau. Under ordinary conditions, with a normal man involved, the scene would have been dramatic. But now, as the headless man stood in the doorway, there was a feeling of unreality about it all. It was as though they were experiencing the suffering of a monstrous nightmare.

"That's what you think!" Jimmy retorted.

"We've still got laws in this country!" Frank added.

Together, both of them heard the headless man say to them, "But there is no law which can prevent an adult person from doing as she wishes, is there?"

"Who says Aline wants to go with you?" Jimmy asked.

"Ask her yourself," the headless man said.

Frank turned to his sister. "You're not going off with this guy, Sis, are you?"

Aline stiffened imperiously. Her face showed no emotion. She stood there in front of her former fiancee and brother as though she were confronted by complete strangers.

"Are you going with him, Aline?" Jimmy asked.

Both of them waited for her reply. The air was electric with suspense. It crackled with the tenseness of pent-up emotions, of incipient decision. Jimmy could stand the strain no longer. He looked over to where the headless man was standing. He could see, from the attitude of the body, that there was self-assurance in the stance.

"Well, Aline?" he demanded.

There was a short pause. Then, Aline said in a cold, emotionless tone that was frigid with disdain, "Yes, I am!"

THE news of Aline McDonald's decision hit the populace like a bombshell. Even the thousands who had favored the contest became incensed at the turn of affairs.

"What right has that headless guy got coming here and grabbing off our women?" was the concensus of protests.

Editorial writers in most of the country's leading newspapers sounded off in the same vein. Radio commentators took up the hue and cry. Willis Ford, the "Voice of Romance," pleaded with his audience day after day until he was able to form a vast group of people who objected to the turn of events. Thousands of telegrams of protest were sent in to officials in Washington all of them demanding that something be done about allowing the headless man to leave the country with Aline McDonald.

And, in all this furore, Jimmy Hart remained aloof. "I've washed my hands of it all," he told Frank who had sought him out in one of Newspaper Row's taverns. "I've told Ryan I don't want anything more to do with it. Because if I start in shooting off my mouth objecting to Aline's going, they'll all think I'm doing it because she was going to marry me!"

But thousands of others in the country had no such qualms. A thousand Chicago women—the same ones who had clubbed together when the headless man had appeared in their midst a short time before — got together a petition and, a thousand strong, went to Washington to picket Congress bearing signs which read: "AMERICAN GIRLS FOR AMERICA" . . . "WE WANT NO HEADLESS HORRORS HERE" . . . KEEP ALINE McDONALD IN AMERICA."

Finally, because they felt it was their duty and also because they, themselves, objected to the whole business, Congress set up a commission to study the the affair. It was held one Monday morning, a week after Aline had made her momentous decision. The committee room was crowded with reporters. The general public, because of threats of murder against the headless man, was excluded. The headless man, himself, sat at the table. At his side, dressed in stunning, silver-fox furs, sat Aline McDonald, her face a cold, expressionless mask.

Jimmy and Frank were seated in the press box gloomily witnessing the proceedings. Jimmy's eyes were focused on Aline. He stared at her and tried to study the thoughts that moiled about behind the mask she was affecting.

Senator Goss of Alabama opened the proceedings by delivering a scathing denunciation of foreign monstrosities and wound up with a flowery defense of American womanhood.

Then the headless man was questioned. Once again his replies were wordless but were transmitted to all who were seated in the committee room and to millions of radio listeners by means of thought transference.

"I am a citizen of the Kingdom of Haar," the headless man insisted, "and my reasons for coming to your country have been entirely legitimate."

"But what about this 'body beautiful' contest you conducted?" one committee senator asked.

"Is there anything illegal about a beauty contest?" the headless man asked in reply. "Because, if there is, then there have been hundreds of illegal acts performed."

That retort bridled another of the senators. Leaping up from his seat, Senator Tom Gaines of Oklahoma, snorted out: "But the promoters of none of these beauty contests insisted on taking the flower of American womanhood out of this country and taking them to some unknown country of headless savages in the wilds of Central America!"

THERE was a long pause between this statement and the reply made by the headless man. Finally he was felt to say, "In the first place, I do not insist in taking Miss McDonald out of this country to my own country of Haar. And in the second place, my country is not populated by headless savages. I can assure you that, in most ways, we Haarians are far in advance of you Americans, scientifically, economically and otherwise. I suggest that instead of questioning me, you ask the woman in the case, herself. Surely, at twenty-one years of age, she should be able to know her own mind. I'm positive that there is no statute yet written in your country that prevents any adult from doing exactly as he or she sees fit. Why not ask her what she intends to do and why she intends to do it."

All eyes turned to Aline as she sat stiff-backed at the committee table.

There was something out-of-the-world about the way she sat there, a reflective Mona Lisa smile curling her lips, her eyes seemingly staring into distances far beyond the confines of the committee room.

"Do you voluntarily wish to leave this country?" Senator Goss bellowed at her, "with this . . . this man who is lacking a head?"

Aline looked coldly at her questioner. Then she turned and looked at the headless man and smiled. Her head nodded slightly. "Yes," she said, "of course I do."

"But why?" the senator thundered.

"Because I want to."

"Do you realize what may result from such a rash act?"

Aline's lips curled. "Do you?" she retorted, "know anything about the Kingdom of Haar?"

The questioning continued through the morning with nothing definite accomplished. When the proceedings were adjourned for lunch, Jimmy left the room, followed by Frank, and wound up at a tavern where he began to drink himself stupid. Frank saw what was in the cards and succeeded in getting Jimmy out of the tavern and into their car. There, he turned on the radio and started to drive aimlessly around.

Jimmy sat next to Frank, slumped deeply in the seat, moodily listening to the proceedings of the committee over the radio. It became quite obvious that the entire committee was dead set against Aline's decision to leave the country. From the line of questioning, an attempt was going to be made to force the headless man to return to Haar without his "body beautiful."

"Looks like they're going to force Aline to stay here," Frank commented. He got no response from Jimmy, so he looked down at him. "There's still a chance for us," he added.

Jimmy snorted. "Meaning what?"

Frank started off on another track. "Look, Jimmy," he said, "you loved her once, didn't you?"

"So what?" Jimmy snarled.

"You still do!"

"So what?"

"She's in trouble now," Frank said quietly, "and this is one helluva time for you to welch on her. You know yourself that she's not the same Aline we used to know. Something's come over her since that headless guy took over. He's got something to do with it. Maybe something to do with hypnotism, or thought transference, or something. Whatever it is, I'm sure that Aline is doing this, not because she wants to but because she's being forced to in some rotten, evil way!"

Jimmy sat up suddenly from his slouch. His lacklustre eyes brightened. "Yeah," he said, "maybe you're right. I've been acting like a kid that's had a lolly-pop taken away from it. Aline's in trouble. And she's going to get into it deeper if we don't do something about it!"

"That-a-boy, Jimmy!" Frank enthused. He stopped suddenly. "Wait a minute!" he said, "sounds like the committee's come to some sort of decision."

They waited silently, listening intently to the auto-radio. From it, they heard one of the committee member's summing up. "So the committee has decided," the voice said, "that it is going to recommend that you shall return to Haar without Miss McDonald. And not until we have been given sufficient evidence that no harm would befall her, in the event that she should be allowed to go with you, will she be allowed to leave this country!"

As Jimmy turned off the radio, the last words heard were those of the headless man protesting vigorously about the curtailing of Aline's personal rights.

"Let's get out to Aline's hotel!" Jimmy said. "She's stopping at the Mayfair. We'll barge into her room and take over. You're her only living relative and we'll insist that she be given in your charge!"

WHEN they arrived at the Mayfair, they found the lobby filled with newspaper reporters and photogs.

"What's up?" Jimmy asked of one of his colleagues.

"They haven't showed up yet," was the reply. "The headless guy snuck out of one of the rear entrances with the McDonald gal. We thought they'd come right out here but, so far, no soap!"

Suddenly, a cry broke out from a newcomer. "Just got a call saying their car was seen driving out to the airport!"

"Yeah!" another added, "I heard they came down here in the headless guy's plane!"

"Then he's going to kidnap her!" Jimmy cried out. "He's going to take her out of this country by force!" He started to run out of the hotel lobby followed by Frank, the mob of reporters at their heels.

"Where we going, Jimmy?" Frank puffed out.

"To the airport!" Jimmy cried as he flung himself into his car. He stepped on the starter and was soon roaring down the street.

"Think we can make it?" Frank asked.

"We've got to!"

"They've got a headstart on us."

Jimmy watched the speedometer quiver up to 75, then 80 and finally pause at 87. "Once he gets her out of this country," he said, "she's a goner!"

THEY reached the airport in ten minutes. Just as they pulled into the parking-lot, they heard a strange, hissing roar followed by a blazing flash of light. Looking into the air, they saw a plane whizzing through space so fast that it was difficult to identify its outlines.

"What's a rocket-ship doing here?" Frank cried.

"It's the headless man's plane!" Jimmy replied. "I knew there was something fishy about it when I saw it landing in New York!"

"There's no plane here that could follow it!" Frank said, shaking his head dolefully. "From what I hear, a rocket-plane that'll work could do over a thousand miles an hour!"

They ran from their car into the hangar area. There, they saw that one of the hangars was lighted up with its doors still flapping in the wind. An attendant stood close by, scratching his head.

"Was that the headless man's plane?" Jimmy demanded of the attendant.

"Was that a *plane?*" the attendant threw back. "Man! I ain't never seen a plane shoot out like that one did!"

"Was there a woman in it?" Frank asked.

"Yeah!" the attendant replied, "a woman an' a guy without a head, the same one I been reading about, an' . . ."

"Where's there another plane we can hire?" Jimmy demanded, "the fastest plane here?"

"What you planning on, Jimmy?" Frank asked.

"We've got to follow that plane and try to keep up with it! It's our last and only chance!"

The attendant started off to a hangar close by. "There's a pretty fast number here," he said, "if you've got someone to fly it."

"I've got a pilot's license," Frank said.

The attendant stopped at the hangar. "By the way," he said, reaching into his pocket, "if you catch that plane, you might give the guy this map or something that fell outen his pocket." He handed the map over to Jimmy.

Jimmy peered down at it for a moment. "We're in luck!" he cried out. "It's an air-map showing the headless guy's route from where he came." He traced a route of arrows with his fingertip. "See, it goes from New York to this spot in Central America. Terrabona, it's called!"

"Us for Terrabona, then!" Frank interrupted.

"That's about 1500 air miles from here so we'd better put in some extra tanks of gas. With that rocket-plane, they'll get to Terrabona in a couple of hours. It'll take us about five hours. The map here shows this guys destination to be somewhere west of Terrabona where the arrows stop. Our only chance is to cruise around the Terrabona area in the hope that we may spot some secret landing field. It's our only chance to save Aline!"

IN A few hours, they were winging their way across the country. Soon they passed New Orleans and found themselves over the Gulf of Mexico.

"This is all new territory to me," Frank said as he looked over the side of the cockpit into the blue waters of the Gulf.

"How's your navigation?" Jimmy asked.

"Fair," Frank replied, "but I think I can take her to Terragona. While we were gassing up, I got some dope from a pilot who's flown the Central American line. Gave me a lot of landmarks and tips. Said it shouldn't be hard to find. Told me, though, to watch out for the mountains. Said there are lots of them around the neighborhood."

"How's the gas holding out?"

"O.K. Depends on how much cruising around we'll have to do looking for that airfield."

After a few more hours, they found themselves hovering over a small, sleepy, Central American town.

"That's it, all right," Frank said, "I can tell by the gas-tanks and the white buildings that pilot told me would be here. Three of them, he said."

"There's three, all right!"

"So, what now?"

"Start cruising in circles," Jimmy said, "widening circles and keep your eyes peeled to the ground for some kind of an airfield—and keep your fingers crossed!"

AN OMINOUS sputtering from the motor, about an hour later, warned them of the predicament that was soon to befall them.

"Oh-oh!" Frank cried out.

"What's the matter?"

"Gas is gone!" Jimmy replied. "I switched on the last tank a few minutes ago. We'll have to find some place to land—but quick!"

Jimmy looked over the side of the cockpit. Down below he saw only vast stretches of almost impenetrable green forests.

"This plane ain't equipped to land on trees!" Frank said.

Jimmy looked ahead. He saw a twin range of mountain peaks looming ahead in the gathering gloom. A tiny valley nestled between the two peaks. At first, he was able to see only a lush, green carpet of trees covering the entire valley. But, suddenly, he discerned something white glistening near the center of the valley's forest.

"What's that?" he hollered at Frank, pointing with his finger ahead.

Frank looked in the direction that Jimmy was indicating. "It's an airfield!" he cried out joyfully, "and just as we were on our last drop of gas. I'll have to take her in on a glide."

"Think you can make it between those two peaks?"

"I've landed in tighter spots than that!" Frank replied. "What's more, if it's an airfield, other guys have done it so I guess I can too." He prepared to maneuver the plane so that he could get her down as gently as possible. Jimmy sat tight as he watched Frank manipulate the controls, his palms moist with sweat. Slowly, almost hesitantly, the big plane came down between the towering crags like a huge, silent prehistoric monster-bird, its wing-tips, at times, grazing against the sides of the wall-like heights that reared up closely on both sides.

Suddenly the plane seemed to lose altitude.

"Easy!" Jimmy cried out.

"Rotten air-currents!" Frank said. "That airfield looks like a postage stamp from here. You'd better get set for a landing crack-up just to make sure."

"Watch out for those trees ahead!"

"If I can clear them, we're set."

Lower and lower the plane settled itself, gradually drawing closer to the tops of the trees that towered immediately in front of the airfield and also surrounded it completely from all sides.

"Hold on!" Frank hollered.

They heard an ominous scraping of branches against the belly of their plane. Then, all of a sudden, the scraping stopped. The plane was in the clear. Immediately ahead of them stretched out a narrow expanse of flat, white runway.

"Here goes nothing!" Frank said quietly.

They both sat tight expectantly awaiting the worst. Instead, they felt a sharp, heavy bump beneath them.

Then came smooth rolling.

"We made it!" Frank cried happily as he brought the plane to a stop in the air-strip.

"Have your gun ready," Jimmy warned; "you may have to use it."

THEY waited for some time before descending from the plane, on the alert for anyone hostile to approach them. But no one did. Meanwhile, they used the time to look around at their surroundings.

"What's that funny doo-jigger doing there at the end of the field?" Frank asked.

Jimmy looked. He saw what appeared to be a canopy of green boughs crossing the entire width of the field at the extreme end. He trained his binoculars on it.

"It's a camouflage top," he said suddenly. "It's supposed to be rolled over the field when it's not in use. I can see the tracks on the side where the rollers glide. That's how come this place has never been discovered from the air. When the canopy of boughs is rolled over the top, the whole thing looks like a forest of trees from a plane."

"Guess they forgot to roll it back this time," Frank said, "or we'd never have found it."

"They must have all gone with the headless man and Aline," Jimmy said reflectively. "Because of the big doings, I'll bet. That's why we weren't met by a welcoming committee." He opened the door of the cockpit. "Come on, guy!" he said. "We'd better get started before anything happens to Aline!"

Followed by Frank, Jimmy hopped out of the plane, prepared himself with his gun and started to walk off to the right where there appeared to be a sort of hangar. They approached it slowly.

By this time, twilight had already given way to night and it was completely dark. Jimmy got out his flashlight and trained its beam on the hangar. They saw that it yas empty. Behind it, they saw a small highway leading directly into the mountain-side.

"No wonder," Jimmy whispered, "this Kingdom of Haar is in a mountain. That's why it hasn't ever been discovered!"

Cautiously, they advanced up the road and into an immense hole in the mountain. They followed the tortuous winding of a huge cavern hewn out of solid rock. They were amazed to discover that the immense cave was flooded with blazing light.

"Some kind of indirect lighting," Jimmy said.

"Gosh!" Frank breathed wonderingly, "indirect lighting an' rocket planes. What next?"

In a short time, still undetected, they had traversed the entire length of the cavern and approached another opening. They went up to it cautiously. Then, when they were certain they were not being observed, they stepped out of the opening and found themselves standing on a high promontory overlooking a tiny valley. To their amazement, although it was night, the valley was illumined into the brightness of day. High up they could see the rock ceiling of an enormous cave. At regular intervals, around the periphery of the valley, they saw immense platforms on which were placed giant flood-lights which threw a brilliant blanket of light, of neon intensity, into every nook and cranny of the valley floor.

"Let's get down," Jimmy said. "There's big doings going on or else we'd never have got this far without bumping into someone. They must be all gathered to welcome the guy without a head."

"And Aline," Frank added.

Slowly, hugging the side of the cave, they descended the steep-grade road. As they went down, they saw finely carved doors and casement windows chiseled into the sides of the cavern.

"Their houses," Jimmy commented.

FINALLY they came to what appeared to be an enormous amphitheater at the end of the road. The air was strangely, ominously quiet although, somehow, they got the impression that a large amount of people were gathered together close by. Throwing themselves on the ground, they inched their way to the rim of the amphitheater until soon they saw that they were looking into a sort of half-bowl scooped out of the valley floor. A great crowd of people were seated in a semi-circle around a raised dais at the flat end of the half-bowl.

"Holy smoke!" Frank whispered loudly. "Look! They're all like that headless guy we saw back home! There ain't a solitary head among them!"

"There's Aline way down there!" Jimmy said, "with the headless guy who came to the U. S."

"What's that they're standing in front of?" Frank asked. "Looks like some kind of an idol to me."

Jimmy adjusted his binoculars to his eyes. He lay there for almost a full minute. Finally, he cried out in a hoarse whisper, "For the love o' Mike!"

"What's up?"

"That's a head they're standing in front of!" Jimmy whispered excitedly, "just a plain, ordinary head of a woman, and with no body attached to it! It's resting on a golden platter with a lot of hair streaming out from behind!"

"This is getting screwier all the time!" Frank sputtered. "What the hell's a woman's bodiless head doing here among all these headless bodies?"

"A dollar to a dime it's Queen Viir!" Jimmy said; "the one that headless guy was always talking about. No wonder she sent him to the U. S. to conduct a body beautiful contest. The gal hasn't got a body herself and she . . ." He stopped short suddenly. "No!" he cried out in distress, "it couldn't be that!"

"What?"

"It just occurred to me," Jimmy explained, "that Aline was brought back here because of her body, because this bodiless queen wants to use it in some awful way!"

"They're starting something," Frank broke in. "Let's us watch and see what happens."

ALINE stood next to the headless man, in front of the bodiless head, and experienced no sense of fear. She couldn't understand it. Ordinarily, she knew, she would have been horrified at the sight of what she was witnessing. Even when she had ducked out with the headless man and driven out to his plane, she had not been afraid. There was something in the back of her brain that seemed to be directing her, that seemed to be telling her what to do and say. Like when she had told Jimmy that she didn't want to see him any more and like when she had told the committee that she really wanted to go away with the headless man. Her first reaction had always been to follow her normal desires but it had always been interposed by the commands given her at the base of her brain.

Standing now in front of Queen Viir, she could sense the pull of the directionalizing even more. But a horrible fear did creep over her when she saw the eyes of the head on the golden platter roam over her entire body almost

lasciviously. There was evil in them.

"You have done very well, Naar," the queen said to the headless man who had brought Aline.

The headless man bowed. "She has the most beautiful body in the entire United States," he said.

The mouth in the queen's head grinned widely. "Let us waste no time," she said. "I want my surgeons to prepare the operating table immediately. I want to have her body as soon as possible." She turned her eyes to Aline. "You are not afraid, little one?" she asked.

Aline shook her head. "No," she said, and she wondered why she should be speaking the words. "I think it's an honor for me to have my beautiful body desired by Queen Viir, who has such a beautiful face!"

The queen smiled. "With your beautiful body and my beautiful face, I shall be the most beautiful person in the entire world!"

They were interrupted by the sound of a commotion coming from the extreme end of the amphitheater. A mass of the headless people were milling around with long-fingered arms flailing the air.

"Who dares interrupt me?" the queen demanded.

A headless man came running up to the dais and fell to his face, with his arms outstretched. "We have caught two men with heads!" he conveyed to the queen through thought transference.

"Two men with heads?" The queen became incensed. "How did they manage to get in? Who are they? Have them brought to me immediately!"

The messenger left. In a short while he returned, followed by a group of the headless men. Their long, prehensile fingers were coiled around Jimmy and Frank. They had been surprised as they had peered over the edge of the amphitheater. For, suddenly, they had found themselves being leaped on from behind. Long, octopus-like fingers curled around their bodies, preventing them from fighting back. And soon they were helpless and being dragged to the raised dais where Aline stood in front of the bodiless queen.

Aline was almost startled out of her wits when she recognized Jimmy and Frank. Something deep within her went out to them in their predicament. But a stronger, hidden censor seemed to force her to squelch the feelings of sympathy. Instead, she found herself becoming incensed at their actions. She looked down at them, lying in the dust, coldly, as if she resented their intrusion.

Behind them, a mass of headless people menaced them, their angry, elongated fingers coiling about nervously like the hair-snakes of Medusa's head.

Then the queen spoke. "What are you doing here?" she demanded of them.

SLOWLY Jimmy raised himself up from the dust and looked up to where the voice was coming from. He was startled to hear a human voice break into the awful silence of the headless people.

"Well, answer me!" the queen insisted.

Jimmy arose from the ground and slapped the dust from his trousers. "We followed the girl here," he said, "to make sure that nothing would happen to her!"

"How did you land?"

"On the airfield. One of your people must have forgotten to pull back the camouflage."

The queen smiled ironically. "It will do her no good," she said, "nor you either. There have been only a few

people with heads who happened to wander into this country. But they died hideous deaths—just as you two will soon die. Nobody has come into the Valley of Haar and lived to return to the outer world in all the thousands of years that I have reigned over it as Queen Viir."

"What about the girl?" Jimmy asked.

"She came here of her own free will," the queen replied.

"I'm not so sure of that." Jimmy looked around at all the headless people and saw that all of them had some sort of harness or necklace around their shoulders. The thought suddenly occurred to him that the necklace the headless man had placed around Aline's throat, which she still wore, had something to do with the radical change that had come over her.

"That necklace you gave her, I'm sure it had something to do with her coming here."

The queen smiled. "You are right," she said, "but the information will do you no good now."

"What do you intend to do with her?" Jimmy asked.

"Use her," the queen replied. "That is, I intend to use her body only. As you can see, I haven't got a body. I was born without a body thousands of years ago just as my subjects, the men of Haar, were born without heads. And because I possessed the only head in the entire community, I was made queen of the Haarians. I am their head both in spirit and in body. I am their mass brain. They are unable to think, because they have no brain, unless I transmit thought processes to them, by means of the necklaces you have observed that they wear."

"That's why you had your man give the girl the necklace," Jimmy said.

"Exactly," the queen replied. "Actually, that necklace is a powerful receiving apparatus, devised by our Haarian scientists, which contains a tiny needle at the back. The moment this needle pierces the body, there is a direct connection made between my brain and the body of the person wearing the necklace. And that person becomes the slave of my brain."

"You still haven't told me what you intend to do with the girl," Jimmy said.

"I tolerate you and answer your questions," the queen replied, "only because I know you won't ever be able to use the knowledge. Because you will soon be dead. You and your friend and the girl. But her body will not die. Only her spirit will be killed. Because I want her beautiful body."

She turned her eyes and looked at a number of the headless men standing around attired in surgical white clothing. "As you see," the queen continued, "my master surgeons are waiting to detach the body from her head and, in turn, attach the body to my head. You see, I'm a woman and, being a woman, I sometimes entertain the whim of desiring a beautiful body. I have had a number of other beautiful bodies attached to my head, bodies of beautiful girls whom my subjects captured for that express purpose. But, being human, these bodies all withered and died. Now, I have the desire for another beautiful body. And that body, as you know now, will be that of the girl you followed into the Valley of Haar."

JIMMY tried to think fast but no solution came. Finally, he decided to play on the romantic element. "She was going to marry me," he said.

A mocking smile flashed across the features of the queen's head. "That is quite interesting," she said. "My plans were to have you and your friend killed immediately. But I think I'll let you live a while longer. To allow you to

marry her—after I have had her body attached to me at midnight!"

The smile disappeared from her face. It was supplanted by a look of vicious cruelty. At the same moment, she gave some orders to the headless men, through thought transference. Jimmy and Frank found themselves leaped upon suddenly. Once more, the octopus fingers of the headless men insinuated themselves like live snakes around their arms and legs. And, although they fought hard to extricate themselves, their strength increased by the awful realization of Aline's fate, they were unsuccessful. And soon they found themselves being hustled into a small cave in the side of the valley, a short distance away from the amphitheater. There they were flung into the narrow confines of a dungeon. Then a barred door was locked behind them.

"What now?" Jimmy said. He got up from the stone floor and looked around the stone cave. From the extreme top came a thin shaft of light streaming through a barred hole. Other than that, and the barred door, there was no other opening or means of escape. The room was bare of furnishings.

"Looks as if this is where we write finished to everything," Frank said gloomily.

"Think of what's going to happen to Aline!"

"Yeah," Frank replied, "and think of what we thought of her when it was really that damned necklace she was wearing that made her act the way she did."

"We've got to do something!" Jimmy said as he paced the floor. "We've got to find some way of getting her out of this jam!"

Frank seated himself on the floor. "What?" he said.

Jimmy started to go through his

pockets. Everything had been taken away from him. "How about you, Frank?" he said. "Got anything in your pockets they missed?"

Frank searched his pockets and brought nothing up as well. Suddenly, a grin suffused his face.

"What's up?" Jimmy demanded.

"It should be in my watch-pocket," Frank replied, "and, if it isn't, we can just as well lay down here and die!" He raised his hand slowly to his watch-pocket and tapped it hesitantly. "Be there, please!" he said prayerfully.

"Don't tell me it's a collapsible tommy-gun!"

"It may help just as well!"

"Well?"

"Yeah!" Frank said with a grin, "I got it!" He stuck his hand into his pocket and withdrew a knife. "I stuck it in there just in case," he said.

JIMMY looked around carefully and stepped over to the barred door to make certain they were not being watched. Then he went back to Frank and took the knife. It contained a long, sharp blade. "So far, so good," he said, "now we've got to get a chance to use it."

"I'm hungry," Frank suggested.

"Swell," Jimmy replied. "Let's set up a holler for some food. They'll have a guard hanging around even though most of them are hanging around for the fireworks to begin at midnight. What time is it now?"

Frank looked at his wristwatch. "Eleven-thirty."

"We've got half an hour."

"Suppose we do knock over the guard?" Frank asked; "how the heck are we going to get away with a measly little knife against all those headless monkeys out there?"

"I've got an idea," Jimmy replied thoughtfully. "I got it from the queen.

I've got a hunch it'll work. But if it doesn't, it'll give us an outside chance, at least, of trying to do something to save Aline!" He hid the knife in his pocket. "Start hollering for food!" he said. "Then, when the guard comes in, you stand in that corner and I'll stand here. I'll have the knife ready and jump him when he goes over to you. Start hollering!"

Frank walked to the opposite side of the cell and began to holler for food. For a while they heard nothing but the sound of his voice reverberating through the cave. Then, after a few minutes, they heard approaching footsteps. Jimmy cautioned Frank to get ready and prepared himself at the opposite end of the cell the while he fingered the open knife in his pocket.

Soon they saw one of the headless men appear at the door. By means of thought projection, he demanded the reason for the uproar.

"I'm hungry!" Frank complained, "I haven't had a bit of food all day!"

The headless guard hesitated at the doorway. Then, without a word, he turned and left them.

"Do you think——" Frank began.

Jimmy hushed him, shaking his head and pointing to his mouth as though telling him not to talk. They waited for some time. Soon they heard approaching footsteps again. This time the guard appeared with a jug in his hand. He unlocked the door and walked over to where Frank was standing.

The second the guard's back was turned, Jimmy withdrew the knife from his pocket and leaped at the guard slashing first at the headless man's fingers. Fortunately, the knife-blade was sharp and it cut off the guard's forefinger cleanly.

Meanwhile, Frank had leaped on the guard and had pinned him down to the floor as Jimmy continued to slash at the fingers sawing them off one by one on the stone floor. Only when he had cut off all ten writhing fingers did he put the knife aside and go to the aid of Frank as he lay on the floor struggling with the headless body. Together, they managed to dispose of the guard so that soon they were both seated on top of him breathing heavily from their exertions.

"What'll we do with him now?" Frank asked.

Jimmy began to rip off his shirt. "Take off yours, too," he said, "and we'll tie this bird up. We haven't got much time to lose. They'll soon be started on that decapitation business!"

Soon they had the guard completely trussed up. "Lucky we don't have to gag this guy," Frank cracked, "I've used up all my cloth in tying his legs."

JIMMY motioned for him to be silent. Then he pushed the body into a dark corner and made for the cell door. After peering up and down the corridor, he beckoned to Frank and, with knife in hand, started off down the dark corridor, followed by Frank.

They hesitated for a while when they came to the entrance of the corridor leading to the side of the mountain through which they had entered. They listened for tell-tale sounds. None came. Instead, they heard weird music issuing from the amphitheater a short distance down the road.

"They left only one guy to watch us," Jimmy whispered; "the rest of them are down at the big doings. We've got to be careful from now on," he added. "I've got to get to the head without being caught. If we can do that, my hunch tells me that we can get ourselves out of this mess."

Jimmy started forward and opened the door. He peered through the crack.

No one was around. Then he opened the door wider and saw that the road leading down to the amphitheater was deserted.

"We're still in luck," he whispered. He stepped out of the doorway and started off down the road. Frank followed behind, making certain that they, in turn, were not being followed. In a few minutes, they again found themselves at the rim of the vast amphitheater looking down at the proceedings. This time, though, they were only a few feet from the raised dais.

They flung themselves down to the ground and watched what was going on. "I can make it," Jimmy whispered, "with a little luck!"

"What are you going to do?" Frank asked.

"Look," Jimmy replied, "as soon as you see me jump up and make for the head, I want you to follow right behind me and try to stop anyone who tries to stop me. The point is this: I've got to get to the head before they get to me!"

Frank interrupted him. "Look!" he said, "they're starting the business already!"

Jimmy turned. He saw Aline lying outstretched on an enormous stone sacrificial altar. Grouped around her were a number of headless men gowned in white robes. An array of strange instruments were standing about in readiness. And off to one side, the head of Queen Viir was lying on a long, white operating table, also waiting in readiness.

Jimmy turned and looked at the mass of headless people. From the attitude of their bodies and from the way they were waving their fingers in the air, he could see that they were concentrating their attention on the decapitation proceedings that were going on. None of them seemed to be paying attention to the head of Queen Viir. Even she was staring fascinatedly at the body of the girl lying outstretched on the altar, the body that was soon to be hers.

"This is it!" Jimmy whispered.

"O.K.," Frank replied.

Jimmy got a firm hold on the knife in his hand. He took a final glance at the route he would have to take to get to the head of Queen Viir making a mental note that he would have to push aside two of the headless people who stood in the way.

"Here goes!" he said. "Now don't forget to keep them off my back," he cautioned.

He rose up from the ground swiftly. Then followed by Frank, he leaped over the rim and made for the head of the queen. He shoved aside two of the headless people in his mad rush the while Frank, behind him, prevented another, who had caught sight of them, from leaping on Jimmy's back. At the same moment, Queen Viir saw Jimmy approaching, his knife in hand.

"Stop where you are!" she screamed.

ALMOST instantly the attention of the other headless people was turned on Jimmy and Frank as they rushed up the dais and made for the queen's head. They saw, with their quivering raised forefingers, that Jimmy had seized hold of the queen's head, by the hair, and was holding it at arm's length with his left hand while, with his right hand, he poised the point of his knife almost touching an eye of the head.

"My people will tear you to bits!" the queen screamed. "Let me down, I command you, let me down!"

"Let one of them make a step up here," Jimmy replied, "and I'll stick this knife right through your eye!"

"You wouldn't dare!' the queen cried.

"Test me, then, and you'll see!"

Dangling in the air by her hair, the queen looked around wildly. Finally, she said quietly, "Well, what do you want?"

"That's obvious," Jimmy replied. "First, command your men to get the girl off that altar."

The queen hesitated momentarily. Finally she said, "Untie the girl."

The men grouped around the altar complied. Aline sat up from it and looked around her. When she saw Jimmy and Frank standing on the dais, her lip curled in disdain. "You should not have done this," she said.

Jimmy turned to Frank. "Take that necklace off her throat!"

Frank strode over to the altar, reached up and lifted the necklace up and away from Aline's neck. A change seemed to come over instantly. A violent shudder shook her entire body as though she were throwing off something painful and evil. And when she looked at Jimmy again, the disdain was gone.

"Jimmy!" she wailed. "What's happened, what's happened!"

Frank helped her off the altar and, with his arm around her waist, aided her in getting to where Jimmy was standing on the dais with his arm aloft and dangling the head of the queen.

"Take it easy, honey!" Jimmy cautioned her. "We've got the upper hand now and everything's going to turn out all right. You've gone through an awful experience, but it's all ended now. We're going to be soon headed for home." He turned to the queen's head. "Aren't we, Queen Viir?" he asked.

"What is it you want now?" the queen asked.

"Safe conduct," Jimmy replied. "I want you to warn your people that we're to be allowed to go through them and get to my plane. If one of them moves a finger to stop us, this knife is going to be sunk smack into that little right eye of yours."

Seeing that she could do nothing else, Queen Viir issued the necessary orders. The headless men hesitantly made a wide aisleway through the center of the mass. And when Jimmy saw that it extended to the extreme end of the amphitheater, he made ready to go through it.

"No funny business, Queenie!" he warned. Then he stepped down from the dais. "Follow close behind me," he warned Frank and Aline. "And watch out for anyone who tries to get us from behind. This gal may be sending out orders to them by thought waves to pull something like that. You aren't, are you Queenie?" He shook the head by the hair.

"Be careful with that knife!" the queen hissed from between clenched teeth.

THEY began to walk through the headless men and women massed on both sides of them like two quivering walls of ominous doom. Occasionally, Jimmy was forced to menace the queen's eye with his knife as an obstreperous one would take a step forward as to throw himself bodily at them. But they soon reached the extreme end of the amphitheater where they scrambled up to the rim, almost at the same spot where they had been caught a short time before.

"Warn them," Jimmy advised the queen, "that we don't want to be followed."

The queen did as she was bade. And when he was satisfied that her orders were going to be carried out, Jimmy turned away from the amphitheater and started back up the road that they had come down on. Frank and Aline followed behind.

"What are we going to do now?" Aline asked fearfully.

"We've got our plane waiting for us at the airfield," Jimmy replied. Then he turned to Queen Viir. "I'm not telepathic," he said sarcastically, "but if you're planning on sending thought messages to your aviators, you'd better forget about it. Because I'm going to hold onto your head until we're up and away, until I'm sure we won't be attacked by your rocket warships."

A look of horror crept into the queen's face. "You must not do that!" she said, "my people will be lost without me!"

"That's their look-out!" Jimmy replied.

By that time, they had reached the tunnel leading to the airfield. Standing on the promontory of rock, they looked down behind them and saw the crowd of headless people standing massed together in the amphitheater. Then, without wasting more time, the trio rushed through the tunnel and came out to the airfield on the other side.

"The plane's still there!" Frank cried out.

"Good!" Jimmy said. "Now get her warmed up and let's get out of here!"

"You're not taking me with you!" the queen protested. Her eyes began to roll wildly. A look of frightened terror haunted her eyes.

"Why not?" Jimmy asked.

"You don't know what would happen," the queen cried wildly.

"Do you?"

"Yes!" the queen replied, "it would be horrible!" Then, changing the tone of her voice, she said pleadingly, "Please set me down before you leave and go on your way without me! Don't take me away from here!" Now her face became contorted with fear. Her eyes popped from her head like fiery balls of flame.

"How are you doing, Frank?" Jimmy called out.

In the cockpit, Frank was already testing his instruments to make certain that they had not been tampered with. He had helped his sister up to the seat beside him and had his hand ready on the starter.

"O.K. by me!" Frank hollered back. "I've got her all tanked up with some gas I found."

Holding the queen's head straight out, Jimmy stepped onto the wing of the plane and then swung over the side of the cabin as the queen spouted virulent threats at him.

"You'll regret it, you fool!" the queen raged. "Put me down this instant! I'll have you cut to pieces! My men will tear you apart!"

Grinning, Jimmy swung over into the cabin where Aline pushed over to make room for him. "Think we can make it on this short runway?" he asked Frank.

Frank surveyed the flood-lighted airfield. "I can if I swing her around," he said. "We can start taxiing from that end of the field and, with a little luck, I think I can clear it!"

"Good!" Jimmy replied, "let's get going!"

FRANK pulled at the starter. The motor roared on with a crackling splutter as the propeller whirled. When Frank gave her the gun, the motor began to turn over beautifully. That done, Frank began to turn the plane until he was able to make the straight-of-way to the end of the field. That done, he reversed the plane again. The entire length of the runway confronted them now. Then, giving her the gun again, Frank started the plane down the runway. Soon she was skimming the ground lightly. Up and up she went. For a moment it looked as if

the plane would not clear the edge of the line of trees that came bearing down on them. But with a seemingly super-human effort, the plane lunged upward just as the tree-tops brushed against the bottom of the plane scraping ominously on the aluminum skin.

"Made it!' Frank chortled.

Aline emitted a sigh of relief.

Queen Viir spat in contempt. "What are you going to do with me?" she demanded of Jimmy who was still holding her out at arm's length in the cockpit.

"Take you home," Jimmy replied, "and hand you over to some medical school for examination!"

The queen groaned. "You mustn't! You mustn't do that!" she implored. Tears began to stream from her eyes.

"What would happen if I did?"

"My people would have no leader—no brain. They would run berserk without me."

"I still thing it's my duty to bring you back to America!" Jimmy said.

"You are determined?" the queen said.

"Yes!"

"Very well," she replied. "Then it will mean the end of the glorious race of Haarians. I still retain contact with them through my brain. If you do not release me, return me to my people, I shall give them orders to destroy the entire Valley of Haar, blow it to pieces and themselves with it."

"The world would be better off without them," Jimmy said.

"That means," the queen continued, "that you will lose me, too. You see, my fate is inextricably bound with theirs. When they die, I shall die, too and my head will disintegrate into dust."

"What shall we do, Jimmy?" Aline asked anxiously.

"Nothing," Jimmy replied resolutely. "If what she says is true—and I don't believe it because I think it's just a gag she's trying to pull on us—but, if it's true, then maybe it'll be all for the best. In some evil way, this monstrosity and the monstrosities she has been ruling have managed to live this long surrounded by an entirely normal world of normal people. If they continued to exist, they might conceive the idea of doing away with the rest of the world, like they were going to do away with us, and create a world of super-human headless men of Haar!"

"That is not so!" the queen screamed, "we only wanted to live in peace with the rest of the world!"

"But you were going to murder us and this girl," Jimmy said, "just to satisfy a feminine whim of yours for a beautiful body!"

"She would have become a queen with me!" the queen replied haughtily.

"When all the time she would have preferred being my wife. I'm sorry," Jimmy said with finality. "I'm taking you back with us!"

THE queen did not reply. Instead, she began to weep. And, as the tears streamed down her cheeks, a terrific explosion sounded over the roar of the motors. It was followed by a series of other earth-shaking detonations of enormous magnitude that rocked the plane perilously in the throes of a tremendous updraft.

Jimmy stood up in the cockpit and looked behind. He saw the entire countryside bathed in a weird glow of fire. And far in the distance, he saw the twin peaks of the mountain range they had just left toss and churn like a mountain of molten lava. Then there came a tremendous explosion far greater than the preceding ones, a detonation that seemed to rock the entire world. Jimmy watched with awe as he saw the twin mountain peaks suddenly disintegrate as a vast volcanic spout of flame and billows of smoke shot up into the heavens. When the upheaval had subsided, Jimmy saw that where there had once been two mountain peaks, there was now a flat terrain of rubbled land.

Only then did Jimmy turn away from the scene of horror and reseat himself next to Aline. She had lost control of herself and was weeping with her face buried in her hands. Throwing a protective arm around her shoulders, Jimmy said, "It's all for the best."

Frank stared straight ahead in the night intent on his navigation, a lump choking his throat.

Suddenly, Jimmy looked down to where he had put the queen's head. Instead of a head he saw a small pile of dust, gray and powdery.

"Well, I'll be——" he cried out.

Aline looked up startledly from her hands. Frank turned his attention from navigation and looked questioningly at Jimmy. Both turned their eyes to the little mound of dust that Jimmy was eyeing unbelievingly.

"She went and did it!" Frank said.

"The end of the headless horror!" Aline whispered.

All of a sudden, a vagrant puff of wind blew down into the cockpit and caught the mound of dust. The dust swirled momentarily and then was carried out of the plane into the free air where it was completely lost.

None of them spoke after that for a long time.

Jimmy eventually broke the silence. Bending over Aline's tear-stained face, he cupped her chin in his free hand. "Body beautiful," he said tenderly, "from now on, you're going to be beautiful only for one guy!"

"For you," Aline whispered.

And, in reply, Jimmy lowered his face to hers and kissed her on the lips.

MIDAS MORGAN'S

BY EMIL PETAJA

ILLUSTRATED BY ARNOLD KOHN

**With the gift of the golden touch,
Morgan thought his worries were over.
But it wasn't until he lost his queer ability
that it proved to be profitable.**

I SIGHED wistfully.

Here I was, as usual, waiting for Susie May. The Sixth and Hill Streets corner was a criss-cross pattern of motion. Sleek-uniformed soldiers escorted starry-eyed dames. Cocky pairs of sailors strutted by. And all the warp and woof that makes Los Angeles a city of hodge-podge and varied life.

It was Sunday afternoon.

The sun knew that. It had a special golden sheen.

Susie May had lingered after church. She was the nucleus of a committee designated to furnish eats for the coming Sunday School picnic.

The ladies had got to gabbing, I guessed, and forgot there was such a thing as time. I'd been waiting fully an hour now.

But that wasn't why I was wistful.

Necks were craned toward the Victory House, in Persian Square. It was

GOLDEN TOUCH

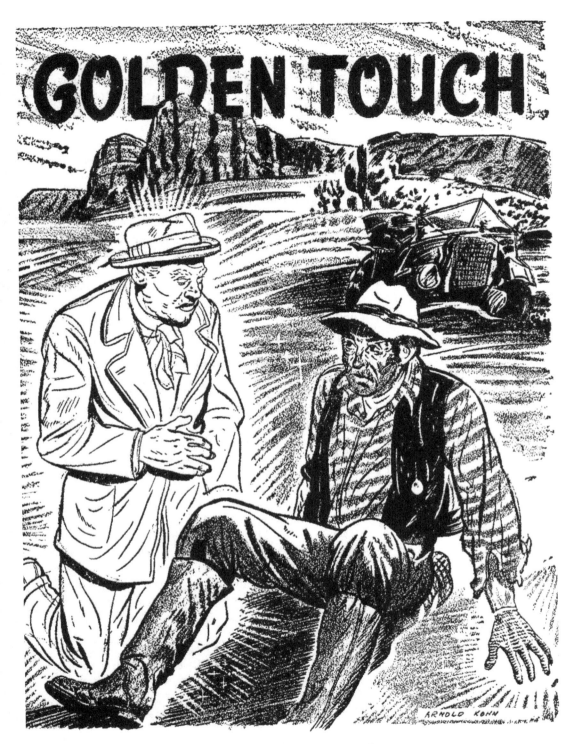

Doc Saunders didn't move. He couldn't—because
he was now an eighteen karat solid gold statue!

163

directly behind me.

I turned, and saw a buxom matron in a bulgy uniform exhorting the big crowd to buy War Bonds, and to keep right on buying them until Mussolini was occupied in digging Hitler's grave in the back yard of Sing Sing, while Hirohito's widow wept on.

The band played the "Star Spangled Banner." My tootsies tingled. That song gets me, way down deep.

"Well, anyhow," I consoled myself meagrely, "if it hadn't been for my cross-eyes and flat feet they'd have took me sure." I dreamed up a quaint vision of my spindle shanks in khaki. "If it hadn't been for my trick pump, my hay fever, and that lonesome lung of mine."

"Nice day," somebody shattered my reverie. Somebody with a raspy dry voice.

"Susie May'll be along any minute now." My mind repeated, over and over, like a busted phonograph record.

I drummed my fingers absently against the stone railing that enclosed a clump of banana palms. I ignored the voice.

"It *is* a nice day," the dry voice persisted petulantly. "That old sun up there looks 'zactly like a gol-danged million dollar gold piece!"

I TURNED.

The voice exuded from a tangle of wiry dirty-white whiskers attached to an oldster. He was attired in ancient dirt-shiny overalls held up by a length of clothesline rope.

I scanned him from top to toe.

His face, besides the whiskers, was more wrinkled than the last prune in the box. I couldn't tell whether it was more dirty than it was tanned by sun and wind, or vice versa.

That goes double in spades for his feet, which were frankly unshod.

His matted hair was without hat. His denim-shirted arms were shoved down under his overall bib, and he stood there rocking on his heels and grinning at me somewhere under that shrubbery like a Cheshire Cat.

"I'm Morgan," he offered cheerfully, spitting a little brown lake in front of me. "They call me Midas Morgan."

"Is that a fact?" was all I said.

"It shore is!" he affirmed, wiggling his toes. "Would you like to know *why* they call me 'Midas' Morgan?"

"No."

"All right then." He took hold of my arm, and led me over to a crowded bench, where he squeezed out room for us to sit. "I'll tell you."

"I'VE hunted for gold all my life," the bearded one began, holding my skinny arm in a vise-like grip. "I guess you'd call me an old desert rat."

"I'd like to call you more than that!" I muttered, but being a sway-backed runt of a bookkeeper wearing thick bifocals, I wanted no trouble. I waved my arms in a gesture of futility, muttering, "Here we go again," under my breath.

"All right. So you're a rat," I said testily. "And where was it you did most of your gold-hunting?"

"In the Mohave Desert," Morgan replied, grinning, and loosing my arm. "And my father hunted gold there afore me.

"I could talk on for hours about our years of living on salt pork and beans, sleeping in any old kind of a crackerbox, grubbing and grubbing away like a couple of gophers. Always hoping we'd strike on to a rich vein.

"There wasn't much pay dirt, only durn plenty fool's gold, and heart-cracking disappointments. But we kept at it, year after year. We never lost hope. . . ."

His hirsute chin quivered. I noticed a fierce fanatical glitter in his sunken off-color eyes.

"What's Midas got to do with all that?" I obtruded.

"Keep your pants hitched, Sonny, I'm acoming to it!" He glowered me into sullen silence.

"Before I buried Paw out under a pile of boulders so those varmints and buzzards wouldn't get his carcass—he used to tell me the story about that old king who wanted gold almost as bad as we wanted it, and who got his fondest wish—that everything his hand touched turned to gold.

"When I was a colt I used to lay down under Mohave's diamond-starred sky at night, goggling up at the moon ablazing up over the Joshua Tree forest like a barrel of melted nuggets, and I'd wish and wish and *wish* that I could have what King Midas had.

"Why if *I* had the Golden Touch, I'd handle it *right!* I used to figger out how I'd make myself the most important desert rat this here world ever saw!"

Morgan cast a vehement sigh, it was almost a snarl.

"T'warn't for nigh onto fifty years that I finally got my wish!"

"YOU speak figuratively of course," I put in. "You don't actually mean—"

"I don't, don't I?" Morgan blared up. "Just keep that fly-trap of yours closed and hold on to your hat, while I tell you!"

I was squelched.

"My shack warn't but a mite bit bigger'n a apple box, aclinging to the top of a red-rock cliff out in the middle of Mohave. Quite a view I had from it, though.

"I was atunneling down into the cliff itself, and of an evening I'd sit me down at the mouth of the mine, cut myself a chaw of Beechnut, and look out over a tremendous big dry lake.

"When the desert sun went down, in a glory of red and yaller, a mist would spread out over this here dry lake, and the tops of lower hillocks looked like blue and purple islands on a great silvery sea.

"And on t'other side of me was a forest of gnarled Joshua trees, looking like fifty old witches pointing lots of black fingers out, up to some devil's mischief.

"Must of been working that mine ten years or more.

"Then, one lonesome February night, the *critters* came. . . ."

"Critters?"

"Shut up!" Morgan hinted, disgorging his chew.

"It had just got dark, so's I had lighted my little kerosene lamp. I was aheating up a pot of pork and beans on my little crack-topped wood stove, for my supper.

"Had just got back from Barstow, where I'd gone in my 1911 Flapper-model jallopy, to buy my monthly supplies. That means a slab of salt pork, a case of canned beans, and a couple sacks of salt.

"I stirred at the beans with a long table spoon, and sniffed hungrily. In my other hand I held a much-thumbed Fourth Grade reader what told all about this here King Midas.

"I was areading and astirring, when all to once a blast of noise and fire sent me aflying under the table.

"The cabin shook like a giant was abooting at it.

"My cracked dishes, and a bottle of catsup scooted on to the floor, busted in a million pieces. Likewise a calendar picture I had framed under glass, of a cat and dog lying together, called 'Pals.'

"I clapped my hands over my ears,

and yelled out. I was scared fit to bust my britches. I shut my eyes tight. That there light what came was so terrible it cut right through my eyelids.

"But after while the noise went away, as well as most of the blinding light.

"I opened my peepers and goggled up from my roost. I was still shivering like a worm-et dawg.

"And after I'd opened my eyes, I wished I hadn't. What I saw made me plumb sure I'd been knocked over the cliff into another world—and I don't mean Paradise!"

"WHAT was it you saw?" I ventured, when Morgan paused.

"Why—*them*, of course!" he retorted. "The critters.

"They was tall as chimneys, and sort of purple and black colored. They had big barrel-like bodies, and dangling arms what had big cups on the ends of them. Their heads was like watermelons, set with a whole row of blinking eyes.

"They stood there blinking and staring at me—the whole three of them—after they'd stalked into my shack. Or what was left of it.

"This was the weirdest thing of all. Those critters tromped in out of a contraption what looked like a magnuficent airoplane all shiny and glittery. And this here airoplane had blown the side of my shack clean off. The open cliff side!

"That there contraption of theirs was hanging in midair, over the side of the cliff, calm as you please. And my little shack was ahanging with it.

"I could feel the studdings gently pulling loose, like it was going to topple over any minute.

"First I was too scared to move. Then, seeing my little shack, what I'd built with boards I hauled sixty miles in my jallopy, torn open like a shucked

pea, made me madder'n a wet hen. For a few minutes I didn't care what those critters did to me. I was bound to give them what-for!

" 'Why, you ornery moon-eyed sons of Beelzebub!' I lit into them. 'A million miles of nothing out there—and you had to pick out my shack to bust down on!'

"My face got red, and I dove for my father's old squirrel gun. It was already loaded for varmints, and I turned it plumb on them three.

" 'Now, you cussed critters,' I told them. 'Get the tarnation out of here, and take that blasted airoplane off my shack, afore I blow you to kingdom come!'

"They put their ugly heads together, and I commenced to hear a funny buzzing sound. I guess they was talking about me.

"And while they was atalking, my streak of courage began to fade. Finally it fizzled out like a bum fire cracker. My hands shook, and my knees commenced to do a hula-hula impromptu like.

"I dropped Paw's old squirrel gun, and tried to run.

"Those critters was so allfired *big!* Of all the strange critters I ever heard tell of, them there critters was the most God-awful to have cluttering up my shack, and pulling it down into the dry lake.

"Did you ever feel like you was a cooked goose if you didn't high tail for tall timber—and yet when you tried your legs buckled under you like they was rubber?

"Well, sir, that was me.

"I couldn't run, nor lift even a finger. I just stood there staring at the critters, while the floor under me rocked ominously.

"My little desert cabin was teetering on the rim of the cliff. In another minute it'd be over and gone, and me with it!"

MIDAS MORGAN paused, and borrowed a cigarette from a passing marine, and then a match from an aircraft worker in a tin helmet.

I watched impatiently while he placed the smoke c a r e f u l l y in his bush, scratched the match along his overall leg, and brought the fag to action.

"I hate cigarettes," he said, puffing luxuriously. "Like a pipe, or a good chaw."

"Another minute and that shack of yours is going over that cliff!" I gritted.

Morgan's cheeks crinkled into a self-satisfied grin.

"Suddenly t h o s e critters realized what was going to happen, too. They stopped buzzing. One of them ran back into the shiny contraption, and fussed around with metal gadgets fitted on its wall.

"And when he did, the shack stopped teetering, and raised clean up in the air, a foot at least! And, along with the shiny contraption, it scooted away from the cliff until there wasn't any danger of us falling.

"The shack eased down on the ground again, like a flower falling in a brook.

" 'Hey!' I yelled. 'What in tarnation—?'

"All to once I commenced to hear voices—inside my mind. It was the critters talking to me, only not saying anything. You understand?"

"By telepathy," I guessed.

"Yup," Morgan said, slapping his knee. "That's what!

"Here's what they told me:

" 'We have come from beyond your world, from another dimension. We intend no harm, and are very sorry that we have ruined your abiding place. We read from your mind that we have made you unhappy, and are therefore sorry.'

" 'W-who are you?' I exploded, getting more curious than scared.

" 'Who we are can scarcely mean anything to an humble Earthling like you,' they said. 'Our dimension is more vast than yours, and far more significant.'

" 'Say, if you fellows are on the level,' I told them excitedly. 'Let me take you down to Barstow in my flivver, to meet my pal, Doc Saunders. I bet lots of them there scientists and perfessors'd like to talk to you!'

"But they didn't seem interested.

"One of the critters, who seemed to be the leader, tromped over toward me —like Frankenstein in that there movie.

"I jumped back, scared again.

"Saying nothing, he raised his hands up to that big bulby head of his, and pulled the durn thing off!"

"NOW listen, Morgan," I broke in. "Enough's enough!"

"Thought I told you to keep your trap shut!" he hissed. "Like I just said, the leader pulled his head clear off.

"And he followed that up by taking most of his body off, too.

"You see, the critters' bodies—the big bulby ones—were pure *camouflage!* When they 'undressed' themselves they was really little shrimpy red fellows, with long flexible noses. Those big bodies of theirs were fitted with radio apparatuses, and were moved mechanically from inside.

" 'Why?' I asked the critters, terribly surprised.

" 'Like we have told you, we are scientist searchers from another dimension. On one of our exploring parties in a primitive dimension like yours, we encountered malignant primitives like yourself, who endeavored to harm us. It was after that trip that these protective coverings were designed, to frighten off would-be assassins.'

"After asking me quite a few questions about our world, the leader finally said 'Thank you' very politely, and that they'd be going back to their world.

" 'Why not stick around a while?' I suggested. 'We got lots for you to see in this here dimension. Maybe you might even find some of those things you been searching for so long.'

"They all laughed at that.

" 'You are to be thanked again for your offer,' the leader said, 'but I hardly think that—'

"One of his pals interrupted.

" *'Zorfu!'* he yelled. *'Zorfu!'*

"I turned.

"He was ameddling around my cupboards, holding something up for the others to see, and pointing at it with his flexible nose. Gosh, but he was excited!

" *'Zorfu!'* he hollored again.

" 'No!' shouted the leader, in unbelief.

" 'Shucks,' I said. 'Taint nothing but a common old ten pound sack of salt.'

"But those critters all examined it, and the other sack I bought in Barstow that afternoon, and shouted gleefully. It seemed as how salt was 'zorfu,' and that's just what they'd been hunting for a powerful long time.

"They asked me would I be willing to part with so rare a treasure.

"I chuckled.

" 'You're ajoshing me!' I said.

" 'But most negative indeed!' the leader insisted, his flexible nose vibrating like a windmill. 'In our entire dimension exists not one single grain of zorfu, nor of the potent chemicals that compound it.

" 'For many years our people have suffered greatly because of a vast deathly plague. Thousands have perished.

" 'Finally our greatest scientists, of which I am one, determined that a chemical compound that we designated as 'zorfu' was needed to free our people from this sickness.

" 'We combed the dimensions, every one into which we could penetrate. Your dimension was our last hope. So you can readily see how frantically happy we are to have discovered zorfu in your world!'

" 'Well, I'll be a horned toad!' I exclaimed.

" 'If you'll allow us to take this wonderful compound back with us, we will reward you in any way we are able,' the leader went on.

"THE other two nodded with their noses, buzzing excitedly.

" 'Furthermore,' piped up the smallest and shrimpiest of the lot. 'We owe you something anyway, for demolishing your abode.'

" 'True!' cried the others.

" 'Shucks,' I blushed. 'This old shanty don't amount to a hill of beans, nohow. And if that there sal—zorfu'll help your folks, you just take along all I've got, and welcome.'

"They all thanked me again.

"Then they asked me what reward I wanted. Anything, they said, that was within their power. And from the looks of them that extended pretty doggoned far.

" 'You old desert rat,' I told myself. 'This here's the chance of a lifetime. Think fast, and think *good!* It's your golden opportunity!'

"So I pondered a spell, scratched my whiskers, and thought on it some more.

" 'Your *golden* opportunity!' The phrase ran over and over in my mind.

" 'That's it!' I hollored out, even though they read it all in my mind. 'I allus wanted to be like King Midas. That everything I touched would turn into gold. And that's what I'm asking —if you're able to give that power to me. But maybe I'm askin' too much?'

"Their noses dropped down queerly. I stared from one of them to another. I felt the dismay in their minds.

"My jaw fell down a foot.

" 'Just my dang-fool luck,' I muttered, 'to pick something you can't give me!'

" 'It isn't that,' the leader spoke up, after a moment. 'Only—why do you ask such a thing as this? Certainly we can accomplish this. We are masters in the art of transmuting to metal. But, gold is such a non-important substance! Why that, of all worthwhile things?'

" 'I dunno,' I grumbled sheepishly. 'Only that's what everybody on this world wants. And that's what I want!'

"They put their snaky noses together, and confabbed a spell. Finally the leader sent one of them back to where they came from, in the contraption, and spoke to me.

" 'Since you wish to duplicate the power of mythical King Midas, you shall have that power, scientifically.'

"In less than an hour the fellow he'd sent back returned, carrying a pair of gloves. They were like gold mesh, and shone out like polished lightning.

"I STARED at them stupidly, when the leader held them out to me.

" 'They have already been treated, and are in perfect order to accomplish your desire. They will transmute anything in your world to gold!'

" 'Gimmee!' I hollered, happily.

"I reached out for them, greedily.

"The leader hesitated. 'You might not find this Golden Touch as marvelous as you think,' he warned.

" 'Shucks,' I poo-pooed.

"As I grabbed again, my hand stopped in midair.

" 'Wait!' I cried in alarm. 'First, tell me—they won't turn *me* into gold, will they?'

"He laughed in his mind, sardonically.

" 'No,' he assured me. 'The wearer is immune to their power, so long as he keeps them on. But remember this one thing, it's most important. The potency of these transmuting gloves increases with use. In other words, the longer you wear them, the quicker the transmutation process operates!'

" 'That's okay with me!' I grinned. I had visions of a great big storehouse, filled with gold boulders.

"He slipped the gloves on me. I was so excited I hardly noticed when they put their big bodies back on, and made ready to leave.

" 'Farewell forever,' the leader called back, somewhat sadly. 'Remember— now that you have the gloves on you'll have to wear them always. They can't be removed!'

" 'Hey! How am I going to *eat?*' I yelled.

" 'You must find out how the gloves work for yourself,' he said, closing the door to their contraption.

"In my mind I heard the three of them say, 'Farewell!' as the shiny contraption faded into nothingness, in the cold gray dawn.

"I LOOKED down at my gold-gloved hands.

"Suddenly I shivered. It was cold, what with my shack ripped open, and the desert sun not up yet. . . .

" 'Who cares!' I chuckled, my teeth clicking together. 'I'm rich! I've got the Golden Touch!'

"I thought I'd try it out. I picked up a stool with one hand. I held it up for a spell, near the oil lamp.

"Then I yelled out with fury.

" 'It don't work!' I shrieked.

"In panic and disgust I seized hold of the stool with both hands, and shook it savagely. Then I flung it away, against the stove. It clanged, metal on metal.

"I ran over to it. The stool was gold —pure gold!

" 'Sure it works,' I crooned gleefully. 'Only I've got to touch a thing with BOTH hands.'

"I pondered on that. I figgered there must be some scientific action between the gloves that made it necessary to use both of them.

" 'So much the better!' I congratulated myself. 'That means I can eat, or do anything else I want to without the transmutation taking effect—so long as I do it with only one hand!'

"I came back to building a fire. Thoughtlessly I let both hands rest on a chunk of wood, as I eased it into the stove. It turned to gold.

"I chuckled.

" 'Drat the pesky stuff,' I told myself gleefully. 'More gold'n I can shake a finger at!'

"Still chuckling, I built a one-handed fire. Then I went to bed. I was dog-tired, and quicker'n a wink I was snoring.

"I WOKE up uncomfortable. The tick mattress under me hurt my back. I rolled over, pounding at my pillow. I durn near busted my hand.

"I snapped open my eyes, then. I remembered everything, and realized what had happened. I grinned.

"Sure enough, the pillow was shining gold. And the mattress was gold. And the blankets, and the bunk.

"I blinked around sleepily. The old late afternoon sun came right into my cabin, and what I saw nearly knocked my eyes clean out of my head.

"*My shack, and everything in it, was turned to solid gold!*

" 'Jumping sand-fleas!' I yelled, tossing the gold blankets aside, leaping off the gold bunk onto the gold floor. 'How did all this happen? Did I walk in my sleep?'

"I scratched my whiskers bewilderedly, noticing casually that my old bleached shirt was now made of radiant spun-gold fabric.

"It was easy to see how my bed covers and mattress had been turned to gold. My hands couldn't help touching them, while I rolled around in my sleep.

"But these other things? How did *they* turn to gold?

"Then one of the last things the leader said afore they skedaddled simmered through my noggin. 'Remember, the potency of those gloves increases the longer you wear them!'

" 'Jupiter!' I spluttered. 'The process works its way right through things —as long as my hands are touching something!'

"I was hungry as a winter coyote. But there warn't a thing to eat, on account of the beans was all gold.

"For the first time my new power began to rankle. It was a long hot drive in to Barstow, on an empty stomach. . . .

"I WENT outside. The sight of all that glittery metal began to hurt my eyes.

" 'I got enough gold right now to last me a lifetime,' I pondered. 'Besides, if I go to work and make too much of the pesky stuff, its value will drop way down. I'll just call it quits, take the gloves off now—afore I do something worse than changing good pork and beans to gold!'

"So I tried to take the gloves off. I tried every way I could think of. But they felt like they was growing on my hands. They wouldn't budge so much as a hair's breath.

" 'The leader critter was right,' I sighed. 'They won't come off.' I gripped my hands into fists. 'I think I'll go in to Barstow, and see my pal, Doc Saunders. I bet he'll think of some way to get these tarnation mittens off!'

"I ambled over to my old topless jallopy, abaking in the afternoon sun. It wasn't much for looks, but it beat walking.

"I piled in, and turned on the motor. But I was very careful not to touch anything with both hands. It was awkward, but I managed.

"As usual, it wouldn't start. It had to be hand cranked.

"A-cranking and a-cussing, I happened to glance back at my shack. There it stood in the sunlight, solid gold. A king's palace couldn't of been no prettier.

"Finally the old jallopy jounced into action. I leaped in, still cautious about using only one hand on the wheel.

"We were off, in a cloud of desert dust.

"My right hand steering, I managed to send her a-crawling over the rocky road all right. Then we came to a sandstone grade that stretched alongside a dry wash.

"There was a sharp u-turn in the road. It was a dangerous place. More than once I almost sent the old flivver crashing into the wash, twenty feet below. My brakes was nothing to brag about.

"And right there, at that bad turn, like a bat straight out of hell, came that other car.

" 'Doc Saunders!' I hollored, recognizing his old coupe. Doc was an old codger like me, and we played a lot of rummy together of an evening.

" 'Look out!' I hollored, trying to swerve.

"And then I put both hands on the steering wheel . . ."

"I knew it!" I cried. "I knew that was coming! It had to!"

Morgan glowered.

"There came a jolt that jarred my teeth loose. My old jallopy was transformed instantly into a golden chariot, and there was no stopping her. Off it went, over the grade, into the dry wash!

"I caught a last glimpse of old Doc Saunders poised near the brink, standing up in his seat, yelling like a banshee.

"Subconsciously I jerked my hands off the wheel, and let myself get thrown out of the car. I flew through the air with the greatest of ease—until my poor dang-fool head smacked against the red dirt at the bottom of the wash.

"From then on I didn't know from nothing, for quite some time . . ."

"GO ON!" I prodded Midas Morgan, when he stopped, sucking air in between his sparse yellow teeth. "What next?"

"The worse was yet to come," he averred, shuddering. "I hate to even think what might have happened, if I'd been killed."

"How awful!" I quipped. "You'd be dead!"

"So would you, Sonny!"

"What do you——"

"Just gimme time, and I'll tell you. . . .

"Well, when I finally came out of it, it was morning again. Very early morning. The sun only hinted at heat, back there behind the purple range of distant hills.

"Don't let nobody bamboozle you with songs about 'Until the sands of the desert grow cold'. The desert's as cold as a haunted tomb around four-five in the morning!

"I lay there a spell, with my head nearly cracked open, shivering and groaning. I felt stiff icy hands on mine.

"I looked up.

"It was Doc Saunders. He was try-

.ing to lift me up by the hands, so's he could help me. But he couldn't budge me. He couldn't move a muscle—because he was turned into an eighteen karat solid gold statue!

" 'Doc!' I yelled, panicky. This here was something I hadn't even thought about, in spite of King Midas's daughter.

"I yanked my gloved hands from under Doc Saunders' gold ones, and stood up shakily.

"My head throbbed like a dynamo. I shook it, so's I could focus my eyes properly, and rubbed my half-frozen hands together.

"I gandered crestfallenly over at my jallopy. It was nothing but a junk-heap now. A golden junk-heap.

"I rubbed my eyes and looked around. My head cleared slowly.

"There was Doc's coupe, up at the top of the grade. It should be dark blue—but it looked yellow. Yellow!

" 'Jumping Judas!' I hollered. "It's turned to gold, too!'

"I gandered around me some more. A feeling of stark horror began to jab me at the top of my spine. A sinister suspicion, that grew slowly into a fact . . .

"The greasewood bushes to my left clinked slender metal leaves together in the low morning breeze. They were gold! The sandstone grade, and the whole twisty dry wash glowed dully. It was gold! Even a little gopher, scared out of his hole, was poised pertly on his haunches, ready to run. But he'd never run again. He was gold!

" 'Lord Almighty!' I yelled out, like a prayer. My voice echoed faintly along the wash.

" 'Now I've gone and done it!' I cried.

" 'Gone and done it!'

" 'Done it!' said the echoes, right back at me.

"I'm no mental wizard, but I had imagination enough to see what had happened. The leader of the critters from that other dimension said the power of the gloves increased rapidly.

"So all the while I'd been unconscious there at the bottom of the dry wash, with my hands plunked up against the ground, they'd been busy at work. The worst mischief I could possibly do had been started, and nobody could stop it. The critters had said positively they wouldn't never come back . . .

"It was plain as the nose on your face that *the entire world and everything on it was slowly turning to solid gold!"*

"THAT *is* too much!" I exclaimed, when Morgan paused to borrow more cigarettes. "It's preposterous!"

"Yup, it was too much for me, all right," he agreed, waving away a cheap Mexican cigarette scornfully. "It's authentic, too."

"Anyway, you've got me where you want me," I muttered. "Go ahead and finish your fable."

Midas Morgan puffed meditatively on a perfumed cork-tipped fag he had mooched from a gentleman in a top hat, then continued.

"There wasn't nothing I could do about *that* situation! I couldn't walk forty-six miles into Barstow. I started off miserably over the gold desert toward my shack, four miles away.

"I hated to leave Doc standing grotesquely there, but I had to. I couldn't lift him nohow.

"I got back to my little gold shack, pooped, starved, and all sick inside. My damned wish had back-fired on me. Now I wished those critters'd gone to hell afore they came to this here world.

"The more I thought about what I'd done, the sicker I got. I was so hungry I could have ate almost anything. Any thing but gold—which was all I had.

"And I was sick to death of the sight of gold.

"All I could do was lay down on my gold bunk, bury my face in the gold pillow, and wish that I was dead.

"I fell fast asleep.

"Then I had a most peculiar dream. At least it *seemed* like a dream! I dreamed that the leader of the critters from that other dimension was standing right in the middle of my shack, just where he stood after he'd put the gold-making gloves on me. His long nose waved around, and his buzzing voice spoke. My mind caught the word he kept repeating, over and over.

"That word was, *'Fire!'*

"I jumped off the bunk, wide awake.

"'Fire!' I hollered out. 'That's what he said! And he's trying to help me out. Or—maybe he left that word imprinted on my mind somehow!'

"But, what could it mean? It didn't make much sense. Just that one word. Did he mean, maybe, that I could *burn* the gloves off my hands?

"I ran for my cupboards, to find matches. But there wasn't any I could use. Only useless gold ones.

"I ran outside, and headed out toward the main road. I almost ran, over the gold that shone like fire in the blazing dawn. Finally I reached sage that was sage, and Joshuas that were green and brown, and I knew I had reached the edge of the gold menace.

"Then I came to the highway.

"I sat by the side of the road until a big Diesel truck lumbered along. I flagged it down.

"'Toss me down a couple matches?' I begged the driver. And when he did, and started to say something about my gold clothes, I ran away fast as I could.

"With one hand clutching the precious matches, and the other arm loaded down with wood and dry brush, I went back to my shack.

"I kindled a merry fire in the gold stove.

"'Here goes!' I gritted, and stuck my left hand down into the fire.

"I EXPECTED it to about kill me with pain. But it didn't burn. It didn't hurt me at all. My gloved hand just *melted!*

"Wherever the glove was right up against my hand, it was gold underneath—not flesh and blood any more. But when I stuck my hand in the fire too far—*ouch!*

"Before long my left hand was all melted away. I pulled my arm out, and looked down at it ruefully.

"I built up the fire, and was about to give my right hand the same treatment, when I noticed something that made me whoop out with joy.

"The glove on my right hand didn't glitter any more. It was solid black! And when I tugged at it hopefully, the glove came off easily.

"I tossed it in the fire, flexing my bony, live fingers with ecstasy. I had saved one hand, at least!

"Then, glancing around, I got another surprise.

"The cook stove was dirty black iron. The table and bunk were wood. The bed clothes, and my own shirt and pants, were raggedy cloth.

"And when I looked outside, I saw that the Joshua trees were real trees again. My shack was a lop-sided board one, half-blown off.

"After while, in the distance I saw Doc Saunders' coupe, his dark blue coupe, raising dust my way. He was all right.

"Tears ran down my whiskers, I was so glad. Glad to see everything just the way it had been before. Glad I

(*Concluded on page 192*)

A couple of guys were down on their knees trying to drink the gutter dry

THE CONSTANT DRIP

By BERKELEY LIVINGSTON

WHEN liquor started flooding the streets, MacCarey had to go into the next dimension to repair the leak!

THE Mazda glow of the Golden Bar restaurant shed a circle of light over the corner of State and Van Buren Streets. To the south, on State, were the cheap honky-tonk clip joints. Dime beers and fifteen cent whiskeys; and a couple of strong arm boys all set to relieve the sucker of his hard-earned green stuff. To the north, just off the corner, was the White Way burleycue house. Its huge sign enticed the passerby with a promise of "Fifty Gorgeous Gals Glamorously Gowned."

Here, whiskey was king, and man lived only to relieve his thirst. And here, too, across from the Golden Bar, Marty had his liquor store.

ILLUSTRATED BY LEW MEYER JR.

Marty was one of those guys whom nature had overlooked. Undersized in every physical way, he also had the heart and manner of a weasel. His hangout was behind the cash register. People often wondered how he managed to tear himself away from the coin box long enough to wait on a customer. But as Marty put it, "With me, everything is hokey-dokey."

Marty had a single weakness, however. And if a customer happened to stumble on that weakness, the happy patron would discover a new Marty. One who treated and treated, so long as the customer listened and agreed. Marty was a Utopian, engaged in building newer and better worlds.

Tonight, Marty was at his best. The only customer in the store was sitting with mouth agape and eyes dulled from the effect of the flow of Marty's talk.

"And so," Marty said in conclusion, "mine opinion is like this. The only good world is another world."

The customer, realizing that his thirst could stand another beer and that Marty had about run dry, broke in with a slyly querulous:

"What d'ya mean, another world?"

"What do I mean, another world?" Marty grunted. His mean, little eyes gleamed balefully, from behind steel-rimmed glasses, at the offending questioner.

"Another world, like this earth," he explained loftily; "like from where the whiskey came."

"Like from where the whiskey came?"

There was an honest curiosity in the customer's voice.

"Sure," Marty said, then, as he saw the man was still in the dark, continued, "Say, wasn't you in Chicago, when it happened?"

"When what happened?" the customer asked impatiently.

Marty was off on his best story. "Why, my friend," he said, "it all started right here in this store. I had that magnum sized whiskey bottle right there in my store windows——" Marty pointed to the window in question—and felt his face go pale.

As for the customer—he simply slid from his seat, down onto the floor. What they had both seen, unbelievable as it was, were pieces of paper floating down to the display window floor. The amazing feature of that was—the papers were appearing from empty air.

Marty recovered first and leaped forward to gather them up as they fell. But the customer was only a step behind. As Marty picked them up, he handed them to the customer to hold. It was then they noticed that the sheets bore numbers. For two hours the papers fell; then, as mysteriously as they had appeared, they stopped coming.

Marty began to read, after he had placed the manuscript—for that was what it proved to be—in order:

"This is the tale of Harry Mac-Carey——

IT ALL started in Marty's Liquor Store. Y'know, right across from the Golden Bar. And how I got mixed up in the business is very simply explained. I was sleeping off a drunk on the receiving ramp of the Maxon Shoe Store, next door to Marty's. So it wasn't till the whiskey or Quesquebah, as we—but, hell, let's start this story the way it should be started. With Officer Finnegan.

After all, it was he who discovered the Flood. Finnegan, off duty and pleasure bound to the Golden Bar, stopped off at Marty's, across the way, to admire the new advertising display old Ant Nose had in his window. The display consisted of a magnum-sized whiskey bottle tilted on a set of wires so that it spilled its contents into a shot glass on a ledge below. Finnegan, his red, beefy face pressed close against the window, was intrigued by the set-up. The whiskey, pouring in a slow, steady stream into the little glass, never overflowed. Yet, despite the fact that the display had been going for twenty-four hours, somehow the bottle remained full.

Finnegan, his eyes squinting in his effort to concentrate, suddenly noticed something take place that was all wrong. The glass had overflowed. What was more, the bottle had begun to spout out the liquid in large foaming spurts. Even as he watched, fascinated and bewildered, the window floor began to show a film of wetness.

Finnegan knew that if it continued, there would be damage done to the stock in the window. So he went over to the corner cigar store, which stayed open all night, and called Marty. It was two in the morning, but he knew Marty would be down in ten minutes.

A sleepy, querulous voice answered the ringing of the phone:

"Hello, damn it, what's the idear of waking——"

"Shut up and listen," Finnegan broke in. "C'mon down to your store before you have a flood."

"Say," Marty asked suspiciously, "who is this? And what's this flood you're talking about?"

"It's Finnegan, the cop," Finnegan said impatiently, "and f'r the love of Mike, cut out this gabbing. I said get down here, quick!"

Marty, evidently realizing that something was wrong somewhere, got down there . . . but quick. In five minutes, by Finnegan's watch! He joined the policeman at the window. Already the window floor was two inches under whiskey. And still it came from out of the bottle.

"Holy smoke," Marty yelped in consternation, "that's impossible!"

"What's impossible?" Finnegan demanded.

"The bottle. It hasn't got that much water in it," Marty said.

"So. The whole thing is a fake," Finnegan said in a satisfied tone. That's what he had thought in the first place. The whole thing was a fake.

"And when I see that display salesman," Marty ground out savagely as he put the key in the lock, "I'm going to tell him where to put that gadget!"

He turned on the light switch and as he groped for the control switch for the display, he threw an explanation over his shoulder to Finnegan:

"Y'see, Finnegan, it's what they call an optical illusion. The whole thing is a continuous pipe—from bottle to glass and back again. So it can't overflow. That's what the salesman said, the jerk!"

AT LAST his fingers found what they were seeking. Finnegan heard the click of the switch being snapped closed. They both turned to see how much damage had been done to the inside of the window.

And found the bottle still sending its contents into the little glass below.

"Hey," Marty said wildly, "that's impossible. I've got the current off."

"Try it again," Finnegan suggested.

Marty did. Several times. But nothing happened. The flow never stopped.

"Well," Finnegan said, after they watched the display for a few minutes, "If you don't want your joint ruined, you'd better disconnect that bottle."

Marty almost broke the inside door down in his haste to reach the bottle. With a single pull he jerked it from its supporting wires—and dropped it from suddenly nerveless fingers.

Finnegan crossed himself hastily,

when he saw what was happening. Marty almost fell out of the window in his haste to get away.

They both stared, speechless with fright, at what was going on from where the bottle had once been. A large stream of liquid was pouring from the empty air. Neither Marty nor Finnegan could see any hole or opening anywhere. The liquid was doing the impossible! There it was, shooting out in an ever-widening stream from the emptiness of the center of the display window.

"Oh my God!" Marty groaned, as he saw the growing flood on the floor. "How are we going to stop that leak?"

Finnegan was on his way to the phone at the rear of the store. He knew this was something beyond his control. But maybe the desk sergeant at the station might have an idea.

After the call, they waited around for as long as they could for something to happen. It wasn't long in happening, either. With a crackling of splintered wood the window on the inside of the store window burst and the whiskey flooded the interior. By the time the fire department — the desk sergeant's idea — arrived, the flood had forced Marty and Finnegan outdoors.

And almost drowned me!

I WAS sleeping—or rather, taking a couple of hours rest from bending my elbow—on the ground floor receiving platform of the store next to Marty's. I was awakened by a tickling at my nose; it was the undeniable and heavenly odor of whiskey which was titillating my nostrils. I lay there on my back and let the flood which was beginning to crawl up around my chin, have its way.

Then I realized what was wrong. I was being drowned! In whiskey! I scrambled about on my hands and knees

for a few seconds, and slipped once or twice—luckily. For, in slipping, my mouth filled with the nectar which was running in such a lovely river down the alley. And of course I swallowed some. My deepest fears were immediately realized. It *was* whiskey. But whiskey such as I'd never tasted. There are not enough superlatives to describe that whiskey.

Then I discovered something else. My mind, usually dull, seemed to be clear; even more, I was thinking in a manner of years ago. Just then, however, I was interested in one thing. Getting in touch with Charlie Moran, a saloon-keeper with whom I had a sort of nodding acquaintance. I was usually found nodding my head over his bar seven nights a week.

Luckily I found a nickel in my pocket. Usually I had to go to someone else's pocket. And not always luckily.

Charlie's whiskey soprano answered my summons.

"Ugh, grhh, huh," Charlie began. I didn't wait for the rest.

"Look, lug," I said coming right down to cases, "do you want to make a lot of dough?"

Charlie's English immediately improved.

"How?" He didn't even bother to ask who was calling.

"Just come down to the back of Marty's Liquor Store, and bring a couple of empty whiskey barrels with you," I said.

Charlie became suspicious then.

"Say," he demanded, "what's this all about? And who the hell is this, anyway?"

I took a chance. After all, if Charlie came down, I'd get a couple of bucks for the tip. All I had to do was get him to come down. The evidence was there. And it was mellow.

"Now listen, rum-pot," I explained,

"there's a small river of the best whiskey in Chicago running loose out here. How it got here, I don't know. But if you don't get here, someone else will. Don't ask any more questions. Just get here. And don't forget the barrels."

I hung up. Just like that. And went back for another drink.

As I say, my mind was clicking on all eight. Now, without boasting, I had at least a quart of yocky-dock during the day. And the three or four healthy swallows I'd just taken would have made another quart. Yet I felt fine.

Not sober, understand. Yet not drunk. I hadn't noticed the crowd out in front of Marty's, when I went to the cigar store to make my call. But leaving it, I did. The crowd, the police, and the fire department. Also I saw that the street looked like a water main had burst. The smell wasn't from water, though. I saw Finnegan, the cop, looking important as an alderman at the Hod Carriers' picnic, talking to Marty and his sergeant.

I high-tailed it back to the alley. Charlie pulled into the alley just as I got there. His smeller was working in high gear. He was sniffing around like Bugle Annie looking for Lionel Barrymore.

"Well, what do you want?" I asked politely—"an invitation?"

"Huh," Charlie countered masterfully.

I'd always known he was a little solid between the ears—but this was too much. I opened the rear door to his car and rolled out the barrels—without music. It wasn't hard to fill them. I simply set the bung hole down to where the whiskey could flow in and waited until the barrel filled. It only took ten minutes. Then I rolled them back to the car. As simple as that.

"Thanks," said Charlie. He was leaning against the building, puffing comfortably at a fat cigar, watching me.

"Huh?" I said. It was all I could think of just then. It wasn't till Charlie got in the car and rode away that I thought of other things. None of them pleasant.

"There goes the 'fin' I was going to get," I thought, as I walked around to the corner again, "and I thought he was solid between the ears. Well, well, Mac-Carey, the wisenheimer."

A WHISTLE of surprise escaped me, when I reached the corner. This was going to be a red letter night for State and Van Buren Streets. The street was a foot deep in the stuff that was pouring from Marty's store. And from the number of drunks who were on their hands and knees, gathering in handfuls of whiskey, it looked like every joint in the whole area had been emptied.

I was so interested in what was going on I forgot my own thirst. Not some of the others, however. Even the cops and firemen would slip now and then and sneak a drink. I venture to say it was the biggest drinking party ever staged. And free!

I waded over to the large group, with looks of frustration on their faces, parked in front of Marty's. Marty, himself, was explaining something to the fire marshal.

"Now listen, Mr. Fire Marshal," he was saying bitterly, "everything was hokey-dokey when I leave tonight. Then Finnegan calls me. So what happens? I come down and find this. What's with my store and stock? Everything'll be ruined. I'm telling ya, Mr. Fire Marshal, someone's goin' to pay for this."

"Say, Chief." A fat man in a blue uniform, wearing a cap marked 'Captain,' came bustling up importantly. "Look. How's about opening the sewers and letting the stuff out that way?"

I had recognized the captain. He was head of the Loop station from which Finnegan was dispatched. I had had several small dealings with him before. So I sort of remained in the background. The fire chief had turned wearied eyes in his direction. His voice matched his eyes as he said:

"Listen, Corrigen. That stuff coming out here is whiskey. D'ya understand? Whiskey! All I want you to do is rope off the whole damn area. Before someone drops a match in it. That's why I can't let it run down the sewers. Too much of a fire hazard."

Finnegan was standing guard in front of the store. I sort of sneaked over and whispered:

"Hey, what're they gonna do with all this? Start a distillery here?"

Finnegan looked down at me disgustedly. "Isn't there enough trouble here without you giving me any more?" he demanded. He fixed me with a stony look. But I didn't stay fixed. I peered into the window.

Then it happened. The stuff was coming through a hole in the empty air that was all of two feet in diameter. Suddenly a body had come shooting out. A *green body*. I wasn't color blind or drunk. It was a *green* man.

Finnegan's chin hit his chest so hard he almost lost his lower plate.

"Hey, what's this?" he demanded.

I wasn't there to answer. I was already through the open door.

The green man was on the floor of the store, gasping like a fish out of water. A hand—Finnegan's—pushed me out of the way.

"Where the devil did you come from?" Finnegan demanded, as he lifted him from the floor.

Our strange visitor mumbled something or other in reply. His eyes fluttered open and I noticed they were an ordinary, everyday brown.

"C'mon, c'mon," Finnegan commanded, all the while shaking him as though he were a damp towel. "Open up, you queer-looking goon! Where'd you come from?"

The brown eyes in the strange green face were curious and unafraid. But definitely bewildered.

"Mumble mumble mumble," were the only sounds he made. Then twisting away from Finnegan, he tried to get back to—well, as far as I could see— back to the hole in the air. And that was when I got it. The air, I mean.

A HAND—heavy, meaty and firm— was placed on my shoulders. A voice, pleasant as a drill-sergeant's, thundered:

"So it's you, is it?"

My height is, as I say, "a good five feet five inches." When I heard that cherubic voice, it was just five inches.

"Uh, yes, Captain, it's me," I stuttered.

Captain Corrigen turned me about until I was facing him. He glowered down at me with the gentle look of an executioner.

"Well, what are you looking for, some free whiskey?"

I looked down at the alcoholic flood around my ankles.

"Wouldn't have to look very far," I cracked.

The hand on my shoulder tightened and another grabbed my pants where they were loosest; and then . . . why, I was outside, looking in.

The last words I heard, as I sailed through the door, were:

"And now for that freak in the green paint!"

Realizing there was no further use in hanging around, and knowing, too, that my sleeping quarters were probably flooded out, I made for Skid Row. Charlie Moran's place wasn't far off.

And he did owe me something for the tip I gave him.

For once, Charlie played the Good Samaritan.

I slept the rest of the night in one of the back booths. And when I got up, the day bartender threw me a buck, saying:

"That's for the tip, Harry. Charlie told me to give it to you."

That was more like it. I hadn't had a buck in my kick for so long it felt uncomfortable. Maybe my luck had turned.

The newsdealer on the corner obligingly turned his head long enough for me to snatch a paper. And over coffee and sinkers, I read the news.

The flood occupied the whole front page. The stuff, according to the papers, was still pouring out. The National Guard had been called out. A quarter mile section of the Loop had been roped off from all traffic. And they had decided to pipe the stuff off into tankers. To quote the news account:

"Fire Marshal Allerton has appealed to the various oil companies to rush every available tanker down to the lake front. The mayor, this morning, issued an emergency proclamation, and asked the public to stay from the area.

"The railroad companies, realizing the seriousness of the situation, have volunteered the free use of all their tank cars.

"Already huge pipe lines are being laid to carry the highly inflammable liquid off to tankers in the lake and tank cars waiting in the freight yards."

All this made very interesting reading. But what about the green man? I found him tucked away in a corner at the bottom of the second page.

The squib merely said the police had arrested someone who, evidently taking advantage of the excitement, had tried to pilfer some of the liquor stock. It also said the police thought he was a lunatic because he was dressed in a crazy get-up and had painted his entire body green. Further, the thief had pretended he could not speak English. The police were holding him for further questioning.

"Pilfering. Can't talk E n g l i s h. Nuts!" I exclaimed. "Why, Finnegan knows that's a lie. And I know he can speak English because I heard him. He kind of mumbled, but I understood him. He said: 'I pressed too hard; now I must get back again.'"

I MUST have looked very silly, sitting there with coffee drooling from my open mouth. I had just realized the meaning of the green man's words.

He had come shooting out of a hole in the air. But beyond that hole, there must be a tangible, real world. A world of—— I became a little dizzy from the thoughts taking shape in my brain. But one thing I knew: I had to see the green man again. And if possible——

I suddenly became very drunk. I upset the table as I got up, and dishes went tumbling and flying about. As I staggered around, trying to recover my balance, I stumbled into a man carrying a tray full of food.

The manager helped us to our feet, and while apologizing to the customer, yelped to one of the countermen too:

"Get that cop on the corner and I'll have this bum thrown in the can!"

The cop took one look at me and no questions were asked. We waited on the corner for the wagon to pick me up. I'll bet the manager of the restaurant would have been amazed at how quickly I had sobered up though.

"So! Drunk and disorderly again, huh?" the desk sergeant growled, on seeing me. And continued:

"Well, I'm going to do just as I

promised you. You're going to mop up every cell in the station."

The sergeant couldn't see my grin. It was all inside. But the plan I had begun to formulate, took in that promise.

Fat Larry, the lock-up man, took me in tow. His eyes, behind their fleshy walls of eyelids, twinkled merrily as he said:

"Whiskey floods, green man, martial law: everything happens here. But no matter what happens, at least twice a week I play host to my old friend, Harry the Lush."

Our footsteps echoed hollowly down the stone walk which led to cell sixteen.

"Green man?" I asked. "What green man?"

"Oh, that freak they got locked up in number twenty. They found him in Marty's. Seems like he can't talk English. So we're holding him till the captain finds time to question him."

So he was in twenty. That was good. Beyond that cell, about twenty feet, was the receiving door at the end of the basement. While Larry went to get me the mop and bucket, I thought over exactly what I'd do.

"Better do a good job," he warned, handing me the stuff. "The sergeant's hotter than a pistol."

I knew the lock-up man's desk was at the turn in the corridor. So I would be hidden from view until I wanted to get into a cell.

Larry was barely out of sight when I was at the receiving door. I breathed a sigh of relief when I saw the lock which kept it closed. A simple latch.

In ten minutes I was ready to go into cell twenty. Larry noticed my nervousness as I waited for him to open the door.

"Don't worry," he said. "That freak is harmless. Just sits there and talks to himself. Listen to him. Sounds nuts. All part of his act, I'll bet."

It may have sounded that way to Larry. But what the green man was saying when we came in, was:

"I must get back to the Fault. Soon the locks will be repaired——" He broke off his soliloquy at our entrance.

I WAITED for Larry to leave.

"Now if I can get you smartened up, somehow, we'll blow this joint off fast," I ruminated aloud.

"What?" he said.

"I said, if I can——" and stopped. Wonder of wonders, he understood!

"Hey," I said turning swiftly toward him, "I thought you didn't understand English?"

We were a study in bewilderment. Green and white.

"But you are speaking my language," he whispered.

I whispered back:

"That's something we'll talk about later. Right now all I want to know is, do you want to get out of here?"

He nodded his head in a vigorous affirmative.

I told him what to do. When he signified his understanding, I handed him the mop and called the fat lock-up man.

I asked Larry to come over to the far corner where I was standing.

"Hey," I said in a conspiratorial voice, "c'mere and look at this."

I was bent over as though I was examining something on the floor. My friend the green man was leaning against the bars, the mop held close to his side.

It didn't take long.

Larry walked in, tripped over the mop handle which the green man thrust between his legs, and fell flat on his fat gut.

I didn't waste any time. Before Larry could recover his breath, I had taken his service gun from the holster around his belly and shoved it up against the side of his skull.

"Listen, fat man," I confided to him, "I'm going to show the freak our town and I don't want you around. So behave and you won't get hurt."

In the meantime, my friend followed my instructions to the letter. While I held the pistol to the thoroughly frightened Larry's head, he pulled off the fat man's trousers and shirt. Then, using the policeman's handcuffs, I fastened Larry's wrists behind his back. I used a handkerchief as a gag and another to tie his ankles.

They wouldn't miss him for at least fifteen minutes. That was enough time for us. The copper's clothes kind of lapped over in a few places. But they covered the green body. And with my hat jammed low over his forehead we were a strange-looking pair, but at least on the normal side.

I headed back for Marty's. I wanted to get back there before they started to put the pipe in. We were just in time. Workmen had already started to swing huge three foot sections of iron piping through the front window of the liquor store. Van Buren Street looked like the subway was being built above ground.

We mingled with the workmen. It was an easy matter to get into Marty's. Laborers kept walking in and out of the joint.

That is how we walked in. I suppose they're still waiting for us to walk out.

"Take off your clothes," Yerka ordered. That was the green man's name: Yerka. I did. He followed suit. His shorts were prettier than mine. He walked up to the leak in the dike, with me right behind. And plunged into the flood.

I had a prayer on my lips but luckily I'd learned the crawl. The water tasted good. A little high in alcoholic content but I didn't mind that. I'd never swum against a tide of such force. Although, to tell the truth, I didn't have to do much swimming.

Because just as we leaped into where the Quesquebah came out into our world, Yerka clouted me on the chin. Maybe it was the punch which knocked me out. Or maybe it was the strange unearthly force—the sudden cosmic release from this world through the fourth dimension—which seemed to do the trick. But suddenly my brain felt as though molten fire had been poured on it. My body felt like it was going through the bends. My mouth and nostrils were filled with the "quesqui" as we call it; I felt Yerka's hand grasp my hair—and knew no more.

I CAME to consciousness and found myself floating in a tank. But such a tank as I could never imagine existed.

Of some metallic material, it stretched as far as the eye could see, to all sides. At regular intervals on the bastion-like walls, large batteries of complicated pump machines were mounted.

I thought I was floating. Then I felt Yerka's hand around my chin. I twisted about and began to swim with him. He turned his head at my motion, smiled, and said:

"Well, my friend I didn't know whether we'd come through, but here we are—in Corna."

I was too busy looking about me to give an answer. He was heading for a landing stage, set against the smooth surface of the metal dam.

Several small boats were bobbing about below the ladder of the stage. I could see half a dozen men in the three boats looking toward us. One of them, noticing us at last, called something to the others and the three boats were speeding toward us.

In a matter of a few seconds Yerka and I had been lifted into the largest of the three boats. And they set out for the landing stage.

I was getting a little dizzy from the overpowering odor of the quesqui. People had always said that "Harry Mac-Carey must bathe in the stuff." But even I was beginning to feel that too much is ditto. I had started out by wading around in the stuff, then I was dragged through a river of it; now I was swimming in a lake of it.

Just then all I wanted was a drink of water. I said as much:

"How about a drink of water when we land, Yerka?"

A silvery voice said:

"Why, it speaks our tongue."

A voice answered:

"Holy Dorothy Lamour! It's a woman."

I recognized the last voice. It was my own.

It was sacrilege to couple Miss Lamour's name with Loo Loo's. The sarong made Lamour famous. But Loo Loo would have made the sarong's wear obligatory. About Loo Loo— more later.

Yerka spoke up:

"Yes, he speaks our tongue. And if it weren't for him, I would still be in that other world into which I was plunged."

He went on throwing the stuff around: how I saved his life, etc. But my attention was centered on the luminous eyes of the girl who was seated under me.

Oh, I forgot to say I was stretched out lengthwise in the boat and my head was in this angel's lap. Her fingers were caressing my cheek, and my heart was thumping a bass accompaniment to the music her fingers were making.

For the length of time it took the boat to reach the ladder, I was content to lie there.

As Yerka boosted me up to the first rung, he said:

"Now I shall show you the wonders of my world."

"Thanks, pal," I said, as I clambered up the ladder, "but I've just seen the wonders of your city. Well anyway, one of them."

About half way up the almost sheer side, Yerka pointed out a projection in the metal, saying:

"Push hard against it. It's a door."

SO IT was. After opening it I stopped, my eyes almost popping from my head at what I saw.

What we had first come up into, was the Quesquebah reservoir in the city of Corna. I stood upon a huge concrete abutment and looked over the city. My dizzy eyes beheld a city whose homes, palaces, stores, boulevards and streets were an amalgamation of the most grotesque and goofy designs my eyes had ever seen.

Whoever was responsible for the city's planning must have gone to the insane asylums for ideas.

Stucco vied with rococo. Gingerbread with Grecian. Victorian and vacuous. I saw homes with gabled windows on the ground floor and a Gothic upper story. And vice-versa. What I saw, in fact, made me decide I preferred the nightmares of Charlie Moran's yocky to the reality of living in Corna.

But it was too late. Already Yerka and Loo Loo and the rest were behind me, pushing me ahead.

We came to a stairway which led down the slope of the abutment. Even as I walked down the steps, Loo Loo beside me, I wondered what the hell I was getting into.

I wasn't long in finding out. As we walked along Loo Loo kept looking at me curiously.

"Look, honey," I said after a few moments of this inspection, "I'm real. You can stop looking at me like that. I can't help it if I'm a little pale. Maybe the change of climate will bring a little *color to* my cheeks. Green color."

I never thought I'd fall for a dame whose complexion was on the olive side.

"Tell me," she began—I was glad to see her teeth were white and even— "how did you meet Yerka, and what happened?"

I told her.

Her eyes, a sort of golden shade, were speculative as she said:

"So that is what happened? Yerka, in trying to stop the leak, was sucked through the break and evidently through a space fault. The evidence of that, is you. For obviously you are from another world. Perhaps from a universe which our scientists have never suspected existed. Further, that the universe of which you are a part speaks the same language as we do. That brings up several interesting questions. One, is that sickly pale color, natural pigmentation or is it a sort of protective coloring, as some of our animals have acquired through the centuries? Another question—"

"—is this," I interrupted her. "Are all the girls in this place as gorgeous as you?"

I was going to add a supplementary "and as gabby?" but didn't.

I discovered then, what Loo Loo looked like when she blushed. Her face was suffused with a lovely orchid glow. I had to admit the effect wasn't bad.

But the lady known as Loo Loo stopped me cold with this oldie:

"Oh, you!" the gorgeous goon whispers. "I bet you say that to all the girls. Now, confess—don't you?"

My weak riposte, "Nope; don't know all the girls," set her into a gale of laughter.

I thought that was going to end the game of Ask Me Another—but not with Loo Loo. Oh no; all she wanted to know was, where I was born, why; do all the people wear the same kind of clothes, why; what were cultural pursuits, why? And just—why.

I DIDN'T tell her about the Dodgers, though. It would have been too much of a job explaining the natives of Brooklyn to her. I was pumped almost as dry as the W.C.T.U. Finally we reached Yerka's little palace.

It was nice-looking, six-story job, done in yellow and blue and designed by an opium eater from something he dreamed up.

The interior, however, wasn't as bad as I thought it would be. Looked something like the lobby of the Chicago theater.

Yerka had managed to rid himself of the borrowed police clothes. He was wearing what he did when he first came sliding in out of the fourth dimension: a pair of skin-tight brown shorts and a close fitting helmet over his hair. The number eighteen coupon would have been useless in Corna. In so far as I could see, nobody wore shoes in this town.

I still had on the shirt and trousers which I had worn ever since Charlie Moran decided he was through with them. And that was a long time ago.

Yerka remedied that situation. He personally brought me to my room and after telling me, "Take a bath and I'll send you a servant with proper clothes," he left me.

"Take a bath? Holy sea cows, I've been living in one ever since last night," I groaned aloud as I disrobed.

The bathroom had one of those sunken tub affairs. When I turned on the water, a foaming spurt of warm quesqui came out. So it came to pass that what the people said about me was true. Harry MacCarey took a bath in the stuff.

The servant Yerka spoke about came in, bearing a pair of shorts and a helmet. He put them on the huge triangular-shaped bed, which was in the center of the room adjoining the bathroom. The servant, too, wore shorts and a helmet. Come to think of it, all the men I had seen wore these swim pants and helmets.

Shrugging my shoulders philosophically, or something, I slipped into the clothing.

Yerka walked in while I was enjoying the effect.

"Well, my friend," he said, as he seated himself on the bed, "do you think you'll like it here?"

Something about the way he said it made me ask:

"You sound like it's going to be permanent."

"Yes," he replied, "I think it is. You see, they fixed the crack at the bottom of the reservoir."

I thought this was as good a time as any to start asking questions. The Lord knows I'd answered enough.

"What is all this about? How did you get to the bottom of that tank? Come on, give me the lowdown."

"To begin properly," Yerka began, "you are in the city of Corna, one of the cities located on Orafa, a planet located in the third cycle of universes—"

I stopped him right there.

"Never mind the astronomy," I commanded. "Just give me the local history. And how is it I understand you and what's with the crack in the tank?"

"I'm sorry," Yerka said contritely, "but I was just explaining what every school boy knows. About the third cycle of——" He took a look at my face then and hastened on to more pertinent matters.

"About the crack in the tank. That was something which was discovered a few days ago. The constant movement of the quesqui had worn a crack into the foundation. And a leak developed. Our scientists realized the seriousness of the situation and asked for volunteers to repair it."

"What's so important about this quesqui?" I asked.

He looked horrified at my question. "In that reservoir is the city's drinking supply," he said.

I WHISTLED in surprise. Some city. And what some people will drink instead of water.

"And," he continued, "if we lost all the quesqui it would take hundreds of years to collect enough again. The only way we have of getting it is in the form of rain."

"You mean it actually rains this stuff?" I asked.

"Yes," he replied; "and not very often. So it was necessary for immediate repair work. Of course, I volunteered. And you know what happened then."

"But how did we get back?" I persisted.

"That is a question I have no answer to. I can only surmise that we are able to penetrate the fault."

"O.K.," I granted, "but how did I get through? After all I'm not from your world."

He looked at me, his forehead knit in thought.

"Perhaps," he suggested, "there is an unknown catalyst in your chemical makeup which acted upon the quesqui. As a result, although outwardly you are unchanged, in some mysterious fashion a change has taken place. For you came through, as I did. Therefore you are one of us."

"I guess that'll have to satisfy me until a better explanation comes along. But how about the crack?"

He sighed deeply then.

"We were very lucky, my friend. Those men who came to meet us were five of the greatest scientists in Corna. And they were debating with my sister Loo Loo, as to how much more time they would allow for my reappearance. We came back just in time.

"For in another few moments it would have been too late. You didn't see what happened. But they carried a cement of their devising; a cement which effectively sealed the crack."

And also sealed the entrance back to my world.

We sat there on the three-cornered bed, each lost in his own thoughts. At least I was.

I broke the silence.

"Now that I'm here, what are your plans for me?"

I had to admit Yerka's plans for my welfare exceeded my fondest hopes. This guy was Mr. Big of Corna. This little shack we were in was just his city house. He had several other places scattered about. The first thing he had planned for me was a banquet. To take place this very night.

"What about clothes?" I asked.

"Why, wear what you have," he answered.

"You mean these glamour pants?"

"But of course."

"That's all right with me. I just thought I might be out of place."

"Oh no," he assured me. "The rest will be dressed as you are."

He meant undressed.

IT WAS a little gathering of about a hundred and fifty people. I've never seen so much epidermis since the last time I was at the beach. I liked especially the drape-shape halters the women wore. It did a better job of revealing than concealing. But who was I to complain.

I was seated at a table for six. It could have been a table for six hundred. As far as I was concerned there was only one person at the table, Loo Loo.

Green complexion or no green complexion, I went overboard for her. She was seated between me and some guy who was giving her a good play till I sat down. He *was* handsome—in a sort of repulsive way. But the moment I sat in on the party, Loo had eyes only for me.

"Marta," she said to him, as I sat down, "this is the man who, by his resourcefulness and intelligence, made it possible for Yerka to return to Corna."

A pair of cold gray eyes looked me over as though I were something a chicken digs up.

"Really?" the owner of those eyes said.

I could see he didn't like me.

"Harry," she went on with the introductions, "this is Duke Marta, my fiance."

The smile left my face. This big lug was her boy friend. And he was a Duke. A fine chance I had of getting anywhere here, with a Duke for competition. But there was something about this Marta bird I didn't like. He was a little too shifty in the eye. And a little too haughty in manner.

"I think I'll take you down a peg or two," I thought, "before long."

Loo took over the conversational reins, as usual. I was content to sit back and listen to her carry on. But my eyes and brain were busy casing the banquet hall.

It was obvious, from the manners of many of those people seated at Yerka's table, that they were of the nobility. And it was also obvious that Yerka himself was a leader of some kind, from the attention paid to his remarks.

Servants arriving with trays loaded with food, brought my attention back to our table. It had been a long time since I'd seen so much food.

I speared what looked like a breast of chicken. It was watermelon! I'll swear that I was chewing on watermelon. But when I took up what looked like a tomato, and founded that it tasted like Filet Mignon, I gave up.

What a joint to land in. The meats tasted like fruits, fruits like meats, the finest whiskey I ever drank was used for bathing and drinking, and the woman I loved was going to marry a Duke.

The future didn't look too rosy. So I proceeded to lap up on quesqui. After four or five water-glasses full of the stuff, things looked brighter.

"Y'know," I said to Loo by way of an opening gambit, "no one ever accused Harry MacCarey of professing a fondness for water, but right now I wouldn't mind a glass of the stuff."

Loo was puzzled.

"Water?" she said, "What's that?

I explained as best I could.

She was still puzzled.

Everything would have been just fine if the Duke hadn't opened his kisser.

"Oh come now," he said condescendingly, "that is a little too much, you know. Really, there is no such thing."

"Look, mushmouth," the quesqui in me said, "are you calling me a liar?"

He smiled and said:

"You must admit you're pulling my ear a bit."

I leaned over the table, snarled, "Nobody calls Harry MacCarey a liar," and crossed my right to his jaw. . . .

I OPENED my eyes and saw the lovely face of Loo looking worriedly down at me. My head was in her lap. I began to wonder if every time I opened my eyes, I would find myself in her lap. The future began to look more promising.

Then I saw the circle of wondering faces surrounding me. I got up slowly and shook my head free of the cobwebs which had suddenly enmeshed my brain.

The Duke Marta was standing by the table. I walked up to him.

"I'm sorry, Duke," I apologized.

His smile made me forget the balance of the apology.

"I'm sorry, Duke," I began again. "I'm sorry I led with my right. The next time I'll use my left."

And walked away.

His laugh, nastily soft, followed me.

Yerka came up to my room in a few minutes.

"What happened?" he asked.

I told him.

He shook his head regretfully.

"Marta can be a very nasty person," was his comment on our fight.

"How come a jerk like that is going to marry your sister?"

"My father was responsible for that," Yerka explained. "In the beginning, two families ruled Corna. Mine and Marta's. Gradually my family took over most of the ruling power. But my father didn't think that condition was just. So he promised Marta's father if one had a daughter and the other a son, they would marry; thus uniting the families again. So Loo Loo will marry Marta because of a promise our father made. And then he will gain control of the city, as he has always boasted he would do."

I looked at him bug-eyed.

"You mean he's bragging of what he's going to do when he get's married?"

Yerka nodded his head.

"What's his marrying Loo Loo got to do with ruling this town?" I asked.

"When the princess marries, she becomes ruler. I hold only temporary powers until the day when my sister weds. And on that day, Marta's ambition will be realized."

Yerka sat silent, while I mulled over this interesting bit of information. I didn't like it.

"By the way, Harry," Yerka broke into my thoughts, "what is this water you speak of?"

I didn't feel like going through the business of explaining that again. So I told him if he wanted to taste some to get me certain necessary articles and I would distill some from the quesqui. It was a lucky thing I remembered some of my high school chemistry. The architects and engineers of Corna may have been a little on the queer side when it came to designs and color schemes. But the scientists of Corna were as modern as any in Chicago. Yerka's palace has as good electric illumination as could be found. And with electricity, it's a simple matter to get water from alcohol.

YERKA sipped reflectively at the colorless liquid I had brought from the retort. He took another sip, then emptied the contents down his throat. He stood silent for a few seconds, then after hiccoughing softly, handed the glass to me, saying:

"Delishush, lesh have another."

I turned and started to draw another glassful and almost dropped the glass. I turned back to him and slowly asked:

"What did you say?"

"I shaid that wash deli—deli—very good. Wash more, I'll have anozzer drink."

"Not before I have one," I replied. And filled the glass again. But all I could taste was . . . water. What the hell was going on here?

The door opened and Loo walked in.

Yerka, his head lolling at an absurd angle, watched her approach and said:

"My dear shishter. My friend Harry and I agree that Duke Marta ish a— wha d'ya call him, Harry?" he asked, appealing to me.

I told him.

"Thash righ'," Yerka went on. "Marta ish a jerk. Why? Becaush there ish shush a thing as water. Harry made me shome. Here, Loo Loo, have a drink."

With that he thrust the glass of water at the girl. She went through the same business as her brother. First, the sip, then the whole glassful, then another glassful. The second glass finished the contents of the retort. Yerka had fallen across the bed.

"Thish ish a wunnerful drink," she said, pausing deliberately between words, "and I think you're wunnerful, too."

Then she stood up. She could take it better than her brother. She at least was able to walk.

This was something I hadn't planned. Or even thought of. But there it was. I watched her weave across the room. At the door she turned and blew me a kiss. I blew one back and the door closed behind her.

I let out the air from my lungs in a soft whistle. Yerka and Loo both drunk —on water. And all the whiskey in this world was free for the asking in that steel dam behind the city. I lay back among the soft pillows and permitted myself the luxury of a few daydreams.

MacCarey and Loo Loo, the luscious king and queen of this wonderful country. Of course, I'd let Yerka be the actual ruling head. We'd empty the reservoir of quesqui and fill it up with water. The dream didn't go into any details as to how that was going to be done. That dream ended with Loo Loo and me having a high old time on a couple of glasses of water.

THEN I had another dream. Not so pleasant! Marta, dressed in a sort of Buck Rogers outfit and carrying a ray-gun as big as a house, had me prisoner. I was standing with my back against the wall. All around me were the soldiers who had fought for their Prince and Princess, Yerka and Loo Loo. They weren't of much use. They were dead. All of them; even Yerka. Beside me and held shelteringly within my strong right arm was Loo. I was bleeding from half a dozen wounds. Weak from my wounds and reeling with the fatigue of battle, I faced Marta. On my lips, tightly drawn in a thin line, a grin hovered. I saw him approach through a pain-filled haze. His lips were sneering and scornful.

"My friend," he said, "it is all over but for the shooting."

I laughed in his face. Harry Mac-Carey, the hero.

"Why don't you throw that gun away?" I said.

He did; then came at me with bare hands. I waited until he was almost on me. Then—I led with my right again!

Somewhere, I heard a voice saying:

"MacCarey, get up! Come, man, get up."

I shook my head dazedly. Damn it, I was always leading with my right.

"I'll get up," I yelled, as I struggled to get up, "and when I do——"

I felt someone tug at my shoulder and opened my eyes.

Prince Yerka's face swam into view. That was all wrong. He was supposed to be dead. My eyes made a circuit of the room. It had all been a dream. But what Yerka was saying now wasn't a dream.

"Quick, Harry," he said as I sat up. "Marta has gone crazy!"

"So what," I said, yawning widely,

"what do you want me to do? Get him the latest in strait-jackets?"

"Damn it, man!" Yerka yelled.

He shook me so hard the IQ of my wisdom teeth fell off to zero.

"Wake up! Marta is trying to over-throw the government. Already his forces are approaching the palace."

I wrenched myself loose from the wrestler's grip he had on me.

"Take it easy, pal," I said. "Do you want all of me, or just certain parts? I'm ready. What do we do?"

One look at his puss told me he was in a fog. I would have been, too, if I had as much water in me.

"All right, chum," I said, "let's go out and take a look at the brawl. Maybe I can figure out an angle on how to stop it."

There was the God-awfullest noise to be heard as we came out on the balcony. It sounded like a New Year's eve at State and Madison.

The streets below were packed with struggling figures. I looked on the scene bewildered, then asked:

"Say, who's who? How do we tell what side we're on?"

Yerka, his arms folded across his chest and looking like Hamlet waiting for a cue, replied:

"The men in the purple shorts are ours."

That was nice to know. Especially when Marta's men seemed to be dressed in dark blue shorts. But in all this struggling, shouting and confusion I couldn't see any sort of weapons being used.

"Where are their rods?" I asked.

Yerka put on his favorite expression, the blank look.

"Their guns — weapons?" I said hastily.

"We have no weapons," Yerka explained, "they have been outlawed here."

I STOOD there for a few seconds, lost in thought.

I looked beyond the struggling figures, to the sprawling city. It's goofy-looking architecture suddenly pleased me. I liked the haphazard arrangement of things. The way the homes looked. Yes, even the way the hydrants looked. The hydrants! I suddenly remembered a scene from a movie.

Quickly I told Yerka of my plan. And, as quickly, had it acted upon. We waited on the balcony to see what was going to take place. As we stood there I felt a soft, warm hand slip into mine. Startled, I turned and looked into the golden eyes of Loo Loo. One look was enough. Marta had lost his fiancee. And when I looked down I saw Marta was going to lose his battle.

Yerka had followed my instructions implicitly. They were coming from all directions, their sirens wailing hysterically. All the fire departments in Corna.

I had noticed the battle royal was taking place in a little square in front of the palace. So I had told Yerka to get the fire companies out. And use the hose on everybody. Already every hydrant on three sides of the square had pieces of hose attached to it. And in a short while it was all over. They practically washed the whole battle right out of the square. Of course, it took a hell of a lot of quesqui to do it. But finally it was all over.

The three of us walked back into the room. Yerka was out of the world.

"Harry," he babbled, "it was sheer genius, that thought." He laughed aloud.

"How funny they looked when the quesqui struck them."

To tell the truth, I wasn't paying too much attention to him. I was too wrapped up in Loo. We were holding hands like a couple of moonstruck kids. Then he popped up with:

"And tonight we will celebrate this victory. A banquet. That's what we'll have."

Loo leaned over and whispered something in his ear. He turned to her, surprise on his face.

"But, sister," he said, "that can't be. He's a commoner."

Loo whispered something else to him. A big smile appeared on his face and he gave me a whack across my shoulders that sent me staggering.

The banquet hall was jammed again. I noticed something new this time, Yerka was sitting at a long table placed against the wall. With him were twelve men. They sat facing the rest of the people. After the meal, Yerka stood up and went into a long spiel about how I saved his throne.

While he was going on about me, I leaned over and whispered to Loo:

"What happened to Marta?"

"He escaped. The guards are searching for him."

Suddenly there was an interruption. A guard dashed in and ran up to Yerka. We could see that the guard's message was important, because Yerka instantly went into a confab with the men seated with him.

Yerka called one of the servants over to him and gave him an order.

The servant came over to our table and said.

"Sir, the Prince Yerka wishes to speak to you."

THE smile I had on my face went away when I came to Yerka's table. Whatever had happened was damned serious, from the looks on their faces.

"Harry," Yerka began, "it looks as if Marta is going to have the last word."

"What do you mean?"

"Marta went to the reservoir with several of his men and broke the cement which closed the crack."

"So what?" I said. "Have your scientists make more cement."

"That is the trouble. It may take too long."

After a lot of arguing back and forth, they came to a conclusion. That it would be the best thing for everyone concerned if they sent Harry MacCarey back to where he came from. He'd caused enough trouble.

My throat felt dry. If only I had a drink. Even water. Then I had it. The solution, I mean.

"Look," I said. "If you were to get a substitute for this quesqui, would that solve the problem?"

That gave them a good laugh. But I wasn't done yet.

"Well," I demanded, "would it?"

"Of course," one of them replied, "but where is this substitute to be found?"

I told them about water. Yerka objected, however:

"But you made the water from quesqui," he said. "And soon there will be no quesqui."

I laughed and shook my head. "I can do something more wonderful than that," I said. "I can make this water from the very air we breathe."

Now the scientists laughed.

We all had a good laugh together. Then I told them to get me the apparatus I wanted. It was a good thing Yerka was for me. In a half hour I had assembled what I needed. I played it smart and made only a couple of quarts of water. Just enough to get the scientists tight. After that, I could ask for almost anything and get it. They finally got together enough cement for the crack. I went down with them and just before the finishing touches went on I slipped these papers through. So tell the boys that Harry MacCarey—excuse me, Duke Harry MacCarey is going to marry a princess and live happily ever after in a house with gables on the top and bottom and Gothic in between.

But it will seem funny to see people get stiff on water.

THE END

MIDAS MORGAN'S GOLDEN TOUCH
(Concluded from page 173)

didn't have so much as a one-ounce gold nugget to remind me of those pesky gold-making gloves . . ."

"I THINK I understand," I frowned, thoughtfully. "The affinity between the two gloves was what brought on and controlled the remarkable transmutations. And with one glove destroyed, the other became useless—and all the molecules of the materials that had been transmuted quickly rearranged themselves into their original atomic form!" I sat dreamily cogitating on this for the space of two minutes. Then I bounced up, glaring down at Midas Morgan. "Say, you don't think

I really swallowed all that!"

"You got to believe it," Morgan insisted, blinking his deep-set eyes. "It's gospel truth. And I figger that the leader of them critters let me have my wish, knowing what was going to happen, just to teach me a lesson. And not only me, but everybody on this old planet!

"That's why I go around telling folks about it—to teach them the lesson I learnt. Not to be greedy."

I sat down again impatiently, rubbing my chin.

"For instance," Morgan went on blandly. "I'll bet you got ten bucks in your pocket right now you don't need, but somebody else does."

"As a matter of fact," I admitted, "I have an extra ten spot. I'm saving it for another bond."

I tugged out my carefully folded ten-spot to reassure myself.

"Give it to me," Morgan whispered. "I'll make good use of it."

"Look here!" I snorted. "That cock-and-bull story of yours was just—"

"Was it?" Morgan broke in, very softly.

He tugged his left arm of his overall bib, solemnly. He pulled back the ragged sleeve.

I gulped.

His left hand was missing, cut off at the wrist.

Midas Morgan stood up dramati-cally. He grabbed my proffered ten-spot, and stalked majestically down the street.

I stared after him.

A nearby old man with a droopy sombrero sniggered.

I whirled on him sharply.

"That guy Morgan has sure got it!" he chuckled.

"Got what?"

"Why, the Golden Touch, of course!" the man with the droopy sombrero said. "He just touched you for an easy ten-ner, didn't he?" He closed his half-open eyes, and mumbled off sleepily, "The las' time Morgan tol' it, he lost that hand saving a little girl from a Bengal tiger what broke loose from a circus in Hoboken . . ."

The OBSERVATORY by THE Editor

(Concluded from page 6)

that fact. And we guarantee that, whether or not you believe a word of the story, it strikes us as mighty fine material for AMAZING STORIES.

WHY do we die? What is gravity? How did life come to Earth? Are there beings on other worlds? Did ancient Mu exist? If you have any of the answers to these questions, they are either wrong, or inadequate! The *true* answers are contained in the TRUE STORY OF LEMURIA! And when we have completed the assembling of a mass of sensational theory and fact and a thrilling story of adventure, we intend to present it to you, take it or leave it. But *we* believe it to be *true!*

WHERE did we get this amazing manuscript? Well, it's not a manuscript—it is the *memory* of one of the most amazing men we have ever had the good fortune to encounter—a man who *re-members* (through that process we call "racial memory") the whole story of ancient Lemuria, and further, remembers many of its scientific se-crets! Watch this column for more definite de-tails!

IN "DISCUSSIONS" for this issue you will find an innovation in prize contests. The startling success of our new discussion policy has had one result which tends to throw us out of direct con-tact with your opinions on the stories. Thus, we are now instituting a $10.00 monthly prize (to hold true also for our sister magazines, *Fantastic Adventures* and *Mammoth Detective*) to the reader who writes the best letter of not over one hundred words telling us what he likes most about the magazine and what he likes least; and submits a list of the stories he has read in the issue in the order of merit. The way you list the stories has nothing to do with your eligibility for the prize. The contest will continue until further notice. So step in, you readers, and register your likes and dislikes. It's not often you get paid for either praising or kicking. "Discussions," of course, will continue entirely independently, being the place where you can air everything from soup to nuts.

AMONG those soldiers who visited us recently on furlough were Lt. William Lawrence Ham-ling; Lt. Russell Milburn; Lt. Jack West; Sgt. John Sharp, and Sgt. Sylvester Brown, Jr. Two authors, one artist, and two readers. It certainly makes us feel good to realize that these boys think enough of us to give us some of their furlough time!

WE HAVE just received word that the second Martin Brand story—"The Justice of Martin Brand"—has gone to the typist, and author G. H. Irwin finally concedes that it satisfies him! Then it must be something! This "most-asked-for" se-quel in several years will appear just as soon as our schedule can accommodate it! Even if we have to tear it all apart. Be seeing you. . . .

Rap

Scientific

THE GREAT TEMPLE OF KARNAK AT THEBES TO AMEN (WHOSE SON WAS OSIRIS, A HISSING-SOUND NAME, SYNONYMOUS WITH THE SERPENT, OR DRAGON) WHO WAS THE "VEILED ONE," LORD OF TWO LANDS

AMEN

OSIRIS

FACIAL PAINTING OF AMERICAN MAYA PRIEST SHOWING THE HORIZONTAL STRIPING OF THE DRAGON TOTEMS, SIMILAR TO THE VEILING OF THE MODERN MAYA

SHOSHONI

TANOAN KIOWA

CREEKS

CHOCTAH

CREEKS

PIMAN

ATHABASCAN APACHE

YAQUI

MAYO

HUICHOL

NAHUA

AZTEC

MAYA

ARUAKS

UTO-AZTECAN GROUP OF LANGUAGES

MAP SHOWING DISTRIBUTION OF THE TRIBES OF THE DRAGON IN-FLUENCE IN CENTRAL AMERICA

FOOTPRINTS OF THE DRAGON

By L. Taylor Hansen

The trail of the Dragon can be followed over all the Earth and through the legends of many isolated races of humankind.

WE HAVE seen how, in trying to track down to its lair, the ancient colossus of the seas, the giant Dragon Totem, the weight of much evidence seems to point to two very important conclusions: 1) that the long-headed peoples of the Americas, who occupy the refuge-locations (thus indicating an early strata of population) also seem to carry the strongest suggestions of very ancient Dragon ritual, and 2) that the ceremonies and legends which these isolated tribes hold in common, apparently center in the Antilles.

These facts certainly do not fit in with the centralization of the Dragon Totem in Asia, where it is at present carried largely by a round-headed population. Furthermore, if the Dragon entered Amerind ritual from Asia, then we would expect to find its traces through the Northwest of North America and down the Pacific Coast. This is not true. The Wolf Totem is the most powerful in the Northwest with Coyote-Man the first figure in their pantheons. The Great Bird is second, but even the Whale Totem is more powerful than the Reptile-gods. In face, in no other part of the Americas, with the possible exception of the Southwest part of So. America, are the Reptile-gods as weak as they are in the Pacific Northwest.

Yet certainly there is some meaning in the pattern which the distribution of Dragon-ritual presents, rippling outward as it does from the Antilles, and resting most strongly in the *Uto-Aztecan* family of languages which number most of their members from Mexican tribes. Just as there is most certainly a meaning behind the three main types of face-painting and the distribution of each. The division of the face into two halves originally indicated the Totem of the Eagle, or the Great Bird. This is most strongly characteristic of the hawk-nosed disharmonic Old Red Race which is largely crowded into the eastern part of North America. The painting or tatooing of the face into concentric whorls or circles is typical of the Spider Totem and is scattered through the South Seas and up some of the South American coasts. The horizontal banding of the face indicates The Serpent or The Great Dragon Totem. (The various colors stand for the four directions, which differ from tribe to tribe.)

For a moment, let us concentrate upon this horizontal banding which some authorities have noted is so typical of the wild tribes islanded in refuge-locations, that they have suggested it may be typical of hunting tribes in general. The various Karib peoples of the Antilles, including the Aruaks who speak a tongue akin to these Indians of the Caribbean, wore nose-bands or in some manner indicated a horizontal line across the cheeks. The Itzaes[1] wore a hollow tube through the septum of the nose into which breathing holes had been punched. At the present time the Mayas wear a veil across their nose and mouth at night. When questioned about the matter, they insist that the night air is poisonous, and they must protect their air passages. (The Ancient Mayas by Stacy-Judd)

It was an old Indian sage who gave the present writer the needed hint which might serve to unravel this mystery. In remarking upon the continual connection between the horizontal banding of the face, in ritualistic dances of the Veiled-One (if not actual veiling the features) and the other characteristics of the Great Serpent or Great Dragon as compared to those of Egypt, he suddenly remarked: "Was the 'Veiled One' of this Ancient Egypt, always known as Ammon-Ra?"

"Why, no," I answered thoughtfully, "that was the joining of two sun-gods into one. Ra came into Egypt from the east while Ammon or Amen came from the direction of the Atlantic . . . " But my mind was leaping ahead of my words. Was this Egyptian Amen the Zamna of the Mayas, the Tiaman of the Guatemala tribes—even the Tanama "Trembling-One" (Earthquake) of the Apaches?[2] Tanama had once walked

---

[1] *Itzaes, "First Conquerors of Colhuas." They founded the Mayan Golden Age. In turn were conquered by Tutul-Xius.*

---

[2] *For Apache legend see E. L. Squier, "Children of the Twilight."*

among them, teaching them how to live. (Apparently this was a confusion with a later culture-hero, similar to the Quetzalcoatl legend.) Yet if this remark was thought-provoking, the next observation by the old sage was almost startling.

"Of course, he does not always go by the same name. He is the god of breath or life. Therefore he sometimes goes by a name with a hissing sound."

"Osiris! The god of life and learning! The Egyptian son of Amen!" I gasped.

OTHER names were flashing to my mind. Some of the names of the ancient cities which history records once belonged to those mysterious veiled Tuaraks who rule the Lybian desert. Tafassaset! Khamissa! Essouk! And the mysterious secret society of the Sahara whose wasm[3] is the Serpent—The Senussi! Did the hissing sound of the serpent cause it to be early connected with breath and life? And the veil which the Tuaraks of today place upon a boy at puberty and which thereafter no one sees him without —they explain its presence by saying that they wish to protect their nasal passages from evil spirits! What connection did that have with the fact that Amen was known as "The Hidden One?"

There was another fact about Amen—"The Two Horned" which kept pounding itself rhythmically to my attention. Amen had been known as the "Lord of the Two Lands." Sometimes he had been spoken of as being seated upon the "Throne of the Two Lands." What were these two lands? And what did the Tuaraks mean when they pointed to the Atlantic as their homeland?

Possibly all of this was mere coincidence. Yet there were the curious little three-sided stones found on both sides of the central section of the Southern Atlantic. Both Northern Africa and Central America had yielded them. On one side was a face, on the other side feet, and in the center the peak. They are distinct representations of a man buried under a mountain. What could they mean. What ritualistic significance did they have or what story were they trying to tell?

And then from both sides of the Atlantic at this point was the legend of the warrior-women —women who had removed the right breast in order to better handle their bows? Upon the American side there was the legend of the women warriors who met the men of another tribe upon the certain designated night of each year and at that time returned all male infants born to them during the previous twelve months. The Spanish did not find the legendary tribe. Yet they did find that the Karibs had fighting women. These women fought beside their men in battle, did no work and were very strong in

all tribal councils. The work was all done by captive women from other tribes.

Strangely enough, the French priests travelling up the Mississippi River during the following century, discovered that the Choctaws, who painted their faces with the sinuous horizontal of the Serpent, and who boasted that they were immune from snake-bite (evidently an ancient remedy, since all Serpent peoples the world over seem to share this knowledge) had a legendary woman-chief who had been a particularly savage warrior. This is the most notable case of the Serpent Totem being found outside of the Uto-Aztecan block of languages with the exception of the Antillean group. As the relationship of the Antillean group is as yet very little understood, it is quite possible that they will be found to be connected, while the Choctaws, speaking a Muskhogean tongue related to the Creeks, share with the Creeks their legend of a Mexican origin.

AS YET so little is known of these various Indian tongues in their relation one with the other, that the investigator must be cautious and creep over the paths which in another hundred years with the subsequent investigation of Central American and South American tongues and comparisons of them all, will, we hope, no longer be obscure and uncertain paths. Certain it is, that here in the Americas, there is more knowledge of the ancient figure of Ammon-Ra than the old world has known since the burning of the great Egyptian and Alexandrian libraries. Yet that knowledge is in the form of fragmentary legends held in the memory of a priesthood which is gradually losing the fight against the encroachments of a much younger religion.

If this priesthood decides to die with their lips still sealed, then our scientists will write in blissful ignorance that the Red Man had childish notions of nature worship, and the last strands which connect the Americas to untold millenniums of forgotten history will fade away under the very spectacles of twentieth century science without that august body even suspecting its existence.

It is time for science to stop riding comfortably upon the theory of entire Asian migration. It a theory which will no longer fit all of the facts. As more is learned about Amerind thought, it should become increasingly evident that THE AMERICAS ARE CULTURALLY CLOSER TO ANCIENT EGYPT THAN THEY EVER WERE TO ASIA!

It is high time for some young scientist with vision, to begin a life-time pursuit of this figure of Amen from tribe to tribe. His names may vary but his characteristics are the same. He will spill over the barriers of the Uto-Aztecan tongues into the Athapascan Apaches of Arizona where he is Tanama, or the Muskhogean Creeks and Choctaws of the lower Mississippi River where he is the fire-god and Master of Breath—

(Concluded on page 210)

---

[3] *Wasm, Arabic for trademark or signature.* See De Prorok, *"Mysterious Sahara."*

DISCUSSIONS

WHO'S THIS GUY, SINATRA!

Sirs:

I am a comparatively new fan, though I have always thirsted for S. F. I have beside me now, two issues of AMAZING STORIES QUARTERLY and enjoyed both to the utmost. I think the best two stories are "Warrior of the Dawn" and "That Worlds May Live." I mistook the former as belonging to Burroughs.

Now down to business. I would like to acquire some back issues of AMAZING STORIES QUARTERLY. I also wish you would contact me through my address as I don't have much hope of acquiring any AMAZING STORIES any other way.

One thing I might suggest: More novels, less serials, more Juggernaut Jones and more space stories.

But, all in all, I can't complain, but I do get a kick out of some of the letters in Discussions. This is the first fan mail letter I ever wrote, and this is the first magazine that got me excited enough to do it. And, brother, that's something! And keep up those kind of back covers coming along.

All the illustrations in my latest ish were good, in fact splendid except the ones for "Victory from the Void," "Ard of the Sunset People," and "Bring Back My Body!"

As I say, I would like to get my hooks on some of those back ish's of AMAZING STORIES QUARTERLY. I am 13, and the only guy at my school who doesn't swoon over comic books, in fact the only kind I like are Walt Disney's comics. And I am the only one who could sit down with one of your big ones and really read it! I have, I believe, one of your books dated 1933.

Well, I guess this is my limit, so so long 'til next time.

EDWARD KYTTA,
Townsend Harbor, Mass.

We wouldn't want you to swoon over AMAZING STORIES, but the implication flatters us anyhow! As for back issues of the Quarterly, so sorry! All out! But you'll find a list of the available monthlies at the end of "Discussions."—ED.

HIGH PRAISE FOR WILLIAMS

Sirs:

I must tell you how much I enjoyed the novelet "The Machine," found in your winter quarterly of 1943. This story was written by Robert Moore Williams.

A more stirring and fantastic drama could not be found elsewhere, except in AMAZING STORIES magazine.

In my worthless opinion, it has put your publication at the top of fiction magazines.

There wouldn't have been a better way in which to tell one of the progress and unlimited powers of the machine.

I would like to congratulate your talented author, Robert Williams. Also congratulations to your editors for turning out a story that is truly a great masterpiece.

Let's have more stories like "The Machine." I know your vast reading public enjoyed it also.

HOWARD WEASE
Box 105
Clarkdale, Arizona.

Your editors agree absolutely! Williams commands our deep respect.—ED.

OH, MISTER SERENE!

Sirs:

I have been reading your magazines, AMAZING STORIES and *Fantastic Adventures*, since somewhere around 1932, and have enjoyed them very much. Some have been excellent and some not so good, but usually very good.

The very excellent were "The Black Flame," "The Eagle Man," "The Mystery of the Lost Race," "Doorway to Hell," "That Worlds May Live," "Warrior of the Dawn," "The Last Warship," and last but not least, the newest "Intruders from the Stars."

This was very excellent as it is one of those stories which sticks with one and causes a good deal of consideration; it could happen, therefore it causes one to think about its possibilities. More by Rocklynne, please.

Magarian is superb, why not a cover by (her?). Her work is an art and a pleasant relief from so much machinery, slimy beasts and spaceships. Mc-Cauley is very good, as are St. John, Finlay, Paul and Fuqua.

The authors, I've already mentioned Rocklynne, so on to Wilcox, Burroughs, Bond, etc. All very good. What happened to E. K. Jarvis ("The Mystery of the Lost Race") and Frank Patton ("Doorway to Hell")?

Discussions is one of the first departments I read. However, I don't agree with Mr. Jos. G Serene of Pa. when he says rule out all cigarettes, swearing

and drinking. Especially smoking. I have always noticed that your authors try to make their characters as human and convincing as possible, because for a story to go across to the public it has to be convincing enough for the reader to imagine those things could actually happen to him or her.

As for Mr. Serene's reference to the "Mad Robot," what could have been more natural than for Rick to light a cigarette for Rita and himself? Besides it relieves the tension, in many cases, of a fast moving story.

So I say do not rule these things out just because one reader wants you to; let the rest of us have our say.

I'm hoping you'll print this so as to get an idea of what others think.

Before I close, how about some more stories applied to today's war and its outcome? I'm sure a great many could be written around it such as Rocklynne's was.

JOE ALMAN
Corpus Christi, Texas.

*Magarian, unfortunately, is lost to us by the pressure of other work, so even the interior illustrations we have we are doling out slowly to make them last. E. K. Jarvis is in the air force, but he'll appear next issue in our special Fighting Force written issue! Frank Patton is still working, and has promised us a long yarn soon. As for Mr. Serene's letter, your editor was completely swamped by protests and indignation by the readers. Before such a flood of mail we can only bow, and say with heartfelt sincerity, "we'll be goddamned!"—*ED.

WHO DROPPED THAT BANANA PEEL?
Sirs:

Altho I know darn (*Damn, not darn! Please! Our readers will mow us down!*—ED.) well you won't publish my letter I have a bet. (Remember my remarks are all in the nature of constructive criticism.) Here goes:

In the first place you seem to have a flattering opinion of your magazine. Tho you claim your stories are so thrilling, the majority of them are plainly mediocre. However you do publish a good story occasionally.

A good story is hard to define. Nevertheless it holds its interest all the way and the plot is not cluttered up with cigarettes, ray-guns and green-skinned Venusians. In other words a good story has something of originality and a plot with hair on it.

Also, why be so darn (*sic!*—ED.) serious in a story? Why not mix some humor into it? After all the reader pays his quarter to be entertained.

Let's have a few space stories. Interstellar and intergallaxy tales. Venus, Pluto, Callisto, etc., could stand a rest.

Personally I think your writers are overworked with a few exceptions: Ross Rocklynne, Robert Moore Williams, Eando Binder.

By the way, you could fire your whole bunch of so-called artists and save on paper thru the discussions they create. Bother the cover and hire one 10th rate artist.

If you trim the edges (they need it) this paper could be resold.

I hope my letter proves instructive and that you will publish it.

Please remember there are thousands who judge a good story merely by reading it.

> D. C. FARNEY
> 129 W. 3rd Street.
> Newport, Ky.

The day we first picked up a copy of AMAZING STORIES *(18 years ago) we formed a flattering opinion of the magazine. We've still got it. Only now, we get letters every day reminding us of that opinion, so we can't see how we can abandon it and still be honest! We challenge you to show us a "clutter" of cigarettes, ray guns, and green-skinned Venusians! Take this issue, for instance? Humor? We* INVENTED *humor in science fiction! And we've run more humor stories than any other pulp in history (outside of a few magazines up to 50 years in the field)! There are* TWO *in this issue! Your last sentence is very interesting. How do those thousands judge a story who* DON'T *read it? How* ELSE *do you judge a story? And we bet you lost your bet! But all kidding aside, we'll give you intergalactic stories, and humor, and everything else you want, when we can. We hope next time we'll please you better.—*ED.

BOY, ARE YOU GOING TO BE MOBBED!

Sirs:

Would you help a devoted STF fan?

Meaning *me!*

If so print this:

I have located some old magazines which some of your readers might be interested in securing.

They include some old AMAZING STORIES, both quarterly and monthly and "Air Wonder Stories," and a few "Wonder Stories Quarterlies" about 15 years old.

I thought we might run this sale as auction but if you wish, quote a price you'd be willing to pay.

It might be of interest to collector fans that one of the mags containing Hugo Gernsback's book "Ralph 124C 41."

> C. S. GARRIQUES
> 720 Stenney St.,
> Inglewood, Calif.

*Okay, you collectors, jump all over him! He's a rarity, these days—a fan with precious old issues to sell!—*ED.

STORM OVER SERENE!

Sirs:

For the first time since I have been reading your magazine (which is a good many years) I am unable to resist the temptation to make a few remarks about one of the letters in the Discussions Dept. I refer to the letter in the March issue, from one Jos. C. Serene—

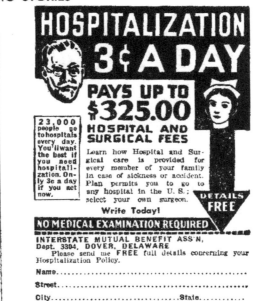

You Also Serve

If You Work Efficiently in the Home Trenches

Really, Mr. Serene, you should come out of your shell and face the facts of life! At first I thought that I might be reading a letter written by some preacher or minister, but as I thought back, I could not remember a single one (and I might add that I have known many) that was so narrow-minded and short-sighted. Tobacco is not a vice, merely a stimulant, and liquor can be regarded bad only when taken in excess—but after all these columns are hardly the place to discuss the relative merits or sins of such items, nor does it seem the proper place for an impromptu little sermon such as your letter was.

Now, after all, the stories you will find in magazines such as this depict men of action who live hard, work hard, play hard and on occasion pray hard. Now such men (you will find many of them in the armed services today fighting for your, and all of our, freedom) are not prone to speak among themselves in a vocabulary that would seem to come from a third year reader or a monthly religious magazine. No, not even the brave chaplains, who go into the fiercest of actions, bearing no weapons, so that they may bring the solace and comfort at the time of greatest need. Even they, my dear Mr. Serene, whom I'm sure *you* could not censor in any way, are prone to lapse into a bit of good old fashioned "cussing" when circumstances suggest such a course.

I can say one thing about you—you are well named, for you must have lived a very serene life not to have encountered a situation where uttering a really heartfelt "DAMN" would be the most natural thing in the world. It is easy to see that you have never had to fight for your life or anything else that was very dear to you. I wish that all of us could be so fortunate! But unfortunately such is not the case. If you had ever lived among men being trained in the fine art of killing—or thrust a bayonet through a dummy in practice for live dummies in the form of Japs or Germans, or marched in the hot sun 'til your feet were blistered and carried a rifle 'til your shoulder was sore; all of this, mind you, merely in training to become a man of action, much less live through the actual hell of battle for your own life and what's more the very existence of your country and your mode of living, then you would understand why men may talk profanely, and smoke a cigarette or perhaps (don't let this shock you *too* much) take a drink once in a while.

In the pages of any science fiction magazine or book, you will find such men as these portrayed, men who are pioneers just as much as those great but rough men who wrested the west, in fact the entire of what you choose to call your U.S.A., from the wilderness. If you are unwilling or possibly are unable to stand the shock of what would be the natural speech and mode of living of such men, I suggest that you look elsewhere for your reading matter. There are many worthwhile religious magazines and papers available (of which I have read my share) that would be only too glad to gain your support. I, for one, would be unwilling to read about thousands of saintly space travelers wresting worlds from their native inhabitants by quickly passing out copies of the New Testament. When I want religion I'll go where I have been going for it all my life—to Church—but when I want amusement and fanciful, yet true-to-life reading, I'll continue to come to the pages of such magazines as AMAZING STORIES.

C. P. SUREAU
P. O. Box 2733
Hollywood 28, Calif.

All your editor can say is that this column is called Discussions, and since Mr. Serene brought up the subject, be it on his own head! However, many readers got the opinion we agreed heartily with Mr. Serene. Well, we do, when profanity is used for profanity's sake, or just as an amateur attempt on the part of a writer to attract attention. And we also do, concerning cigarettes, when the author has a policy of adding 500 words (at regular rates) to his story by having his characters smoke incessantly. THAT'S making a sucker out of us, and like any ordinary human, it gripes us! Damn it, how it gripes us!—ED.

YOU LOSE, MR. COX

Sirs:

I have a few things to say about the January issue of AMAZING STORIES.

First there are the covers, which are remarkably good. Fuqua's covers are quite good, but I can't say the same for his inside illustrations in all this issue. I like the idea of both covers to illustrate a story. Why don't you get rid of "Stories of the Stars" and have both covers depict a scene from one of the stories?

As for the stories—they're better than the stories in the preceding issue. "Intruders from the Stars" takes the ribbon. And coming up neck and neck are "Island of Eternal Storm" and "The Mad Robot." GIVE US MORE LIVINGSTON!!!! (The rest of the stories weren't bad, either!)

All in all, I think AMAZING's pretty good!

ARTHUR COX
Rt. 8, Box 5617
Sacramento, Calif.

Sorry, Mr. Cox, but the readers say "no" to the idea of using the back cover in any other way than we have for years—for a special feature.—ED.

OH SAY CAN YOU SEE—DOES THAT ERROR STILL GLARE?

Sirs:

Egad, editor! I have just finished reading Vance's "The Needle Points to Death" in the Jan. issue. Now I am not one to criticize, but I found a glaring mistake in it and thought I'd let you know about it. It seems that Jeff Morgan (our hero) is explaining the purpose of his latest invention to his wife Ann. To quote: "Anyway, this device isn't particularly complex. It's simply a means to determine the temperature in space at any given time. You know, of course, that the temp-

erature in the void is always pretty close to absolute zero; but it would be a great help in rocket construction and navigation if we could know that temperature exactly, especially in areas like this where there is considerable variation." If I know my physics and astronomy correctly, absolute zero is the point at which all atomic and molecular motion or vibration ceases. Since heat is molecular motion then if this motion stopped, the substance at that temperature, i.e., absolute zero, could not become any colder. Now outer space is believed to be void of all matter (of course, except the stars, sun, planets, etc.). The only thing space is supposed to contain is ether. As Webster defines ether, it is "a medium postulated in the unadulatory theory of light (and radiant heat) as permeating all space, and as transmitting transverse waves." The parentheses are mine. Since space is void of matter, therefore, also of molecules, which are essential for certain forms of heat, how can it have any other temperature other than absolute zero? The heat comes to the earth from the sun via ether. Any body in space which would intercept such waves would either absorb, reflect, reradiate or transmit (or perhaps a combination of two or more of the operations) the heat waves. Even in the immediate region of such a body the temperature of space itself would be absolute zero. Take the moon for example. The moon itself (on the sunward side) would have a temperature of perhaps 200°. But, if possible, you measured the temperature of space, say 1 inch above its surface, you would find it, theoretically, to be absolute zero. I say "theoretically" because actually the thermometer would absorb heat radiated by the sun or reradiated by the moon (via ether) and, therefore, record this. Radiant heat is transmitted through space the same way light is. In fact, radiant heat is of the same vibratory nature as light only of longer wavelength.

All this goes to prove that outer, or interstellar space has and cannot have any temperature other than absolute zero.

My letter, however, does not reflect my views of your magazine. On the contrary, I enjoy it very much.

DONALD MARY
751 Convention St.
Baton Rouge, 8, La.

Egad, Mr. Mary! We have discovered a glaring error in your hypotheses. Since Webster has "postulated" (the quotes are ours) ether to be a medium that fills all space, said medium being nothing, we hold that in all true scientific spirit you cannot draw a single one of your conclusions from a postulation. The fact is, we don't know what space is filled with (or not filled with) so we further hold that Mr. Vance has as much right to give space any temperature he wants other than (or identical with) the one you give it! However, entirely unrelated from this letter and its editorial reply, we ask that you keep an eye open for a story mentioned in our editorial column this issue—it will present, among other things, a most sensational idea concerning what space is filled with! And we have a funny idea scientific investigation will find itself hard put to shrug it aside!—ED.

IDEAS ON PROPULSION METHODS IN SPACE

Sirs:

In practically all the stories I have read about interplanetary travel the driving element has been rockets. Why not have some other method that does away with all that weight and machinery? Couldn't centrifugal force or the opposing gravitational forces of some other planet or a beam of energy shot from some station on earth to a small resistance in the vehicle push the ship like a sailboat? I should think these methods would work if only in a science fiction story. I'm only 13 and just starting to read science fiction so maybe I should just sit back and keep quiet, but I'm bound to get my say in now, so here goes.

The popular conception of the rocket ship is a long, thin, cigar-shaped vehicle, and that is because, says Chad Oliver, of Cincinnati, Ohio, of air pressure. Well, unless the ship is used specifically for travel through an atmosphere, such as on earth, the distance traveled through air would be negligible, say 500 mi. at each end against the millions of miles traveled through a space utterly devoid of air. Thus a ship that was square, round, hexagonal, or any other shape would do equally well.

According to A. Brown in his letter, and I quote, "For with no air in space to create friction, a ship could travel on inertia, theoretically." That's all very well, and one could probably travel to one's destination with plenty of inertia left over, but air isn't the only thing that can exert pressure.

I think it's a pretty well-known fact that radiation exerts pressure. Even barring the light and heat radiations from the various stars the cosmic radiations alone would suffice to stop the ship after perhaps billions of years.

You and Pvt. Ralph Blumenthal seem to have had quite a chat about travel on Jupiter. Besides the fact that astronomers believe Jupiter to be in a semi-gaseous-liquid state, just cooling down, I think both your ideas could be improved upon. Your idea about having a propellor or screw under the surface is as bad as his tractor idea. Why not have a propellor up in the atmosphere like the similarly driven marsh boats used by our army today. It would provide less friction than a screw to hold the craft back, and certainly no more weight to push it down. If your idea of Jupiter is that Jupiter has no atmosphere, you can use rockets or my energy-beam idea.

ARTHUR Z. BROWN
19 Cubberly Place
Staten Island 6, N. Y.

Once more we've got to say that we can't really propound anything but theory, since we don't know what we'll find out in "space." Maybe it's empty, maybe it isn't. But dealing with known factors, it is scientifically best to shape our spaceship in the form of a cigar or projectile. Our forth-

coming true story of Lemuria will contain some intensely interesting thoughts on this very subject. When we present that, we'll have a lot more to say we can't hint at now!—ED.

MANY STORIES ON HAND!

Sirs:

Don Wilcox's "Earth Stealers" is the best science fiction story I have ever read. I have never written to any magazine before but I just had to let you know how much I enjoy all the works of Wilcox. "The Great Brain Panic" was also very good, but somehow it did not measure up to "Earth Stealers." As a writer of science fiction Wilcox is tops! Please print as much of his stuff as possible. AMAZING has always been an especially good magazine and it is getting better with every issue. Keep up the good work.

DON MERWIN
160-15 7 Ave.
Beechhurst, N. Y.

You'll get your wish. We have a great number of Wilcox manuscripts on hand, ranging from novels down to shorts.—ED

WE DON'T DO IT—YOU DO!

Sirs:

Keep AMAZING STORIES going. AMAZING is now the only bi-monthly S.F. mag on the market. There is still one monthly mag, but that—er—stinks. Your mag has three times as much content and the stories are much better, yet the monthly is the same price as AMAZING. I don't know how you manage to do it, but you're doing it.

AMAZING STORIES is now, in my opinion, the 2nd best mag. Keep it up, AMAZING.

MONROE KUTTNER
41-16 51st St.
Woodside, N. Y.

You readers asked for more stories, and we gave them to you! But you meant to say AMAZING STORIES is the best magazine, not second best, didn't you? A typographical error, no doubt.—ED.

CORRECTION

Sirs:

I read your very interesting article in the January, 1944, issue of AMAZING STORIES, attempting to describe why the indentations or craters are upon the moon's surface. I am not attempting to discredit it. I think your reasons are very plausible and I agree with you in every respect, but one. In your last paragraph you mentioned that the hail of comets destroyed everything. "The very air burned," you said. I have only taken one term of chemistry in college and I learned that the air is composed with other elements, of oxygen and oxygen does not burn, it merely supports combustion. Perhaps I am wrong. I probably am, but would you please let me know.

MELVIN JANOVE
701 Crotona Park North
Bronx 57, New York City

Our explanation was inept. What we meant was that the very air was destroyed (as air) by burning. If you'll check, you'll find that "burning" is the process of oxygen combining with another element to produce an oxide. Rust is such an oxide. Thus, all the Moon's air (oxygen) entered into chemical combination with other elements, due to the "burning" and became heat, light, oxides.—Ed.

YOU ARE PRIVILEGED!

Sirs:

Why do people, when they see somebody walking down the street with a science fiction magazine under his arm, shake their heads regretfully, and mutter something about "Such a nice young fellow, but he has to read that rot. . . ."

This is supposed to be a practical nation, but why don't you people realize that some day there will be spaceships and other marvels of science? Why, one hundreds years ago if a man had talked of flying, he would have been considered crazy. If he had actually built a flying machine, he would have been burned at the stake for witchcraft. Yet today great airships span the ocean in a matter of a few hours. Will people of the future look back at 1944 and say the same thing about us?

This is supposed to be an enlightened age, but do people profit by past experiences? No. They continue to ridicule the visionary. They scoff at one who actually believes there will be such things as spaceships one day.

I believe that I read some time ago that the English Rocket Society (or some such name) stated that after the war when materials are again plentiful, they could actually build a successful spaceship.

Such advances are bound to come, and scoffing people who believe such things impossible are due for a surprise. The two or three people who read science fiction in this "town" are considered slightly off the beam because of it.

Of these and many other indignities practiced upon the readers of your honored magazine, I protest. I am sure there are many others who feel the same way.

ELTE BAKER
Oswego, Kansas

Unfortunately, most people are not gifted with imagination, the factor which is entirely responsible for all man's progress. Readers of science fiction are especially gifted, and they should pay no attention to those who scoff at and look with scorn upon a true gift. So next time they shake their heads, ask yourself which you'd rather be—a man with ideas, or a man without.—Ed.

NO MORE WESTERNS!

Sirs:

Because this mag seems to be the fashion for small brats to read, I am growing highly indignant. (I speak from the full weight of fifteen summers (15) also five months, four days, 3 hours, ten minutes and 37 seconds!)

I'm not going to say this magazine is my favor-

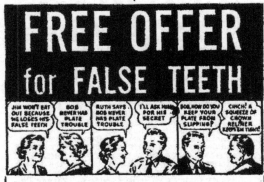

ite. It isn't. (For this hard, blunt statement this letter will probably be burned in the black of the wee sma' hours with the full military honors accorded Tojo's funeral by the U.S. Navy.) I do, however, appreciate F.A. a little more than A.S. as I don't go for explanations of great scientific value.

Inform the misguided child that wrote "The Sheriff of Thorium Gulch" he is in the wrong field. He should write for "The Woolly West Weekly."

I like and miss the stories of old where some fella with a fist full of rocket guns goes and gets real hard (Something like "Crusade Across the Void"), and a lot of amusing shorts.

My favorite all-timer is "Blitz Against Japan." Bouquets to Mr. Williams and while on the subject also to Messers. Wilcox, Bloch, McGivern and Yerxa. And Bond. E. R. Burroughs was good while he stuck to Tarzan.

> HENRY B. KING II,
> Lutherville, Md.

Yes, your editor is slightly red-faced. We'll not try it again! Also, we ran a "western" cover on Fantastic Adventures, *and boy, did we get panned! But it goes to show ya, your editor is human too—and sometimes how! So long for now.*—ED.

BACK ISSUES CORNER

Each issue we will publish the following list of copies of back issues of *Amazing Stories* still available. They can be secured by addressing the Circulation Department. Cost of all issues more than six months from date of this issue is 30c; less than six months previous 25c.

1940	1941	1942	1943	1944
Jan	Jan	Jan	Jan	Jan
Feb	Feb	Feb	Feb	....
Mar	Mar	Mar	Mar	Mar
Apr	....	Apr	Apr	....
May	May	May	May	
....	Jun	Jun	Jun	
Jul	Jul	Jul	Jul	
....	Aug	Aug	Aug	
....	Sep	Sep	Sep	
....	....	Oct	....	
Nov	Nov	Nov	Nov	
Dec	Dec	Dec		

READER'S PRIZE CORNER

EACH issue, until further notice, this magazine will pay $10.00 for the best letter of not more than 100 words stating simply what you like best about *Amazing Stories*, and what you like least. Such criticism may include suggestions for changes. Winner will be announced in the issue immediately following. The decision of the editors of this magazine will be final. In case of ties, the award will be made on the basis of neatness and clarity of presentation. Closing date will be the 10th of the month preceding the date of this issue. Each letter should be accompanied by listing, in order of preference, of the stories in this issue (coupon below may be used, or a reasonable facsimile). Only stories read need be listed.

EDITORS, AMAZING STORIES

540 N. Michigan Ave.

Chicago 11, Ill.

Sirs:

I rank the stories in the May, 1944, issue as follows: (Indicate preference by numbering 1 to 6 in squares. Mark X for stories not read.)

MURDER IN SPACE ☐

I, ROCKET ☐

THE FREE-LANCE OF SPACE ☐

THE HEADLESS HORROR ☐

MIDAS MORGAN'S GOLDEN TOUCH ☐

THE CONSTANT DRIP ☐

Name ....

Address ....

City .... Zone .....

State ....

ROCKET WARSHIP

By MORRIS J. STEELE

Our back cover carries James B. Settles' heroic concept of the rocket-firing warship of Neptune, giant world of our System

THE most sensational development of modern warfare has been the introduction of the rocket and its application to offensive weapons.

Perhaps first to come was the famed "bazooka" of the U. S. Army, a small rocket projectile fired by an electrical spark, capable of knocking out a heavy tank.

Next the rumored giant rocket guns of the French invasion coast, reputed to be able to smash London from a great distance, and held up by the Germans as a propaganda threat.

Latest is the Allied jet-propulsion plane, not technically a rocket at all, but popularly called one—and the new German rocket bomb which is launched from a plane and steered by radio.

James B. Settles, inspired by these new inventions, has envisaged a giant Rocket-firing Warship of the planet Neptune, where he assumes its people use it to wage war on a scale even greater than on Earth. Although it is purely imaginary, let us consider the possibilities contained in the ship he has painted for us. We must remember that this magazine forecast the jet-propulsion plane, and rocket bombs, and even the bazooka, as long ago as 1926 to 1928. Therefore, the imaginings of our artists and authors are worth serious consideration. They usually become actualities!

Using artistic license with the known astronomical facts regarding Neptune, Settles has pictured his Rocket Warship as a sort of giant launching barge, heavily armored and streamlined; propelled by gigantic paddle wheels to permit a great area of propulsion, which, coupled with an extremely shallow draft, permits great speed coupled with firm steadiness.

Powered by atomic motors, this ship is capable of speeds of one hundred miles per hour, and is as steady as though a part of the land, insofar as rocking and steering deviation is concerned. This is necessary to launch the rocket-torpedoes so that they will not attain too great an elevation, nor plunge down into the water.

Our ship carries three rocket-launching sleeves, open at the top to permit immediate release of the gases and smoke and flame attendant upon firing of the rocket itself. The rocket rests freely in the sleeve, and is initially aimed by the navigator of the ship itself.

The high speed of the ship carries it instantly free of the smoke and flame of the rocket's takeoff.

Set off electrically from the firing cabins located atop the ship, the rocket leaves with a tremendous roar and in several miles on its way before it is corrected in its course by radio impulses from the firing cabins. Thus, if the ship being attacked changes its course (on Neptune the effective visible horizon range of the rocket would be as high as one hundred miles) the rocket torpedo's course could be corrected to compensate.

Since the rocket's speed would be well in excess of one thousand miles per hour, it would take only six minutes at the most to reach a ship at the limit of visible range. Ordinarily this would be sufficient time to make maneuvers which would be impossible to compensate for, due to the speed of the projectile, except for the fact that it travels so close to the water that its approach would not be noted until three-quarters of the distance had been covered. Then no ship could change its course sufficiently to guarantee avoidance of the oncoming danger.

However, more potent possibilities are contained in the rocket blasting of larger, stationary targets, such as enemy coastal cities. These cities could be attacked from much greater distances than one hundred miles, since the range of the rockets would conceivably reach as high as four to five hundred miles.

In such attacks, the ship would take up its aiming position by triangulation to an infinitely delicate degree, wherein the stability of the great barge-like craft would enter. Once properly aimed, the speed and timing of the projectile's course could be definitely regulated so as to drop it directly into the center of the city, or upon any single target whose latitude and longitude had been exactly computed.

Radio devices, such as radar instruments, could be built into the rocket, and could be used to keep the rocket at a prearranged height from the water. Any deviation would be flashed back to the mother ship and instantly corrected by radio.

Approaching the enemy city, distinctive landmarks would register on the radar, and corrective changes made in the rocket's course to compensate from wind-drift or speed changes due to atmospheric conditions. Also, changes in direction of approach would make it impossible to locate the attacking ship.

These rockets would carry as much as a hundred tons of high explosive, and would be capable of blasting an area a mile or more in diameter.

Before this war is over, we may see such an idea as this applied to our own naval tactics against Japan. We sincerely hope so!

SCIENTIFIC MYSTERIES
(*Concluded from page 196*)

Esskata-Emishe, or he will supervise the dancing ceremonies of the Matto Grosso, with his long whip and his banded face.

It is time for some young intellectual to raise the pertinent question—"If it is true that the god of a people is a deified culture-hero, and the oldest records we have from the archives of Ancient Egypt, tell us that this Amen once sat upon the throne of TWO LANDS, are we any longer justified in accepting the long-held belief that these lands were Upper and Lower Egypt?" WHAT WERE THOSE TWO LANDS? Is it not possible that one of them was the lands which today we so ironically call THE NEW WORLD?

REFERENCES

Daniel G. Brinton: "The Maya Chronicles," "The Annals of the Cakchiquels." (*More recently discovered ancient Amerind books which had been rewritten with the Aryan alphabet.*) Published in Philadelphia 1882 and 1885. Now out of print.

Brasseur de Bourbourg: "The Manuscript Troano." Studies on the system of writing and the language of the Mayas, claiming to translate the original. Published in 2 vols., "Historical Researches," "Archæology and Languages of Mexico." Published in Paris 1869-70. Now out of print.

Stacy Judd: "The Ancient Mayas." A Creek migration myth by Gatschet. Published in D. G. Brinton's "Library of Aboriginal Lit." (*Now out of print but on ref. in many libraries.*)

E. Squier (not the scientist): "Children of the Twilight." (*A collection of legends.*)

Clarke Wissler: "Indians of the U.S." (*for Uto-Aztecan*).

De Prorok: "B. Mysterious Sahara."

De Prorok: "Byron in Quest of Lost Worlds."

PRINTED IN U.S.A.

TO MEN WHO WANT A NEW BODY *FAST!*

I'll Prove I Can Make You a New Man In Only 15 Minutes a Day!

I F YOU are like the thousands of men who have written to me, I know that you want a body to be proud of — one rippling with muscular strength, full of roaring energy. You want a physique that will point you out as a HE-MAN, that will draw looks of admiration wherever you go. If these are the things you want — and want FAST — then I'm the man to help you!

I myself was once a 97-lb. weakling — flat-chested, self-conscious, ashamed of my appearance. Then I discovered the secret of developing sinewy bands of muscle on every part of my body, of filling out my arms and legs, and broadening my shoulders. I changed myself into the man who has twice won the title of "World's Most Perfectly Developed Man."

Dynamic Tension Makes New Men

What's my amazing method? *Dynamic Tension!* And it has shown thousands of fellows how to become New Men — new in husky, muscular body, new in health and energy. In only 15 minutes a day — right in the privacy of their own homes — they have added powerful ridges of muscle to their stomach, biceps and legs, welded their entire bodies with sinews of strength!

What My Method Will Do For You

I'll prove I can do the same for YOU! If you're frail and skinny, I'll add weight and muscle to the spots that need flesh and strength. If you're fat and flabby, I'll streamline you into a picture of well-developed, radiant manhood. I'll put smashing power into your back, make your arms and legs lithe and powerful, give you a fine, deep chest. Before I get through with you, you'll be ALL MAN!

CHARLES ATLAS
Twice winner and holder of the title, "World's Most Perfectly Developed Man."

Here's Proof! Atlas Champions!

What a difference!

F. S., of N. Y., wrote. "Have put 3½" on chest (normal) and 2½" expanded."

GAINED 29 POUNDS

"*Gained 29 pounds!*" says T. K., of New York. "When I started I weighed only 141. Now I weigh 170."

FREE BOOK
Gives Full Details

My FREE book, "*Everlasting Health and Strength*," tells all about *Dynamic Tension*, and shows PROOF of my success in building MEN. It's packed with untouched photos of fellows who developed into Atlas Champions with powerful muscular development and vigor. Let me prove that what I did for them I can do for YOU. For a body that will win respect and admiration, mail the coupon NOW. Don't delay. Address me personally. CHARLES ATLAS, Dept. 9-D, 115 East 23rd Street, New York 10, N. Y.

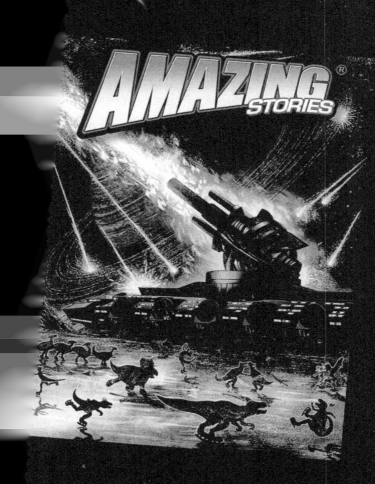

Made in the USA
Coppell, TX
26 October 2020